DARE TO MOVE

GARRETT NICOLE WOOD

Merrimack Media
Boston, Massachusetts

ISBN: 978-1-945756-20-7

Published by Merrimack Media, Boston, Massachusetts

DEDICATION

All the women out there searching for themselves: this is for you. To the twenty-somethings struggling to pay the bills and the thirty-somethings still dealing with Mr. Wrong: read on. To the forty-somethings missing the one who got away: read this and you'll find peace. For those of you who are lonely: this book will prove that it's a temporary feeling. I hope you find a part of yourself in Dare To Move—the part you need to own to get to the next, better phase of life. No matter the struggle you face today, don't forget to enjoy the ride.

ACKNOWLEDGMENTS

I don't remember when I started writing this book, yet, I very clearly remember divulging my desire to put my story on paper, to my mom Laura Wood. From the second I shared this with her, she cheered me on, first by agreeing that my story was valid. A few months into writing, my mom spent hours indulging me in long conversations about the flow, organization, essential parts and potential woes of taking on the challenge of book writing. Mom, you are the sole person who kept me from giving up in the earliest phases of *Dare To Move*. Knowing that you believed in me, and that you enjoyed the story means so much to me and I cannot thank you enough for helping me emotionally, mentally and even financially on this journey to self-publish. Thank you for taking the time to read the God-awful early drafts, and giving me constructive criticism, always.

About six months into writing *Dare To Move,* I thought I had it down, finished, totally complete (I didn't know it would take me nearly three years to complete). Naturally, ballsy me thought I could write some letters, get quick representation and nail down a publisher because I wrote a book. But not so fast. In the initial phases of my journey to find a literary agent, I went down a rabbit hole on MeetUp.com and stumbled upon a writer's group. Fearless, I decided to share my work with the strangers of said group, and head to a meet-up one late Tuesday night. I didn't know it right away, but the writer's group leader would become my unofficial agent, mentor, book coach, and support system.

Jenny Pivor, thank you very much for guiding me to my editor, coaching me through the self-publication process and even more for telling me that my story showed promise on the very first night. I appreciate all the time and energy you've given me and my book.

To my Beasley (Jeff), thanks for becoming my daily cheerleader. Somehow as soon as I shared my goal of self-publishing with you, I knew it would happen because you wouldn't let me fail. From offering to pay editor's fees and reading chapters for me, to printing rough drafts so that I could edit them by hand and hugging me everytime I needed it, thank you. You've become my rock and your encouragement has allowed me to stay a dreamer. I'm entirely grateful for your patience with me, this process and the story itself. Love you to the moon.

A key player in the story of *Dare To Move* is my marvelously patience and keen editor Elise McIntosh. Together we spent over two years sharing drafts back and forth, trying to understand the story and make people feel all the emotions of *Dare To Move.* Nonjudgmental and always persistent with good grammar, Elise coached me to be a better writer. She gave constructive, honest criticism and challenged me to show not tell. Elise, I truly appreciate your patience with me and this book; and I know that it wouldn't have happened without your guidance. Thanks for all the upbeat comments that kept me going, the "I think you can do betters" and your genuine interest in *Dare To Move.* You are my writing hero!

When it came down to the wire and the production of the manuscript was wrapping up, I needed to get the opinion and advice of one of my best friends, Nicole Theodore. After working for the well-respected publication of *Playboy,* I knew she knew a thing or two about writing and I've always loved her unique writing style. In late 2017, Nicole took the time midst traveling to edit and give advice on Part One, leaving helpful critiques were able to be carried throughout the entire piece. Thank you, Nic. You are #goals.

To all my family and friends who've given your listening ears and motivational pep talks: Thank you. I'm grateful that I have friends and family to lean on, and share my high and lows. Thank you for caring. For all the people who've believed in me, those of you who pre-ordered *Dare To Move* early, I sincerely appreciate your support.

Working on this novel was a coming-of-age task for me, a cathartic journey and the greatest learning experience of my entire life. The greatest takeaway is this: I love the writing process and cannot wait to write more!

PART I.

REAL WORLD: CHICAGO

CHAPTER 1.

ROCK BOTTOM

Boston, August 2014

One lyric, two notes and some familiar vocals can bring me to tears. More than anything, music brings me to my memories, good and bad. A few seconds into one song and you're back there, standing in front of that Chicago skyscraper—the one you stood in front of three years back, craning your neck to see the top, wondering if perhaps this would be your city for years to come.

Maybe a song doesn't bring you back to a physical place, but instead transports you to an emotional embrace with a person you never saw leaving your side. Romantic songs carry me the furthest.

It wasn't until I moved to Boston that I realized music's true power. Not only did I realize it, I began using it like a form of public transportation—as a free train ride to go back in time. And it was not just in my mind. I wanted to be physically overcome by emotions that I missed and wanted to feel again.

The memories weren't always joyful, but loneliness hurt more. When you move to a new city alone, loneliness becomes your MO, and isolation was killing me.

A month into a new life in Boston I found myself grateful for music while driving to a photo shoot. At the perfect lull in the drive, the song "19 You and Me" by Dan and Shay came on the radio and I felt my mind start to get on the memory train. I gripped the wheel tighter, like a child holding on to a bench, refusing to do what his mother asks. I didn't have time for emotions that day.

Covering my sadness was a mask of perfectly done makeup; I hoped my tears wouldn't drizzle it all off. I needed this photo shoot for my new fitness blog to go well—it was me taking a step into the future. Moving on.

The song ended five minutes before I arrived at the photographer Lucie's studio, giving me enough time to gather myself and get a grip—this was my new life. A grip I had, but the emotional wherewithal I lacked.

I'm sure I greeted Lucie kindly, but all the changing of outfits, backdrops and poses remain a blur. Well, all but one moment that stands out: me standing in front of a blank white backdrop, shirtless, and looking at the photographer behind her camera. Instead of feeling confident, "Take my photo, I look amazing," I felt shy and exposed.

"Can you make it look like I have abs?" I said.

I actually asked her that.

I felt like a "C" average; my arms were just normal arms and I wished I'd dieted more for the shoot so I was skinnier. Yet, as uncomfortable as I felt, I didn't want the shoot to end. I didn't want to go back to my new "home" in Back Bay.

My friends were in Chicago, my family was in Indianapolis and all there was for me in this new city was my apartment. I had an office in Rhode Island that I commuted to for my real estate job, but it was a holiday week and I was working from home.

I'd go anywhere but back to my apartment. It was beautiful, but it made me feel like a prisoner in a foreign country.

When the photo shoot concluded, the sweet photographer let me see some of the images on her laptop so we could filter through the shots I loved the most (read: remove the ones I hated). It turns out, though, she was a magician, and I could see some ab definition in a few of the photos. But what I really saw was a dejected, unsure girl hiding behind good makeup and a pretty smile.

On the drive home, I felt a hole in my heart and another in my stomach. I wasn't sure if what I felt was a side effect of loneliness—or from my recent breakup.

Months earlier, I opted out of going through the motions of a breakup, even though healing my broken heart would've been a cinch since we'd been in a long-distance relationship. Making the heartbreak even easier to sweep under the rug was the fact that I was mentally preoccupied with the idea of moving to this wretched city, saying goodbye to my friends in Chicago, and preparing for life in isolation.

It was as if I'd mentally closed the "relationship" file folder and moved it into someone else's brain for a few months—and now my brain wanted to reopen the file. Like I said, the power of music—thirty seconds into another song after the photo shoot and I was yearning for those memories.

What else could I do on that sunny Monday in New England instead?

Here were a few of my options:

1. Work out (again).
2. Wait at my computer for emails to come from my unresponsive boss, Mr. Bates.
3. Listen to music or watch a dramatic movie and reminisce about my long-gone ex-boyfriend.

My choice? None of the above.

Instead, I decided to cry in the car on the way home, pissed off that it was so sunny outside. Pretty days are meant to be enjoyed with others or outside having fun. I didn't even know what people did here for fun yet. *Would I ever?*

After the tearful trip "home" to Back Bay, I wrote fitness articles via voice record on my phone so that my brain could focus on anything but loneliness and heartbreak.

CHAPTER 2.

SEEKING FITNESS SANS SIX-PACK

Indianapolis, June 2013

Sitting on my BFF's couch in sweats (you know, preferable *Bachelorette* viewing attire), I felt myself daydreaming about my imminent move to Chicago. I looked 12, felt 18 and wanted to be 25 already.

After going away to college and spending my summer vacations working in other states or countries, I knew very well I'd never get homesick, nor would I want to move back to good ole Fishers, Indiana, in my twenties. Sure, I wanted to get married and have babies, but not yet. Carrie Bradshaw of *Sex and the City*, Lauren Conrad on *The Hills* and Kate Hudson's character in *How to Lose a Guy in 10 Days* dropped sparkles in my eyes like fun, flirtatious fairy godmothers inspiring me to pave my own way. Being a boss babe on my own in Chicago was the dream. Making my own money and embracing adult life were so close I could taste it—which made my two-week post-grad stint in Fishers watching *The Bachelorette* get old very fast.

You'd have thought I had an extraordinary amount of eagerness for a 22-year-old kid who was about to be supporting herself financially, but having locked down a full-time job months in advance, I was ready to jump into the Real World headfirst and fast! I'd accepted a sales position at Digital Media, a company that sells ad space on Google. Since that was taken care of, it was time to focus on landing a side job teaching fitness classes: spinning, TRX, something, *anything* fitness-related.

While watching *The Bachelorette* on my last Monday in Fishers (yes, I was counting down the days until my big move), I Googled this fitness place my childhood friend told me about called Tread Seven—or at least she'd thought that was the name. A place called Tred11 came up first on Google. I called immediately at the first commercial break.

I didn't know if this boutique fitness studio was big or small or even relatively popular. I simply read the company's info page, noted that it was in Lincoln Park (close to where I'd be living), found the number and called. Like I said, I was stupidly eager and possibly entering the ballsiest phase of my life. The girl on the other end of the line told me to email Sally, the owner.

The next morning, I spent ample time scouring Tred11's website. I had no idea what this place was really like—only that my friend said it was cool. The sexy ripped trainers on its website showcased a posh workout place where models and celebrities trained—like you have to be famous or have a six-pack to get in. Needless to say, it looked intense. However, I was a naive little firecracker and I wanted this intensity. I desired the posh, cooler-than-rural-Ohio (where I went to college) vibe. Tred11 looked like something I'd never tried before, something that would push me to my limits.

As if my passionate energy summoned her, Sally responded five minutes later!

The front desk girl was right—Sally worked quickly! Within minutes, I had a meeting set up with her for June 29. She also arranged for me to take a free introductory Tred11 class before the meeting.

* * *

Two days remained until the big move when I'd pack up my stuff from my mom's place and leave for Chi-Town. But after receiving Sally's email, I procrastinated packing. Feeling a little flabby and sluggish from guzzling too much wine during *The Bachelorette,* I was beginning to second-guess whether or not I was cut out to be a Tred11 instructor. There was no way I'd have shredded abs like Sally's by my interview in four days.

To cover my bases—and further delay packing—I walked over to my mom's Mac and Googled "TRX Chicago" to see what other opportunities my new city might offer, just in case Tred11 was too much for 22-year-old me to handle.

A small kettlebell gym called Flash Fitness came up first.

Thank you, SEO.

I called right away. A middle-aged-sounding guy named Mike answered the phone and, sadly, told me they weren't hiring.

"Damn!" I think I accidentally sighed out loud on the phone.

"But, hey! Come on in once you're all settled; we would love to meet you. We want to start letting trainers work as independent contractors in our space with their own clients. Come by, see the space, meet my co-owner and we will talk more," he said warmly.

I had no clients in Chicago (yet), but I told him that I would come by on June 28, which was the day after my move-in. But he didn't need to know that.

I couldn't wait to get to Chicago.

I couldn't wait to meet these fitness people.

I couldn't wait for this new adventure.

CHAPTER 3.

LOCKING DOWN JOBS

Chicago, June 2013

The first full day I lived in Lincoln Park, Chicago, it was uncomfortably hot. Sweating from nerves, sweating from the actual climate and adding in the sweat from working out made for a whole lotta not looking so cute. Day two forecasted the same weather and there was nothing I could wear to my interview at the kettlebell place that would keep me cool enough. While minimal clothing would've been best, I would've chosen a large muumuu, if it were socially acceptable.

You see, days after my college graduation, we took this crazy, two-week trip as a family—my dad, stepmom, grandma and brothers—before it was time for me to move into the Real World and for my brothers to head back to college.

We traveled from Indiana to California to Hawaii, and then from Hawaii to New Zealand. In New Zealand, we drove from Wanaka to Queenstown and then flew from Queenstown to Sydney, Australia. From Sydney, we hit Hamilton Island, then flew back to Hawaii and then home. My dad, who's a former F-16 fighter pilot, flew us the whole way in his Citation Sovereign, which seats about 10 and doubles as a corporate jet for his automotive company and an aircraft for family adventures.

There was a whole lot of eating during this adventure and the weight I'd gained was not the kind that can come off in two weeks. Now preparing for a high-pressure meeting at Flash

Fitness with Mike in the Real World, I squeezed my tummy fat while getting dressed and felt a whole lot more guilt. Despite remorseful feelings about the second helpings and superfluous cocktails, I had to pick a darn outfit.

Thanks to my mom's help during the move, I dug through my freshly organized drawers to find the only workout clothes I deemed "fitness teacher worthy" for their fat-sucking-in qualities: salmon-pink-and-black Lululemon capris with a backless, black spandex tank top that may have shown too much skin/back fat.

Once my clothes were squeezed on, I realized that not having a full-length mirror in my room was going to save me a whole lot of time and negative self-talk this summer. Knowing that dwelling on this "not good enough" feeling was a waste, I moved on to tackle the next big hurdle of my first real day in Chicago—packing my bag.

If you know me, you know that "packing my bag" has been a thing since junior high. I was always packing for something back then. First, it was for gymnastics practice and band concerts and then 6 a.m. cheerleading practices and football games. By college, I had to pack for spin classes that led straight into real classes that then concluded with sorority meetings. Despite all this time I spend packing, I'm still not a natural at it, and "packing my bag" has become a very well-known "Nicole thing" my family and friends tease me over because it's an event most days.

For the meeting with Mike, I packed a leather binder full of resumes, a change of clothes, extra pens, my wallet and hairspray. I have no idea why I decided to pack hairspray. Of all the instances when I've taken my nerves out by freaking out on my hair and straightening it 10 times, it's ironic on my first day in the Real World, I left my hair surfer-girl wavy and down. The only thing I didn't have to pack that I wished I had were business cards, though I'm not sure what they would've said at this point in my life. "Nicole Winston: 'Bachelor' critic, stay-at-home wine drinker."

I did not really feel "ready" to go to a fitness interview but I went anyway. In order to feel more amped, I grabbed a 5-hour Energy shot at a convenience store on Diversey Avenue about halfway there and chugged it.

A gaping hole in my stomach formed as I walked toward a gym I knew nothing about. After staring at address numbers on the rickety old buildings with faded signs on Clark Street, I finally found Flash Fitness. Inside, I saw a burly guy sitting behind a desk.

"Hello?" I said as I nervously opened the double-glass door.

"You must be Nicole," the burly guy said. He seemed pleasant but serious.

There was another young-looking guy who was vacuuming toward the back of the gym, which was really one oversized, warehouse-like space. I sat on a couch next to the glass windows at the front of the gym as I began telling the burly guy behind the desk—who turned out to be Mike—about myself.

I probably spoke too fast.

I probably seemed like a teenager to him.

To my luck, he didn't seem fazed by the sweat that was breaking at my hairline from the 90-degree weather outside combined with nerves of my first day adulting.

He told me again, very bluntly, they were not hiring.

"But, hey, let me show you around so you can see the space. What you could do is form your own LLC, get your personal trainer's insurance and use our space to train your clients," he said as if we were sitting at a café trying to decide on one dessert or another and figured we should just get both because, well, why not?

Flash Fitness seemed empty compared to most commercial gyms I'd seen.

There was a huge row of kettle bells and weird jargon written on a giant whiteboard that hung on one of the walls.

On another wall, there were the gym's community principles, which Mike made sure to point out.

"We are a part of the StrongFirst community," he said proudly.

StrongFirst? What the heck was that? Uh-oh, had I walked into some cult-like exercise club? The floors were a weird black-mat type of rubber material. There were signs that said, "No shoes." There were about 12 broomsticks without the broom heads leaning against the wall in the corner.

What was going on here?

Uneasiness of the Real World crept over my skin as I remembered my great-grandmother's warning: stay away from shady businessmen in that dirty city!

He went on about StrongFirst and I was distracted. I was trying to see what else this gym had to offer. I saw a pull-up bar, some dumbbells and kettlebells, and that was it.

Then Mike pointed to the younger guy vacuuming.

"Come meet my co-owner," said Mike, leaning into his next stride and waving his hand to invite me to the back area of the gym.

Mike introduced me to his co-owner, KG, moments later.

KG was strikingly handsome, in a simple way.

For some reason, he reminded me of my brothers' friends. It might have been because he was built like an all-American athlete. He had ridiculously gorgeous blue eyes and a calm but closed-off demeanor. After I smiled and shook his hand, I awkwardly walked past him to see the rest of the gym and felt butterflies, which increased my nervousness.

After the brief tour, Mike explained how they wanted to improve the gym, which was barely a year and a half old, in the coming months as they were trying to build the community and space.

Mike listed the 17 million steps I needed to take to get myself ready to train my clients at his gym.

I'm not sure what my face looked like as I tried to take in all the information, word by word, detail by detail, but I can imagine the awkwardness because I was concentrating so hard, wondering why he was giving *me* this opportunity. But I wasn't going to question it. I wanted the shot and knew I would rise to the occasion.

I shook his hand and said I'd get on it right away. He told me that while I was building my own business, I should learn more about kettlebell training; this way, I could use their kettlebells with my clients and not just the TRX suspension trainers.

Before I left, I looked back over my shoulder to give a farewell smile to KG, but he was too busy vacuuming to notice. I shrugged into myself like a turtle in a shell, but still hopeful. Perhaps I'd take one of his classes sometime ...

Focus, Nicole!

* * *

Walking out of the gym, I felt a weight had been lifted off my back. I left on such a high! I'd won the lottery nailing this opportunity to work with knowledgeable guys who seemed to be so passionate about their coaching and their community. And I couldn't help but wonder when I'd see KG again!

After five minutes spent daydreaming about KG, I wanted to run home and begin researching how to form an LLC in Chicago. But not so fast; I had 100 resumes I'd planned to go pass out to other gyms in Lincoln Park.

One mile down Clark Street and two hours later, I'd strained my neck from looking over my shoulder, scanning the streets for more fitness studios. When I made my way to Lincoln Street, I stopped at two different Jim Karas studios. I also hit up three XSport Fitness gyms, two different FFC gyms and an LA Fitness. I continued to search for more gyms until I was so sweaty I started to look unprofessional.

"OK, Nicole," I told myself. "Time to stop now. Nobody will hire the sweaty girl."

Besides, I wanted to go for a run and do a workout of my own in the park before my meeting at Tred11 the next day. If you saw the photos of the shredded trainers on the Tred11 website, you'd want to run a marathon really quick before the interview, too!

CHAPTER 4.

LULULEMON POSSE

On my second full day in Chicago, I woke up ready to hit the ground running. Before the sun rose over Lake Michigan I went for a quick run down Lincoln to Lakefront Trail, hit a few miles along the beachy trail and ran back home.

I showered while my roommate, Becca, was still asleep. Genuinely hoping I wouldn't wake her, I tried to keep quiet but I had no time to tiptoe around.

The summer weather was the kind where you get out of the shower and towel off but wonder why you can't get dry, only to realize it's because you can't stop sweating. *Not cool, Chicago!*

My choice of fitness-teacher-worthy clothing that day was a pair of bright blue leggings, a yellow sports bra and a colorful tank top that matched my headband. The lululemon gear was nicely chilled from my dark walk-in closet. The outfit had suited me—I Snapchatted the look—but only the outfit, not my face. The selfie thing still seemed weird to me at the time, but I definitely needed to show off the electric-blue leggings because they rocked!

When I arrived at the Tred11 studio in Lincoln Park, I stepped into a packed room full of women. Most of them appeared to be stay-at-home moms, given the 9 a.m. time, and were gossiping and trading fashion tips before the class started. Never had I seen so many people donned in lululemon—the latest and greatest trend in athletic wear. My electric-blue leggings felt like old news, but at least they were the right brand. It was as if there was an unofficial uniform required to take the class. After spending four years on a college campus in the middle of nowhere in Ohio and only recently finding out about the brand, it was shocking to find that what I thought was a cool, under-the-radar workout line was really the average young mom/yuppie outfit in Lincoln Park.

After signing in on the sheet for Greg's class, I saw whom I assumed to be Greg talking boisterously to a few women about the imminent workout. He seemed overly confident.

My confidence, on the other hand, waned, as if the electric-blue leggings faded to regular blue. I was an outsider ... Eek!

What if Greg knew I was coming and was going to evaluate me?

I got this.

As he walked around the class, his presence was almost too cocky for his gelled-hair-and-cropped-pants look. It took all but five minutes for me to realize why he was so vain: The people in the class were more than just participants; they were members of his unofficial lululemon posse. He had a fan squad—a harem of women. And I was there too, posing as a wannabe member but not sure I'd really fit in. These posse ladies had wedding rings the size of small weights.

The class was at maximum capacity, and the space felt small with 26 people inside. Remixes of Britney Spears, Justin Timberlake and Bruno Mars songs and, of course, Robin Thicke's song of the summer, "Blurred Lines" put a little pep in my step while calming my nerves.

Mid-class fatigue set in and my mental toughness waned; I thought that I couldn't do another step-up until Greg came up behind me, gently placing his hands on my shoulders, forcing me to relax them as I stepped up onto the bench with dumbbells in my hands, my glutes screaming at me. *Oh, yes: I could do one more rep. I had to do one more rep, even if the sweat was stinging my eyes.*

The air conditioning was kind of a moot point in the studio, which had more floor-to-ceiling windows than walls. I sweated so much that I drenched my stink-proof headband.

After class, all of the women flocked to Greg as I quietly exited the exercise room, all senses activated. I wanted to make sure I didn't miss meeting Sally or any other Tred11 managers. Disheartenment came over me when I couldn't find Sally; I took one last, quick scan of the waiting room, noting the fancy merchandise for sale, before I reached for the door to leave. Just as I placed my hand on the handle, a tall, fit guy grabbed my arm.

"Are you Nicole?" he asked.

"Yes, I am. Is Sally here?"

"She will be. I'm Jay. I instruct here," he said.

Seconds later, Sally, an adorable brunette who looked about 27, greeted me with a warm hug. Her long, lean arms let go of the embrace as she said hello with a huge, white smile that contrasted with her tan skin and black pigtail braids.

"Come back to my office; let's chat! You're from Indiana? I went to IU," Sally said with a cheery voice.

"When did you graduate? All of my friends went there!" I said.

I felt so adult now that I was out of school.

"Oh, sweetie, I graduated a long time ago. I am 36," she said in a sweet tone with a know-it-all demeanor.

I blushed.

I followed her into her office, wondering how she was so lean, tan and toned. She could rock braided pigtails like nobody's business.

Inside the office, which barely fit two desks, I told her and Jay about my experience coaching group fitness classes at Miami University in Ohio. I told them I was hungry to teach and I would do whatever it took to work for them.

"I saw that you have 5 a.m. classes; if you need me to teach those, I'll do it," I said boldly. "I used to teach spin and TRX classes for the Division I women's basketball, swimming and volleyball teams during their off-seasons at 5:45 a.m."

Jay smiled wide when I said that.

"I am the 5 a.m. teacher. I love a good morning workout," he said passionately.

His voice had a musical, meditative tone—like I wanted to wake up to take one of his early classes just to hear him speak. I had a feeling he was an uber-motivating coach.

"Why don't you come audition for us this Saturday morning, and you can meet my counterpart, Tawny. If you do well, you can teach your first free class Monday night," said Sally.

"I would love to," I said, trying to hold back my excitement.

The fact that my very own housewarming party was planned for the night before the audition didn't worry me the slightest bit. I was ballsy and invincible, remember?

CHAPTER 5.

FIRST REAL-WORLD PARTY

We'd been living in the city for just a few days and already my roommate, Becca, and I had received invites to the same five housewarming parties. Although we'd both been sorority girls at Miami, studied at the Farmer School of Business and had about 10 mutual friends, we'd never actually hung out before living together. The fact that we were equally stoked about the same five housewarming parties proved we were going to get along just fine.

Considering the upcoming weeks would involve similar parties with the same people, we figured we should get our own housewarming party over with before people started getting sick of them. We called everyone we knew in Chi-Town.

The afternoon of our party, we threw paintings on the wall as Florida Georgia Line's song "Round Here" played in the background: *Hammer and a nail, stacking them bails ...*

The night of the party, I accidentally put on too much perfume while Becca contemplated which black top she would wear (they all looked the same to me). We sipped vodka drinks while we waited for friends to buzz the doorbell to our new apartment.

Becca claimed she didn't have as many friends in the city as I did, but I called her bluff when 20 people I didn't know showed up that night. I was shocked at how random some of the guests were.

When it was all said and done, the party included: a friend of mine who played basketball at Miami, some high school friends from Indiana, some of the Alpha Phis from the pledge class below mine and 10 girls from my actual pledge class.

The "Boyz" (the name written on Apartment No. Four's mailbox) from upstairs came by with huge speakers for us to borrow, and Becca and I looked at them lustfully with the "I wonder if we will hang out or date these boys" kind of eyes.

Once most of the guests cleared, I was feeling high on life as I lay on my new couch chatting with these quasi-strangers, who happened to be Becca's work friends. I also was feeling tired and pretty buzzed, but that wasn't going to stop me from getting up at 5 a.m. to prepare for my Tred11 audition.

The Real World was so cool.

CHAPTER 6.

HUNG-OVER AUDITIONS ARE OK AT 22

On the second Saturday of the Real World, I had a sick feeling in my stomach when my alarm went off.

Crap! Was my red tank top clean?

I'd been running outside in the summer heat so often all my "dirty" workout clothes were not the kind of dirty you could shake out and wear again; they were the kind that was still half-damp and smelled like mildew from being wadded up in my hamper.

Please let it be clean!

Phew! The red top was in my newly organized top drawer and recently laundered.

I was impressed—that never happened. One week later and that drawer would look like a bomb went off.

The red top was perfect for the audition because it showcased my shoulders. I paired it with short, gray spandex shorts. My legs were my favorite body part because, for my entire life, they'd earned me countless compliments.

I stood in the kitchen drinking coffee and closing my eyes, pretending that the living room was the Tred11 studio.

"Treadmills, we have speed work today. Please start your inclines at four percent. Our warm-up will be five minutes."

"Floor! Grab your weights!" I said more loudly, beginning to walk around the imaginary studio, talking with my hands, trying to remember the way Greg had coached at the only Tred11 class I'd taken.

I paused, feeling slightly idiotic.

Crap.

I had no clue what I was doing. My only hope was I would come off as confident and motivating. I needed my personality to prevail.

Anxious to get to the interview, I almost forgot the actual workout I'd written that morning. Hours of "packing my bag" the day prior, and yet I still walked out of the apartment without my notes.

Chill, Nicole.

The walk to Tred11 was peaceful, but as I got closer and quickened my pace, I felt my hairspray, perfume and deodorant instantly melt off. I could *not* be the sweaty girl! I might've gotten up hours before any other girl my age on a Saturday morning in July, but pretending that I hadn't partied the night before wasn't an option as the ringing in my head was too loud to ignore.

Ballsy.

Luckily, my bag was packed with a 5-hour Energy.

Recovery.

Since age 16, I'd been a pro at chugging caffeine, and now it came in handy.

Ready.

I walked by a few stroller-pushers as I approached Tred11 and tried imagining how I'd ever get to that stage of life. Before I could let my brain go down that rabbit hole, I looked up to see the awkwardly shaped corner brick building and spotted the Tred11 logo on the window.

As soon as I walked in, I could hear music coming from the studio room. The doors were open, and Sally poked her head into the lobby. She summoned me, and I knew it was now or never.

Go time.

Tred11 got its name from the idea that clients will do six 11-minute rounds of exercise during class. Clients either begin on the “floor”—really a bench set up with dumbbells underneath it—or they start on the treadmill. The entire class is timed and the clients only have 30 seconds to switch positions in between rounds.

There are 13 treadmills in the room and 13 floor spots, making the trainer’s job quite difficult. Coaching all 26 people simultaneously, with half on the treadmills and half on the floor, is not something you can learn without just diving right in.

I was told to have an 11-minute round prepared for class. Tawny started on the floor first; Sally was on the treadmill. This way, I had to prove that I could coach two groups at once.

“Three, two and one! Let’s get this party started! Runners, your speed should be a four to a six and your incline five percent,” I said in my deep, cheerleading voice.

Thank goodness all of those years of cheerleading taught me how to yell from my belly.

“Floor, after 30 more seconds of lunges, you will grab two medium weights and begin bicep curls,” I coached, continuing to use my diaphragm to speak.

About six minutes into the first round, Tawny stopped me.

“OK, that’s good. We’ll switch spots now,” Tawny said, adding, “Call the treadmills, ‘treads’ or ‘treaders,’ not ‘runners’—not ‘if you are on the treadmills.’ Got it?”

Sally and Tawny quickly switched places and tightened their ponytails for the next round.

Walking back to the center of the room to instruct, I noticed the three of us were not alone. Because I’d been so nervous about getting the mic situated, I hadn’t noticed a woman and two little kids sitting in the corner of the studio. They were family friends of Tawny. I had an audience.

After my rough rehearsal, in which I was convinced I spoke too fast and my directions were not concise enough, Tawny reamed me.

“You need to be precise. Your floor segment needs to flow like a good story. You have to control the room.”

Her ponytail fiercely swung as she gave me this constructive criticism. Then she demonstrated just how it should be done, mimicking the moves I'd just tried to coach.

Catching a look at myself in the mirror-walled room amid her instruction, I saw that my face looked like my coral-red sports-bra top and, still short of breath from teaching, I knew it wasn't gonna fade anytime soon.

Tawny paused, looked up at me from lying on her stomach, demonstrating my swimmer move, and said, "Make sense?"

Seconds later, she hopped up, smiled with her hands on her hips and said, "Very well done, though! You need to work on those things, but you'll be great."

I swallowed, thinking, *"Great" is good!*

"Yes! You are so motivating, and your voice is really good—not too high-pitched sounding," Sally chimed in. "I can tell you were a cheerleader. And your legs look amazing!"

"Nicole, do you have family in Indiana related to Tom Winston? We are from there originally. When I saw your last name, I wondered ..." said the woman watching in the corner.

"Uh." I fumbled with my words. "I do. That was my grandpa actually," I replied.

Everyone knew my family from our car business in Indianapolis.

"Wow, small world!" exclaimed Sally.

"Too funny. Anyway, we will plan on having you teach a free class Monday night at 8. Bring as many friends as you can!" said Tawny.

They gave me hugs and showed me out. They seemed to be pleased with my work. I couldn't wait to tell my mom how it went!

I walked out of there on cloud nine, not really sure what just had happened. The weather no longer felt so steamy, my clothes didn't feel so tight and my head had stopped ringing.

"Start before you're ready" was quickly becoming the theme of my year.

The Hustle had commenced.

CHAPTER 7.

THE HUSTLE

My first Monday morning commute to my Real-World job at Digital Media was spent feverishly planning my Tred11 workout for the free class I'd be teaching that night. Not only was I strategically planning what exercises I wanted to coach, but I also was writing down the names of people I needed to text to remind them to come!

I loved the whole "being on my own" thing. There was a certain novelty to the freedom it bestowed upon me. No longer did I have to attend a class because it was mandated. No longer did I have to go to chapter meetings for my sorority or practices for cheerleading. I got to choose my apartment, my lifestyle, my workload and my extracurricular activities! I wanted to make the most of every second. There was so much I wanted to do, see and eat in Chicago. But of all the exciting things to come, I loved the idea of making extra money with fitness, my favorite hobby. My brain kept toggling between these thoughts of gratitude and "holy crap" moments of "is this real life?!" during my first morning commute to my Real-World job.

I'd interned at Digital Media the previous summer at its old office in Glenview, Illinois, spending the majority of my time writing blog posts. Although I kind of enjoyed the work—writing came naturally as a former journalism major—that summer taught me I'd prefer client-facing sales work since it would be more social and lucrative.

After expressing my interest in sales to my former mentor, Digital Media hired me to begin its first-ever inside sales team. I use the term "team" loosely since I was the only person in the division that first summer in the Real World.

The plan was for me to first learn inside sales (i.e., cold calls) and earn my way into outside sales within a few months.

When I arrived at Digital Media's new office on Day One, I immediately remembered another reason why I accepted the job offer: The people were so kind. The company's relaxed office environment made me feel at home. I especially loved the down-to-earth, always-frazzled secretary/office manager, Mallory.

After Mallory guided me to the new waiting area, I scrolled through my phone pretending to check emails. After 10 minutes, Tim, the VP, appeared, also looking a bit frazzled—kind of like he was running late and also forgot that today was my first day.

Nevertheless, he handed me my own company laptop and told me I wasn't going to be working in the actual Digital Media office.

What?

This was a bit unsettling.

Goodbye, comfort zone!

As he escorted me two blocks away to what would be my actual place of work, Tim explained that he'd arranged for me to work at a company called Alessor, a cold call center where companies outsourced their inside sales sectors, so I could receive inside sales training.

"Learning from this cold call center will be the perfect place to begin. In a few weeks, we hope that Alessor will provide us with some team members for the account too, so you aren't working alone. But for now, you are the only inside sales rep for Digital Media. We want you to work on selling our paid search services to potential new automotive clients nationwide. We want you to tap into potential clients our small outside sales team hasn't yet been able to reach on foot, in person. But enough of that for now. Your temporary boss, Graham, who helped start Alessor, will go over your goals more in-depth with you this afternoon," Tim said as he kept hitting "Ignore" on his beeping cellphone.

When we arrived at Alessor, I was a bit daunted by the hundred-plus cubicles in the big office and casually dressed employees walking around wearing headsets, talking with their hands or tossing mini Nerf footballs in the air. There were some bored-looking employees surfing Facebook and some people gathered around a TV in the café showing "SportsCenter."

I hid behind not-so-tall Tim like a scared child on the first day of preschool as we waited for John Blackwell, the CEO, to come meet me and help me get settled. I was studying the people around me. If I had to guess, I'd say 70 percent of them were between the ages 22 and 30.

"Hi!" someone with a booming voice yelled from down the hall. "I'm John Blackwell. Nice to meet you, Nicole," he said from about 30 feet away.

How did he know me?

"Hi. Thank you," I said, pretending not to be shy as I stepped out from behind Tim.

"Nicole, Tim tells me you went to Miami. I think there are about 15 people here who graduated from Miami and, like you, my daughter just graduated from there a few months ago. You might know her. Her name is Molly. You're gonna fit in here so well," he said with a charming smile.

In that moment, I realized how powerful and important personal interactions between business leaders and employees truly are. All it takes is one good leader expressing interest, care, concern or faith in a person to give him or her purpose and motivation.

Noted.

John walked me to my new desk and told me that my new quasi-boss Graham would be over soon and that he also went to Miami of Ohio.

Great! Another Midwesterner, I thought.

I pretended to check my email for 15 minutes, too nervous to look around at the desks surrounding mine. I knew nobody. *What did people do in awkward situations before cellphones?*

When I met Graham, he was as warm as you'd expect a Miami of Ohio grad to be.

"I know your situation is a bit different since you're technically a Digital Media employee, but I'm really excited for all of DM's goals. I've been talking with Tim and I think we can help you crush it for DM big time," he said.

At lunchtime, I ran to the elevator and walked outside across the street to David's Tea with my personal laptop. I had 55 minutes to form an LLC for the guys at the kettlebell gym.

Twenty minutes and one coffee later, I had an employer tax ID for Illinois, I'd completed the personal training insurance Mike suggested and possessed the correct forms for filing my LLC.

Crushed it.

As I walked back into my new office, I noticed that even though there seemed to be young, fun people around, the office life looked grim.

I was thankful to have something else—fitness—to look forward to.

I was standing by the copy machine, waiting for Graham to introduce me to my new team. I looked down at the mint-green eyelet capris I wore. The fact that they came up uncomfortably past my belly button was disguised by my white peplum top. In order to look a little bit more professional, I also wore my gray J. Crew suit jacket, only to realize I was definitely too dressed up for Alessor's casual environment.

Two young guys clad in collared shirts and khaki pants walked past me, each with a bag of golf clubs over their shoulders like they were heading out to have some fun. They said hello with warm smiles.

"Hey, are you new here? We heard you went to Miami. So did we! My name is Evan and this is Pat. We both report to Graham, too," he said with a smile so big, it was like a puppy greeting his owner. If he had a tail, it would've been wagging.

I was happy to say hi but didn't want to be too friendly; I wasn't going to be there long—only temporarily. I was there only because I had to be, a necessary step to becoming an outside sales rep for my company. I felt the need to tell them all of that but, thankfully, I resisted.

After my first day at Alessor, the first three weeks are slung together in my brain. I was as consistent with my schedule as the sun, spending as many waking moments thinking about or doing fitness training as possible and keeping to myself at Alessor.

Every morning in the break room, I reminded myself I was not there to make friends; I was there to make calls, learn how to sell Google strategies to car dealers on the phone and hopefully move to outside sales sooner rather than later. I wasn't even interested in getting to know the two Alessor employees whom Graham assigned to be my teammates.

A part of me felt like I was better than these people—or like I was luckier in some way that this was only a temporary situation, a mere hurdle to becoming an outside sales rep who hopefully would make six figures within two years.

There was one girl at Alessor—Michelle—who seemed interesting, though. She always had a cheerful pep in her step and wore sundresses in bright colors. I knew this because I had to walk by her desk every time I went to use the bathroom, which was way too often with the copious amounts of caffeine I drilled into my veins to survive 4 a.m. wakeups and the water I chugged to stay hydrated.

One day, she complimented me on my outfit. The next day, I complimented her on her coral-pink summer dress. She seemed jovial and friendly, and I liked that.

Before long, our casual smiles at each other became funny faces accompanied by hand gestures each time I walked by her desk.

One Thursday on the train home from work (we also shared

part of the same commute), we had a very passionate discussion about our mutual disdain of kitten heels, and next thing you know, she asked me to get lunch. It was a nice offer but my gut instinct was "hell no."

It wasn't that I didn't want to go to lunch. I just had better things to do—like plan Tred11 workouts—and so I wasn't ready to give up my productive lunch hour just yet.

Although I didn't need friends from work, eventually I agreed to go to lunch with her, mainly to keep a good reputation. A week later, I kept my word and reluctantly went to Whole Foods. She didn't judge me for bringing my own lunch.

From the moment we sat down, we hit it off, laughing about weird office happenings and contemplating which Alessor men we found the most attractive. Lunch on Monday was followed by lunch on Tuesday, Wednesday and Thursday. Our lunches were giggles galore and by the weekend, we had a list of inside jokes that could fill a fifth-grader's secret diary.

CHAPTER 8.

RUNNING RHYTHM

Chicago, August 2013

By August, I had more than a thousand cold calls under my belt for Digital Media. I also had a good fitness groove going. I loved my Monday, Wednesday and Friday mornings when I'd run down Lincoln Avenue all the way to Fullerton and take Fullerton to Lakefront Trail. Sometimes after an early run, I'd go to the 6 a.m. kettlebell class with KG or Mike.

The summer mornings had a distinct smell. If you'd made me close my eyes while running, I could tell you where I was in Chicago based on what I smelled.

For instance, if by chance I slept in on Friday (Thursday nights were for fun!) and ran on Saturday instead, I'd smell the nauseating aroma of stale vomit outside a bar contrasted with that of frying bacon emanating from the best brunch spot on the next block.

On Mondays, some blocks carried the scent of stale pizza mixed with the muggy summer air, which was sometimes smoggy from auto shops on Lincoln Avenue. The air just before Lakefront Trail often smelled of fresh rain in the morning.

I loved my morning runs—most of the time. Running always helped me find a sense of power and control and added serenity in my life. But some days, I ran because I thought I had to. Sweet potato fries on Friday nights, pizza on Sunday evenings—these were the guilty pleasures of the city forcing on me the guilty *need* to run.

After all, running was the only way I'd known how to control my weight throughout college—that and taking spin classes. Because it helped me lose weight back then, I had tricked myself into loving running because I thought it had to be a part of my life or else I would be fat again—like I was in seventh grade. Oh, seventh grade. You couldn't pay me to go back. I was less steady in my skin than a soda can on the hood of a car racing on the highway.

As routine as all of that running had become, it was sometimes a very calming, tranquil release, but mostly exhausting, especially the times I felt I had to do it for the sake of my waistline. Luckily for me, my intense running regime was about to change.

Still sweating from a three-mile run on a Saturday morning in August, I walked into the kettlebell gym a bit early for class. Mike's co-owner, KG (remember, the cute one?), was teaching a class when I walked in. We locked eyes as I began to stretch, starting with attempts at a deep squat. I cowered in pain. My flawed squat stuck out in the crowd of talented lifters.

My hips hurt badly from all the sitting I was doing—sitting on the train, at work, at lunch—coupled with not stretching after my 55-minute run before class. I knew the Real World would be hard, but I didn't know that one of the hardest parts would be finding ways not to be sitting all the time!

KG came over and began performing some soft tissue massage on me. He began with the back of my neck, rubbing down my shoulders and scapula, as I held on to a pillar in the gym to keep my balance. Just feeling his physical presence close to my body—never mind the touch!—made me feel like I was experiencing the adult version of the feeling you get when a boy in your fifth-grade class hands you a note … erotic butterflies!

My shoulders began to melt downward and my chest opened up as he used his hands to push my shoulder blades downward, forcing me into a healthier posture. I wanted to let my eyes roll into the back of my head but quickly remembered that I was in public.

As his hands moved around my body, he kept repeating, "Breathe. Breathe. Again. Breathe. Now squat holding on to the pillar, breathe at the bottom and stand up."

He was a muscle miracle worker. My heart pounded while my other muscles relaxed.

As his hands started on my upper back and worked their way down toward my IT bands—the sides of my strong quads that become super strained from running and not stretching afterward—my heart felt like it was in stilettos, walking on a tightrope between feeling mortified and excited, pain and pleasure. Then he asked to see me squat again and checked my ankle mobility (I had no idea what "mobility" even meant).

"Nicole, you gotta stop running; it is ruining your ankles and hips; you can barely squat," he said with concern.

"I can't stop running; I'll gain weight," I said, exposing my hidden insecurity.

"Well, how is your nutrition?" he asked earnestly.

I had such a crush on him; my thirst to impress him augmented every minute spent in his presence. He was the most handsome guy I'd ever seen in the Real World. For the past three weeks, I'd basically fallen in love with him simply from watching him coach. Every Tuesday night, I'd be in the back of the gym coaching a small group while he coached a class in the front area, and I lived for the moment when I'd peek around the corner and watch him join in the workout with his dedicated clients.

"It's perfect. I mean, I eat superfoods every day. I eat a lot of protein and I make all my own meals when I can," I said.

"OK, great; then you can stop running now," he said with a smile as he walked away to return to teaching.

I pretended to agree in that moment, but it was a few weeks before I finally gave up being a slave to running. The transition was easier than I thought because in 2013 I was constantly moving. I walked to the train. I walked to my office. I walked to the gym.

Just with doing distance runs once a week and quick sprints on the treadmill at Tred11, I was getting leaner and feeling more and more confident about my body. I had never felt so consistent with my nutrition.

After years of restricting my diet and then binging, coupled with exercising like a fiend simply to combat a bad diet, I was getting the lean body I'd always wanted without excess running. Less extended amounts of cardio made for a less intense appetite.

I wanted to tell the world about my discovery because I knew I could help people.

If only being a full-time fitness coach could be my job! I'd say to myself while I lay in bed at night.

The summer of 2013 was a formidable time in my life. I felt supported, encouraged and surrounded by friends and learning opportunities. My biggest struggle was deciding which fun activity to do on the weekends and trying not to have FOMO if I couldn't go to all the activities to which I'd been invited.

I was stupid happy with my life. If laughing made money, I would have been able to purchase a condo in the Gold Coast of Chicago on laughs alone.

CHAPTER 9.

DIVERTED

I caught a look at myself in the mirror one last time as I drenched my lips in lip gloss before heading to dinner. My dad and stepmom, April, invited me to join them at a steakhouse dinner for car dealers. My grandfather's dealership, Tom Winston Automotive, now run by my father, was a part of a national Jaguar group of dealers who were all in town for the yearly group meeting. My dad and April said I could tag along.

I'd had nothing else to do on a Sunday night, and it was a great excuse to wear a fun outfit. I threw my wristlet around my arm and reached for my keys on the kitchen counter.

Thank goodness I'd agreed to let April buy this jacket for me, I thought as I threw on the neon-yellow, three-quarter-length blazer we'd found when we were in Sydney. I remember thinking it was an impractical color in the storefront, but April was buying, so I let her.

To match the neon blazer, I'd thrown on these adorable floral shorts with yellow and gray flowers that were an appropriate length to wear with wedges and a white, drop-neck halter top—hence the need for a blazer.

I might not have been headed out for a hot date, but I felt like I was becoming the Carrie Bradshaw of Chicago, throwing on the perfect end-of-summer evening outfit, because my closet and body rocked. I had to soak up this body-positive moment—these didn't happen often. I was investing in myself in all facets of life and feeling confident that evening, and my perfect espadrilles were a good reminder of this.

As I grabbed the doorknob to leave, I remembered to grab my necklace. I lunged backward into my bedroom (literally, it was one step from the apartment door) and put on the silk-and-gold choker my parents bought for me in South Africa. Tonight was the perfect opportunity to finally wear it.

I walked outside to hail a cab. The steakhouse inside the Ritz Carlton downtown was way too far to walk to. It was a warm evening but not sweltering. Fall felt near.

As soon as I stepped outside of my cute little walk-up apartment in Lincoln Park, I tried to hail a cab. My friends would've laughed if they could've witnessed my futile attempts to hail the old-school cars in Sunday evening traffic while telling me I should just download Uber. At the time, I was still unsure about this relatively new technology.

Just then, my friend's mom called me. I totally forgot we had a scheduled call for that evening.

The week prior, my little brother Wyatt's friend had texted me to see if I knew anyone looking for a job in Chicago.

"We all just graduated. I'm sure I know some people still looking for jobs," I replied ever so confidently.

"What about you?" he'd asked.

"I'm good. I have a sales job and a trajectory. I am not looking."

"Well, can you just talk to my mom? I think it's a good offer."

I obliged and said that I would be free in a week. And now she was calling.

"Hello? Hi, Mrs. Fleming," I said as I raised my arm and squinted my eyes, still searching for a cab.

She was kind, friendly and, boy, was she convincing! She told me a story about a real estate company formerly made up of three men named Green, Macklemore and Swam. That firm was now dissolving and Swam was venturing out on his own, taking the majority of the employees from the previous firm. Despite the manpower he maintained, he also wanted young blood. I got the sense from Mrs. Fleming that this guy gets what he wants. He wanted someone without any pre-existing ideas about how to develop real estate.

He wanted me.

But he didn't even know me.

I told her how I was thriving in my full-time job, smiling to myself as I pictured Michelle and me giggling during our lunch breaks. It'd only been about a month, but I felt comfortable with the lifestyle I'd cultivated in such a short time.

As Mrs. Fleming congratulated me on my recent postgraduate successes, I thought to myself, she doesn't know the half of it! My TRX classes at the kettlebell gym were picking up; heck, I even had a Facebook group to market them!

The fact that I could do both DM and fitness made me think, *I don't need to bother with this real estate business stuff,* as I continued looking left and right for a cab.

The part I didn't tell her was Digital Media existed in the automotive space, the same industry as my family's business. What I also didn't tell her was I wanted to learn the automotive industry by working for other big dealers in the country before working inside my family's company someday.

And that was the truth (since age 5): I want to help my family's business someday. In 2013, I had the perfect plan, a flawless trajectory.

Mrs. Fleming convinced me to meet with their star employee, Mr. Bates, in the company's Chicago office.

"I didn't know you had an office here," I said. "I could be interested in that! But I thought you lived in Indianapolis?"

"We do. We have offices in Chicago, Rhode Island and Indiana. The Indianapolis office is the home office," she said.

"And Mr. Bates runs the office here in Chicago?"

"Kind of," she said with an "it's confusing" tone. "He is kind of working everywhere and needs help," she added.

"He is a very successful and motivated guy. He was the president of his fraternity," she said.

I was the president of my sorority, so at least we had that in common. If this Mr. Bates character went to Indiana University and was the president of his frat, he had to be cool. And maybe he was cute?

Yes, I was boy crazy and not ashamed of it.

I obliged to meet Mr. Bates in two weeks. I was trying to be polite while trying to put it off. I honestly had no interest. I also had no time.

* * *

After finally flagging down a cab, I arrived at the Ritz and was greeted by a fancy bellman's hand reaching in to help me out of the car. Two more bellmen opened grandiose double-glass doors and all of the summer evening's light dissipated as I wound through the dark hotel lobby looking for the bar-restaurant.

"Nicole!"

I turned around to find my dad's old friend, the brand-new vice president of Tom Winston Automotive, John Winston, standing behind me. It was entirely a coincidence that he had the same last name as I; we weren't related. I hadn't seen him since he'd begun the new role in the company, but I'd known him forever.

I felt young all of a sudden. Something about wearing canvas wedges with floral shorts and talking to a man in a suit made me feel underdressed and immature.

When he asked how I was, I began with the most recent news: I was pretty sure I was just offered a job with a real estate development firm based in Indianapolis. I gave him a hug and skipped the small talk; he'd known me since I was a little girl.

Since John came from a real estate background and now worked in Indy where Swam and Associates was located, I asked him to look into it for me. I trusted him.

The next day, he called and told me that the job was worth considering if I was interested. He didn't know much about Mr. Swam, but the former company—Green, Macklemore and Swam—seemed legit and that I should give it a shot.

"Don't worry about hopping jobs right out of school. It's all about the story you tell," he said.

CHAPTER 10.

DECIDING ON THE STORY

"I am going protein-only for the next five days; don't judge me," I said to Michelle as we perused the Whole Foods salad bar in Evanston during our lunch break.

"Why? Are you dieting? You're already skinny, goof," she said.

"Well, I'm 'fit,' sure, but Sally told me yesterday I have a photo shoot for Tred11's website in like 12 days, but who's counting?" I said. "You've seen their website, right? They all have shredded abs, and I do not."

"You will be fine. Just do the diet as best you can; you'll look great."

"During lunch tomorrow, can you help me look for some sports bras and lululemon stuff to wear for the shoot?" I asked.

"Of course. Shopping is my favorite," she said in a girlie tone.

We sat down with our tiny lunches and made a lot of jokes about our odd employee comrades at Alessor. When the laughing stopped, she paused and said, "Can I tell you something?"

For some reason, I sensed she had a lot to say. The floodgates opened for the next 35 minutes.

Her boyfriend wasn't "The One."

Her apartment had a rat problem.

Her job didn't pay enough.

Her parents weren't nearby to help her.

The list went on ...

I felt her vulnerability was inspiring and genuine, and right then and there, we made an escape plan for Labor Day weekend, two Saturdays from then.

The light at the end of the tunnel was the relationship developing between her and Evan, the guy from Miami whom I'd met the first day of work—the smiley one.

The three of us had cubicles near each other at work. We were close enough to make silly faces and mouth words to each other. Inside jokes were developing day by day.

He didn't know she had a boyfriend and, in fact, I'm almost positive he wanted to date her. Michelle told me that Evan promised to help her apartment-hunt that evening, and then she promised they would come to my TRX class at Flash Fitness.

After the game plan was set, I began telling her all about my crush on KG at the kettlebell gym to lighten the mood. We made way too many inappropriate "kettleball" jokes and laughed for the rest of lunch.

* * *

Evan and Michelle stayed true to their word and came to the gym promptly at 7 that night. Because I had taken the 6 p.m. class with KG, I greeted them with flushed cheeks and then introduced them to some of my college friends, whom I'd also convinced to take my TRX class. When Michelle walked in, she gave me dramatic, embarrassing hugs along with sarcastic "Oh my God, I haven't seen you FOREVER!" squeals.

Michelle also made some not-so-discreet hand gestures in a pretend whisper voice about KG.

"Is that the cute guy?" she said, not using her inside voice and pointing at him conspicuously.

She was the perfect amount of embarrassing that a good friend is—when you know they are being sincere but also are aware they secretly want to give you crap.

After the TRX class, Evan, Michelle and I walked toward the

train together. They thought KG seemed nice and perhaps interested in me, too.

"Really?" I asked. "No way! P.S. We need to find out how old he is! What if he's too old for me?"

"Girlfriend, he clearly doesn't care how old you are! You should not care about his age because he is beautiful!" Michelle said dramatically. "But, we should look up his age. You know, just because, yeah." She smiled again. "I bet he's 28! Shoot! What if he's, like, secretly 40?"

"Oh my God, you are the worst!" I said, rolling my eyes but actually hoping that wasn't the case.

"Love you, too!" she said with a smile.

"Next week, let's all go get pizza together after class," I said right as they pulled out their CTA cards for the train.

As I turned down my street and was almost home, I felt warm inside.

Evan and Michelle were great people, and I was so glad to have met them and that I felt close to them already. They were what I guess you'd call "fast friends."

Finding a sense of community was something I didn't realize I would need to find after graduating college. In college, you are always surrounded by a community of young people. Not a lot of people find that again in their new cities right away. Lucky me.

CHAPTER 11.

MR. BATES WAS NOT CUTE

I felt like a cumbersome offensive lineman as I walked through the narrow hallways of Swam and Associates' Chicago satellite office building carrying my work bag on one shoulder, gym bag over the other and a lunchbox in the same hand as my running shoes. But of course, I was a lot cuter than any of the Chicago Bears, dressed in brightly colored crop pants that straddled the line between summer and fall.

"Have a seat," said Mr. Bates as he ushered me into his office.

Although he was semi-handsome, he wasn't as tall as you'd expect for a guy with his air of confidence. He looked like he was strategically dressed down, like he was most certainly a man who always looked nice—even on his casual days. The goal was "simple, casual," I'm sure, but to me, it was not effortless.

Geographic maps of Chicago and Denver hung on the walls.

"Hello and welcome," he said like a friendly robot after he took his seat across from me.

Mr. Bates jumped right into telling me about how Swam and Associates researches populations, land, municipalities, etc., to discover which areas are best for their clients—big pharmacy and gasoline companies—to buy or rent to build stores or gas stations. He went into such intricate detail of how the work is done that I stopped listening completely and stared at his ears. They were kind of peculiar.

Looking back now and remembering his references to string maps, script counts, aerials and prices per square foot, he made sense. But at the time, it sounded like another language to me.

I thought for a second that I was going to have to schedule my own flight to take photos from special airplanes to get "aerial shots" if I took the job. It was all a bit overwhelming.

When he finished talking, I looked him straight in the eye and cut to the chase.

"I am sorry, Mr. Bates, but this is simply going to come down to money for me. I have a job. I'm happy with my trajectory, and unless this position can offer me more than I currently make, I'm not interested. What you do sounds neat; it sounds like a chance for me to learn a lot about many things of which I haven't got a clue, but I just took this other job and there's little pull for me to leave."

"The salary is not up to me," he replied.

I was a bit embarrassed that my confident, bold, "I don't give a shit, this is all business" statement backfired. It also made me realize he didn't seem to want or need me to work there, despite the fact that Mrs. Fleming had said I'd be hired to work for/with him.

There was an awkward silence and I began to stand up.

"Thank you for your time. I guess perhaps I have more to discuss with Mrs. Fleming," I said.

Then in his friendly robotic tone, he stood up, gave me a wave and said, "Good luck and thanks."

As soon as I was in the elevator, my mind went off to la-la land; I couldn't wait to get to the kettlebell gym. I scurried off to the Red Line train, which luckily was right near Mr. Bates' office. Only 30 minutes until class with KG started. The train better be fast!

CHAPTER 12.

REROUTING TO THE ROAD LESS TRAVELED

Mrs. Fleming called me promptly at 6:15 the morning after my meeting with her star employee. I was in my pink robe, drinking my favorite protein shake with a towel on my head, still sweating from Jay's 4:45 a.m. class. I knew this time might seem early to ask for a call, but it was 7:15 a.m. her time and she'd agreed. I figured it might make me look crazy, but I didn't care; I had zero faith in Swam and Associates' ability to pay me enough to incentivize me to leave Digital Media.

As we talked, I had to whisper a little because Becca was still asleep. She was the kind of 22-year-old girl who got up five minutes before she had to leave for work.

Even though Becca and I generally got along well, I think she kind of hated my epic morning routines. When I wasn't teaching Tred11 classes at 5 a.m. or lifting kettlebells with handsome KG, I was still up and at it. I loved to take the early morning Tred11 classes with Jay on Tuesdays and Thursdays. Inspirational quotes and mantras spewed out of his mouth like a showerhead on full force.

An animal in the studio, Jay barked fitness challenges and screamed with passion when clients killed it. My Tuesdays and Thursdays weren't the same if I missed his morning class. He had this inspirational aura, and if you got close enough to him in class, you'd leave feeling like you, too, could conquer the world.

He rewarded good efforts with powerful words, and I witnessed how his words, high-fives and exercises changed people's attitudes every morning—and consequently their lives.

Equally inspiring were the 8 a.m. meetings John Blackwell would hold at Alessor. Every day, he'd gather all 100 employees, catch us all up on office happenings and individuals' accomplishments and set group goals for us. On Tuesdays, he'd bring in a guest speaker. At the end of the group meeting, with all of us circled around the cubicles in a great room, he'd pause, then yell, "Now let's go set the world on fire!" and we'd all clap and disassemble.

I myself would often feel invincible after being motivated by Jay and John. Maybe that's why I had taken such a brazen approach with Mr. Bates the day before.

"So, what did you think?" Mrs. Fleming asked in an excited "how could you not like Mr. Bates" tone.

I told her that Mr. Bates was polite and informative and then paused.

"And?" she asked.

"He explained the job fairly intricately; it sounds awesome. I could learn a lot. But I told him it would come down to money. He told me the salary stuff was up to you."

"He's right; I am in charge of that," she said with a bit of cheer in her voice.

I was nervous now. I had spoken with my trusted financial adviser (aka my mom) about "what if she asks me what I wanted to make?"

We'd decided I shouldn't ask for too much, but perhaps a little more than my current job at 100 percent of my sales goals.

"So, what do you want to make?" she asked.

It was happening—and fast. The Real World had no chill.

I went with the strategy my mom and I'd schemed, but I wished we'd discussed it more thoroughly. I was kind of shocked this conversation was actually happening and not sure if it was formal or informal; lines seemed blurred, seeing as though she was my brother's friend's mom.

I went ahead and told her I wanted to make $52,000 because that's what I'd make at 100 percent of my quota at my sales job (base salary plus commission). I thought it would be nice to make $52K flat, no matter what.

"OK," she said.

Damn! I should have said more.

That day, I gave my two weeks' notice to Digital Media.

* * *

I was not ready to tell Michelle about my decision. The more I thought about the job, and the more frustrating cold-call life became, the more excited I was to shift gears professionally. Out of about 100 calls I'd make a day to sell paid search and marketing services, at least four general managers of auto dealerships would ask me if I was related to Tom Winston of Tom Winston Automotive. I couldn't lie and answered yes. Then all of those conversations turned into:

"Why aren't you working for your family?"

"You don't need to work; why are you calling me?"

"Did your dad make you do this?"

It was all very frustrating. Despite being over 400 miles away from my dad, the family business was always an elephant in the room.

And in the lull of my first week in the lame-duck phase, I passed the time on Gchat with Michelle, where we'd joke about KG. We made more inappropriate jokes about "kettleballs" (alluding to his junk, which had to be impressive given his great looks) to get through the monotony of cold call sales—and for me to avoid telling her about my new job.

After our lunch break, Michelle sent me a message about how I should seduce KG. We'd flirted enough; it was time to actually hang out with him. Her plan had something to do with staying late at the gym.

I had a better idea.

"My rough plan is to somehow meet him out one night when we are all out together, like pretend to accidentally end up at the same bar," I said.

"Perfect. Let's do it this weekend!" she said.

"OMG, no! I'm not ready. What if he's not interested? What if he has a GF?" I typed into Gchat.

But I knew Michelle would be an excellent wingwoman. After meeting him in person, she totally understood why I was crushing so hard.

"You know I will help you, girlfriend," she said.

After work, I took the train to the Fullerton stop instead of Diversey. I walked into Benefit Cosmetics to get a spray tan for free since Tred11 had a deal for instructors and my photo shoot was just a day away. I got sprayed, instantly felt like I'd lost 10 pounds and gorged myself on chicken and sweet potatoes in the cab on the way to the kettlebell gym. I was following some "photo shoot prep" from bodybuilding.com and needed to carb up since my photo shoot was the next day.

Darn it, there was a TON of traffic and I was anxious to get to the gym because I had 10 people signed up for my TRX class and also antsy because I felt extra-sexy with my spray tan and black spandex outfit. I called the kettlebell gym and KG answered.

"Hi!" I squealed like a 13-year-old girl talking way too fast. "This is Nicole. Can you tell any of my clients who walk in that I may be a little bit late, please? Thank you!"

I nervously hung up before he finished saying yes. I got there only two minutes late, but punctuality is my mantra, so I felt a bit flustered.

Evan and Michelle were already there, chatting it up with KG. I swear his jaw dropped when I walked in wearing black spandex booty shorts revealing my tan legs. I had pulled down the black straps of my tank top off of my shoulders so that they wouldn't leave marks on my freshly sprayed tan, and the padded bra I wore made the "girls" appear much larger than they actually were.

My night got even better when 12 people showed up to work out with me; it was an inspiring mess of fun, but the main thing I remember was sneaking glimpses of KG in the front of the room right as he would sneak a peek at me around the corner that separated the front of the gym from the back part. He kept coming over to shuffle songs at the sound system area conveniently located near where I was coaching. The frequent eye contact created crazy tension.

After class, Evan, Michelle and Evan's friend, Sasha, went with me to my favorite place for pizza, Mista's. I was ready to eat a full pizza since I strategically placed the carbs into my day. The photo shoot was less than a day away and I had been counting my calories and macros to the gram. I also read I should dehydrate the night before a photo shoot ... so, naturally, we brought four bottles of wine.

In fact, that's the second reason I adored Mista's. It was BYOW (bring your own wine)—a cheap way to get drunk with the best pizza in Chicago.

When I walked in, Ben the host said, "Nicole's here for the big order!" The four of us sat down and I scarfed down my salad with chicken and a glass of wine more quickly than most people take to pull out their chair and sit down.

It was easy to eat so quickly because Michelle was the one chatting.

"KG is so into you, Nicole," Michelle cooed, emphasizing every vowel. "Who are you kidding? He couldn't take his eyes off of you tonight. If you don't win him over this weekend, there's no hope for the rest of us," she said with googly eyes.

I was tickled. I definitely felt like he was interested, but I didn't know how to get to a point where I'd see him outside of the gym.

"I need you guys to be my wingmen this weekend," I said as I took a huge bite of pizza.

"Here's what we will do ..." Michelle began.

I stopped listening to her mapping out our master plan aloud when I saw the second pizza I ordered coming our way. I had ordered two, just in case I was extra hungry.

My first pizza was a gluten-free, dairy-free "Heart Smart" pizza and I had planned to eat half. But after two plastic cups of wine down, who was I kidding? I was absolutely about to eat the entire pizza. After 10 days of eating very little, I just had to succumb—the smell was too tantalizing.

Strangers walking by the giant windows would smile at us—and not because they knew us, but probably because we looked so happy. After two pizzas and three glasses of wine each, Sasha, Evan, Michelle and I were laughing like there was no tomorrow.

Just after Sasha said goodbye to go meet up with a new crush, my old fling and friend from college, Jesse, walked by Mista's. It was not uncommon for me to know at least one person walking by every time I ate there.

I smiled and waved. Jesse was shocked to see me and came in and sat down where Sasha had been eating.

He was on his way home from the gym, but we convinced him to have wine with us. I leaned over to Michelle and whispered too loudly, "Jesse was my rebound after my long-term college boyfriend and I broke up senior year—like a year ago!"

That's when I knew I was drunk.

Somehow, I stumbled home after another glass and set my alarm for 4:15 a.m. I had to take Jay's 5 a.m. class in the morning at Tred11. I wanted one last sweat session before my first-ever fitness photo shoot.

* * *

My alarm went off at 4:15 a.m. sharp.

In a daze, I got up and saw KG had just sent me a message.

Why was he up? I wondered and then asked.

"I can't sleep. Why were you drunk last night?" he replied.

Shit, I drunk-texted him.

Immediately, I remembered Michelle's elaborate dictations of what I should text KG. In our drunken stupor, we thought it was a smart idea to prime KG for a weekend meet-up.

Our first non-professional conversation was happening *right now,* and I was still too foggy at the early hour to process it.

"I can't sleep. Going through some stuff," he said.

I wasn't sure what that meant, but whatever it was, my 22-year-old self was sure I could fix all his problems if he'd just give me the chance.

"I'm sorry. At least you weren't drunk at a pizza place last night and now heading to work out at 5 a.m.!" I replied.

By the time I put on workout clothes and began to jog to Tred11, he already had responded.

"You're still drunk, aren't you?"

A little dramatic for him. I definitely wasn't drunk, but I was 100 percent exhausted. The wine was not a good idea.

Although I didn't like that he thought I was drunk still, I knew he wouldn't be texting me if he wasn't interested.

"Have a great day!" I replied quickly. This conversation was getting weird.

* * *

I survived class, detoxing my body from an entire bottle of wine via treadmill-induced sweat. When I got home, I spent two hours doing my hair and makeup for the photo shoot. The added pressure of the camera made me want to use every item of makeup I owned, twice. I ended up layering on the makeup, taking it off two times and redoing it through bouts of frustration.

When it was all said and done, the makeup looked fine, I was proud of my body and excited for the shoot. Like a mom, Sally was at the shoot to be supportive and give positive feedback about posing.

"She can wear the short shorts; her legs are flawless," she said when I arrived and the photographer asked where my mandated black leggings were.

After the shoot, I strategically ran by the kettlebell gym before going into the office for a half-day of work. I wanted KG to see me all dolled up. I wore extra perfume and pretended I needed to pick up more liability forms for my TRX clients to fill out. I'm not sure if my plan worked, but it made my day to see him.

When I got to the office in Evanston, Michelle was standing at my desk like a puppy dog awaiting a treat.

"Give me details now, drunky!"

I burst out laughing.

As I pulled out my rolling office chair to sit down, she started laughing harder than I was. The morning had been such a whirlwind I'd forgotten about how tipsy I'd felt leaving Mista's. Looking at her smile, I got the feeling she was laughing at me and not with me.

After we both gathered ourselves, I started to ramble about the shoot.

She was staring intently at my face.

"Nicky," she said, pulling her hands over her mouth, trying to hide a smile too big for her face. "Um, did you, well, how do I say this? Well, um. I think you drooled last night in your sleep and now you have a huge white streak on your face. How did you not see this?" she said, bursting out giggles like a bubble machine.

"NO WAY!" I said, trying not to raise my voice too loudly.

"Go look, NOW!"

She was right: The drunken-slumber drool had undone my spray tan like a glacier creating a canyon, forming a white streak from the corner of my mouth to my jawline.

OH MY GOD.

How did the photographer not notice? Maybe my bronzer was hiding it all that time and hopefully when I saw KG, too!

OH MY GOD.

After a surplus of laughs, we both paused and there was a

more serious silence. There was a looming awkwardness in the imaginary room at my cubicle: the new job opportunity I'd taken. We hadn't fully discussed it yet. She hadn't known I'd put my two weeks in with Digital Media. I'd been procrastinating having this conversation because I knew as soon as I told her, it would feel more real. I wasn't ready to leave the fun with Michelle at Alessor yet.

"Nicky, I wouldn't say this if I didn't mean it and, trust me, I *want* to be selfish here, but you have to take that job. It's such a better offer and sounds like a great challenge for you. And don't worry, we will be friends no matter what."

I sighed because I knew she was right. My days at Alessor with Michelle were numbered.

CHAPTER 13.

THE SEDUCTION PLAN

September 2013

"What's our plan, girlfriend?" I typed on Gchat, imagining what my Friday night might possibly entail.

"I'm emailing you the plan now," Michelle replied immediately.

I remember opening the attachment quickly with "oh my God, how ridiculous is this going to be" anticipation.

The plan was to commence after work. Thank God it was a Friday; this plan was too good to wait for.

Step 1: Grab KG's attention in a sexual way.

I knew just what to do. Friday afternoon I took my very Oompa Loompa spray-tanned self and ran shirtless as fast as I could for a quick one-mile run to the kettlebell gym. With every step, I got faster, entirely too anxious for this so-called "Seduction Plan."

The steamy, 85-degree weather didn't help my nerves or my running. The sun's intensity had dwindled, but it was still the kind of weather to work up the perfect light sweat—the kind that you don't notice until after you stop for rest.

Walking into the gym quickly, like I was still kind of running, I kept my eyes down, pretending to keep a low profile from the other clients, fully understanding that there was no way KG would miss me in my bright-orange sports bra, black spandex shorts and my tank top in hand.

I'd made it to the cubbie area quickly without making eye

contact with anyone. I removed my running shoes first, then pulled my tank top on over my sticky body. There were no mirrors at the kettlebell gym, so I had no idea whether I was a glistening goddess or if I looked like a 5-year-old kid after a soccer game in August with sweaty, red cheeks.

It didn't matter—in my peripheral vision, it appeared I'd caught KG's gaze.

Other clients stretched around me as I sat nervously waiting for KG to leave his desk and begin class. Would I grab his attention further? Would he notice me? Did it look like I was trying to get his attention?

Be cool, Nicole. Be cool.

I had to begin class assuming I'd completed Step 1. Part of me wasn't sure, but then I remembered the way he looked at me on Tuesday when I taught class in black spandex with my fresh spray tan. I was on his radar.

Step 2: Figure out if he has weekend plans.

The first part of every kettlebell class involved mobility work. While I was intensely trying to pry my right knee outward in a Cossack squat, a lateral type of lunge to stretch the groin, KG walked over and stood right in front of me. He bent down to my level and murmured, "Go to the water cooler."

Puzzled, startled and excited all at once, I obeyed, trying not to let him see my heart jumping out of my chest.

At the water cooler, I found a T-shirt with the name of his gym on it.

I looked over my shoulder with an "Is this for me?" look.

"Put it on already," he mouthed with a smile.

He stared at me until I disappeared around the corner to try on the dark-colored T-shirt quickly. I looked back and he'd repositioned himself, staring at me with a grin, to sneak a peek at me in a sports bra, again, as I removed my tank top to try on the shirt.

After I rolled the edges of the charcoal shirt down my sweaty body, KG looked away. I hustled back over to the group, doing backflips and high-kicks in my head. Excited but unsure why he gave me the special attention via the T-shirt gesture, I began to feel a bit mortified.

What are the other women thinking? Is it obvious that I have a crush on him? Do they think he has a crush on me? Does he?

Crap.

What if they think I'm reading his friendly advances as romantic and they think I'm a dumb, young girl?

I shouldn't care what others think. I *did* have a crush on him.

Thanks to KG's T-shirt advances, I found the confidence to ask him what he was doing for the night (according to plan!) after everyone finished putting the kettlebells away at the end of class. People trickled out, but I stayed pretending to fiddle with my shoelaces. I was not going to fail at this mission. *I got this.*

Walking toward him to ask the big question, I was thankful that during class I overheard his best friends discussing where they should go out that night. I stood across from his gym desk, conveniently located by the exit (in case I needed to run away), and asked what he was up to later, trying to hide my urge to pant heavily.

He told me he was going to Monsignor Sur, a bar in Boystown near the gym—a place quite close to where I lived, too.

"Oh, I've never been!" I said.

"It's fun. Nothing exciting, but it's fun, I guess."

"Nice. Yeah, I might meet up with Michelle later," I said, thankful that he actually knew who I was talking about. Then I ran out the door.

I didn't care that he hadn't technically invited me—I texted Michelle immediately: "You, me, Evan—Monsignor Sur tonight, let's go." I loved that she knew exactly what I was talking about and, without question, replied: "Meet you by the Mexican restaurant across the street at 8:20."

Step 3: Meet him somewhere outside of the gym and flirt with him.

At 8:20, I nervously combed my fingers through my hair,

smacked my glossy lips together several times, hoping I still looked like I did before the 12-minute walk to the Mexican place. Walking in heat can drastically change things. You leave your apartment feeling like a Pantene Pro-V hair model done up with professional MAC makeup and then you get to your destination looking like a sweaty, deflated Dolly Parton. Melting makeup sucks, as does humidity.

I nervously glanced at the time on my phone. It was 8:22. Michelle, Evan and Evan's friend Sasha rounded the corner. As they approached, I excitedly skipped toward Michelle and gave her a hug.

"Calm down, girlfriend. It will be fine!"

Michelle and I led the pack as we crossed the street right into the bar where we knew we'd find KG.

Monsignor Sur is one of those narrow bars where you're either bellied up to the bar or at a table against the wall and there's only a tiny aisle in between. In the back, there was a tiny dance floor area. I saw KG and his friends at a small table across the bar about 35 feet from the entrance. He saw us immediately as we walked in. Michelle and I looked away.

Yes, both of us looked away like we didn't know him. More like embarrassed junior high girls scared of talking to their high school crush, we avoided eye contact and walked down the aisle, right past KG and his friends. Although I had mentioned to him that I might come by, it wasn't like I had texted him, "Hey! I'm on my way!"

And now there we were.

When we got to the end of the bar, there was a door that led to a packed back patio with no room for us.

Michelle and I gave each other that "Oh, crap!" look out of the corner of our eyes, trying not to look defeated or nervous.

"What do we do?" she asked me.

As if I had a plan?

"I don't know. I'm scared. I feel like an idiot."

"Me too!" she squealed, grabbing my hand and squeezing it.

She was the one who had been encouraging me all along! If Michelle was scared, what should I be?

"You're supposed to tell me it's OK right now, goof!"

"But it's not OK! We are being such nerds; we are so awkward."

"I know," I said.

"Let's just go back," Michelle squeezed my hand as if to signal it was time to move.

As soon as we turned around, we laughed because Evan and Sasha were standing there, breaking the ice and talking to KG and his two friends—like normal human beings who know each other from the gym.

As soon as Michelle and I reached the table, good ole Evan dismissed himself to go buy shots.

"Hey, guys! We didn't see you there!" I said, trying to act too cool.

Evan returned with the shots—not one, not two, but three for each of us. We downed them within minutes.

"How old are you, anyway?" asked KG's friend Pete.

Not sure why, but I lied. "I'm 23," I uttered nervously.

"No, you're not—you're 22!" said KG.

Crap! He had my client information sheet. Everyone started laughing.

"It's one thing to lie about your age, but by only one year? How does that even help you?" asked KG's roommate, Adriel, chuckling.

I had no idea. I had hoped 23 sounded a bit more mature. But that backfired 100 percent. After the age mishap, I don't remember much.

The little I do remember was this: We all progressed to the dance floor, where I tried to dance sexy.

Keyword: "tried."

I was a sweaty, drunk girl, doing all kinds of hair flips and pulling moves that made an onlooker wince for too long. KG must have thought I was going to bite it at any moment. Drunk dancing is never as sexy as it feels.

But like any good drunk, I had superpowers that not only kept me from falling (OK, I might have fallen once) but allowed me to somehow have the guts—and the aim—to reach for KG's face, grab it, and make out with him.

He was drunk enough to accept my advances and kiss me back.

Twenty minutes of drunken dancing later, I'm assuming he thought it was time for me to go home. But being the mentor and new friend he was, he suggested "we" leave the bar—at least that's how I sort of remember it.

From the bar, we walked up and down my street for 15 minutes, looking for my place. I told him I didn't know where I lived. The next day, I was embarrassed that my inebriation allowed me to forget my address, but in retrospect, I think it was all a strategy from Drunk Nicole's motivated brain. KG eventually gave up trying to get me to find my apartment and took me to his place.

CHAPTER 14.

REAL WORLD HICCUP

I woke up naked in a pitch-black room, gasping. As I panted heavily, I felt a hand reach for my shoulder.

"Shhhh. It's OK, Nicole. It's me, KG. I'm right here." I continued to breath heavily, assuming that we had done what I thought we had done.

Shit. I skipped Step 4.

Step 4: Get him to kiss you and ask you on a date.

It seemed as though we'd skipped the date and landed straight in bed, thanks to shots of Fireball and tequila.

He grabbed me and pulled me closer.

We started kissing and his hands wandered.

My senses were heightened in the pitch-dark room.

He began to breathe heavily with me.

His fingers went inside me, and as I began to moan, I wondered exactly what we had done the night before. Waking up naked, I assumed we'd had sex, but I didn't totally remember leaving the bar.

The sound of me accepting and enjoying his advances turned him on further. We were moving together and he was like a boiling pot about to blow.

"What the hell. We already did this last night!" he said as he threw my naked body on top of him.

For the next thirty minutes, we were like animals. It was the most intense sexual experience I'd ever had. Clawing. Scratching. Screaming. We sweated, we gasped, we grabbed each other and it was a miracle we didn't fall off the bed.

As soon as we were finished, he turned on the lights so I could get dressed and go home. It was a Saturday morning and he had a busy day of packing ahead.

Apparently, Labor Day weekend in Chicago is a popular day to move: Both he and Michelle were moving that weekend. I found it peculiar that he was moving locations with the same roommate, but I barely knew him on a personal level, so I simply wished him luck as I stood up to get dressed.

As I was reaching down to grab my shoe, I leaned my right hand against his dresser. There, right next to it, I noticed what looked like a woman's necklace. Although it was still rather dark in the room, a tiny glimmer of light shone through the cracked doorway from the hallway. I was fairly certain it was a woman's necklace.

Oh my God, he has a girlfriend.

All of a sudden, I felt nauseous. I pretended not to notice as I stood up, signaling I was ready to leave. He smirked at the stilettos I was about to wear on my walk home.

Crap! I hoped he didn't live far from me. As he led the way out of what seemed to be a basement bedroom, we walked upstairs and I could hear someone in the kitchen.

Both of us got dizzy as we arose to a very bright family room with huge bay windows and a white carpet.

There were boxes everywhere.

Wow, my head hurt.

His did, too. I could tell because he brushed some moving boxes off of a couch and sat down for a moment.

There wasn't room to sit next to him so I straddled him in my outfit from the night before.

"Morning Adriel!" he yelled into the kitchen, unenthusiastically.

The dejected hung-over look on his face would not lead

anyone to believe he'd just had mind-blowing sex. I could hear the water running in the kitchen. This was awkward. I knew Adriel; he always took classes at the gym. And now he potentially knew me on a more personal level.

Great.

Sitting on KG's lap, I could stare into his baby blue eyes, but I couldn't study them for long. I looked away sheepishly after a moment, trying not to be too embarrassed. He kind of had a sheepish look, too. When I looked back at him, we were both half-smiling.

"What the hell? I thought you were like a virginal, quiet, reserved girl. That was nuts," he said.

"I don't know what that was," I replied with a smirk.

Bottom line: We couldn't deny there was chemistry.

"Shit, I have to pack. I'll text you later?"

I quickly ran out the door and realized I knew exactly where I was—just a block from my street.

I ran home in my outfit from the night before as fast as I could, hoping no bystanders would witness my stilettos, shorts, strapless shirt and sex hair. I tried to ignore the fact that what just happened was absolutely, 100 percent against the plan. And while part of me was still in shock at how amazing it was, somewhere in the back of my head I knew that was not how you get the guy. I also hoped that in three days things wouldn't be awkward at the gym.

After I got into my apartment, I sighed with relief I hadn't seen anyone I recognized on my jog-sprint down Diversey Street. I quickly plugged in my phone, took my birth control (almost four hours later than my usual 5 a.m. time, crap) and called my mom.

Thank God Becca wasn't there to taunt me about my very apparent walk of shame. I didn't need any added stress; I had to be at Michelle's place to help her move in 30 minutes. Or at least that was the original plan; but so far things were slightly derailed.

My mom didn't answer, but my call would signal to her that I was in fact alive. I dialed Michelle next. She answered on the first ring with a giggle.

"What did you do last night, girlfriend?" she asked like she already knew the answer.

"I'm sitting here in the same outfit I was wearing last night. What do you think?" I said coyly.

"I think that you just wanted to wear it again!" she said, messing with me.

I heard someone in the background giggle.

"Wait, are you with Evan?"

"No, you tell me what happened first!" she said.

"Let me tell you all about it when I get there. When do you want to meet?"

"Come over to Evan's in an hour," she said.

* * *

When I arrived, I realized she was still feeling just as crappy as I was. We quickly debriefed each other about what had happened the night before. I was happy to hear she had gotten herself into the same exact situation with Evan as I had with KG. We both were concerned about the consequences of our actions—Michelle used protection, but she's not on the pill, and I was worried about the effectiveness of my birth control since I took it four hours late. Before we could get on with our day, we had to make a stop.

Right before arriving at her soon-to-be old brick apartment building in a tired area of Chicago north of the downtown area on North Sheridan Road, I made a fast turn into a narrow CVS parking space.

"Nicole!"

I didn't look at her.

"You totally just bumped that car!"

I tried to hold in a giggle, avoiding eye contact.

"It was just a love tap! I thought if I didn't say anything, it was like it didn't happen," I said.

Cue the song "I'm a Hazard to Myself."

"I just love you," said Michelle.

"Let's do this," I said.

Entering CVS, we beelined for the pharmacy counter.

"Hi, we both need Plan B, please," I said nervously.

I threw two big bottles of water on the counter and paid.

Once back in the car, we quickly opened the pills.

"Bottoms up!" she said and I repeated.

"How did our 'master plan' turn into Plan B in the parking lot of CVS somewhere near Evanston?" I asked.

We looked at each other, just tickled, and laughed until we cried.

* * *

Fortunately KG was too busy moving to hang out Saturday afternoon, I needed a day to process my own actions. However, I truly hoped he'd want to see me again during the three-day weekend. Whether or not it was my own insecurities or a sixth sense, I perceived an unwillingness from KG to see me one-on-one anytime soon.

My nerves led to probably too many texts, and somehow, I ended up convincing him to see me the next day. Sunday afternoon, I bought a bottle of vodka and some lemons and put them in a lululemon bag. I put on my shortest white jean shorts and a blue, capped-sleeve T-shirt with a pink bra underneath. I liked the way the bra made my boobs look, even if it could almost be seen through the shirt. I wanted to look good, and since the summer heat would not allow my hair to stay straight, I was not about to walk in 95-degree weather to his new place that was a half-mile farther than the apartment I'd skipped out of the day before. I went to hail a cab.

The two-minute walk down to the end of my street to find

a cab made me sweat. Nervous sweating on top of actual heat sweating are a bad combo. Thankfully, I was able to get a cab, but two minutes later I wished I hadn't …

The driver complimented me on my perfume as soon as I closed the door. As he obnoxiously smacked his lips while munching on a family-size bag of Doritos, I pretended not to hear him. I could not stop worrying about how this afternoon was going to play out. I was sober, KG was probably going to be sober, and I hadn't seen him since I woke up at his place. Looking back, I'm 99 percent sure we were both still drunk when we'd awoken.

I still couldn't focus. That sound! My goodness—it was like the driver couldn't get enough chips in his mouth at once. With all of the Sunday afternoon Labor Day weekend traffic, we were only traveling about five miles per hour, but my heart was racing as I thought about KG. I couldn't wait to see him. I hoped the feeling was mutual.

The driver finally swallowed enough chips to take a breath and I watched as he reached down for a drink to wash it down. I looked up as he threw his head back to get more of his drink down the hatch. The large bottle was an actual "drink": a 40-ounce beer.

My cab driver was drinking a 40-ounce beer. You can't make this stuff up. I wasn't sure what was worse: his nasty chewing or the fact that he was drunk driving. At least this ridiculous encounter took my mind off of KG. I needed an extra 10 minutes to take some deep breaths and gather myself in the air-conditioned car before seeing him. Plus, anything is better than showing up sweaty, I guess.

* * *

KG was quiet in the elevator; it was that somber side of him I'd seen a glimpse of when he was hung-over Saturday morning. I'm not sure why, but he seemed either really hung-over, really sad or both. He didn't have a lot to say. And my giddiness was pushing out my Chatty Kathy side, whom I could tell Somber KG did not want to meet.

As soon as we got into his apartment, he showed me the claw marks I'd left on his back from two nights prior. His back was obliterated. We joked about that night as he began chopping lemons for our drinks. We made vodka waters with lemon and began kind of play-wrestling in his big open family room space while listening to music, talking and checking out the views in his new high-rise apartment.

The place was a stark contrast to the pitch-dark room I'd woken up in two days before—the floor-to-ceiling windows made it full of light. This place was a new start for him, I surmised. Beyond the looks of a fresh slate, it made sense when KG revealed that his ex-girlfriend had lived with him and Adriel in the last apartment for almost two years. I cringed for a moment thinking about the necklace...

Facebook is a great tool for stalking when bored at work, and I'd definitely seen some photos of the two of them together: her at Flash Fitness, with his family on holidays and in an apartment living together. She was most likely older than I was, and she was a brunette. I've never been the jealous type, but knowing there was another woman, who might possibly still be in the picture, made me feel like I had competition—like I had to prove myself. On top of that, I wanted to know more:

Why had they broken up?

Was he hurting?

Do they still talk?

Did she want kids and he didn't?

Be quiet, I told myself. *Stop thinking so hard.*

All of these thoughts were running through my head as he silently looked out his window. Before I could say anything, he pulled me onto his lap. We made small talk about my family and my past relationship for some reason. I think I was trying to be vulnerable in an effort to get him to open up.

After one drink, he picked me up and carried me to his bedroom. This afternoon was going exactly as one would've expected, given our recent encounter and the fact that we were drinking vodka waters alone in his apartment. This was further from The Plan than I could've imagined, but it was 10 times more exciting.

CHAPTER 15.

THE GRIND, INTERRUPTED

Chicago, September 2013

On a two-week stint of unemployment (read: waiting for a new job to start), I imagine most 22-year-old city dwellers would savor every last second of sunny September, sleeping in and day-drinking with friends. But I wasn't your average 22-year-old woman. Sure, there were tons of friends still job hunting in whimsical Chi-Town with time to hang, but I wasn't going to be hangin' with them. Rather, I kicked it off Monday morning with a coffee date with John Blackwell, the CEO of Alessor. He agreed to meet me after I left Alessor; and as he put it "many people use Alessor as a stepping-stone." I sought advice on veering away from the car business, my future goals and leadership. After all, he was the coolest Real-World leader I'd ever met. Validation fell over me when he said, "I knew you'd only be here a few months after your first week of work. You have crazy drive."

But aside from the business-related coffee date, I planned to grind. I'd only been in the Real World for two and a half months and the thought of not having a regular paycheck for one pay period freaked me out. Sure, somewhere in the back of my head, I knew I'd be OK, but I'd spent a lot of my college graduation money buying "essentials" for the apartment and felt the weight of my rent and cable bills hanging over my head.

Despite what was in my family's bank account, my parents had never handed me money (besides paying for school), and I highly doubt they'd be stoked to help me with my third month's rent as an adult—nor would I have been stoked to ask. Years of watching my single mom support three children ingrained in me a serious level of self-reliance; therefore, the week leading up to this two-week post-grad vacation from work, I scrambled to assemble five "jobs"—what would later be the beginning of a time I refer to as "The Grind."

The Grind actually began thanks to Facebook. The first job came after I posted a video to Facebook showcasing me doing backflips at an adult gymnastics class in Wrigleyville. A wealthy woman from the North Shore saw my flips and reached out to see if I could teach her daughter and her daughter's friend some gymnastics skills for $100 an hour per kid. I didn't know it then, but that was the first of many gigs that would come to me from me simply being me and documenting my life on social media.

Between coaching gymnastics lessons on Mondays, personal training on Tuesdays at Flash Fitness, extra Tred11 classes, Nic Fit TRX boot camps and outdoor park workouts, I was overbooked. A busy schedule stresses some people out, but I liked that this "business" of five jobs belonged to me. I was in charge.

How do I even have time for a Real-World job? I wondered, perusing my schedule on Google Calendar that first Monday of The Grind after coffee with John. If Swam and Associates wasn't offering great benefits and a reliable salary, I probably could've made it work doing fitness alone. But business classes in college made me feel obligated to go with the safety net of a "real" job. Conservative business schools don't promote risk; plus, you can't teach someone to be ballsy.

Sipping on more coffee at my home desk, I caught sight of a weird note buried on my calendar for that day and actually choked a little: "Meet Dad and April's friends' son." It even included his phone number.

What?

Apparently, the son of my dad's friends from Nashville was going to be in Chicago and our parents wanted us to meet. I'd agreed to this rendezvous back at the steak dinner in August. I knew which "friends" from the car business these were; I'd met them before at a summer party in Indianapolis. But I'd never met their only child—I'd only heard stories. To be honest, I barely remembered my parents' friends, let alone what they'd shared with me about their son. I was sure he was just *awesome*—the only child is always "awesome."

According to my calendar, I'd agreed to take time out of my day to meet this guy for lunch. I sent him a text, hoping he'd want to cancel.

"Hey, this is Nicole. Do you still want to do lunch?"

He responded right away.

"Hey! Yeah, that sounds rad. What time do you want to meet?"

Rad?

"I can meet you if you can make it to the Brown Line Diversey stop by 1 p.m. I have to teach at 2:45. Do you know how to use the trains?"

You could call me a jerk, yes.

I did feel a little guilty about not helping him out more, but a part of me hoped that it would decrease his desire to meet me, that we'd both send a cordial text about meeting another time, *in another universe*. I was busy, you know! Plus, it really irked me that my perfect two-week plan was already being rattled by an impromptu lunch.

He replied with what I interpreted to be a kind of snotty remark: "Yeah, I know how to use the trains. It's not that hard. I'll be there at 1."

Since he's a dude, I figured he'd be late, but that wouldn't halt my punctual side. At 12:56, I walked briskly down my street wearing black leggings, knee-high boots, a pretty cream-colored scarf and a neon-green, sheer workout top over a black sports bra—my "athleisure" look (though, that's not what they called it back then). When I arrived at the doors to the train station at 12:59 p.m., there he was, right on time.

When he rounded the stairwell corner and walked through the

turnstile, he lowered his sunglasses as if to show me, *Yes, this is the guy you're waiting for.* As he came toward me, he spoke about 10 steps too soon, winked at me and said, "Hey what's up? Nice to meet you."

He reached out toward me, and I knew it then: He was totally a hugger.

Before we actually embraced, time froze and I took him in like you'd gawk at a wild animal you'd never seen before. He was shockingly tall with great hair and a British rock 'n' roll style.

On second thought, he sort of looked like he could've walked out of a pop music video.

His jeans were super tight; if he were on camera, they would've looked perfect. If I'd had time, I could've contemplated for a good 10 minutes just how he pulled them over his quads.

He was chatty from the first embrace. I didn't thoroughly listen to his small talk, though. I was too busy studying him.

He wore a jean jacket, rugged, leather, lace-up boots and a long silver necklace. His bold style confused me. I tried not to like him. I didn't understand his big hair and cutting jaw.

"Want to grab lunch at that little place on the corner over there? I've never been, but I hear it's good."

I actually hadn't heard it was good, but I knew it was a popular bar on Friday and Saturday nights and hoped they were open for lunch. I simply wanted to go somewhere close to my apartment that wouldn't be busy.

When we sat down at a patio table outside, the waiter approached us immediately and asked for our drink orders. I prompted him to go first, looking to see if they had Diet Coke.

"I'll have a whiskey," he said. "Do you have Jameson?"

Taken off guard, I ordered: "Um, I'll have a water and your cider, please."

I didn't want him to feel like he had to drink alone for some reason.

He smiled at me and said, "Last night was wild."

"What are you in town for again?"

"Ah, the Warped Tour," he said, like it was something he'd been looking forward to. "I was up until four this morning."

I couldn't even comprehend that. I'd gotten up for The Grind that morning only 15 minutes after he went to bed.

When our drinks came, he made a toast and, as we clinked glasses, I noticed his Rolex.

"Who do you like? What are your favorite bands?" I asked.

"Well, I was totally a huge rock/punk guy when I was in high school. I loved metal," he said while making an air-guitar hand gesture and a crazy face.

"I really like all music, but a lot of these bands are friends so I came to hang backstage with them. I recently ended a tour in Japan with a band called Every Avenue," he added as if it were nothing.

Apparently, he was a drummer, but five minutes later, I learned he was more of a college student studying finance who paused school to go on a music tour.

But wait, then he said he wasn't sure he still wanted to get an MBA and law degree anymore—he might just stay in music.

Wait, no, then he explained he was actually more of a musician who had dropped out of Belmont University to rebel against the frustrating music industry, then went to Lipscomb to study business and get his bachelor's degree and MBA until Every Avenue needed a drummer.

Now here he was, not in school, and the band had just broken up.

All he wanted to talk about was cars and my family's car business. He grew up as a car business kid, too. I spent the next 20 minutes talking about how my dad never wanted to be in the car business. (Yes, my dad runs the business now, but only because my grandfather signed the papers over to him when he realized cancer was going to be the only thing he couldn't win against.)

For the next 30 minutes, while we ate bacon-wrapped dates and drank whiskey and cider, he dropped about 40 different facts about the luxury car business and several names of celebrities and bands. It was hard to take him seriously.

Who was this guy?

Yet, his stories were interesting. It didn't matter what we were talking about, he knew something about everything. He was the Renaissance Man—Ren Man.

I told myself he wasn't my type, though. My last boyfriend had an 8-to-5 job as an accountant; he was simple and easy to understand. Ren Man was hard to grasp.

It wasn't that he wasn't my type necessarily, because he was actually quite attractive. It was maybe that I'd never met a beast like him before.

He was intellectual but not condescending. He seemed charming but personable and genuine. He dressed well and had a great body but drank whiskey at lunch. He had nice things but didn't seem too snobby. At least, I hoped not. I most certainly didn't drive a Lexus or own a Rolex.

During our entire lunch, the voice in my head was begging:

How is he not working?

How does he have the money to do this?

Where does he get the money for his nice clothes and travels?

The more stories he told, the more I felt like he was 100 percent financially supported by his parents and that wasn't attractive to me. The wink Ren Man gave me, though, was hot.

Hopping into my beat-up Volkswagen Touareg after lunch to head to coach gymnastics, I called my stepmom, April, to tell her that I'd met her friends' son and I didn't think we were a match. He seemed like some type of trust-fund kid, I explained.

The Grind had me drawing up plans A, B and C to make ends meet. Dating a guy who lived off his parents wouldn't even make the cut for Plan D. He might have been one year older, but I was one year ahead of him in the Real World.

Also clouding my ability to see Ren Man as a romantic candidate that day: the fact that I was starry-eyed over KG, who was 10 years my senior. I eventually found out he was 32.

I thought about KG during the entire gymnastics lesson—he was an easy obsession—and even sent him videos of me spotting roundoff back handsprings. I told him I had to teach a Tred11 class afterward, and for the last 30 minutes of the lesson, I said little prayers that he'd send a text saying, "Come over after."

When I checked my phone after the Tred11 class, I'd had a series of texts—all from Ren Man. Frustrated they weren't from KG, I didn't even read them until I was home 90 minutes later and my phone buzzed again.

"Hey, my friend is in class all night."

"I am just hanging near Loyola."

"Let me know if you want to hang later."

"I can come to you."

Hang out? Who had time to "hang out"? What? At 9 p.m.? Was he going to come over to sit on my couch and try to make out with me?

Absolutely not. I was not interested. If I were going to make time to "hang out" with anyone, it was going to be KG.

I was so annoyed and needed his messages to stop, so I replied:

"Hey, sorry. I have to go to the grocery store, do laundry and plan my workout for tomorrow's class. Have a safe trip back to Nashville."

"Sounds really important," he replied sarcastically.

"Actually it is; have a safe flight."

I sent the text thinking I would never see him again.

As I frustratedly folded laundry, I kept checking my phone, hoping KG would respond to my texts and maybe invite me over; after all, we'd hung out the past two Monday nights. Looking back, I wish I hadn't wasted so much hope on him. But during The Grind, hope is what kept me going.

CHAPTER 16.

BARKING UP THE WRONG TREE

September 2013

Every time I woke up at KG's place, I felt empty inside. There was no morning hug or kiss. There was never even a murmur of "good morning."

The first week of hanging out with KG—the week after Labor Day weekend when I drunkenly seduced him on the dance floor of Monsignor Sur's bar in Boystown—was fun. It was flirty. There was a lot of sex.

We cooked dinner together a few times a week for two weeks. He called me pretty. He even gave me a toothbrush to keep at his place.

After one of my Tuesday TRX classes at Flash Fitness, we ordered pizza to go from Mista's. I felt comforted when he rubbed my head as we lay on the couch.

"You need to slow down, Nic. You're burning the candle at both ends," he told me with concern.

"I can't stop! I love coaching at your gym, and Tred11 makes me so much extra money. It's nice and it's a taste of the fitness-only lifestyle," I explained.

I knew it was crazy to stay up with him, in bed, and then get up at 4 a.m. to drive to teach a Tred11 class. And talk about the bag-packing. I could barely handle packing all the different workout clothes and wondered how I'd do it all when my new job started.

But I appreciated his notion to care, even if he wouldn't care when the sun came up the next day.

That night, he kissed me with the smallest amount of passion, giving me an ounce of hope that the late-night hangouts, flirty texts and midnight trips to his place would turn into something. It'd been three weeks, but who was counting?

By the middle of September (OK, so, yes, I was counting), I was determined to win over his heart by way of his belly, making my mom's undeniably incredible white bean chicken chili accompanied by her homemade beer bread. The fact that he invited me to hang on a Sunday was a big deal and I was not going to arrive empty-handed. After buying all the ingredients that rainy morning, I schlepped over to his place with a backpack full of spices, a heart full of hope and a belly full of butterflies.

I was totally going to win him over.

When he opened the door with a plain look on his face, my tail stopped wagging. I could've been the second cousin of his down-the-hall neighbor based on his reaction.

Maybe he was just hung-over from Saturday night. Maybe he was tired?

I made my way through his small kitchen, heart pounding in my chest, and got to work, grabbing any bowls and utensils I could locate in his disorganized kitchen. After the chicken and spices were set up in a Crock-Pot and the savory aroma had me salivating, I took a deep breath and walked over to watch the Bears game with KG ... and his roommate.

Perfect timing. The game was just starting. As for the chili, learning how to make it while trying to seduce a man on the same day was not my best decision. For the first 10 minutes of the game, I stared at the screen, contemplating what major ingredients I could've missed. And the timing! I hadn't realized that it would take the chicken so long to cook, and that good chili is made over several hours so the spices set. Oh well. They would just have to be patient. And so would I.

I cuddled with him on the couch as the cool fall breeze flew in from the cracked window. His roommate—Aloof Attorney Adriel—was there, kind of. Physically, Adriel's presence was known. He was 6-foot-3 with crazy, curly, brown hair. Yet, despite being a monstrous man with the body of a fitness model, he was very quiet unless spoken to—or when he had a strong opinion. He intimidated me. To me, he was the 30-something type of man who wouldn't think twice about dating a 20-something girl, but what did I know?

At about halftime, the smell of homemade beer bread permeated the family room and Adriel perked up. "Hot damn, what you cooking, girl?" he said with a smile and a funny sniffing face.

For an articulate attorney who read at least five books a week, his quirky comments coupled with his semi-hipster, quasi-homeless man style sometimes made him sound like a homeless person from the South.

I smiled. "Adriel, I'm making beer bread and white bean chicken chili! It will be done soon. Are you hungry?"

As the chili and beer bread came together, I began to relax and focus on the positive: Here it was, the perfect fall day with my favorite fall foods and a cute, older guy.

* * *

I was hopelessly infatuated with KG, endlessly waiting for his texts, dropping everything to come over when he said "when" and sacrificing my own sleep and workout schedule to stay at his place. I was well aware that I was chasing him—which, for a girl, is never a good place to be—but the fleeting moments alone with him made me want to continue to throw those rules out the window.

Aside from our perfect Sunday hangout and a few other late-night rendezvous filled with sparse conversation, my relationship with KG was purely a physical one. And it wasn't mindless sex. It was more than clear that we both craved each other. The sex was that good! We'd get lost in his bedroom. Sex where you don't know which way is up or down, have no conscious idea of time or direction, but every inch of your body is engaged, turned on, wet, hot and oblivious to anything else. Every. Single. Time.

When we weren't at the gym together, there really was no "we." "We" only existed late at night, behind closed doors, and sometimes lying together on his couch. "Nicole and KG" were both coaches at Flash Fitness, profoundly professional and cordial. The dichotomy in space and time with our relationships wore on me, though. I was becoming more and more on edge around him at Flash Fitness. Because he didn't want me in public life, it made me wonder why he even wanted me in the bedroom. Because I felt inadequate, I began to be less engaged in bed; we could both feel it, I'm sure. Without sex, would we have anything?

Feelings of regret often would seep in during the late hours of the night at his place when he'd go to sleep without acknowledging my presence; it was like I'd had my 10 minutes of fame and now I was a nuisance. These nauseating feelings would fill me up to the brim until my skin actually would throb, keeping me awake like a loud clock on the wall.

One early morning, I heard him stirring from across the bedroom. I opened my eyes to find him staring out the window at the foggy haze over Lake Michigan.

"What's wrong?" I asked. "What is going on with you?" I said as I sat up.

"I have baggage. I have a lot of dark stuff going on," he said without turning from the window.

His short answers and lack of eye contact proved his apathy. He didn't care to let me in. I didn't need to know why he was the way he was. I was nothing to him.

I assumed it had something to do with his ex-girlfriend; I knew that he still texted her; and how could I forget about the necklace I saw in his old apartment?

On top of his dejected persona and closed-off demeanor, he

never wanted to know much about me. Plus, he did recreational drugs sometimes and loved to drink. I knew he was a former bartender, but I dared not suspect he was an alcoholic. I only wanted to see the good inside him.

Despite feeling sad for him, I knew he wasn't incapable of loving someone; he clearly had been in love before—several times, actually—and the girlfriend before me was in the picture for a little over two years. Thank you, Facebook, for clarifying.

I was constantly vying for his attention and perplexed as to why he was guarded like a castle with a stockade and moats. I was the heroine that could change him, help him, save him. I just needed time.

And in the meantime, I'd thought I could be tough—handle it—even if sleeping next to him was like lying next to a ghost sometimes.

The flammable physical chemistry we shared when we had sex duped me into believing something would come out of this relationship. But the truth was that being there in his darkness felt like a vacuum sucking more and more life out of me.

Why didn't he want me? Was I not good enough?

The logical part of me still knew I was a catch, but he made me feel like an indigent, like I was irrational and hopelessly needy for wanting him.

Deep down, I knew it needed to stop—rather, I needed to stop pursuing him. But I wasn't yet ready to stop wanting him.

PART II.

RENAISSANCE MAN

CHAPTER 17.

UNDEFINED ROLE

October 1, 2013

Day one of my new job was a big deal because it involved traveling to New England. If you're thinking that the night before I was busy packing my bag, you're wrong.

I should've gone home to my own place after country-themed night at Cornstock, I thought while lying naked in KG's bed. It was a bad call on my part since I had a midmorning flight to catch to Rhode Island for new job training. I quietly peeked at my phone, which was lying next to my face; it was 6:15. I had time.

When I heard KG get up to shower, I pretended to be asleep. There was no use in revealing I was awake; he wouldn't say "good morning."

And let's be clear, he wasn't mad at me; I'd done nothing. But it was a feeling, an energy I perceived, a nauseating, negative aura.

The pit in my stomach grew like an expanding sponge as I heard his footsteps trailing down the hallway to the bathroom. I clenched the sheets in my fists as my eyes welled up with tears. As soon as I heard the bathroom door shut, I let out a tiny but audible cry.

I'd had it with this—whatever "this" was.

I jumped out of bed, my vision blurred with tears, and fumbled around for a pen and some paper. I scribbled down my feelings hurriedly, writing all the things I had almost texted him before but refrained. It was like one long drunk text—embarrassing but all true.

I remember writing so fast, hoping to get it all out before the shower turned off. My tears fell on the paper as I wrote the heavy-hearted note I feared he wouldn't even read.

It was a note about what a great coach and teacher he was.

It was about how I saw him being an incredible father and husband someday.

It was about how I believed in him so much—as did his clients—and that he needed to believe in himself.

It was about how I had no idea what I'd done wrong to deserve this type of treatment.

I made sure to tell him that regardless of whether or not he wanted to date me, I would be there for him.

I'm not sure why I said that.

Maybe it was a Hail Mary attempt at getting his attention?

Truly, more than anything, I wanted the best for him. His darkness was depressing. I deserved bright and happy. Despite this mess, the levelheaded part of me knew I needed more respect, but I still couldn't understand why he didn't like me.

I wasn't buying the whole "I'm not emotional" or "I don't want to date."

It was me. I wasn't "the one" for him. And I hated that. It affected my self-esteem. Half of me felt like the best catch of the sea and the other part of me felt like the scum of the earth, knowing he didn't want me.

I signed the note and put it on the floor of the doorway to his bedroom so he wouldn't miss it. Then I shut the apartment door behind me as quietly as possible, hoping I'd never go back there again. That apartment made my heart hurt. A lot.

In two months, I'd felt a gamut of emotions—highs, lows, uncomfortable uncertainties. It seemed more like a year than two months.

Was I crazy? I wondered during the longest elevator ride ever.

During the ride down, I stared at the cowgirl boots I was

wearing at the bar Sunday night when KG summoned me for a late night rendezvous. I'd had them since high school and wished for a second that I was still the pure, idealistic, hopeful 18-year-old who had sweet, kindhearted Indiana boys taking her out on picture-perfect, G-rated dates.

Relief fell over me when the elevator door opened at the ground floor.

Made it out. Moving on. New chapter.

Stepping foot outside in my cowgirl boots and jean shorts reminded me that I was still 22 years old. I giggled as I pictured myself wearing a business suit the next day at my new job in the Real World. If they only knew what I wore to a bar Sunday night …

* * *

I didn't know it when I ran into my apartment to kick off my cowgirl boots and throw suits into a garment bag that morning, but that first day of my new job with Swam and Associates would be the beginning of my adult transformation.

Was I ready? I was about to find out. My training program was broken up into four weeks and kicked off with a trip to Swam's New England office in Lincoln, Rhode Island.

Week 1: Work in the New England office

Because Lincoln is a 20-minute drive from the Providence airport, I had to rent a car—a big Real-World experience for me.

I found the rental car center very easily but was stressed out when I had to pay for the car with my own debit card (the company hadn't yet given me a corporate credit card to use).

It was the first time I'd ever rented a car and, for some reason, doing so with my own debit card made me feel very nervous and also very "adult." I think the rental car agent could tell I was having a "moment" when my eyes widened while signing the contract.

In true Nicole fashion, my cellphone—and, thus, my GPS—died five minutes into the drive and I knew I was missing either the common-sense piece of adulthood or the responsibility component. Check "needs work" under both boxes. Though I could see the city skyline a few miles away, I exited the ramp off the highway, wandering through backcountry roads before finding a deli where I could charge my phone.

The hotel wound up to be much fancier than I expected. I rode up to my seventh-floor room in an elegant elevator and opened a big cherrywood door to find an enormous corner-room suite with a king-size bed.

The room was filled with classic New England decor: long valance drapes, a headboard bigger than the bed itself, plush white bedding and a cozy white robe that hung on the closet door. The bathroom had double doors and a double sink in an actual hand-carved wooden vanity. There was a glassed-in shower and a separate bathtub, too. Impressive.

* * *

The next morning, you could say I was nervous as I sat in the rental car in a gas station parking lot approximately one mile from the office, killing time until I could walk into the office at an appropriate, not-too-early time.

Slowly sipping my third cup of coffee, I studied my surroundings. Unfortunately, there was nothing too thrilling on a Tuesday morning in Lincoln, Rhode Island. Lots of moms, kids and school buses. At 7:40 a.m., I left the gas station parking lot to go wait in the office parking lot.

Ten minutes and two country songs later, it all began to feel "real" when I saw the man who turned out to be the head of the New England office walking into the building.

Peter was as plain and "white-collar male" as you could picture. Not a hair was out of place and his crisp white shirt was ironed perfectly under his sophisticated gray suit. Something about his walk screamed "rule follower."

I followed him inside, heavy briefcase-bag over my shoulder, a few steps behind him, and paused at the front to let him get settled. Three minutes later, he greeted me with a warm smile and firm handshake.

Peter explained he wasn't clear on what I was going to be working on but told me to wait for Kathy, the woman whom Mrs. Fleming said would be training me.

After 10 minutes of small talk—the amount of chatting that extends just long enough to seem substantial—Peter guided me to an office that would be mine for Week One. It was small and bland but well lit by a large window.

"You are welcome to hop into my 8:30 a.m. scrub meeting with John from First Aid Farm to listen in. That will most likely begin before Kathy arrives," he said invitingly before leaving me on my own.

In my new little office, I stared past my computer screen into the hallway. It felt wrong to close my glass office door. The place was silent, and I made sure my computer speakers were turned off. I told myself to refrain from opening Facebook, but after five minutes of scrolling through Instagram on my phone, I realized I had nothing else to do, so why not?

Four quick Facebook messages later, Kathy arrived. Before she even said hello, she paused at my office door and said she needed 15, that I could come in her office after she was settled. I worried that my early arrival annoyed her, like she kind of forgot I was coming.

But once we started talking about work and personal stuff for about an hour, I could tell we were going to get along just fine. Kathy spent about half the day giving me a crash course in real estate deals. We talked about due diligence periods. Permit periods. Extension periods. Geotechnical testing. Lawyers' roles in deals. Engineers' roles with projects.

It was like playing volleyball against a really tall team with your hands tied behind your back. Everything she said flew over my head.

I tried to read through all the sample LOIs—which I learned that day stands for letters of intent—that she gave me and also the project booklets. I wrote down several questions and vocabulary words that I would come across during the day.

The rest of my first day was spent discussing nutrition with Kathy, who had miraculously lost almost 100 pounds on her own. By the end of my first day, Kathy knew all about my Chicago fitness activities and endeavors. Maybe I shouldn't have been so eager to talk about my passion outside of work—but passion outweighs logic.

The second day there, I met the other new guy on the job with me—Larry—who was 10 years my senior, was married and had two little girls. He had the thickest Boston accent and spoke to me like I was his little sister.

He was hired to be in the New England office full time and work as a construction manager. Basically, from what I gathered after the meeting with Peter on Day One, as soon as my job was finished—meaning I closed a deal and managed it through the permitting and breaking-ground phases—Larry's construction role would commence.

Nobody in the New England office seemed to know what exact projects I'd be working on or what to tell me to start doing. The whole week was a resounding "I don't really know what your job is yet either; you'll have to wait and see what Mrs. Fleming has you work on."

"I am not sure what you are doing, but my guess is that you'll be helping Mr. Bates."

So many unknowns. At least the weather was nice—and so was my salary.

* * *

My first week on the new job, I heard from KG zero times. Each time thoughts of him crept up, I tried to remind myself that I wasn't a thought on his mind and blocked them out.

It'd been a few weeks since lunch with Ren Man and he'd been texting me incessantly. The first 10 texts went unanswered on my end, but my disinterest only fueled his fire. Soon, he was inviting me via several texts over three days to a party his parents were throwing:

> Ren Man: My parents are throwing a big bash, it's '60s-themed. You should come.
>
> Me: No response.
>
> Ren Man: Their parties can be nuts, and it's kind of fancy. Your parents are coming, so you will know people.
>
> Me: What's it for?
>
> Ren Man: It's the grand opening of the new Lexus dealership. I think you should really come. I can show you Nashville.

Even though I wasn't really interested in Ren Man romantically, I did find him to be a little intriguing. And the idea of escaping Chicago didn't seem unappealing, especially when I was trying to avoid bumping into KG after that Hail Mary Heartbreak Letter I'd left him.

I realized Ren Man wasn't lying or exaggerating either about how fancy it was going to be when low-maintenance April called me and told me she was already searching for a dress.

"Nicole, we are totally happy to pay for your plane ticket if you want to go," she said. "It could be fun."

"If I can get a dress, I will totally go," I replied.

"Let me know what you find—and book your ticket," said April.

I planned to do all of the above but didn't feel the need to tell Ren Man right away. He'd find out eventually ...

CHAPTER 18.

STILL TRAINING

Indianapolis and Chicago, October 2013

It felt so good to walk back into my Chicago apartment after a week in New England. The garden apartment wasn't that spacious, but it was big enough. With updated appliances and a big cozy couch (a generous graduation present), it wasn't ratty, it wasn't fancy, it was just right—especially when I only had the weekend to enjoy it before heading to Indianapolis for Week Two of training.

Swam didn't tell me when I was hired that I'd travel often, but, boy, did I travel. I'd put money on more nights away from Chicago than in Chicago. In fact, it became so ridiculous I started keeping track: Between October 2013 and the end of May 2014, I'd taken 78 flights. Each time the flight touched down in Chicago, it felt more like home—probably because I wanted it to feel that way. But before Week Two of training, I anticipated none of this, and heading to Indy was a nice chance to see my parents and lie low.

WEEK TWO: WORK IN THE INDIANAPOLIS OFFICE

Another week without working in the same vicinity as Mr. Bates meant I had literally nothing to do. Professionally, I'd be cc'd on emails from Mr. Bates on occasion, which I'd skim and pretend to understand. But there were never orders or tasks clarified. I was told to "study" my notes from my time with Kathy and stay up to date on anything Mr. Bates sent my way. But reading a few emails a day made 9-to-5 unbearably long.

Sitting at a desk with zero tasks gets old after a few hours, as does small talk in an office of four other people. I'd rattle my pen, pick my nails and get annoyed at the office microwave beeping until I couldn't take it. I'd go outside to the parking lot and walk for 15-minute increments. This could not be the Real World, salary-making office life.

I left the office by 4 p.m. each day. Since I was "in training," and Mr. Bates was traveling somewhere in the country, the two ladies I was reporting to didn't mind if I left early. They'd even admit there was nothing for me to do. There was nothing even left for me to pretend to do!

* * *

When I got back to Chicago Thursday night, I planned to go to the kettlebell gym first thing in the morning after teaching a 5 a.m. Tred11 class. When I arrived at Flash Fitness for the 6 a.m. class, KG walked up to the entrance holding a coffee cup from Starbucks. There was a girl I'd never seen before walking alongside him. She kind of held back when he approached the doors to open the gym and saw me.

I glanced back to look at her again and noticed she was holding a Starbucks cup, too. It had been two weeks since the Hail Mary Heartbreak Letter.

My stomach churned.

He was sleeping with her. I knew it.

I was about to train next to this woman and pretend like I hadn't spent the last two weeks conditioning myself to stop thinking about the man she was sleeping with.

Lifting kettlebells next to her in a small, six-person class was nauseating. Following KG's coaching orders without acknowledging his presence was a heavy burden, too. Out of nowhere, a migraine struck me and I left class early and jogged home. When I walked through the door, I went straight to my computer, then texted April: "I just booked a flight and emailed you the confirmation. I'll see you in Nashville!"

* * *

WEEK THREE: WORK IN THE CHICAGO OFFICE

My third week on the job, I finally got to work in what would be my permanent office in the Gold Coast of Chicago, much closer than Alessor's office in Evanston. It was nice not to have to cart all my workout stuff, notebooks and laptop onto the Express L to Evanston every morning. I also loved that Mr. Bates arrived early and left early when he was in town—my kind of schedule!

Mr. Bates' instructions for Day One: Arrive at 11 a.m. for new company headshots. When I walked into the long, narrow office building at 10:40 a.m. feeling wide awake (thanks, Starbucks), it felt like I'd spent the morning playing hooky. But let's be real, I'd been writing Tred11 workouts, sending protein shake recipes to clients who wanted help and paying bills. The Grind never quit!

Meandering through the quiet, poorly lit office building to rediscover the Swam and Associates space, I held my coffee cup with every desire to find a trashcan fast. I couldn't be the millennial walking into Day One with a Starbucks cup. But my mind got lost in the dark and sad hallway; no part of me could imagine working there for years to come. What was I supposed to feel? Anything? The stench was like an old library, and it made me wonder what other types of companies existed behind these walls.

Suddenly, Mr. Bates appeared out of nowhere, like a phantom floating through the building.

"Hey, good to see you again. I have a key for you. Let's go downstairs and see if the fob works on the exterior building," he said in his cordial-robot tone.

"Hi, thank you. OK, sounds good." I followed him in his fancy-casual attire to the creaky, old doorway, ditching my cup in a trashcan by the elevator, hoping he didn't notice it.

The keys worked and, for some reason, I felt like when he handed them to me, I was supposed to feel this kind of "forever feeling," like these are the keys I will use each day I build my career for the majority of my life, or at least most of my young-adult life. But I felt nothing. If anything, I felt like I was holding keys for a temp job, even though I'd received an email about the enrollment period for a 401(k) with Swam. No part of working for Swam and Associates had grabbed my heartstrings yet.

Before skipping out to catch a flight, Mr. Bates led me into the front area of the office where there was a photographer set up with a backdrop you'd see at an elementary school picture day. I was as excited and nervous for these photos as I used to be in elementary school—a Real-World professional headshot! Woo!

There were three other men who worked in the Chicago office: Mark and Cody, who were both new, and Charlie, who had been with Mr. Swam for years when the company was Green, Macklemore and Swam. All three men were married and extremely kind, smart, driven individuals.

Mark asked Cody and me if we wanted to go get coffee at the Starbucks downstairs.

"Sure, I'll go," I said, thankful I'd ditched the last cup so I got an invite.

"So what were you hired for? I mean, I'm trying to take over the Chicago stuff because Mr. Bates is being phased out of that and moving on to other stuff. Cody is taking most of the Wisconsin territory for the client; so, where will you work?"

Well, he wasted no time on small talk. I had no clue—and I'm sure I looked like I had no clue, too.

"How old are you again?" he asked before I could answer.

"I'm 22."

"Wow, you're just a baby!" Cody chimed in.

"No, I'm not!" I retorted. "How old are you?"

For some reason I found him to have a friendly face, so I felt like I could ask him that. Plus, he also looked like he was 22.

"I'm 27, about to be 28," he said like he wanted to be older.

That sounded super young to me.

But they seemed like cool guys. In fact, I'd later find them to be the only supportive guys I could commiserate with when Mr. Bates sucked.

Mr. Bates had left pre-photo shoot, so after the Starbucks rendezvous, they told me to go home at about 1 p.m. Another tough "work" day in the books.

* * *

After packing lunch, drinking my shake and showering post-5 a.m. workout, I twiddled my thumbs. Without a 45-minute commute to Evanston, I had more than enough time to do things before leaving for work, but really, I sat there in my chilly garden-level apartment overthinking everything. All these "Day Ones" created such a buildup, I wondered when I'd actually start work.

At 7 a.m., I walked into the Gold Coast office and greeted Mr. Bates, who was dressed in his fancy-casual attire again; he exuded his calculated, cordial and professional but guarded persona. He did not make eye contact with me, which was either weird or a side effect of being uber-busy. I wasn't sure yet. For a while, I wondered if maybe it was because he was around a year older than me. Regardless, it made me become awkward, too—awkwardness breeds awkwardness.

I was there to listen in on a "tracking call," which involved about 15 people on the line discussing about 20 different deals in Chicagoland. I took as many notes as I could: due diligence periods, cap rates, triple nets, toxic aquifers, gross rents and percentage deals. I had no idea what half of the words meant or who any of the people were, but I pretended to care. I kept a serious, concerned look on my face for a whopping 90 minutes—not an easy task!

As I sat across the wooden desk (the same one I'd stared him down across at our first meeting before I had a clue of who he was), not sure where to keep my gaze, I eventually settled for staring at the office phone itself or my notebook as I wrote. We looked at each other for milliseconds when I'd ask a question, but there were few moments that allowed for it. Mr. Bates explained some of it to me as we went.

After the call, I continued to sit in the chair directly across from him, feeling like a chore, a hurdle, an annoyance as he explained that their newest client was a gas station client, Oil City. When he first joined the company—when it was Green, Macklemore and Swam—he lived in Boston and worked on the First Aid Farm client, doing pharmacy deals; basically, he'd scoured the markets and knew the New England territory well. In fact, that's how Swam ended up landing the Oil City client, a New England-based gas station company. I began to think that maybe Mr. Bates was actually a few years older than I was. I was going to guess he was like 28, even though he acted 35. Once you enter the Real World, guessing ages can be hard because there's no criteria for how to act, and I think that's when you start living in your soul's age.

Post-tracking call, Mr. Bates told me he would copy me on emails to the brokers out there on the gas station stuff (not knowing what that "stuff" entailed). Looking back, though, I don't think he really had a plan for what I was going to be doing. He excused me to leave at 3 p.m. like a person who doesn't want to talk on the phone anymore clears the awkwardness by saying, 'I'm going to let you go so that you can …"

He told me to come back the next morning to accompany him on a site drive with a Chicago broker.

"What time should I arrive, er, um, when will you be in?" I asked.

"Uh," he said, itching his ear, "you can get here by like 8:30;

I'll be here about 7:15 but somewhere around 8 is fine," he concluded.

There was no way I'd be a hair past 7:15 a.m.

* * *

After a hellish first week of sitting across from Mr. Bates waiting for the clock to tick …

Just kidding. It wasn't that bad leaving by 4 p.m. each day. And that Friday, I had a hell of a night with Michelle. We danced, she and Evan helped me try to hit on guys, and we drank a little too much vodka. I had it in me to sweat it out on Lakefront Trail the next morning, but three measly miles were about all I was capable of. Come 10 a.m. the next day, I checked my text messages. I had 10 texts from Ren Man that he sent at 2:30 a.m.

"Hey."

"What's up?"

"Are you there?"

"?. K."

"I am drinking whiskey what are you drinking?"

"Have you decided if you're coming to the party?"

"You should come."

"Your parents are coming."

"OK, maybe you aren't there."

"Hello?"

It seemed he might have been intoxicated but, nevertheless, interested in me, which made me perk up. How refreshing it was to have a quasi-mysterious and uniquely handsome guy in Nashville chase me. Reading his texts and then stalking him briefly on Facebook made me realize that I might, in fact, be slightly sexually attracted to Ren Man, too.

That morning, I decided to bite the bullet and verbally commit to the Nashville party. (Just because I had a plane ticket didn't mean I'd actually go!)

"Hey, sorry. I was out last night and my phone died. I'm actually going to come to the party. I get in late Friday night."

"OK, great! It will be fun, even though I'm missing the Predators game for it. I was going to go to that, but maybe we can do both."

All of a sudden, he didn't seem so interested.

"Uh, I'm not going to wear a cocktail dress to a hockey game, but you can go! I'll hang out with my parents."

Whatever.

I had his mother's number and texted her to ask her what type of dress to wear.

When I found a beautiful silk, black cocktail dress with a plunging neckline, I sent a photo of it to his mom and, apparently, she showed it to Ren Man.

Ten minutes later, I got a text from him: "Hey, my mom said you found a dress. Don't worry. I won't make you go to the Predators game in that dress. But maybe we can leave the party early if it's boring. One of my friends is also having a birthday that night. Should be fun."

Diehard hockey fans don't sign up to miss a game when they have box seats, so the text was peculiar; nevertheless, the apologetic, backtracking text made me feel a little less dumb.

The text's polite tone starkly contrasted the slew of drunken texts the week prior. I later learned there was a reason for that: Ren Man didn't send them! The truth came out later; the initial 10 texts were actually from his father.

While smoking a cigar with his dad, Ren Man admitted that he didn't think I was interested in him and his dad called bullshit. Ren Man then surrendered his phone to his dad, saying, "Say whatever you want; she won't respond."

And then I got those 10 messages.

And respond? Clearly, I did not.

CHAPTER 19.

THE ELEPHANT IN THE ROOM

November 7, 2013

Chicago tour dates when we'd take clients to see potential sites for their projects were like secret missions—at least that's what I called them. Mark and Cody would copiously plan the perfect route, make sure the i's were dotted and t's crossed on the letters of intent for each property and then we'd all set off in a large black Escalade. The backseat is where I laid claim, taking notes verbatim, observing how the men spoke, and watching Cody and Mark be demoralized as Mr. Bates would rearrange their carefully planned tour while also taking liberty to pitch their sites.

Another reason I called the tours "secret" missions was because the clients Swam and Associates worked for did not know about each other—something I discovered when I made the mistake of asking Mr. Bates about an email from First Aid Farm in front of Oil City's real estate directors during a tour in New England during my first month on the job. He shushed me so hard you'd have thought I asked him if he'd committed murder.

The day of the November 7th tour, it was negative 15 degrees Fahrenheit in Chicago and I had to be at a random Marriott near O'Hare Airport by 7 a.m., according to Cody. Mr. Bates was too busy to fill me in on the agenda.

Uber got me to Union Station by 6 a.m. and onto the train in my lucky stilettos, wool tights, my lucky maroon wool pencil skirt and a fancy, Romanian houndstooth jacket. It was such a warm coat—perfect for Chicago during a winter that would become known as "Chiberia." My hair looked pretty good for trying to curl it at 4:50 a.m.

When I got off at the Rose Park stop, I walked a bit off-kilter because my cross-body leather work bag containing my heavy laptop was awkwardly slung over my shoulder. Stilettos weren't my best choice, as I had to walk in the snow about a quarter-mile to what I thought was the correct hotel. Turns out, I needed to go two blocks further down. Snow covered the sidewalk, or what I thought was the sidewalk, so it was hard to tell what the shortest route was. It was dark outside and slightly eerie. Since I couldn't find the correct doors, I ended up walking an entire lap around the hotel in negative 15-degree weather in high heels. My face was numb. I feared I'd freeze to death. *No, I'm not being dramatic.*

Despite all this, I was the first one to arrive to the hotel lobby. Cody appeared soon after me, followed by Mark. Both looked handsomely professional.

I tried not to laugh when we got a mass text from Mr. Bates: "I'm in the hotel driveway."

Of course, he would text us that he was there, like we were unimportant and in the way of his tour. He never made us feel like team members, but rather like inferior interns swarming him like annoying gnats.

We got into the large black Escalade and headed to the airport to pick up the two Indianapolis-based real estate pharmacy directors—or, as I called them, The Directors. I was nervous to meet them because they were rumored to be very intense, hard to work with and opinionated. Awesome.

I didn't have to crawl way to the back of the Escalade until The Directors got in, but when I did, my knees were bent up to my face. I said a prayer that my pencil skirt wouldn't rip at the seams.

Shallow breaths, Nicole.

When we brought them back to the hotel for a nice breakfast, The Directors were fixated on me—like I was a muse at the table for them to enjoy. I was the only woman and also the only person under 28. I felt like they saw me as a child, like my ears were too young to listen to real business matters. For them, they could procrastinate starting their work day by inquiring all about me; for Mr. Bates, I was a completely inappropriate distraction, I'm sure.

His irritation was becoming evident as he tried at every break in the conversation to change the subject.

Mr. Bates was always all business yet so suave that he had this ability to naturally work in some interesting story about a deal he did somewhere and the concert he went to afterward, the celebrity he met there or the cool fact he learned about the town mayor. He knew how to bullshit so well that you couldn't even call it bullshitting—he was just that good. Sometimes I wondered what he was like guard-down.

One of The Directors mentioned he had a son who went to Lesley High School.

"My baby brother, Wyatt, went to Lesley," I said, excited to finally be able to chime in about something. "And I went to Shomberg High School."

"Your brother is Wyatt Winston? No way. Great athlete. My son knows him. My son played soccer at Lesley."

Then they made the family connection.

"So, wait, you're related to the Indianapolis Tom Winston car business then?" he asked.

"Yes, I am," I said.

"Well, why the heck don't you work for your old man?" he asked rather brashly.

Ugh, that irritated me. No matter where I was or what I was doing, the family name followed me.

Instead of indulging him in car business facts, I told him about how I'd had a job at Digital Media, a company in the automotive space, but the connection was too close to the family and I was interested in learning more about real estate.

It's all about the story you tell, right?

That day, we went to three sites in downtown Chicago, ate lunch at a fancy Italian restaurant near Michigan Avenue and then made our way to the burbs.

Me and the dudes.

That day, The Directors rejected almost every site.

Was this normal?

Was I bad luck?

After we dropped The Directors at the airport, there was no team meeting nor goal-setting debrief discussion, just small talk and goodbyes.

Finally at 7 p.m., after we'd been at it for 12 hours, Mr. Bates slowed down just enough while approaching a red light for me to jump out of the car near a train station. Cody and Mark had taken a different train to the burbs.

My first tour was ... something. Not sure what I was ever going to be doing for this company, but so far I made a good, quiet muse. Something about riding around in a black, tinted-window Escalade, making secret stops in pharmacies as secret shoppers, and talking about multimillion-dollar deals was interesting to me. At the very least, despite the intercompany drama, I learned that I liked the subject matter.

CHAPTER 20.

LEONARDO DICAPRIO

November 2013

The week after my first tour with The Directors was the week of the Nashville party. But before I could set off for Nashville, I had a quick 10 hours in Boston for a real estate tour with Mr. Bates, a bumpy flight back home, four Tred11 classes and two kettlebell classes to teach and one late pizza night at Mista's. By Friday afternoon, I was wiped and in no way ready to "party," whatever that means in Nashville terms. It'd been one of those days when everything seems to move in slow motion. Remarkably busy with The Grind, I felt like I'd been living on my own planet.

Yet, when 5 o'clock struck and I caught a whiff of the chilly Chicago air outside my somber office, I felt re-energized. Magic was in the air. And that's what I loved about Chicago—if you ever paused to breathe for just a moment, you could smell it, feel it, maybe even see it. The energy exists.

To get from Lincoln Park to Midway Airport, I took the Orange Line. Had I known just how many flights of stairs I'd have to take, I might've considered not wearing my favorite wool stilettos. I'm sure I was quite the blonde spectacle as I hobbled up and down those damn flights of stairs, trying to balance a huge Vera Bradley bag over my shoulder with my purse and cellphone in my hand.

By the time I landed in Nashville, I still had a hopeful vibe with each step in my stilettos, showcased by a little swing in my small hips. Nervous about Ren Man picking me up (or not), I sighed with relief when I saw him pull up in a Lexus SUV I knew his parents must have given him—they are Lexus dealers after all.

I tried not to laugh as I stared at him approaching. *How typical—Nashville guy arrives in cowboy boots.*

Somehow, he still vibed the rock 'n' roll look with the cowboy boots, something I'm sure only he could pull off.

"Hi, you look great!" he said with a smile, arms reaching out for a hug ahead of time like he did back in September. His scent was borderline mystical—captivating and delicious. After the embrace, he opened the car door for me, and so began the chivalry.

"Hope you are hungry! We're going to meet our parents for dinner at BrickTop's," he said with another smile. Luckily, the ride was short enough to dinner that all we had time for was small talk.

Together, we walked into the upscale, darkly lit but homey restaurant. Once we were seated, it appeared that we'd arrived at a strategy meeting for an arranged marriage.

Being the only "kids" at the table, the conversation was weird—focused solely on us. Growing up with two brothers, I wasn't used to all the attention, but I didn't mind. After awkward small talk among the six of us, Ren Man and I ordered the same thing.

"They are just so similar, these two," his mom said in an audible whisper to my stepmom.

April is cool and, as I suspected, she would not play into the giddy-mom role. She just nodded and started a new conversation.

After dinner, all six of us gathered in the lobby; I'd anticipated a few awkward goodbyes and "see you tomorrows" before grabbing my bag out of Ren Man's car and heading to his parents' home with my parents. But before I could say anything, my dad gave me a hug, followed by my stepmom as she said, "Have a good time with him tonight."

"What? I am not staying with him," I whispered in April's ear as I hugged her goodbye.

"It's fine," she said. "His parents have other guests staying with them, so there's nowhere for you to sleep—even the pull-out was taken. Sorry, boo. Ren Man was supposed to tell you on your way here. I forgot."

I walked away, holding April's gaze as the four parents waved goodbye to us. I'm sure my eyes said, "OMG, what is happening?" She just mouthed, "Text me if it gets weird."

The moment Ren Man hopped into the driver's seat, his cologne spewed my way and I became enthralled; his energy screamed, "The night is just beginning."

He began with a driving tour of his beloved hometown. It's seldom you meet someone who speaks of their hometown like a starry-eyed tourist. Energizing.

He drove me by Taylor Swift's apartment, pointed out his favorite bars, then over to Music Row and up Broadway to see the neon lights.

During the drive, Ren Man was the DJ with ADHD. You'd think he was nervous at first, but he was just amped about letting me hear *all* of his favorite songs. He played the Civil Wars and Betty Who. He played Keith Urban. He played old songs from his friends' band called Bonaventure and told me the stories about how each song was written, who wrote them or why he loved them. I sat quietly absorbing it all; I learned things like Kacey Musgraves' green-room wishes and quirks and Blake Shelton's favorite hangout spots.

When "Small Bump" by Ed Sheeran came on, Ren Man sang along. He was the first guy I was ever attracted to who actually knew the lyrics of the song.

"I actually have perfect pitch but hate my own voice," he said matter-of-factly.

After a few more stories and songs, Ren Man took me to his condo, where he carried my bag in for me and, of course, held all the doors. The first thing I saw was the guest bedroom (thank goodness) and I let out a visible sigh. He led me past the guest bedroom and plopped down on his cozy couch, inviting me to have a seat in his perfectly decorated condo. Next on the agenda? Sharing a bottle of wine from country star Kix Brooks' winery. No big deal.

To find out more about each other, we told childhood stories and took turns pulling up our own Facebook profiles to share photos. He talked about his plethora of hobbies, including but not limited to: photography, cigars, distilling alcohol, building, guitars, songwriting, interior decorating and fitness. Next, he showed me the bar he built himself. He followed that up with stories about how he had learned to distill alcohol on his own and had to sneak into the science lab at Lipscomb University to get the right equipment. He wasn't just talk. But, boy, he could speak well.

"I like to learn things," he said, stating the obvious.

He also showed me his guitar pedals, his handcrafted bar stools and his newest guitar. His eyes widened when he picked it up. As he strummed a few chords, leaning the guitar against his tight jeans, I let my eyes wander away from his strong legs around the place; his apartment smelled amazing—a combination of amber and nag champa. (I know this because years later I found a candle that smelled just like his apartment and that was the description.)

When I told him his place smelled amazing, he replied, "Thanks. It's quite the challenge to get it just right, but when you do, it's *nice,*" he said, putting the emphasis on "nice."

After staying up until 2:30 in the morning, he walked me to the guest bedroom. He tried to make eye contact with me and I dodged it as I leaned into his strong side body to give him a hug good night. My head came just about up to his shoulder and his hands touched me mid-back—an appropriate place—as he side-hugged me back and closed the door behind me.

"Sleep well," he yelled through the door before I heard him walking back toward his bedroom.

I remember lying there, staring up at framed hockey jerseys on the wall, kind of wishing he had kissed me good night. It must have been something about his chivalrous side and the way he treated me like no man had before. But then there was a boyish part to him that also reminded me of my brothers—like he was in no way, shape or form ready for a relationship.

Let's not think about that now, Nicky. Just go to sleep.

* * *

The next day, we decided to go to the mall so he could get new running shoes on our way to the YMCA to lift. He was so adamant about getting shoes that it was kind of odd. But I didn't care. Out of my own city and element, I had no agenda, and that was a first for me in the Real World.

On the drive to the Green Hills Mall, we got on the subject of my parents and their divorce. I don't mind telling that story, although I'm always nervous when I open it up with: "It actually makes me believe in divorce."

Ren Man listened as my story, which began way back at age 5 to explain what happened before the divorce at age 7. He allowed me to dig into some heavy details before asking very thoughtful questions.

"When I was little and they broke the news, the decision made a lot of sense. Plus, since I was used to my dad's absence because he traveled for work, not much would change. Now looking back I feel so thankful not to have grown up with two parents living under the same roof while hating each other. Divorce was the right decision for them. But, it oddly makes me even more passionate about a good marriage for myself someday."

Ren Man wanted to know about my mom. It's weird, I know, that I remember this, but when you meet someone who breaks the mold entirely of everything you've ever known, the first moments, serious conversations, physical interactions and scenes cement in your mind. You'd remember their untied shoestrings if you saw them.

That morning, he also wanted to know about my grandmother—both of them, actually. Then he shared his parents' love story.

Not for a moment was there a guard up between us; we spoke like we had nothing to lose and everything to gain.

Even his "listening" face was sexy. His hold-nothing-back attitude was delicately balanced with a respectful tone. More than anything, I knew he was listening; and trust me, I know what men look like when they're pretending. There was something about him—he was so thoughtful. In less than 24 hours, I knew that I'd never met someone as calm and relaxed yet so Type A with exercise training. He had an emotional, intellectual side. Multifaceted was his MO.

When we got to the gym, so did our parents, which was kind of hilarious since none of our parents work out regularly. I think they were stalking us. While our parents pretended to work out next to us and hold a conversation, Ren Man and I were both irked for a second before we realized the gym was a lost cause. Talking turned into them convincing us to join them at a really yummy breakfast place called The Perch. It was the only time I'd ever been excited to be at a gym and not really train or even sweat. I was becoming a bit nervous around Ren Man and didn't want him to see me all sweaty and gross.

What the hell? Was I into him?

When we arrived at The Perch, Ren Man took off his hat and threw it at the guy walking 50 feet in front of us. A strikingly gorgeous man turned around and grinned from ear to ear.

"Hey, man!" he yelled, walking toward us. "So great to see you, buddy! How are you?"

"I'm good, man, just hanging. How have you been? Are you back in town for family?" asked Ren Man.

"Yeah, just to see family for the holidays," he said, smiling. "We should get together this week."

As we walked away, Ren Man told me that his friend was a famous actor—one of many on the list of "famous people I met through Ren Man." I'd also later meet several people, men and women, who greeted him as if they were seeing their biggest crush, with the same ear-to-ear grin.

The weekend was becoming more interesting by the minute, and I hadn't even gotten to the good part yet!

After breakfast, we went to his parents' house to "hang." Former musicians, they had an in-home recording studio that was perfect for listening to new records—and for their drummer son, who liked to play in his spare time. Casual.

Once we were all gathered in the studio with headphones on, Ren Man played drums to songs from Dan and Shay, a new duo, who also happened to be friends of his.

While he played, I flipped through the Nashville Lifestyles magazine on the coffee table, only to find Ren Man in the center spread featured next to Brett Eldredge as one of "Nashville's Hottest Singles." My cheeks flushed. I quickly closed the publication and looked up at him, only to get a smile and a wink when we made eye contact. Winking was his thing, apparently. But actually, so was drumming. I gawked at the sweat dripping off of his vascular body as he played.

* * *

The rest of the day, Ren Man and I chilled out, got coffee at a local spot, made a stop for Twizzlers (his favorite) and I bought nail polish at the grocery store. I was beginning to learn what "hang out" really meant in the Real World and liked the slower pace of what Saturday in Nashville had to offer since I never seemed to slow down in Chicago.

The day took a flirtatious turn once we got back from running around town and it was time for us to get ready for his parents' big party.

I showered first in the guest bathroom while he fiddled with his new guitar pedal. Then, Ren Man showered while I curled my hair. As I starting to paint my nails on his coffee table, he came into the living area and stood to my left, wearing nothing but a towel, as he began playing his guitar; I tried not to appear obvious when I peered out of the corner of my eye to see his abs, which were only five feet away from me.

I don't know if I was more into his hair or his abs—or scared of them both. They were a lot to grasp.

Is this real? This hot, know-it-all, 6-foot-2 guy with great hair is basically naked, playing guitar right next to me like it's totally normal.

Later on, once I felt extra-pretty with my makeup on, I added to the (possibly imagined) sexual tension by pretending to need help with a strap on my dress. He was tying his tie in his bedroom and I felt like I was breaking the rules when I entered, asking him for help.

Before he could say yes or no, I turned my back to him, probably blushing, contemplating whether or not to call his bluff as he took his sweet time and pretended not to know how to fix the strap that really didn't even need fixing in the first place.

After it was "fixed," he lightly brushed my hair back onto my shoulder and pulled my shoulder toward him, turning me around so I faced him squarely, bodies inches from each other.

In that millisecond, I paused with chills, feeling for one fleeting moment something quite entrancing.

Was he my dream guy?

"You look beautiful, Nicole," he said politely. Then, he abruptly added with boyish charm, "All right, let's go!"

He smiled at me and gestured for me to walk out first. I rolled my eyes to myself as I led the way out of his room, worrying that I'd come on too strong.

It was all good, though. When we got outside, he opened the car door for me, again.

It got me every time.

* * *

When we pulled up to the shiny and bright new Lexus

dealership, parked outside were not only fancy new Lexus vehicles, but Maseratis, Ferraris and other luxury vehicles owned by the suave partygoers inside. Per his dad's directions, we parked right up front; a red carpet paved the way from Ren Man's Lexus to the front doors of the new dealership's showroom, where photographers sat waiting for us to smile.

As soon as we made it into the showroom, our parents flocked to us and cameras began flashing. There was a nonstop flow of people coming up to greet Ren Man. I began to feel more and more elated—almost honored—to be his date that night.

Ren Man's father was the general manager of the dealership and the unofficial mayor of Nashville—he knew everyone. People's eyes lit up when they talked to Ren Man about his dad.

As Ren Man led me around the party that night, he was my Leonardo DiCaprio with the perfect combination of articulate language, slicked-back hair, a strong jawline and impeccable fashion.

Meandering through the hallways of the new store before the formal sit-down dinner, he would lean in just enough to discreetly whisper in my ear, "See the guy to your left? He loves cars—go ask him about his Ferrari."

Or, "That man over there is worth billions; he loves horses; go ask him about his favorite horse."

Or, "That guy is the creator of the show 'Doug.' He is the best—let's go talk to him."

Nerves fueled my wine consumption, which turned into martini consumption. Despite lots of conversation, I managed to have four drinks all before dinner—and they were beginning to hit me.

By the time dinner came, I was starving. Thank goodness for bread pudding dessert. I scarfed it down, hoping it would sober me up, disregarding my gluten allergy. Unfortunately and not so glamorously, I had to make a few trips to the restroom because I of major gluten-induced bloating. The trips were noticeable enough that my dad came to wait outside the restroom to make sure I was OK.

After my third restroom trip, I realized Ren Man had been gone for a while, too. My parents were seated at the other end of the center table making small talk, and the cute couple who was seated to my left were up dancing. I decided to sit, sip water and people-watch. As I looked across the room, I spotted Ren Man interacting with five men who must have been 30 years older than he. In that moment, I saw him differently. I don't know what it was about him, but I liked it and I knew it instinctively. I didn't want him to catch me spying, so I shifted my gaze just before he could notice. Five minutes later, my eyes began to droop as the band played jazz. Right before I actually dozed off, Ren Man tapped my shoulder.

"Wanna head out? I told my friend I'd make it to his party. Let's get out of here and go have some real fun," he said.

Weren't we having fun? I wondered.

"OK, sure, that sounds fun! Is that OK with your parents?"

"Yeah, they won't care, or they shouldn't!"

Just then, a flash went off. His mom was trying to take a candid photo of us, of him whispering in my ear.

"Bye, guys, we are leaving!" he said with a fake annoyed smile and wave.

Taking my hand, he led me to the door.

Ren Man put on good music and rolled the Lexus windows down slightly. It was a gorgeous fall night. We drove 10 minutes and arrived in his parents' neighborhood. When he parked right outside of his parents' house, I was confused.

"Are we making a pit stop at your parents'?" I asked.

"No, we are going to my friend Jim's house; he's my neighbor."

Just then I saw a big "Happy 50th!" party sign in the neighbor's yard.

Before I could ask questions, Ren Man stopped me and said, "Blake and Miranda might be inside. Jim is their producer."

I took a deep breath and smiled at the people sitting on the front porch as we walked into her house.

Right as we walked in, a very famous country singer (who shall remain nameless) walked downstairs wearing jeans and Uggs; it turns out she was Jim's wife. Before she made it down to greet us, Jim clobbered Ren Man with a drunken hug from behind. He'd clearly been having a great 50th birthday.

We both grabbed bottled waters from hired butlers, laughed with Jim for a few minutes and then Ren Man and I quickly exited; the party was at that dying-down phase when most guests were leaving and only drunk people and family remained. Plus, it was weird to be in black-tie clothes when everyone else was casual.

Ren Man had aced the black-tie look, but something told me he preferred to ace the casual look. And that he did.

As soon as we were back at his condo on Wedgewood Avenue, I ripped off my tight dress and threw on a pink top with jeans. When I walked out of the guest bedroom, three of his best friends were walking in with beer, and I vaguely remember doing two shots before leaving for the bar. For the record, Ren Man wore even tighter jeans than usual that night, paired with a jean shirt that was lined in leopard print.

Recognizing some characters from the show "Nashville" was about all I can remember from the bar. Oh, and faint memories of thinking I should kiss Ren Man as I watched another girl flirt with him. The cute part was, he could tell I was a bit curious if they were an item (and also maybe jealous), so he took a step closer to me. He secretly grabbed my hip while in the midst of conversation with his childhood girlfriend as if to let me know he was into me, not her.

Not too long later, we left the bar—I think he could tell I was about to get sick.

* * *

The next day, I woke up in his bed with my clothes on, quite startled, nauseous and embarrassed. I rolled over to look at him.

Without pause, he started making out with me. It was weird that he wanted to kiss me because I'd been sick, but I think he knew his time with me was limited.

His head was so big and his jawline was so strong, it was different than anyone I'd ever kissed. He wasn't a bad kisser—just different.

A few minutes into our makeout session, when it started to feel more natural, we heard a knock on the door. It was his mom coming by to drop off the boots that I had left behind at their house the day before. Thankfully, Ren Man convinced her not to come in by saying he had to tend to me because I was sick.

"Shoot! Oh my gosh. I am going to miss my, wait, did I miss my flight?! Will I make it? When is my..."

He interrupted me. "You're fine; we have about 90 minutes."

We lay in his bed for a second, both staring at the ceiling.

I was beyond mortified.

"You tried to kiss me at the bar," he said bluntly. "Then you tried to hit on me when we got back here right before you fell over. But when I tried to pick you up, you wouldn't let me."

OH MY GOD.

I tried to say something, but nothing would come to me. "I ... I am..."

He rolled over and began kissing me again.

Then he paused and said, "You wanna know what your pick-up line was?"

"Oh, no! No! Don't say it. I'm too embarrassed!"

He grabbed me as I tried to roll away from him to hide in embarrassment.

"You told me, 'I'm like a 7 or an 8, and you're a 10 and I started to laugh, but then you started to fall over ..." he said.

I tried to roll away again.

Then he pulled me close and kissed me through laughs.

Fifteen minutes later, we decided I should pack my things

and get going to the airport. Scurrying around from room to room gathering my things—which were sprawled throughout the entirety of his lair—I was giddy and felt like I was watching an episode of a show I didn't want to end.

In the car, Ren Man passed his phone to me so I could watch the silly videos of my drunkenness that he captured during his own drunken stupor that night.

My cheeks reddened as I watched the snippets he filmed of me stumbling in the kitchen, fumbling over myself in the bathroom and trying to sleep in my clothes—all narrated by shirtless Ren Man in his glasses. In each snippet, he made sure to tell the audience what time it was and give a play-by-play of my drunken acts.

"Oh my God!" I threw the phone back at him with shame. "You are nuts," I said, sheepishly.

Ren Man smiled and turned up the radio.

"Oh! This is great! Have you heard of the Bobby Bones show?" he asked.

I tried to think, but my brain was in drunk-sleep mode.

"It's a radio show that just moved to Nashville. It is so awesome; Bobby is really cool. My friend Nada—who you'll meet sometime—is the web girl."

"That's cool! I'll have to find it in Chicago," I said.

"Oh, Chi-CAH-go," he said in his best attempt at a nasally accent. "Gross accent, cool city."

"Don't make fun of my city!" I said, playfully.

He pulled up to the Southwest drop-off area and ran to the back of the car in his bright blue basketball shorts, orange shoes and hoodie.

After grabbing my bag from the trunk, he walked over to the curb, put my bag on the ground and, without hesitation, grabbed my face and stared into my eyes, like he was looking at my soul. Then he kissed me, hard.

Dizzy and disoriented, I tried not to fall over as I turned

around to go check in for my flight. I had real-life heart-eyes, like the emojis all of my girlfriends used in their texts.

As I looked back to see his Lexus driving away, my heart felt like it does when you're on the first big drop of a roller coaster. Happy tears, or maybe sad ones, welled up in my eyes. What just happened?

CHAPTER 21.

CONSPIRACY OR COINCIDENCE?

December 2013

I sat in my own private, 12-by-12-foot office in Chicago and stared at the Boston maps I had hung on the wall, wondering if my leather legging pants and peplum top were too much to be wearing to work. I knew I wanted to wear this outfit to the upcoming Nashville Christmas party I'd been invited to and it was probably best I break in the pants so they wouldn't be so darn tight. On second thought, Ren Man said that Dan and Shay were coming, and they wear the tightest pants, so, hey! Maybe I would fit in just fine!

Midst ponder, a guy named Chris from the Indianapolis office called me. I knew he had a reputation for being really nice, friendly and genuine, so I wasn't nervous to take the call.

Chris and I made a little small talk, which I could have done all day because I really didn't have any work to do. When Mr. Bates wasn't in, it was nearly impossible to get a hold of him, so I arduously studied populations on this special app, but it grew boring after several hours of looking at places I'd never been to.

When you have no point of reference about a city, no motivation to crank out deals because you have little incentive or any superior checking in with you, all your work feels pointless and mind-numbing.

Anyhow, Chris asked me about my dad and how to get in touch

with him. He told me he needed to get my dad an LOI (letter of intent) for some property in Indiana that might interest him.

This was my time! I can be of use! I can be helpful! I can give value to this company!

I gave him John Winston's contact, the same guy who told me I should take the real estate job with Swam if I thought I could learn something.

What had I learned so far?

I set up a conference call with Chris, my dad and John. I helped fill in some minor details on the LOI, which I noticed was for roughly 37 acres and $13 million.

I didn't think much of it except that if my dad needed property, I could hook him up (or at least appear to) and if Swam's employee needed to get a deal done, I could be a middlewoman and at least set up a meeting.

After firing away a few emails, I went back to dreaming about Ren Man and what to pack for the party.

But before I could actually get to Nashville, I had a real estate tour with Mr. Bates and The Directors. And before that? Answer a sweet email from Ren Man.

* * *

By this point, The Directors knew more about me and my family's financial situation than I would have liked, but as far as what I did for Swam and Associates? I think they thought I was just a dumb blonde who worked as an office girl making copies and laminating things—as if laminating still existed!

But I could understand their thinking. I wasn't just the new girl days into the job. I had a few months under my belt but had little to speak of, project-wise.

Still, they didn't respect me the way I deserved to be respected. At a post-tour dinner that night, they asked me my age—again. When I told them it was my 23rd birthday that week, they laughed. Then they asked me who I was dating and for how long.

If I were 30, I would have told those guys to stick it where the sun don't shine. But not yet. Now I was just a girl, or I felt like a young girl. I needed to grow up, fast.

"They had no right to know those things," Cody told me afterward, encouraging me to "fight back next time."

I felt totally stupid, like a piece of ass hired to entertain these guys when I should've been treated as an equal employee.

I hated that night. More than anything, I hated that Mr. Bates not only didn't stick up for me but also that he said nothing about the matter afterward.

CHAPTER 22.

AM I DREAMING?

Nashville, December 2013

When I arrived in Nashville, Ren Man stood as close to the gate as possible, ready to greet me with a kiss.

It was the third time I was back at Ren Man's place (I'd visited the day after Thanksgiving, two weeks prior), and it was still hilariously perfect to me. He had such an affinity for really nice things. Take the night he let me borrow his Versace scarf when I was cold. That was the same night he wore a beautiful long blue Burberry peacoat.

His bathroom closet was my favorite. In it, you would find his watch winder for his motion-powered Rolexes, a tie rack, multiple Burberry jackets, Armani shoes and even a hair straightener.

I'll never forget the day I freaked on my second trip.

"Shoot! I forgot my hair straightener!" I said, rummaging through my suitcase. Without hesitation, Ren Man shouted from the kitchen, *"Oh, I got you."*

Ren Man even had a personal tailor.

But when he wasn't dressed in designer, you'd catch him in basketball shorts and a tee—typically, a free one he got from the local nutrition store. That weekend, he took me there and introduced me to what became a mild obsession for years: Quest bars. Afterward, we rode our bikes back to his condo, down

Music Row in our shorts and hoodies; the weather was lovely in December.

The trip was magical. New relationships are romantic, but falling in love at Christmastime in Nashville was falling in love in Hollywood style. Everything looked, smelled and even tasted perfect.

We saw the Christmas lights at the Grand Ole Opry and helped decorate for his parents' Christmas party.

That Saturday night, old family friends and new musician friends entered through the front door in herds. Not even an hour after Dan and Shay had arrived, they began singing Christmas songs. The casual singing turned into all party guests cozied up together in the dimly lit family room listening to them play songs from their upcoming album. Don't forget, I was in Nashville, so the entire room was singing along—in perfect key—in the warmth of holiday cheer.

Ren Man got pretty drunk, probably the drunkest I ever saw him. I was drunk but stopped drinking once I realized he and I were alone in his mother's dress closet for 30 minutes ....

When the song and dance ended, just Ren Man, his parents and a few friends remained, hanging by the fireplace. Moments into the conversation, the guitar came out again.

I rested my head on Ren Man's shoulder, realizing how The Grind in Chicago starkly contrasted with the slower pace I experienced in Nashville. It made me realize how frazzled my life was becoming with teaching Tred11 classes, traveling to Boston, and dating someone who lived far away.

My body needed a break. But in that moment, I felt like everything would be OK.

* * *

I woke up in Nashville the next day with a text from KG.

"Michael Jordan," he said.

I had no idea what he meant but it was my 23rd birthday.

The text from KG was unnerving, considering that Ren Man had officially begun calling me "girlfriend."

I'd only seen KG twice at the gym since the Hail Mary Heartbreak Letter, and both times his new blonde girl was there, so I kept my distance. It wasn't hard to forget about him since I had Ren Man to think about. However, with all the photos Ren Man's mom posted on Facebook, I'm sure I was all KG could think about. Or at least that's what I wanted to believe. I felt weird about it—I cared about him, and I'm not sure why.

Ren Man was the most loving guy I had ever been with. KG wasn't worth the emotions.

Looking back, I don't think I was totally over KG by my birthday, but I'd convinced myself I had to be.

You always want what you can't have, right?

Before I had time to think or respond, Ren Man rolled over, throwing his strong arms around me and sweetly whispered, "Good morning, babe. What can we do to make you have the best day?"

I smiled as I kissed him.

Naturally, we started our day at our favorite activity spot: the YMCA for a good lift. But just as I began my lift, my email dinged: My Southwest flight was canceled. Before I could panic, my dad called to wish me a happy birthday. Hearing the distress in my voice as I told him about the fact that my flight back to Chicago had been canceled, he offered to bring me home to Indiana on his way back from Florida in his private plane.

Dad to the rescue! That was close!

Until he could pick me up at 4 p.m., Ren Man's parents made me feel special, despite being far from "home" (whether home was Indiana or Chicago, I wasn't so sure at this point). His mom brought a really yummy cake to Ren Man's condo for a mini-birthday celebration. After I blew out the candles and took a photo, both of his parents followed us to the private airport so they could say hello to my dad before I jetted back to Indianapolis for the evening.

As we walked out to the tarmac where the plane was parked and still running, I looked at Ren Man and said, “Please know that I know that this is not normal. It’s just my family. I hope it doesn’t weird you out. It’s definitely not how I live in Chicago.”

“I know,” he said calmly, genuinely not appearing to see me as entitled.

We hugged goodbye and I climbed up into the Citation Sovereign. During takeoff, I tried telling my dad’s COO that I was in love with a guy I had just met without sounding too dumb or immature. His silent stare out the window after a subtle nod made me wonder what he thought—but only for a minute. I was too infatuated to care.

* * *

The night of my 23rd and first Real-World birthday, my heart was broken.

It began when I showed up to dinner to discover my dad and April had invited another couple to my impromptu birthday celebration at Bonefish Grill.

As we enjoyed cocktails, his friends asked me about my new job and I began telling them about my new role.

“It’s my job to venture off to several small towns and cities, scouting the land, getting accustomed to the municipalities and understanding the traffic patterns. After I lay eyes on the perfect site for my client, Oil City, I send a letter of intent to the seller and work to negotiate the economics of the deal, hopefully coming to terms with the seller before attempting to ‘sell’—pitch—the site to the client. If the client gives their blessing, I lead the team of attorneys, engineers and architects on developing the gas station to fruition,” I explained, feeling proud to have such a big-girl role in a small company.

I paused to breathe when my dad chimed in. “So what exactly do you do for work? You work for a pharmacy? Right? Isn’t it a pharmacy that you develop for? Tell them about Tred11. What is that again?"

Had he not been listening to anything I'd just said? Why did he care more about Tred11 than my real job?

Despite the little time I'd spent time with Ren Man's parents, they could tell you what I did for work, what I loved and hated about it, and why it was important to me, and here my dad couldn't even remember what my job was.

I have a brain, Dad. I am smart, Dad. I make a good salary to support myself, Dad. Be proud of me, please, Dad.

Leaving dinner early, I cried to my mom first, then Ren Man on the way home. The floodgates had opened and my entire being was now exhausted emotionally, physically and mentally. My heart hurt, and this time it stung as I remembered that I'd hurt like this before. My dad was not the best at remembering anything important to me and it constantly left me feeling unimportant to him.

For being just a hair past 23, I moved like a powerful freight train—I just hoped I was not a train that was bound to break down. No man could bring me down. Not my dad, not Mr. Bates, not The Directors and thankfully not KG, thanks to the love and support of my mom. At certain points in my life, she was the dad and the mom to me, especially when it came to dealing with men in the Real World.

Ren Man, fortunately, broke the mold I knew of most men. He listened, he remembered things important to me, he asked me questions as if I had something to teach and he never doubted me. Deep down, I feared he might let me down—or be a normal guy hiding in shining armor.

CHAPTER 23.

WORKFLOW

January 2014

As a real estate developer, my job for Oil City was to appear as an extension of Oil City, finding land for them and representing them in town hall meetings through the entire project. Because developers need not be licensed brokers, it's crucial to collaborate with local brokers who not only know the land well, but also the communities. They also have the capacity to facilitate the transaction between seller and buyer.

The broker I was told to work with in my Maine and New Hampshire territories was technically chosen long ago by—you guessed it—Mr. Bates. Stew was his name and chillaxed-dad vibe was his game.

Because of the long-term relationship Mr. Bates had with him, I'd initially worried Stew wouldn't want to work with me, but it turned out, he very much appreciated my timely responses to emails and ability to scout or "drive," as he often called it. The more deals in Stew's pipeline, the more money he could potentially make, and the more experience I'd gain.

Stew was a cool guy—down-to-earth, very sincere and highly motivated. He worked for a brokerage firm that he co-owned with his father and had an 8-year-old son. I've never met someone so enamored with their kid. Stew always referred to his son as "my kid." I didn't learn the kid's name until 2015.

I'll never forget, one month into the job, when I sent Stew an email with several marching orders, basically a list of targets I wanted to hit on the upcoming drive, and I was trying my best to sound like I knew what I was doing.

He responded, "Rock and roll. Let's go!"

Finally! Someone believed in me and wanted to work with me or, rather, gave me a reason to be excited about work—the hope of accomplishing something!

Despite what a hassle it could be to get a substitute teacher for the Tred11 classes I had to miss, getting to Boston and then getting a rental car, staying overnight in Newton, Massachusetts, waking up early to get to Manchester, New Hampshire, all just to "drive" with Stew, it was worth it. He took time to explain things without an ego, spoke to me like an adult when he helped me figure out what territories to focus on and showed general respect to me as a human.

Part of me could sense that he saw me as a freight train, coming in hot and fired up, but what I loved was that he wasn't going to try to slow me down. He respected my hustle and I, his.

* * *

New to the Real Estate Boys Club, little did I know how easy Stew made it seem. He was always professional, but so friendly I had no qualms about meeting other brokers. Confident in my stride, my work ethic and my knowledge of New England (ha!), it was time to meet a new broker, who'd be of help in the Boston markets.

After weeks of corresponding with a broker named Matt Rogue, I was going to be meeting him and his partner, Matt Donahue, in person at their office in Medford, Massachusetts. As it turns out, they would become very influential in my career.

The Matts and I were going to be working the North Shore of Boston together. They were going to be the "Stew" of Massachusetts for me. Since I'd driven to the Boston trade areas during my third week at Swam, I was fired up and ready to get moving on some of the locations I'd targeted.

With the detailed Excel spreadsheet I'd created of potential sites I'd found during my frequent trips to Boston, I bulldozed into their office building with my head held high, too confident and idealistic about my first stab at the new territory.

Matt Rogue welcomed me with his sweet, mellow and loving side. "Nicole," he said, "come in, please. Sit down. Have Mary take your coat. Can we get you something to drink? Maybe coffee or tea?"

Matt Donahue, in a brash, no-bullshit way, said, "You ready to get this thing going or what?" He could be blunt with me because we had a great phone relationship at this point.

Both of them had thick Boston accents and called each other Matty.

"Yes, Matty, I'm ready," said Rogue.

"All righty then, Matty," said Donahue, as he threw his huge portfolio of papers—maps, brochures, site pamphlets and all—on the large conference room table. He wasn't quite "uploaded" into the paperless life yet.

They sat me at the head of an enormous wooden table, facing a giant glass window. It was snowing hard outside.

Rogue started in that quintessential accent. "Nicole, I must say, I really enjoyed your work on this pipeline. I've lived on the North Shore my entire life and seeing the way you look at real estate here really gave me a fresh perspective. It made me look at corners I may not have looked at, so thank you."

He continued, "What we need from you now is just a little more information about your client; we want to know how they work, what they are looking for and how their timelines work. Also, are they in a hurry? With the weather, nothing will happen fast, but we need to know where they are at. Will they ground lease? How much will they spend if they purchase? What cap rate is preferred?"

I felt confident in my ability to answer all of their questions.

Respect felt good, too. I felt important and purposeful, despite the 30-year age difference.

All the annoyances I had to endure to get there—the snowstorm stress, the long hours seated in the rental car and even the suitcase that hadn't made it to Boston when I did—they were all worth it.

Finally, I would be contributing to this company. It was about time! I truly hoped the Matts would trust me, respect me and want to work with me, like Stew did.

CHAPTER 24.

GIDDY AND GRATEFUL

February 2014

It started off like a regular day—me at my gym in Chicago, steadfast in my New Year's resolution of lifting more weight, more often.

While Ren Man was a very prolific lifter and rocked an insanely strong and cut physique, I was a transforming cardio-bunny, sprouting some little muscles. Although I was still a tiny bit worried that I'd gain weight without running or kettlebells, Ren Man inspired me to trust the bodybuilding style of training.

After training, I jogged home to enjoy a rare week without travel.

After an afternoon of sending work emails and connecting with my friends Karly and Michelle to see if we could do an early dinner at Mista's, I received a call from Ren Man.

We were chatting for about five minutes when I heard a knock on my basement-level patio back door. It was a door to the back-alley parking area—a door I never used. I squealed a little I was so startled.

"OMG! I'm so scared. Will you stay on the phone with me? I am scared to look! What if the person can see me looking and they are trying to break in?" I whispered to Ren Man.

"Calm down," he said.

Something was up.

"Go to the door and just see who it is; you'll be fine."

Approaching the door slowly, as if not to make a sound, I peeked through the crack in the blinds and saw a strong jawline and excellent hair, slicked back.

It was Ren Man! He was there to surprise me!

I opened the door in my pink robe and jumped on him, disregarding the chilly air blowing in.

"I was going to wait to surprise you at dinner tonight with Evan, Michelle and Kar, but I didn't want to wait. I want you now."

As he carried me into my tiny bedroom, I nuzzled my nose into his neck—his scent relaxed me and also turned me on. Three weeks was three weeks too long, we decided. But long-distance relationships are characterized by yearning. In fact I believe the lust dies when the love becomes greater than the yearning.

Later that night, the five of us ate pizza, drank wine and laughed about our fun times in Aspen the month before when we all flew out to Colorado for a ski weekend amidst my crazy travels. One real estate tour was canceled; one ski trip had been planned!

The following night, Ren Man and I celebrated Valentine's Day early. A few cocktails in and lots of handholding across the dinner table later, we made our way to Boarding House for after-dinner drinks and canoodled at the bar as if we were in our own private corner booth.

Putting down his tin cup with barely a sip of a Moscow Mule left, he leaned into me and whispered, "When would you want to get engaged?"

The question made me feel safe, secure and at ease. Having had him around all weekend had subdued my stress levels. But really? This soon?

"Do you mean that? I mean, how could you ask that?" I wanted to say.

But I was also awestruck and flattered.

"Babe, I love you, and I want to be with you. But I have to figure out so many things. You know I'm struggling with my job right now and ..." I trailed off.

We both knew how much I had on my plate and how much more he needed on his plate.

"Talk to me in a year," I said, giving him a hug with a kiss on the cheek.

He threw down a twenty, grabbed my hand and said with a wink, "All right, babe. Let's go home."

CHAPTER 25.

MEETING MICHAEL BLOOMBERG, BASICALLY

February 21, 2014

Discussion of engagement can make anyone's head spin, but mine was already spinning from work life—and uncomfortably fast.

Despite traveling almost every week to Boston for work and multiple trips to Nashville, I was stoked to head up in the air one more time that week to meet Ren Man in New York City for his birthday. His parents gifted the two of us the flight and the hotel.

I planned to arrive ready to hit the town. 'Twas the day before Ren Man's birthday and I wanted to knock him dead. I'd ventured to Benefit Cosmetics to get my makeup done by my favorite artist and a spray tan from a sweet Tred11 client who worked there. Never underestimate the power of a spray tan and a good makeup job in the dead of winter. I felt like a million bucks before the flight.

My hair looked good, too, and though my half-leather leggings and stiletto booties may have looked a little overdone for the airport, I didn't care. My outfit was perfect for being 23 and on my way to a weekend with my sexy boyfriend! I hoped to take his breath away.

But, crap! Maybe I hadn't timed things well enough? There was a lot of traffic to the airport. To quell the nerves boiling up inside me as I pictured navigating security at O'Hare (and all that could potentially go awry), I was mindful to take deep breaths as my heart raced.

When I got to the airport and saw that there was no line at the United check-in desk, I sighed with relief.

But shit! I'd sighed too soon. The security line was easily a two-hour wait.

Luckily, a new line opened up and I zipped through security about 45 minutes faster than I would have otherwise. I got to my gate and sat down to do some work I'd slacked on in order to fit in the makeup appointment. Smooth sailing!

As soon as my laptop was out and my snack/dinner (a Quest bar, apple and giant water) were all set up, the airport PA system called for the attention of all passengers on my flight. It had been canceled. Not postponed, not delayed. Canceled and rescheduled for 5:55 a.m. the next day due to "mechanical problems."

What? No, this was not happening.

It was almost 7:30 p.m., and I would now have to catch a long, expensive cab ride back to my apartment just to get up at 3 a.m. and do it all over again.

I'd wasted money at Benefit, on a cab, and on airport food, and was already missing out on the extra teaching money I could've made if I'd taught Thursday night and Friday morning at Tred11.

Jet-black tears fell down my face as I clicked in my heels, trudging through the airport, headed to find a cab, wishing I wouldn't have wasted my time! Remorse fell over me for saying yes again to another romantic getaway when the reality was that I should've sat a weekend out. Sure, most of it was paid for by Ren Man's parents, but shouldn't I be teaching to make money? Was I failing at adulting?

I called my mom and sobbed out of stress and lack of sleep.

"Do you think it's normal to be this upset about this cancellation?" my mom asked me, not in a mean way, but in an "I'm concerned for your stress level" kind of way.

I knew she was right, but I also knew that there was no vacation, no medicine, no sleep, no new job, nor food or drink that would pull me out of this stress level for an extended period of time.

It was a crazy, out-of-control feeling. Spiraling, swaying, shaking: The stress of my job and travel was boiling inside me and my lid had popped off.

This was too much! Too much for something that was supposed to be fun.

I was doing it because I loved him, but I felt like he wasn't going through any of the struggles I was facing for the relationship. Without a full-time job or strict budget, he wasn't making the same financial sacrifices or using up vacation days.

Word in Ren Man's family traveled fast. Once I was in the cab heading back to my apartment, his dad called to try to calm me down. Sitting in the standstill traffic on the John F. Kennedy Expressway, looking at the wet windows as rain poured outside, it warmed my heart to know such a sweet man; but the warmth stung with an afterburn: Ren Man's dad was a reminder of all that my own father was not, at this current stage in my life.

My own dad wasn't capable of consoling me in this empathetic fashion. My dad has never dealt well with my stress—or any emotions for that matter. It's as if he has Asperger's and cannot feel empathy. Or at least he couldn't through my teenage years. When my dad and I conversed, we spoke different languages to each other. If only 23-year-old me knew that someday (soon) we would speak the same language, maybe my heart would've hurt less.

Listening to his dad, I could see where Ren Man got his sweet, empathetic side. It was further proven when he arrived at the airport at 7 a.m. the day before his 25th birthday to pick me up and ride with me to our weekend digs. All was right when I saw him, waiting for me at the baggage claim in his tight jeans and perfectly fitted black tee. With strong arms, a hopeful smile and a warm heart, he scooped me up and hailed a cab to take us to the Ritz in Battery Park.

Upon arrival, we rushed up to the fancy room decked out

with champagne, a flower arrangement and a chocolate-covered strawberry dessert to celebrate his birthday. The morning hours were characterized by nakedness, a yummy brunch and a workout, all before noon.

Next on our agenda: Ren Man took me to an older woman's apartment for drinks. It was a short cab ride to the Upper East Side, and before I could ask questions, we walked into a $14 million apartment and were handed glasses of champagne on a silver platter.

As I sat on the plush furniture in this woman's fancy apartment that overlooked the busy Manhattan streets, I had to pinch myself. *Where was I?*

This older woman worked for a high-powered makeup company; years ago, she'd helped Ren Man's family with a special fashion event in Nashville. Despite the 30-plus-year age difference, she'd hit it off with Ren Man while they worked backstage together. According to Ren Man, he never made a trip to NYC without seeing her. I don't remember much about her except her silvery-white pixie-cut hair, her perfect makeup and her intense eye contact with Ren Man. She barely looked at me as she spoke. My gut told me she would have dated him in another life. But, apparently, as evidenced by the photos on the luxurious table behind my seat, she did date Michael Bloomberg for several years.

As we sat there enjoying some celebratory birthday drinks for Ren Man, I listened as he caught her up on life and us. Ren Man then mentioned a secret luxury-car business venture.

That's the thing I forgot to mention: This trip was for Ren Man's birthday, but it was conveniently occurring the weekend before he and his father planned to present building plans and designs for a potential car dealership in Nashville that they dreamed of owning and running together. The board meeting was Monday morning in NYC.

Very much enthralled with the intricate decor surrounding me, I found it hard to focus inside the tall, echoey grand room in which we sat and wondered if we'd get a tour. The chairs were the old-fashioned, antique style that almost bounce when you sit on them. Plush velvet pillows sat with us and fancy art hung on the walls. The waitress-servant—whatever she was—who'd handed us champagne from a silver platter kept disappearing behind a swinging door and returning with small bites and napkins. It appeared there were two wings of the grand apartment, plus a room behind me that was more of an office space or an art room.

Once I'd spent 30 minutes taking it all in, I became more present in the conversation, but not as myself, but rather as the Nicole I imagined she thought I was—heiress to a large, successful automotive company who can be enjoying small bites and champagne on a Friday afternoon—not the Nicole who was pretending not to be a struggling, new-to-the-Real-World millennial, in anguish about missing work emails.

Tagging along in Ren Man's exciting life galvanized my view of the Real World. You must remember, Monday to Friday (most weeks), I was teaching Tred11 classes at 5 a.m., was in the office by 7 and then working out or coaching after work when in Chicago. A weekend in Chicago meant a weekend full of substitute-teaching classes or coaching strength workouts in the park. If in Boston for Swam, I'd still rise before 6, work out, complete emails and hit the road no later than 7:30.

Straddling the line between The Grind and the Ren Man Lifestyle, I needed stability. However, I saw no way he could provide that, nor was I ready to lean on him. Coming to this realization more and more during our New York trip made engagement seem seriously far off and incredibly silly.

Ren Man had a lot of irons in the fire—and I was his biggest cheerleader. I loved him. But it was like being a cheerleader for all the sports: Some days I encouraged him to get a drumming job with Dan and Shay or take the tour offer with Blake. Other days, I'd reassure him that being patient and waiting to work with his father would pay off. And on other days, I'd slightly reprimand him for sleeping in until 9:30 a.m. and going to the gym for two hours, which is what he did when he was frustrated with not knowing what to do with his life.

A big part of me hoped the project with his father would happen—I knew Ren Man would find the work purposeful—but a part of me resented the fact that, at age 25, he thought he could just walk up to a franchise and become a part owner or general manager; so many people work their entire lives to get to that point.

Ren Man had a lot of expectations in life, and I guess a lot of dreams too, but his dreams were the kind you dream up in Neverland, and I wasn't sure if Ren Man realized he wasn't in Neverland.

* * *

All in all, the first full day in New York City was a good one. After we had enjoyed a good night's sleep, fancy breakfast and steamy shower, Ren Man took me to SoHo to shop for a dress he said I needed for a big fashion show in Nashville in April. Afterward, we hiked over to Central Park just long enough to take a touristy photo of us kissing on the sidewalk. How mystical it was.

The day was capped off with 9 p.m. dinner reservations in the theater district. Nine o'clock dinner seemed so New Yorker to me, and despite the late hour, I was up for it. The only hiccup we had was actually one most girls have during their time of the month.

When it's that god-forsaken time and you feel like a cow, bountiful cocktails and heavy meals make you feel like a cow who ate another cow. Saturday night before dinner, I felt bloated and gross (severe understatement) and couldn't get my dress to zip.

"I'm soooo fat," I yelled from the bathroom, while trying to zip my dress.

"I want to feel like your smoke-show girlfriend. You deserve the most pretty, most beautiful girl. I feel so gross and fat. This pretty dress barely fits ..." I whined and looked away, disgusted with the image I saw of myself in the mirror. I was feeling all of the things that girls feel when we self-loathe on our period.

Beyond physical cramps, our mental sanity is not all there, you know? We decide to list all the things we've done wrong in the recent weeks that could make us "this fat" and further add to our stress and self-hate. My scapegoat of the night? All the travel. All of the not working out. All of the little night's rest. But it was compounded by the recent Real-World stress of fitness photo shoots and pressure to be the poster child of boutique fitness. I still didn't have shredded abs and, sadly, scorned myself for this daily.

Ren Man looked me in the eyes, like he was going to cry, too. Before he spoke, he grabbed my hands firmly.

"Don't talk about my girlfriend like that. It's not nice," he said, looking me in the eyes with a broken smile.

That broken smile struck a chord with me.

I had a lot of insecure moments with Ren Man. Looking back, I don't know if it was because he seemed so perfect, and I felt pressure to be prettier or something, or if all the travel threw off my training enough to make me feel like I was losing my athletic body. Or was my body just a natural gambit for me when I was frequently finding myself in high-stress situations?

Whatever it was, it was not OK, and Ren Man made sure I knew that.

I loved him more than ever at that moment and hated myself even more for making him ride my roller coaster.

CHAPTER 26.

TURBULENCE ON THE GROUND

Sunday night in NYC, we got to sit up in Ren Man's father hotel room for an hour or so wherein we spoke about life, love and their business venture. His father always put me at ease, made me laugh and feel special. That night, he gave me a $100 bill for my cab troubles and flight delays on the way to NYC. The money didn't make me feel whole, and to be honest, I didn't want to take it, but the feeling of having a dad like that—someone who worried about me—that I did want.

I fell asleep peacefully, as I always did when Ren Man was next to me. But waking up before the crack of dawn the next day wasn't easy. In fact, that part sucked, especially when you're in a cozy, warm king-size bed with white linen sheets at the Ritz next to your handsome boyfriend. But I was a powerful freight train and this wasn't my first early-morning rodeo.

Once at JFK, I sighed with relief when there was no security line and that I'd easily make my 5:20 a.m. flight. But my mood quickly changed when I learned my flight was canceled again once through security. This time, it was weather in Florida holding up my plane.

I started to freak out and called Ren Man, only to break him into more pieces than I had three days prior in the white-marbled bathroom. I knew then that breaking him down wasn't going to help me; the weaker he was, the less he could help me. And I needed him.

But even more, I knew I needed to work on managing my own stress in the Real World. Nevertheless, he helped me get on a later flight at 9 a.m. which led to a 10 a.m. Chicago landing, and a cold train ride straight to my Gold Coast office.

* * *

Two days later, I was about to find out just how steadfast, sturdy and sane Ren Man was, the hard way. I had an obligatory trip to Boston for a drive with Stew in New Hampshire—it was time to get some deals going in that region.

New Hampshire's so vast that you can't just stumble from town to town and get a great idea of the lay of the land like you can in Boston. Well, you can go to one town and see all there is to see, but it's hard to know how that town fits into a series of surrounding towns if you aren't from the area. Simply looking at a map won't tell you all you need to know either. You have to drive the towns, study the traffic, observe the community and perhaps talk to locals.

There were four potential sites that Stew had on the table (meaning they were not only targets but also had willing sellers) and I needed to survey these sites before we would make an offer on behalf of the client.

We met at the Panera in Portsmouth, both wearing jeans and ready to *rock and roll.*

For the record, the reason I was so eager to jump on a plane for these Boston trips was that it was the only way I felt I ever could be productive for the company. Maybe it was too much, but you'd see after sitting in an isolated office in Chicago waiting for emails.

At about 3:30 p.m. in New Hampshire, it began to snow as we passed through Kingston.

My flight was scheduled to take off at 7:30 p.m. and Stew

started to get nervous. It could be over an hour to get to Boston with traffic. He started to head back to Manchester, where I'd parked. I thought he was a little premature—until I saw the traffic around Manchester.

We got stuck just trying to get to his car at the Panera, and it was beginning to snow heavily. Stew sensed my heightened stress. We passed a hotel en route to Panera and, spur of the moment, Stew decided to stay overnight at the hotel.

"Take my car to Panera. I'll use the hotel shuttle to get to my car tomorrow morning," he said, quickly hopping out of his car.

"You'll be able to get right onto the highway and I'll avoid the traffic," he added.

The plan worked. I took a deep breath as I merged onto I-93 South, mentally repeating his verbal directions; my phone was low on battery. Traffic was bad, but I hadn't a clue for how long. Thirty minutes later, traffic had moved, and I cruised down I-93 until I was just outside of Boston. It was only 4:45—I was going to be fine ... until it was 5:30 and I hadn't moved more than a quarter-mile on the highway. Once again, I called Ren Man to help me through.

Stressed, I griped about the storm, the traffic, the potential delay, the late night I was about to have before my early morning. Ren Man already knew how shitty this situation truly was.

"Nic, you're gonna make your flight; it's fine," he said soothingly.

"Babe, I don't know that for sure. Plus, if I do make it back, I get in at basically 11 and have to get up at 4 to teach. I am freaking out. I need sleep," I barked.

"You can nap tomorrow," he suggested.

"Easy for you to say. You don't have to be at two jobs in one day," I said in a bitchy tone.

Ren Man took the jab and simply continued to try to calm me down. I felt like he thought I was crazy and I hated that he thought that—even though I knew I was going crazy from all the stress. I appreciated that he wasn't giving up on me. I needed him. But I sure didn't act like it.

Somehow or another, I got close to the airport around 6 p.m. but then the rental car GPS steered me the wrong way. I was confused on where it wanted me to go, and I took a wrong turn about 15 minutes out of the way, all the while still talking to Ren Man. Out burst several F-bombs on the line.

"Stop it, Nicole. It's fine. You will be fine. We can get you another flight or something," he said.

"If you weren't trying to tell me all is right in the world—because it's def not—I wouldn't have missed that turn. FUCK. I cannot believe this. Now I will miss my flight! It's boarding in five minutes. I don't have a sub for tomorrow. I don't have a hotel for tonight. FUCK!" I screamed.

He said nothing.

"Fuck! I hate this."

"Babe you sound like you're going crazy. Call me back so you don't miss ..."

I hung up on him after yelling "fuck you." I was at my wit's end but still on a mission to make the flight.

I missed my next turn for the rental car center again and was furious. Now I was definitely going to miss my flight, dammit. As I curved around the airport again, I wondered, *Why didn't he get it?*

I pictured him sitting on his comfy couch in magical Nashville, preparing for a nice dinner with his parents that night. Then I saw me, at midnight, waiting in a cab line in freezing Chicago at midnight to go home, getting in bed late and then having to wake up at 4 a.m. to teach the 5 a.m. class—if I even made it back!

If anyone had empathy for me, it was Ren Man, yet I resented the fact that he didn't have any of these kinds of stressors in his life.

Was it supposed to be this hard for me, and Ren Man just had it easy? Or was I some kind of fucked-up person for creating this mess? Would I ever have balance like Ren Man? Looking back, I realize I took it out on him when I shouldn't have, but in those moments, I'd lost myself.

After I finally pulled into the rental car center, crying, the guys at Hertz gave each other the "she's having a moment" eyes and immediately hopped in my car and quickly drove me a secret way to the Southwest drop-off area instead of making me wait for the shuttle.

Once there, I ran straight to the security line and lost it when I saw about an hour-long wait. Tears and makeup were going everywhere like a crying cartoon character.

A nice security line worker looked at me and said, "Wow, you must be going through something really rough; you can cut ahead if these people are OK with it."

Nothing was that wrong, except that I was super stressed out.

Sure, I'd spent only eight nights in my own bed that month, I'd screamed at my boyfriend, I'd felt bloated and exhausted and alone, but nobody had died and my family was fine.

I cried my way through the line; people took one look at me and let me by. I felt guilty, but it was 7:10 and my flight was already boarding.

Amidst meandering through security lines and sprinting to the terminal, I hoped I wasn't going to run into Mr. Bates. He never told me when he would be in New England, but a lot of times it would turn out that we were both there. Luckily, there was no sign of him.

After making the last call for boarding, I settled into a row by myself. It was so nice to have the space and, for a moment, I felt like I was back at the Ritz. I lay on my side and quelled my stress with two Quest bars I had in my bag.

What a dark night.

I landed in Chicago at about 9:45 p.m. and cabbed it home.

I unpacked, made sure I had workout clothes to teach in the next day and called Ren Man to apologize. I heard the phone ringing, picturing a subdued Ren Man mad at me, but he still answered. "Glad you made it back safely, babe."

And next? I tried to sleep. Key word: "tried."

The problem was the lack of heat in my apartment. My roommate Becca thought it was normal to set the heat to 56 degrees, even though it was negative 14-degree weather, since she was overly worried about the heating bill. That night, I slept in three pairs of sweatpants, two pairs of socks, a thermal shirt, a sweater and a fleece and tried to shiver myself to sleep.

The cold kept me wired, thinking. I pondered: What would my mantra be if I had my own blog or business? If I were to do something besides this job that has 10 shitty moments for every good one?

I thought about how Ren Man and his friends had this catchy inside-joke thing they'd say called "DTM," meaning "dead to me." It was their way of drastically expressing dislike for something.

"That band is DTM," they'd say.

"DTM" was catchy; for some reason, I liked it.

What if my mantra is "dare to move"?

Like jumping, hiking, skiing, lifting, exercising—just being in constant motion, always trying to make progress?

I came up with a little poem before falling asleep at 3 a.m. "I dare you …" The next thing I knew, my alarm clock was going off at 4 and I had to get up to teach my 5 a.m. Tred11 class.

The poem came back to me …

> "I dare you to move. I dare you to jump.
> I dare you to lift, laugh and play.
> I dare you to flip. I dare you to ski. I dare you to say 'hey.'
> I dare you to resist idleness. Because without movement, we can go nowhere; our bodies are our tools to do everything."

* * *

The energy at the class that morning was unparalleled. I had a 15-person wait list. One hour of sleep? It's sufficient when you wake up feeling like you have a purposeful job to do.

Tred11 was the one place in my life where I felt like I was helping people and making a difference—so unlike my work with Swam.

More often than not, venturing into these tiny municipalities for Mr. Bates' projects that were further along in the development process, you'd see the neighbors banding together to boycott the gas station projects.

But fitness, everyone loves feeling like they are getting stronger, faster and leaner. I had my 5 a.m. crew, the Type A people who have way too much energy and like getting their butts kicked bright and early.

No matter what was going on in my life, I knew everything would be OK as long as I spent that hour teaching that 0-dark-thirty class. More than ever, I realized my heart was in fitness.

CHAPTER 27.

A LIFE-CHANGING PHONE CALL

March 31, 2014

After an entire week in Chicago with nowhere to go but my office and Tred11, it was safe to say I was in a better mood. So. Over. Traveling.

On my way to teach a new-to-me evening class, not even traffic could bring me down. I was soaking up the city, people-watching at traffic lights and anxiously anticipating a packed class.

About five minutes away, my phone rang. It was Mrs. Fleming.

"Hi, Mrs. Fleming. How are you?" I asked, trying not to sound too caught off guard.

Why was she calling?

"Great and you?"

"Good, besides having my bag lost last week and almost getting snowed in in Boston, I am doing well."

"Good, good. I know you've been traveling a lot! There's something I need to talk to you about regarding your lease. I know you emailed me about it."

Oh yes! I had emailed her. I needed to tell my landlord what I was doing—if I'd be renewing or not—by the end of April. When Swam hired me, I was under the impression that they planned to move me out to Denver for a new territory developing for First Aid Farm, but I wasn't sure now—six months in—if that was still the plan.

"I understand that you will need to re-sign your Chicago lease well before October, which will be the one-year mark for your time with Swam." She paused briefly and took a deep breath.

"So what are your thoughts about Boston, like, in July?" she asked.

My body froze at the stoplight of North Halsted Street and West Armitage Avenue in Lincoln Park.

"Boston? Like living in the city of Boston? Moving?" I replied, stunned.

I choked as I proceeded through the intersection, running a red light.

"Um ... My initial thought? My simple knee-jerk response?" I said.

This was happening. How had I not predicted this?

I took a deep breath and made sure to brake for the next stoplight.

"I know it's crazy expensive. I'm not sure how I could make that work because I would be leaving my fitness job here in Chicago."

"Well, economics aside, what do you think? Would you be OK with moving there? I think it would be a great adventure," she said with zest.

There was something about her tone that made me realize this wasn't going to be an "either/or." This was an "absolutely, you have to go."

Shit. For the sake of keeping this job, I'd have to move.

I told her I just wanted to make sure there'd be a financial incentive. She assured me there would be.

Then, more than ever, I felt alone. This was a decision I was going to have to make 100 percent on my own, without considering anything or anyone—not Ren Man, not my family, not Becca, not Tred11.

Being from the Midwest, I naturally hated the East Coast—just because it was the East Coast. I wanted nothing to do with it. It was a door I didn't want to open, a door I didn't need to open.

Yet, it seemed, a door that I indeed would open because I thought I had to.

The next three weeks were irksome. I felt like I was wading through a cold, muddy swamp in stilettos while trying to run away from bad guys but had no idea where on earth I was.

CHAPTER 28.

OH, THE IRONY

Berlin, 2014

Something I had discussed at length with Ren Man: if I should accept my dad's invitation to go to Berlin as his "plus one" for a work event for the Audi franchise.

Ren Man and I ultimately decided that this trip was a huge deal, an opportunity to spend time with my dad and improve our relationship. Ren Man knew that I wanted to be in the family business someday, and we thought maybe this was my dad's attempt at making me feel included in the company.

I will always remember that pep talk. Ren Man was so hopeful for me; hence, I was hopeful, too. We wanted it to be a good trip, but in the end, we didn't get our wish.

* * *

Despite having a decent salary, a good job and a lucrative side gig teaching fitness classes, I felt like an underdressed high school girl as I stood next to my dad in the airport check-in line. I was wearing leggings and an oversized sweater, and had let my hair air-dry.

Hello, waves.

My inner high school girl shone through when my dad left me in a security line with a one-hour wait while he went ahead through TSA PreCheck and I became frustrated.

Couldn't he just wait with me? Weren't we supposed to be spending time together?

Little things he did (or didn't do) were already annoying me.

Uh-oh. Chill, Nicole.

When we got on the plane, I dramatically warned him (half-serious, half-kidding) that I was going to be very anxious when we landed in France for our layover because of all of the horrible, miserable experiences I'd had in the past traveling through Charles de Gaulle and traveling in general. He nodded like he does when he pretends to listen and started to read a newspaper from his bag of reading materials he never travels without.

My father has a huge heart, but sometimes it seems he was born without the empathy gene. He cannot actually feel for others. He is kind and loving, but he doesn't show his compassion in the ways most people show it.

It sounds weird, but having Ren Man by my side gave me more strength when dealing with my dad. It was nice to know that someone else got it. He understood the confusing relationship and was the king of empathy, like his father.

Fearing that my dad and I might quibble more than improve our relationship, I grew anxious and quickly drank two glasses of red wine on the flight to ease my stress and let go of what I couldn't control with work, travel and my long-distance relationship.

Eight hours later, we'd made it to Berlin, but not before a traumatic experience at Charles de Gaulle when we realized we didn't have a continuing flight from France to Berlin and my bag was lost. But I was now numb to these tribulations—like I had accepted the world of travel was out to get me. It was like I wore a sign on my chest in airports that said, "kick me in the stomach," like I was the forever-bullied kid.

Fortunately, we were able to quickly hop on another flight to Berlin without a long layover and arrived in time for the dinner.

However, when we got to Berlin and my bag did not, my dad

and I knew we'd have to rush to shop for some clothing so that I could look presentable for the first evening's events.

Before that, though, we checked in with the Audi Group organizers at the hotel. The nice woman explaining the weekend itinerary told me to arrive in the lobby the next morning for an art tour and then directed my dad to arrive for a special car-driving experience an hour earlier. There was a lottery for all franchisees and my dad's name was drawn.

I was let down.

"Dad, can't you just do the art tour with me so we can be together?"

"Nicole, I want to drive the car. I'm here for work," he said firmly with a tone that made it sound more like "how dare I ask to spend time with him."

From reading about the driving tour in the information packet provided, I saw that my dad would leave at 7 a.m. and wouldn't return until 5 in the evening. My heart sank a bit more as I tried to hold back tears.

"But, Dad! I want to spend time with you."

Ever since I was a feisty pre-teen (when our quarrels began), if I reveal the slightest bit of sadness or frustration and raise my voice, all he hears is me being upset and starts to be combative.

"Nicole, why is everything a fight? Why are you always mad at me?"

"Dad, I just want you to want to spend time with me. I just want you to be my dad; I'm not the kind of daughter who just wants your credit card for shopping. I want time with you. I want to see Berlin with you."

"What? My credit card? You can't have my credit card!" he retorted.

"Dad! You're not listening! I said I *don't* want your card; I want time with you."

"Well, I'm not a bank, Nicole; you're just spoiled."

He still wasn't getting it. He is literally obsessed with thinking everyone is after his money. And yet, we went shopping and he spent over $1000 on clothes, jewelry, shoes and makeup for me since I had no baggage. I would've rather worn a brown paper bag and had a hug from him.

* * *

That first night at the Audi welcome reception night, I felt like Olivia Pope from *Scandal*. I walked into this swanky hotel bar in Berlin wearing a knee-length, white, silk shift dress that came up around my neck with a collar sealed with a pretty gold button at the nape of my neck. I wore my hair slicked back into a high ponytail to reveal the beautiful pink gem earrings my dad had bought me. I was going to put our fight in the past—until the questions began.

With each dealer I met at the cocktail hour, I was asked about my involvement with the family business.

"Are you the vice president?"

"Are you a GM?"

"I bet you can't wait to be in the family business!"

"Why the hell aren't you working for your old man?"

"When are you gonna step in and let your dad take a break?"

Though these endless questions vexed me, I had polite, engaging and hopeful remarks to say at the beginning of the evening:

"I want to learn the business from the outside in."

"I'm currently working on a really neat real estate development job that I believe will help build my business acumen to help the family down the road."

"I can only hope to be a part of it someday!"

"Whenever he will actually hire me!"

"Oh, sometime soon! And I can't wait!"

My eyes would light up as I passionately spoke of the business I so hoped to someday be a part of—the business my incredibly astute grandfather founded, the business I had wanted to work for my whole life.

It carried on—until it didn't. The chatter dissipated, the lights dimmed, people got too drunk and those of us left in the bar kept to our own small groups. The lull in the evening allowed the opportunity for my dad and me to talk about the very apparent theme of the evening at the back bar.

I knew it was my moment to tell him how much I wanted to help, how much I wanted to continue making the business grow and improve, to tell him how proud I was of him.

Very quickly, he shut me down, telling me I wasn't ready.

"You have your whole life to live," he said.

"But, Dad, this is something I want to do, not something that is me taking the easy way out. I don't love my real estate job. I'm passionate about what Grandpa started."

"You are young and you need to go live your life like I did. And you'll want to have kids."

"Dad, I don't want to end up like you, thrown into this business with no clue what's going on in my late forties. I don't want to not know a single familiar face in the company. I want to start at the bottom; I want to know people; I want to earn respect."

"Nicole, you're in your pre-pregnancy years," he said, as if that made me unable to work.

"Dad, that is discrimination," I said in utter shock.

I looked into his eyes with tears welling up in my own. My heart was breaking. Just like it did when I knew he wasn't going on the art tour with me. Just like it did when he didn't know what I do for a living. Just like it did when he didn't know my best friend's name in high school. Just like it did when he told me not to "toot my own horn" when I said I was proud of my grades in high school.

He was starting to cry too, so I continued.

"I'm not even married! Who is to say I am going to have kids right now? I want to help you! I want to be a part of this!"

"You are embarrassing me. Lower your voice; this is a work thing," he ordered.

I looked around. The only people around us were wait staff

from the hotel. I didn't care, until another couple who was part of the event walked up. I excused myself to go to the restroom.

That familiar heartbreaking feeling was so overwhelming; I couldn't hold it together. I cried heavy tears in the bathroom for the 90th time in my life thanks to him. The warm tears on my face felt the same way they did when I was 5 and he left for Korea as an air force pilot, the same way they did when I was 8 and didn't get to talk to him on my birthday, and the same way they did when he said he wouldn't pay for braces when I was 11.

Once I pulled it together, I knew I had to stay at the event a little longer. The night wasn't over. For the remainder of the evening, and the entire weekend, whenever I was introduced to someone new, I told them I had nothing to do with the company; I told them I did real estate development for another company.

The worst part was, they still didn't get it.

"Oh, real estate for your dad? Right?"

"No. Not right. Real estate for a job I got on my own with an unrelated company," I'd reply.

And, of course, just as I said that, I remembered the LOI for a $13 million deal that I delivered in December to my dad. I couldn't run from the company, but I couldn't be a part of it either.

I wanted my dad to respect me and see me as a mature, capable woman. Yet, it was impossible. The way he breaks my heart reveals my weak, sad side.

That night, I cried when I FaceTimed Ren Man while sitting on the floor of the fancy hallway wearing my white dress and black mascara.

He cried, too.

He got it. He understood my sadness. He told me it would be OK, to just let it go. His voice soothed me and my whimpering cry came down to some heavy, sparse tears.

The next day, I went and saw all the famous monuments on my own. I connected with a bunch of new Audi dealers I hadn't yet met. I went to a "dark" restaurant where you eat in the pitch-black—which would have been a neat experience, had I not been alone.

Unfortunately, the blind waiter ended up sitting down to dinner with me—in an effort to hit on me—delaying my meal for hours. I had no cellphone and was worried that my dad was looking for me (he wasn't). I was alone in downtown Berlin without a phone at a dark restaurant, which was located in a dark side alley. I ran through alleys to find a main road to flag down a cab. I remember thinking, if someone abducts me, nobody will know where I went, when I left or where they took me. Awesome.

I finally made it home close to midnight and my dad wasn't even in the hotel room. He was out at the dealer-only dinner. I was sad but not surprised that he wasn't worried about me. He came into the room later that night. I pretended to be asleep as he flicked on all the lights.

At the closing dinner, we bumped into the president of Audi America. My dad introduced us and the annoyingly familiar question rang: "Are you in the business with your dad?"

Knowing that Audi wants to treat the dealers as a way to thank them for their hard work and big sales and that their goal is not to give free trips to random people without interest, I knew the right answer would be to say, "Someday!" or lie and say yes. Instead, I immaturely said, "Nope. Just here to have fun. My dad let me come," quickly, unprofessionally, and then I walked away. Angry was my attitude, you could say.

Heading back to the hotel early, I was greeted with the all-material things my dad's credit card had sowed: new dresses, shoes, some makeup. I only felt more empty and sad.

On the way home from Berlin, I got stuck in Newark, New Jersey. My dad's flight left from Newark to Indy, but my flight to Chicago was canceled due to another "maintenance issue" and I had no idea where to fly to. I tried calling my dad and he said, "Sorry Nicole, I'm boarding—can't talk. Good luck. I hope you make it home."

I ended up going to Nashville for a few days, my bag only arriving on the last day.

CHAPTER 29.

I NEED MORE ON MY PLATE

Chicago, May 2014

Two days after getting "home" to Chicago, I set up a call with Mrs. Fleming to discuss my future with the company and about moving to Boston. Ever since that call about moving, I was having hot-flash-like symptoms about Chicago: Some days, it felt so homey, there was no possible way I could leave it. Other days, it felt like this weird purgatory I didn't want to live in but didn't want to leave either because I feared the alternative. "Home" was becoming a hard concept to grasp.

Yet, it was a tad easier to contemplate a future in Boston as I began to get into a good groove with work. Finally, after taking a little more initiative (assuming that all-knowing Mr. Bates would step in if I had a misstep), I felt like I'd made some progress on several sites. I was very proud of a deal I negotiated in Tewksbury, Massachusetts, which took several calls between me, the seller and both Matts to get done without Mr. Bates. I liked that I was allowed to get the terms of the deal done on my own.

I also somehow managed to get all four sellers in a Gardner, Massachusetts, assemblage project to come to terms with the environmental cost portion of the deal and sign the LOIs. I won't bore you with all the details of what it took to get this intricate deal through, but I'll just say I felt like an orchestra conductor finding harmony for the first time.

I loved the projects I was overseeing, but I was very much

bored with work life when I wasn't in Boston, which led to some serious reservations about the job. The spitfire, 23-year-old me felt that I needed to tell Mrs. Fleming this: I wasn't going to move for a job that bored me to death and didn't fulfill me. I needed to know that I would be given more responsibility and a clearly defined role if I were to move to Boston after only nine months with the company.

She said she'd speak with me in a few days.

When she called the very next day, Mrs. Fleming sounded so pleasant, almost overly happy, when she greeted me. Was she having a good day? Or trying to charm me?

"Hi, Mrs. Fleming," I said, then paused.

I was about to say what an employee should never say. And I said these things secretly hoping she would be so appalled, she'd fire me so I wouldn't have to move to Boston!

"Yeah, thank you for taking the time to talk," I started again. "I guess I'm confused because I feel like I don't have enough work on my plate. I try to help Mr. Bates all that I can, but he is rarely here and never responds to my emails. I never know if I am stepping on his toes in his own territory. Unless I am in New England driving, I don't have a ton to do," I said rather boldly.

"Well, can't you teach more fitness classes?" she asked.

My jaw hit the floor.

Was the COO of the company really asking me if I could find more work in fitness when she was paying my salary? And I was basically telling her I was doing no work for that salary?

What the heck?

"I absolutely could, but since I told them about my plans to move to Boston, they are going to begin to phase me out," I replied.

"Well, for now just do what you can and know that things will definitely pick up once you are out there full time," she said.

"Yes, I know that I will be much more productive, seeing as though I will be able to go drive to a site whenever."

A huge pit grew in my stomach. Was I really about to leave my life in Chicago just to go drive aimlessly through New England more frequently?

"Just be patient. I know this is going to be a good move for you," she said.

"And you want me to go to Vegas for the ICSC convention, right?" I asked.

I had a flight booked and everything, but it seemed weird to me. The reason my company went to the International Council of Shopping Centers convention was primarily to show face for First Aid Farm, which would have a large booth there.

"Yes, absolutely go. It will be fun for you to see the other developers in this company, spend time with Mr. Swam and see how it all works," she said.

* * *

Another flight, another time-capsule session, excusing me from the Real World and instigating a lot of overanalyzing of my life.

To focus on the good during the flight to Vegas, I reflected on the trip I had taken to Nashville at the end of April to attend a special fashion show fundraiser featuring Christian Siriano, the most recent winner of "Project Runway." Ren Man's family, who was a sponsor of the event, helped put it all together.

I couldn't quite figure out what was cooler from that weekend: meeting the fashion designer Christian Siriano himself, members of the country group The Band Perry or country musician Luke Bryan's guitar player. Every other minute spent with Ren Man was an adventure.

During that trip to Nashville, I had a call with the CEO of Swam and Associates, Mr. Swam himself. Ren Man secretly listened in.

The entire duration of the call, Mr. Swam spoke to me about my father. I was still bitter about Berlin, and Ren Man got mad at me when I alluded to my dad's social awkwardness and quirky side during the call.

"I know you have issues with him, but he's blood and you must stick up for him," Ren Man said firmly when I hung up.

Still, we both found it a little weird that the CEO only wanted to talk about my dad. We sat there on his comfy couch in silence, contemplating it.

Then Ren Man brought up the LOI for $13 million.

"Has your dad paid them for that land yet?" Ren Man asked.

"Over Easter, I asked my dad if he and Chris from my office had spoken. I alluded they were using me to get to him. His response? 'As far as I'm concerned, they do not have a cent from me yet.' I doubt that the deal is the only thing tying me to this job," I said, confidently reflecting on all the work I'd been putting in.

I didn't want to admit it, but after Ren Man's suggestion, my conversation with Swam then made more sense. But it would take a year of things getting messier before I'd fully understand.

Now on a plane headed to Vegas, I sincerely hoped my dad and his business would not come up with Swam.

I need to figure out my life.

At a crossroads with my life and my job, I'd committed to making the move to Boston days before the fashion show. As soon as I verbally confirmed, Mrs. Fleming had me fly out to Boston to find an apartment in a day.

Logically, the move actually made sense. I was only productive when I was there, roaming the actual grounds that could potentially be developed. But I'd needed financial incentive to make the move.

A few days after that call with Mrs. Fleming to confirm the move, she'd come back to the table with an offer that would seal the deal: Swam would pay up to $2,000 a month toward rent and increase my salary by $1,000 per month. When she threw that at me, it felt like a bribe, but I made the decision immediately. Less travel, more money, more sanity. Simple as that. I was moving to Boston.

Still, I didn't want to bite the bullet and accept that Boston was really a thing. In my heart, I wanted to be in Nashville all the time.

But if I made more money and traveled less for work, I'd have more money and energy to spend on traveling to see Ren Man, so potentially a move to Boston could help our relationship. At least, that's what I hoped. A rift in our relationship was forming as Ren Man and I were beginning to argue more frequently. I hoped that the move would bring us back to smoother sailing.

But he had work to do too. I wished he could figure out what his plan was. I wanted to rush him, although I knew it wasn't possible or fair. In his defense, he wanted a plan too. He weighed options in the music business—a gig opportunity with Austin Webb, another potential one with his buddies Dan and Shay. Nothing was concrete—it never is in the music business. But I was so stressed out with my own situation that I needed him to know what he would be doing now—like on this airplane now.

When we'd spoken on the phone the night before, I was short with Ren Man. I also couldn't snap out of it and I hated that. It tore me up inside. I loved Ren Man. He was my rock who lived too many hours away.

* * *

It all got worse once I arrived in Vegas. The whole time I was there I wondered why. Why all these fancy dinners? Why cabanas by the pool? Why was I there? I had no meetings, I had no projects and Mr. Bates was pretending to be mute when he saw me. I was basically there to observe.

Don't get me wrong; I'm great at studying situations. But I knew I could be doing more, helping more. I hated being treated like an idiot.

The first day there, I was at a cabana at the MGM Grand pool with my four real estate developer coworkers (all young males, between 30 and 40 years old) and the CEO, Mr. Swam.

Mr. Swam and I sat in the cabana for two hours talking about my father. He dug so deep I teared up at several points as I revealed a bit more about the dynamics of our relationship, hinting at the rough trip to Berlin.

Mr. Swam, a father himself, was appalled (or at least, pretended to be) about my struggles with my dad. He made me feel less crazy for freaking out. He said things like, "If you were my daughter ... "

He mentioned that he'd noticed weird things about my dad's communication skills, which made me feel less crazy. Mr. Swam's concern was endearing but had nothing to do with my career.

Little did I know, it had everything to do with my career. He had dollar signs in his eyes.

CHAPTER 30.

IT HAPPENS IN A FLASH

Chicago, May 2014

I'm not really sure what did it. I don't really remember which fight started it nor why; I just know I was unhappy and on edge about life.

Nicole in May 2014 blamed her unhappiness on a combination of not wanting to move, wanting this romantic guy to grow up a little faster and wanting her job to actually give her work to do. But the actual reason? Fear. She was afraid to leave her fitness and social bubbles in Chicago.

Regardless of the fear and anger and dissatisfaction I felt toward my life, I know I was mean to Ren Man. I yelled at him and cursed at him and spewed cutting words his way. I was like a series of multiple explosive devices. When I went off, Ren Man had no escape; he cared too much.

After a few hang-ups, phone call fights and episodes of crying, one of us said it was over. Maybe it was me. I kind of blacked out, mentally stepping outside of reality.

I told him I was not going to come to Nashville that Friday for Memorial Day weekend. He said, "OK."

I wanted him to beg me to come. I wanted to go see him badly. Whenever I was with him, it was all better.

To try to push him to beg for me to come, I then said I had canceled my flight, which was a lie. I was still going to go. I thought we'd work it out. But he said, "Good then."

The next morning, nothing had changed. I still had a flight to Nashville that he thought I'd canceled and he hadn't asked me to rebook it.

Since I wanted to talk this out with someone, I made plans to meet KG for lunch that day. By then, we'd kind of made amends. Time and space helped us evolve into quasi-friends. At least that's what I told myself.

As it turns out, I wasn't the only one having relationship problems; we both came to the Starbucks on Diversey to vent about our relationships.

"So, you are moving to Boston," he said, boldly staring at me with his blue eyes.

His hair was combed to the side perfectly. His mood was different, relaxed and almost jovial.

"Yes," I said with an anxious tone, looking away from his bright eyes. "They gave me an offer I couldn't resist."

"And? What is the offer?" he asked.

"Twelve thousand added to my salary and $2,000 a month for my rent there."

On a regular day, that would have been the point in the conversation, the zenith, the OMG moment. But not right now. I had other things on my mind for which I needed his ear. The best part was, KG knew that.

"But what's really up? How's Ren Man? What does he think?"

"He knows we aren't at a point in our relationship where his opinion really matters. I mean, I want him to be a deciding factor, but I feel I'm at a point when I need to rely on myself. Plus, we've been fighting. Last night, I told him I wanted him to fight for me to come there this weekend, but I don't think he will. If I don't go there to see him this weekend, it will be over."

I was trying not to cry.

I never knew things could feel so heavy on a cool, sunny spring day in Lincoln Park, Chicago. In order to refrain from crying and avoid making a scene or trying to solve an impossible riddle at a lopsided Starbucks coffee table, I turned the conversation over to him.

"How's your girlfriend? What's her name again?"

"We broke up," he said.

OK, this is weird.

"Yeah, it was for the best. It was just a week ago, but I am OK."

"Well, if you're OK, then I'm OK. I want you to be happy. Are you OK?" I asked.

I needed to go and get back to work. I had to respond to Ren Man, who'd been calling for the past 10 minutes. I hoped he wouldn't be crushed if he knew I was with KG. I gave KG a hug; he hugged me hard. It was good to be able to hang out with him again. For some reason, despite feeling like he didn't listen to me before, as a friend he was pretty damn good.

I called Ren Man on my walk home. I told him about getting coffee with KG.

He said it was fine if he'd helped me. His tone didn't match his words. I knew this wasn't going to end well.

Ultimately, on that sunny Chi-Town day, we decided we'd take a break. When I suggested it first, a huge part of me wanted my suggestion of taking a break to make him want me more. I wanted him to still want me in spite of my anger. He knew I wasn't evil, that I was just depressed, right? That I, too, knew it wasn't his fault? It wasn't anyone's fault.

The thing is, I really missed Ren Man. I wanted Ren Man but was so confused with my own life that imagining how to deal with him felt like I was looking up at Mount Everest and holding flip-flops and a towel.

That evening, there were more calls, hang-ups and callbacks between us. I couldn't let go. But I couldn't stop feeling anger, sadness and frustration, too.

There was another F-you from my mouth as well as a lot of other hurtful things. I wanted him to fight for me, but I knew he wasn't suited for this battle. I knew it wasn't going to turn out the way I wanted. I knew I had to start focusing more on Boston than a relationship with a guy who didn't know what he was doing. At least, that's what I thought was right back then.

As good girlfriends do, Michelle dropped everything and came over for a pasta dinner and wine.

"You're not even sad; you're mad!" she jeered as she walked in. "This is good. This is fine. You will be OK," she added.

Best friends are always right. I didn't look back twice. I texted KG to see what he was up to.

Moments before midnight, KG showed up with a bottle of wine, blue eyes and open arms.

"Michael Jordan!" he said. "You're 23!"

I let him in with a big hug. As he walked down into the garden level, he looked around curiously as he stepped over and through the boxes to get to my couch. It'd been a minute (or seven months) since he'd been over.

"Sad panda," he said grimly.

"What?" I asked.

"It's sad in here. No wonder you feel depressed. This sucks. Why are you packing so early?"

I explained that my crazy friend Taylor was temporarily moving into Becca's room since she left the lease a month early and those were hers. I was going to pack last minute.

Meandering through the boxes in the dimly lit room, we made it to a small portion of the couch and sat very close. I am not sure when, why or how much wine we'd had before it happened, but before long, I was in his lap, straddling him. We'd held eye contact for too long, knowing this, whatever it was, wasn't right. My guess would be that neither of us was ready to kiss someone else, but going there, to that familiar, scandalous place we'd thrived on before was tantalizing, and wine made it unbearably stimulating.

I pulled back to take a gulp of wine and then leaned in just far enough to make it known that I would dare to go there. He held back, and then I pulled back. There was only silence, eye contact and mental stimulation. *Would we go there?*

I leaned in again. This time as I leaned in, I reached back and grabbed his hands, which he'd just placed on my lower back.

He squeezed my hands as he kissed me, then released them to wander my bare skin. I grabbed his head as his hands crept up my sweatshirt and continued to explore my braless back. I couldn't breathe. Our noses pressed up against one another; we were millimeters away from breaking the rules, going further.

The moment was enjoyed, the kisses carried on.

Different than past times, it was better. Like putting on an old favorite outfit or going to see your old favorite movie. It was the drug I needed and the touch I craved. Ren Man and I hadn't been together in one whole month due to travel and I felt farther from him than ever before. I'd also forgotten about the Hail Mary Heartbreak Letter to KG. I just wanted to be in my warm bed with him, disregarding the fact that it was wrong.

Physically pleasing and somewhat unexpectedly exciting, it contrasted with sex with Ren Man, who was safe, loving and incredibly good at sex. I was used to Ren Man's intense pressure and hard and fast speed coupled with love and care. Lying there in bed trying not to compare and contrast, I admitted to myself that KG soothed the way Advil does the trick for a rough hangover. The sex mirrored my life at that point: looking for something to cure the pain.

One month until I'd be leaving Chicago. What would another night hurt? No-strings-attached was the plan—KG could separate church and state. I could not. But that didn't mean that we stopped.

PART III.

NEW WORLD BOSTON

CHAPTER 31.

PURGATORY SUCKS

June 2014

Head throbbing, mildly sweating and nauseous, I awoke with that feeling in my stomach that it was much later than it should be. The sun was shining too brightly through my blinds. My hair was in a low, messy bun, and my floral romper was riding up a little too high. As I moved to adjust it, a business card fell out of my bra. A foggy memory of a young guy who worked for the NHL in Dallas came to me, reminding me that he'd handed it to me at The Underground the night before. For some reason, I had visions that we'd performed at a live burlesque show, but that seemed like a dream. My pillows were rearranged in a way that was surely not my doing.

Crap, it's moving day.

My third "goodbye Chicago" party—which was supposed to be simply a dinner—became more of a drunken soiree with my best friends. It started off with that "we are all best friends who want to get happy-drunk together" energy, but for me, it quickly veered into "I want to drink my sorrows away" for the first time in my life. Apparently, I was depressed. And now I was in bed, feeling even worse.

My crazy friend Taylor walked through the doorway of my shoebox of a bedroom.

"Hey! You're alive! Great! Shannon saved your life last night. After she brought you home at God knows what time, I took care of you. And just so you know, I am usually you—*the drunk girl*—so I barely had a clue of how to take care of you. Glad you're alive. According to Shannon, you and your new dancing burlesque buddy disappeared after you got off the stage. Wait, you dance? Anyways, call Shannon now and order her a thank-you pizza and send it to her work. When she found you, she had to break a guy's nose to get you away from him and had to go to the ER for her hand."

Wait, what? I looked as puzzled as I felt.

"Some guy coaxed drunk you into his hotel room, which was above The Underground bar. You got away for like 10 minutes and then Shannon went to rescue you. When he wouldn't let you go, she punched him in the face and somehow dragged you out of there," Taylor said very matter-of-factly.

I shook my head confused and then rolled over onto my side. I had no time to process all this. Today was the inevitable day. For a few seconds, I played my new favorite mental game where I'd think about all the other horrible things I would rather have happen to me than move to Boston.

Snap out of it! Time to get up!

Once I made it to the kitchen through awkward, dizzy steps, I found my cellphone and called Jet's Pizza, never turning around to view the boxes which lay behind me. My old "home" on North Wilton Avenue had come apart and laid in disarray, never to be the same. But my new life—which I couldn't even picture—hadn't started yet.

I now knew purgatory.

Midst shuffling from one side of the apartment to the other to finish last-minute packing, I called Hunter three times. My younger brothers were late. They were supposed to be there by 8 to help me empty the place before I had to pick up the U-Haul at 9. Then the professional movers I'd hired could lift the heavy stuff.

As I waited for Hunter and Wyatt, I scrambled around to throw what was left in the closets and cabinets into whatever boxes had a little room left. You could tell by how I shoved glass vases into boxes jammed with ski coats that I really cared about this move. *Not.*

Despite having put on an impressive amount of weight in two months (thank you, emotional eating), my white jean shorts kept falling down. I waddled around wishing it were all a dream.

By 10, my brothers rolled up. I could tell by their sunglasses and disheveled hair they'd had a rough night, too. I ordered Wyatt to start moving all of my things from the apartment into the back alley while Hunter and I went to pick up the truck.

"You got it, sister," Wyatt said in a dry, unenthusiastic tone. He was definitely hung-over. I wouldn't know anything about drinking underage, but I imagine the hangovers are twice as bad when you don't know what you're doing. It appears I still don't know what I'm doing either, but since I'm in the Real World and they're not, I'll keep it a secret from them: Nobody has it figured out. Adulting has no rule book, just a Netflix bible.

After finally locating the U-Haul center (we'd actually lapped it three times since it was hidden inside a convenience store at a gas station), I fought with a brash Indian man about how the truck and trailer I'd reserved were MIA.

The saving grace was that I was there with Hunter, who is basically a god of peace and love; his disdain for conflict—and the fact that my company was paying for the truck—helped me to simmer down.

But only for a second. The fact that I wouldn't be able to enjoy what was turning out to be a sunny, temperate summer day in Chicago made me even more upset than the angry U-Haul man. Even worse, he only had a truck one-third the size of the one I'd pre-ordered.

When we got back to my soon-to-be old apartment, my sweaty, hung-over self was determined to make it work. But something about seeing half my stuff in the gross back alley made me more nauseous.

As the movers started lifting the big stuff out, Wyatt got the last few cardboard boxes, and I began using a Clorox wipe to scrub out the messy bottom drawer in the kitchen where I'd kept all of my supplements: hemp seeds, chia seeds, psyllium, oats, flax oil. As I turned to look behind me, wondering what the heck Hunter was up to (he always tried to get out of chores when we were little), he walked in and started using his higher "gay" voice.

"Yes, Sally, what was that?" he said in full-on acting mode, his chest puffed up and left hand dangling out in front of him, half-pointing at something.

I looked at him, giving him the "Hunter, not right now" eyes.

"I said, 'I'm not straight and I'm not gay. I'm not bisexual either. I'm tri-sexual.'"

"Hunter, what the hell?" I asked with my notorious cackle.

We were never going to get anything done if Hunter reverted to his comedic mode.

"I'll *try* anything!" he said, spinning like Michael Jackson as he nailed the punchline.

The jokes continued. Thankfully, they kept me from bawling my eyes out. The boys knew I was sad. Hunter preferred jokes and laughter over hard work and tears, while Wyatt preferred to avoid the emotions and get the work done so we could leave sooner than later.

"Nicole, what's your new place like? You don't have a roommate, right?" asked Wyatt, trying to be positive.

"Nope! I'm very excited. Becca was not the most exciting person to live with," I said, realizing in the back of my head that I'd live with her for five more years if it meant staying in Chicago.

* * *

Loading up didn't take long with the hired help. I hated seeing my place undone and was ready to get the hell out of there.

My brothers and I left the packed truck in the alley for a moment and zipped down the street to Mista's Pizza before heading to Indiana. Hunter ran next door to grab a beer to drink with the pizza. I had forgotten, he'd just turned 21!

While waiting for our pizza, his jests cajoled me into laughing until I cried. There was comfort in crying from laughter; for a few seconds, it blocked out the worry that this might be the last time I'd ever eat at Mista's.

When our pizza arrived and the boys chowed down the hangover delight, the memories came rushing back. I pictured lunches with KG, dinners with Michelle and the TRX crew, the dates I'd had there that I didn't even know were dates (yes, that happened twice; I have bad gaydar). Oh, how I did not want to leave Mista's that day.

After we paid, I closed my eyes for a second before I stood up and imagined ordering a second pizza with Michelle and then giggling our way back to my tiny ground-floor apartment and seeing all my things back where they belonged.

* * *

For the first leg of the sad departure, Hunter drove the U-Haul, Wyatt drove his Jeep, and I drove my Touareg. My hair was still in the low, messy bun I'm assuming Taylor styled for me the night before. I didn't care—it actually meshed well with my oversized, salmon-colored V-neck and IDGAS ("I don't give a shit" for all you non-millennials) attitude.

It was the same V-neck I'd worn with Ren Man the last time we'd been together in Nashville; we'd gone out to lunch with his parents. He'd worn a matching light-blue one that day. After lunch, we held hands while walking through the parking lot of BrickTop's and headed to Whole Foods to grab something sweet for dessert on that warm Tennessee Sunday afternoon. I chose trail mix, and his dad, a pastry. It was a stress-free day the last time I wore this shirt. Now, I just felt pure heaviness.

Time froze when I hit Lake Shore Drive.

I saw late-night food runs in Lakeview, first dates and last dates, high hopes and dreams just beginning as I took in the city skyline in front of me. But all the memories I had of Lake Shore Drive entailed going north, coming into the city. Now I was going the wrong way.

Winding down the shoreline, then looking over my left shoulder out onto the water, I remembered the enthralling energy of entering Chicago on that curvy road wrapping around the tail end of the city, driving between cement and nature—dreams and real life—with Lake Michigan beaches on my right side and skyscrapers to my left, but now everything was situated the opposite.

My first trips to Chi-Town were to see my first love, Paul, who is four years older than I am. There was something about escaping from Miami of Ohio to the big city, speeding like mad to see my grown-up boyfriend that squeezed more life in my veins.

Chicago had always been my drug of independence. Each new experience I'd have there, I'd get high. The long, early-morning runs I'd take down Lakefront Trail to find clarity while growing up were a serene high.

The long walks I'd take on Sundays were filled with laughs to myself as I'd piece together a drunken night of dancing; that was a jovial high.

I was high on that drug the time "I Want Crazy" by Hunter Hayes played as I drove into the city to move into the ground floor of a North Wilton apartment so I could start my life in the Real World.

I needed to turn around. I wanted to get that high of driving *into* the city—not have that bone-quivering feeling of withdrawal that hits you like a ton of bricks when you can't have your fix anymore.

The city was right there. I could wrap my arms around it. On my own now, going completely against the grain made me uneasy and hurt as if everything I'd worked for was unraveled, gone.

The worst part was that whenever I'd left Chicago in the past, I always knew my departure was temporary; I always knew where I was going, for how long, and when I'd be back.

With this Boston adventure, I had no idea what to expect. Technically, Mrs. Fleming had said it was a year, minimum, but you never know. I was as uncertain as the floundering waves splashing up against the Lakefront Trail. Sometimes they splattered as far as Lake Shore Drive, but you'd never know when or which way they'd spew.

It was seriously a bad nightmare, like someone or something was making me change my life for no reason. There had to be a bigger reason.

All I could do was hope.

And drive.

And cry.

And sing sad songs.

And think about KG, hoping he wouldn't forget about me.

We had spent a lot of the last three weeks of my time in Chicago together, only at night.

CHAPTER 32.

STILL IN PURGATORY

Indianapolis, June 28, 2014

I didn't know time could move so slowly.

I also didn't know I could consume so many calories. *Talk about eating your feelings.* I'd spent less than 48 hours in my hometown of Fishers, Indiana, but still trapped in purgatory; two days felt like an eternity.

After my brothers and I had caravanned there in just over three hours, they disappeared to hang out with friends while my mom and I went to dinner. The next morning, I went to the gym and then to have brunch with my college friend Sarah.

I hoped my outlook on life didn't seem too grim to her always Positive Patty vibe. I'd never seen her without sparkles on, and despite still wearing the salmon tee, I may as well have been dressed for a funeral. I looked like death, and felt like a ghost stuck on earth—nothing about what Nicole Winston wanted to accomplish or do was happening. I was going through the motions and making changes that weren't me. The good news was the hardest part of the trip—driving out of Chicago—was over.

The next day, my mom and I were in no rush to leave. We had all day to drive seven hours to Pennsylvania, where we'd spend the night. No point in remembering the town on a journey I wished to be forgettable.

Day Three in purgatory, I put on the same V-neck and white

shorts that I was wearing the day I left Chicago. As soon as we set off, I felt physically ill, sitting in my car while my mom drove the U-Haul in front of me. Turning out of my childhood neighborhood, I drifted off into space, thinking again about my last trip to Nashville right before Ren Man and I'd broken up. The last time I'd seen Ren Man, we'd said goodbye and I was off to sign a lease for my new Boston apartment.

We'd once discussed doing this drive together, and I'd pictured him in one of his almost too-tight workout T-shirts, basketball shorts and bright Nike shoes with really messy hair. I'd imagined him lifting boxes and loading the truck in Chicago, comforting me in Fishers and then knowing he'd be grabbing my hand and squeezing hard as we began the trek to Boston.

Instead, my reality was: me, my mom, country music and tears.

I'd made it to the highway, still in purgatory but getting closer to hell. I choked the steering wheel with my grip, not because I was hyperfocused on the road. I was a 23-year-old with a bruised heart. The bruises on my heart were the kind you don't notice getting. They show up later and you wonder, *Did I fall?*

I decided to think about things for which I knew the outcome: Ren Man and KG. I knew both relationships were over.

Ren Man had been my rock, but my rock had washed away. Would the same happen to my Chicago friends once I was in Boston? I didn't want to think about it, but why not think about the hurt and the things that kind of sucked right then?

I could count on those things to suck because they sucked no matter what. They were predictable. They were predictably sucky. I knew they sucked and there was no question about whether or not they sucked. I wanted to say the word "suck" as many times as possible.

This sucks.

This sucks.

"This sucks," I said aloud to myself, squeezing the wheel and pressing the back of my head into the headrest.

Each time that word came out, I felt relief, like I was jabbing a punching bag.

CHAPTER 33.

THINGS CAN ALWAYS GET WORSE

Massachusetts, June 30, 2014

My mom was the true martyr in this whole situation. Guiding me to Boston in a giant U-Haul without air conditioning during summer? It doesn't get much more heroic than that. I, however, was not acting like a girl in the presence of a superhero. In fact, I was far from present, delving deep in my purgatory sorrows, which were vast and confusing; the misery increased when KG texted me at dinner in Pennsylvania.

Internal dialogue, begin!

I couldn't quite figure out if it made me happy or sad. I fell asleep stewing over it, to avoid thinking about Boston.

At breakfast the next day, still in my brutal reality, I was a ghost without an appetite watching another girl's life change. Officially the second day of the drive, we aimed to make it just shy of Boston, to a small town called Hingham in Massachusetts. There, as Mom had coordinated, we'd stay at her sorority sister's house for one night before driving into Boston the next morning.

After our 5 p.m. arrival to Hingham, my mom's friend invited us to cruise the ocean on her boat and then dock at the harbor for dinner. I hadn't seen my mom's friend in a year, but I'm sure I was as charming as most millennials are when they don't get their way. I'm sure I was even more of a peach when I dropped my iPhone in Hingham Harbor while exiting the boat after we had docked near a nice country club for dinner.

I'd lost it all: my friends (physically they were no longer near me), my love, my apartment, my sex friend and now my phone with all my friends' numbers.

Wasting worries on whether or not KG had texted me overnight was useless, so I shifted my focus to taking control of what I could: my fitness. Counting sheep was replaced that night by visualizations of some adventurous trail run my mom's friend had suggested.

* * *

At 5 the next morning, I got up. The World's End Trail was not only the perfect name for the way I felt, but it was the silver lining of that first full day in Massachusetts. Something about powering up those hills on a warm summer morning, feeling the sweat on my hairline and tasting the salt from my own body made me feel human again. I was not a ghost driving a truck. Part of Nicole who'd handed out 100 resumes in Chicago's July heat one year ago was still there, alive and well.

Hours later, we pulled into Boston. I don't even remember driving into the actual city, but my day got a little better when my dad and stepmom showed up. Not much had been said between me and my dad since the tears I shed in Berlin. But despite the animosity I carried from assuming my dad either a) didn't believe in me enough to want me in the family business, or b) didn't want me in it for other reasons, I knew he loved me. I never doubted that.

In most cases, showing his love was hard for him, and our love languages are very different. For him, being there in Boston proved his love, and I was learning that. He may not have been there for me during first, second, third or fourth grade since he was stationed at various air force bases as a fighter pilot, and he wasn't there for me when I moved into my Chicago apartment either, but he was there—all the way from Indianapolis—to move my 23-year-old self into my second-ever adult apartment.

He put together my kitchen table and mounted a big decorative clock April gave me. Having a dad present to do "dad" things felt nice. *Better late than never!* They couldn't stay long, but they came. They helped. I wasn't alone.

While my dad and April ventured to Target to buy me bathroom supplies, I went with my mom to return the rental truck. We drove there quickly with that "let's just get this over with" speed and mentality. I paid the U-Haul people, returned the keys and then hopped in my Touareg with my mom riding shotgun.

As soon as we went under the sky bridge of Tufts Medical Center, just four blocks from my new place, I started sobbing uncontrollably.

It hit me again.

This was it.

It was a loud, sad, angry, heartwrenching sob.

My heart was beginning to suffer from chronic pain. I felt mad and sad and desperate all at once. Mad at Swam and Associates, sad that I had let them convince me to leave my favorite place and desperate for someone to come save me from all this. If only heroes existed (besides my mom).

There I was, hundreds of miles from my friends in a totally new place for a job I didn't care about without any fitness outlet to work off this sadness.

I belted it out, a painful cry. I felt it on my insides, like the Berlin cry.

"Stop it. Seriously! Stop it. We are here now. It's fine," my mom said stoically.

It totally wasn't fine.

"Mom, this is like a terrible dream." As I said those words, it almost felt like I was a little girl trying to convince her I'd had a nightmare.

"Nicky. Stop. Enough!" she barked.

"Mom. F this. Don't tell me what to do. Please just let me feel this sadness. I need to allow myself to feel this thing I'm feeling right now," I said.

It was if someone had injected me with drugs and a bad high was flowing through my veins. There was no way to stop the feeling—I just had to wait it out.

Her sigh revealed she was more than slightly mad.

"Mom, I'm not asking you to fix anything or say anything. I'm just crying out loud because I can't keep it in. I don't want to do this. I really don't want to do this," I repeated.

I wanted to be sad. I needed to be sad. I hurt everywhere and feared everything.

That night, she and I went to the Whole Foods conveniently located behind my new apartment building and ate dinner at a nice outdoor table. Sitting there, few words were exchanged between us while I studied the passersby, trying to block out the fact that in less than 12 hours she would be leaving Boston. Knowing I'd soon be completely on my own, I looked at each person intently, like, will you become one of my friends? Will I fit in this community?

CHAPTER 34.

WHEN IT RAINS, IT POURS

July 2, 2014

Sunshine and hot weather in Boston greeted me the day after my move.

Enough with all the sunshine!

The 11th floor was not so cool, even with air conditioning. I'd tiptoed around so as not to wake my mom before going on my first-ever run around my new hood.

Forty minutes and one Instagram upload later (we'd made a stop at the Apple store to buy a new phone in Hingham the previous day), I was back in my fancy building grabbing three coffees, two for me and one for Mom. Thank God she was still in my apartment. I shuddered for a second. *What if she'd left early?*

Typically, my mom and I would be sick of each other after three long days together, but we talked in circles that morning, procrastinating on saying goodbye. I didn't want her to leave, and I could tell she was worried to go.

After she took the inaugural shower of Apartment 1114, I took her to the airport. I don't remember any of it, especially saying goodbye. Anxiety had set in, and I didn't know what my next move would be.

Back in my new place, I was all alone in my new world with no new work and a lot of silence, surrounded by white walls. What to do? No clue, so I worked out in the gym below my apartment.

Mid-lifting set, a very old, inquisitive neighbor began publicly grilling me about who I was, what I did, why I moved, etc. and I was not in the mood. Obliged as the new girl, I answered some questions until he told me never to lift too much or else I'd get big. Pissed off, I left the gym early seeking more solitude; so far the building community was not my cup of tea.

Post-gym, I walked into the apartment and fired off a few emails to Mr. Bates, a couple to Stew and one to the Matts and then decided to go drive. After all, that was why I was there, right? I scoured a few markets on Google Earth in Maine; they were two hours out. Nothing was too far when all I had was time.

After driving around in the sunshine, I came back to my desk to a disheartening email from Stew.

"You know it's Fourth of July week; nobody is working. But I like your hustle," he wrote.

I gave up hopes of any responses from Mr. Bates and called the Nike store on Newbury Street to see if there was a Nike Training Club there and if they were hiring, hoping to check off my next bucket-list fitness goal: Become a Nike trainer.

After a lot of passing the phone around on the other end of the line, and pacing back and forth in my new space, a young woman told me to come in and try Boston's Nike Run Club. They didn't have Nike Training Club yet, but they had a running group they needed leaders for. I opened up my empty calendar and penciled it in.

* * *

Stew was right: The real estate world had gone radio silent, echoing the quiet of my isolated apartment. By dinnertime, I'd had enough "me" time and signed up for a class at Stride and Strength, where I had had a preliminary audition back in the spring.

At the end of the Fourth of July-themed class, while we were stretching, I got nervous because I didn't want it to be over. A wave of loneliness crept over me as I high-fived my potential future coworker on the way out.

I walked home in the quiet of the weekend in Boston, taking mental notes on the class. By the time I was back in my Back Bay neighborhood, I had about three hours until the run club. I didn't care if I was tired; I was going to blow off all the steam I could while avoiding the isolation of my new apartment.

On top of that, a friend from college who was visiting Boston for the weekend invited me out. I didn't care if it was going to be the first time I ever got ready alone, sans roommates or girlfriends, I was going to do it! I didn't know what anyone would be wearing, if this guy would even show up, and I was still sweating from the Run Club, but I put on a dress, called a cab and went out. Big-girl steps!

* * *

In movies, it always rains when life gets turned upside down. And my life was like the happy-sad drama with all the rain, minus the happy. By my third day in Boston, it was a rainy, cold day, but I welcomed the storm because it gave me an excuse to lie in bed and watch Netflix—a thing that was going to be a big part of my leisure life there.

Thankfully, I had the wherewithal to delete Instagram for the day. Photos of smiley friends doing festive activities in the Midwest would be depressing. Purgatory's essence loomed. There was no work to do. There was nobody to eat dinner with. There were only so many workouts I could do. I twiddled my thumbs.

I googled "spinning Back Bay" in between episodes of *Scandal* and found a studio one block from my apartment. I signed up and planned to ask for an audition—to have my bases covered in case my final Stride and Strength audition in two weeks didn't go well.

After lying down for a few hours, listening to the rain and

more Netflix, I thought about the last time I felt this isolated, when I lived in Snowmass, Colorado, for an internship the summer after my freshman year of college. To cope with the isolation, I'd kept a fun blog. It was a series of stream-of-consciousness stories any journalism major would want to write about while living and experiencing the world of marketing tourism surrounded by wealth and wilderness.

That's when it hit me: I could start a blog! A fitness blog!

Suddenly, I remembered the poem I'd come up with in Chicago, the one about "daring to move." That was it! A blog about fitness. I was going to do it—I needed to do it. If only 10 people read it, I didn't care. I was going to write a blog called "Dare to Move."

I went to bed listing all the exercise and nutrition posts I'd write—just as soon as this crappy day was over. My blog writing needed to begin on a positive day!

CHAPTER 35.

KG DIDN'T FORGET ABOUT ME

Perhaps distance does make the heart grow fonder? It was too soon to tell.

Monday morning, I was taking a shower after my first workout at Somerville Sweat, a gym I had joined per KG's recommendation. My heart skipped a beat when I saw the incoming FaceTime call through my clear temporary shower curtain. It was KG, and it was a FaceTime? I wondered if he'd done a butt dial. The hopeless romantic in me liked to hope that he'd eventually miss me, but surely KG didn't miss me yet.

Not wanting him to see me with black makeup still smeared on my face, accentuating my dark circles and unkempt eyebrows, I decided to ignore his phone call. Not only would it give me time to rinse my hair and scrub my face, but it also allowed me to contemplate whether or not he meant to call.

Thinking back to the days (or should I say nights?) leading up to my heartwrenching exit from Chicago, I realized KG and I had grown closer. Initially, the hugs seemed tighter and the kisses seemed longer, maybe because he knew there was a hard and fast ending to all of it. I'd be out of sight, out of mind in no time.

To be flustered about this FaceTime call was one thing, but I grew angry fast. Memories of our last hug goodbye, our last brunch together and all the other "lasts" had been thrown into my mental trash bin, and I'd hit "empty" the day I left. Somehow nothing was actually deleted.

To say I was nauseated about the whole thing would be an understatement. The one man I'd coached myself to forget throughout the entire 21-hour drive to Boston was reaching out? *You've got to be kidding me!*

Before I could decide whether or not to call back, KG called again. Guess it wasn't an accident ...

I took an enormous breath, found the right lighting, and said hello, from a downward angle.

* * *

A week of FaceTime calls and some text messages back and forth had my head spinning. Before long, KG had a flight to Boston, courtesy of yours truly. I had the frequent flyer points from work trips to spare, and I wanted to see him, so I booked the flight against my better judgment. Anytime I second-guessed it, I went to the gym and lifted heavy. Kettlebell training was my only release. Building physical strength coaxed me into thinking I could get mentally tougher.

I guess solitary confinement can do that to you. With zero friends (yet) in Boston, I was a total loner. Even worse? I had no real office in Boston filled with young professionals to befriend. KG was literally the only exciting thing going on in my life. Basically, the two best parts of my first month in Boston were leaving Boston for a trip to LA to see my friend Erin and the days leading up to KG's arrival.

When I pictured picking him up from the airport, I wasn't sure if we would kiss, shake hands or hug each other upon greeting. The moment finally came, and my heart fluttered. He walked out of the baggage claim with his hair slicked to the side the same way it was the day I picked him up in my same blue Touareg for one last brunch together. He wore the same crossbody bag that he wore the first time he came over to my apartment in

Chicago (him coming to my place during the day was a big deal after several nights at his place). I loved how it slung snuggly over his athletic body. For a 33-year-old, he had a strong physique. It seemed he was walking history in my new city, proof that the past was real.

To my delight, we kissed upon greeting—an awkward, short kiss— but, nevertheless, a kiss. Since his flight had been delayed, it was almost midnight, and there was no way we were going out to eat or drink. When we got to my new apartment, the popcorn, cheese, wine and crackers I'd laid out sat on the sidelines of our love scene like the third-string quarterback who shouldn't have dressed for the game.

Like all the country songs describe, I learned what it is to be tangled up with someone.

The next day, we woke up and stayed in bed for a while longer. That morning, as he brushed his teeth and combed his hair, I felt uncomfortable in my own space with him in it. For instance, I couldn't figure out what to wear to go work out. I'd always been at his place wearing his T-shirts to bed or whatever I'd worn over. Now he was in my space where I had my closet, my makeup, my stuff, which should have made me feel at ease, but I was pacing back and forth trying on various outfits and unsure of myself.

Regardless, we had a good morning lift at Somerville Sweat that was followed by brunch and a leisurely walk around Back Bay before meeting my cousins, who live in Boston, for cocktails in the evening.

Having him meet my cousins was a big moment for me. But apparently to him, it felt like my cousins and I came in and out of his life like a boring street festival that comes in and out of town that nobody cares about. In my heart of hearts, I knew he wasn't trying to be rude, but his disinterest almost came off as arrogant.

It appeared as if time passed for him like a much-needed vacation from Chicago, as well as a mental getaway from everything, including me. He was just as emotionally unavailable in Boston as he was the previous summer.

The night before KG left, we went to a dinner with his friends, John and Mary of Somerville Sweat. Deep into business discussions at dinner, John looked at both of us, smiled and said, "Wow! You guys are gonna set the world on fire."

As he said those words, I felt a knot in my stomach. John was right—KG and I agreed on most things and shared an insane passion for helping people in the fitness realm, but I knew then, like I knew it when I wrote him the Hail Mary Heartbreak Letter in Chicago, there was never going to be a "we." KG would never love me in the romantic way, not the way Ren Man did. My sips of margaritas turned into gulps.

I guess there's this rite of passage every 23-year old girl must go through. You must lust after an idiot, a jerk, an asshole (whatever word suits him), and you must like him twice, fall for the same bullshit twice and fall hard on your face twice before you realize it's a bad idea. Then you grow up. Unless you're me, and then you decide you want to fall on your face a third time, just to see ...

Margaritas on margaritas on one taco on more tequila at a speakeasy bar and our night turned sexual. Heated but wet and full of angst from me, our physical connection went further, if that was even possible. Intensely passionate and excruciatingly rough, fueled by anger, tequila and traces of what I thought were love, the cold space that sat between us earlier took a 180-degree turn and drunken sex made me feel every inch of every bone in my body that night. It was hot, but only on the surface of a cooled relationship. We would be no more.

We hadn't but an hour together the next morning before he had to leave. It was a silent hour as he gathered his things and I pretended to read emails. When I took him to the airport, he hugged me like a colleague and walked away after a casual wave. That knot in my stomach twisted and turned, and I wondered if I'd even get out of the departure drop-off queue before sobbing.

Bawling the entire way home left me breathless. *How could I've been so stupid?*

Crying to Michelle on the phone when I got home, I followed her orders and ripped the sheets off my bed as quickly as possible to rid my apartment of any trace of him. Just like a sad movie scene, it was raining outside.

I was that typical 23-year-old brokenhearted girl. The only problem was, I didn't have any pictures of us to burn, Boston guys to call to cure the pain nor girlfriends to take me out, get me drunk and drag me onto the dance floor.

Worse, I couldn't bury my head in my work because the last 10 emails I'd sent to Mr. Bates went unanswered. Instead, I did the dishes, listened to "Somewhere in My Car" by Keith Urban on repeat and sat in the comfort of my white-walled apartment like the actor does in his music video. It was like waiting out a really bad case of the flu.

Sure I was sad, but I was also angry. Angry at myself and angry with KG. The most frustrating part was that he had invaded what might have been a sacred place, a fresh slate, a new beginning.

The rain continued to come down that day and the three days that followed, just like my tears and the blood dripping from my heart. Was I being dramatic? Maybe. But I couldn't ignore the physical pain. I wasn't making it up. It felt like I was getting a concussion on top of a concussion.

* * *

In case you are wondering if it could get worse, it did. I had to go back to the gym KG's colleagues owned the next week since I was preparing for a big kettlebell certification and they were my new coaches.

After a set of kettlebell presses that felt way too heavy (sadness takes a physical toll on your entire body), I put the bells down. John grabbed my arm and lifted it back up.

"Nicole, what the heck? Where did you get that massive bruise?"

I hadn't realized I had one but instantly knew what—or who—it was from. The last night of KG's stay, when things got rough, his thumb had pressed really hard into my bicep and apparently left a gnarly bruise—one that ended up lasting two weeks. I choked back tears every time I saw it. KG hurt me, but what's worse is that I felt like I hurt me more. Like I did this to myself. Not understanding which one of us was more to blame was too much to process.

CHAPTER 36.

HURDLES TO MAKE LIFE MORE DIFFICULT

I'd spent about three days crying in my apartment, crying on the road while driving around looking for gas station sites and crying while watching sad movies. Finally, after 72 hours sans KG, my tears were replaced with nerves. I had a mock class ready to go for my Stride and Strength audition and, out of nowhere, I felt uneasy. Not only had I spent less time preparing than I probably should've, but I realized it was the only hopeful, positive thing I had going for me. With only about 10 percent mental energy to spend on the audition, could you blame me? Plus, the success I'd had winging the Tred11 audition the prior year inspired me to skip overthinking it.

I did not, however, underthink if I was even the right kind of trainer for Stride and Strength. In my heart, I'd decided if in fact they followed the same style of coaching as Tred11, it wouldn't be for me. After training for the StrongFirst kettlebell certification and studying the science behind building strength, I was obsessed with lifting and hoped that Stride and Strength indeed followed the principles I wanted to teach. If so, I was all in. But if not, I wasn't going to be that bummed.

I was explaining all of this to my stepmom on my walk to the Stride and Strength audition day. She called at the perfect time, halting my propensity to overanalyze the workout I'd planned. As we spoke, I arrived early and breezed by the studio, keeping a low profile while ducking into the nearest coffee shop a few doors down.

When I walked inside, I found a corner spot with a seat facing the window looking out into the city and continued chatting with April. We probably spoke about 10 more minutes until I realized I should be making my way to Stride and Strength—professionally early but not awkward was the goal.

As soon as I said, "Bye, I love you," I turned around and almost chest-bumped this short guy (I'd guess no taller than my height of 5-foot-2), wearing a hat on backward, dark T-shirt with gym shorts and Birkenstock sandals. He stood there, staring at me as if he'd been waiting to speak to me.

"Hi, my name is Jaylen, and I overheard your phone call. Are you in fitness?" he said in one big breath before I could move.

I was kind of shocked and probably had a bit of a "stranger danger" look on my face.

"I'm in fitness, yes. Are you?" I replied, feeling a little on edge.

"Do you lift?" he said in a high-pitched tone. Despite his prominent facial scruff (a few days and it'd be a beard), his voice sounded like that of a teenage boy. I was completely caught off guard and unsure of where this was going. It was clear he'd been eavesdropping during the entire call with April.

Super awkward.

But I replied anyway. "Yes, I do. I'm actually training to finish the SFG cert by StrongFirst. But right now I'm on my way to an audition at a fitness studio down the street," I answered.

Before I could ask him if he lifted or coached, he grabbed my arm to stop me from leaving.

"Let me see," he said, holding the palms of his hands out, revealing his calluses like he wanted me to do the same.

I showed him the monstrosities on my hands, as if they'd prove my worthiness.

"Yes, you definitely lift," he said in a flirtatious tone, although nothing about it was flirty in my opinion. You could say I was weirded out. But I did feel cute with my hair done up, so the attention was nice. (When the owner of Stride and Strength tells you to "bring your sexy," you bring it!)

"Are you a trainer?" I asked, reaching to adjust my backpack on my shoulder to remove my hands from him.

"Well, kind of. I am actually an online trainer. I train people all over the world."

Whatever that means, I thought, as I pictured him living in his mom's basement making weird exercise videos and doing Skype calls with foreigners.

"But I'm also helping to open a gym in Government Center a few blocks from here, so if you're interested in a gym for lifting, you should check it out."

"Oh, cool. I just moved here and I'd love to try a new place to lift, so sure—I'll give you my card. I actually gotta run right now."

"Nice to meet you," he said, then paused like he wanted my name.

"I'm Nicole," I said.

I'd come to find out later that after our meeting, he made a Facebook post for his thousands of followers that said: "Just met a nice young girl with calluses on her hands; will marry/10."

Apparently, he'd thought I was The One.

* * *

Time to audition. I walked to the studio to crush it.

Compared to the hung-over, clueless, made-up workout I'd auditioned with for Tred11, I felt much more confident. Teaching over 200 classes in a year will do that to ya, and I felt like I had the right to teach at Stride and Strength. (I was a 23-year-old millennial asshole.)

However, the co-owners of Stride and Strength ("S&S" is what they called it, I learned that day) didn't seem so impressed. A few minutes into the mock workout and the looks on their faces told me I was not what they were looking for. Was I totally different from any trainer they had on their squad? Yes, I'm sure everything from the Midwestern tone in my voice to my motivational style contrasted to what they knew.

Could I have taken more classes before the audition? Sure. But I already was training at Somerville Sweat four days a week. I'd been trying as many things as I could to not put too many eggs in one basket—another millennialism, I suppose. Plus, I didn't want to change my coaching style too much from what I believed in. If the owners didn't like me in my most true Nicole fashion, maybe I didn't want to coach there myself!

Millennial me didn't take into account that I'd potentially be a huge risk for them to hire. Why? They already had found the right formula, selling out 42-person classes and charging $30 per head. Their team of trainers had all gone through training together over a year ago. There'd have to be a lot of tweaking to do with my style before I'd mesh well with what the other trainers offered at S&S. Not to mention, the S&S style of workout itself, which was more focused on heavy lifting than Tred11, would take more time for me to learn. But whether the two co-owners, Max and Kevin, were feeling charitable or they just felt really bad for me, they handed me the Stride and Strength handbook and told me I was hired.

They seemed friendly but serious, cautious but also inviting. After the business talk, they made small talk and asked me about my boyfriend. I'd forgotten that in my first mock audition in April, I mentioned him.

"Where is he? He's from Nashville, right?" Max asked.

I had to tell them we were no longer dating and appear like the youngster I was. (Girlfriend today, single girl tomorrow.) The weird part was, in that moment, it was hard to figure out how to tell them why, so I blamed it on the move to Boston.

I left with the Barry's handbook, carrying it close to my chest as if it held the power to my survival in Boston.

CHAPTER 37.

A NEW GRIND

August 2014

Max and Kevin started off having me teach only one class a week, Thursdays at 8 p.m. in the summer, so a small crowd. To quell my loneliness in Boston and keep busy, I continued to throw myself into my kettlebell training at Somerville Sweat.

The StrongFirst level of certification still sat high on my priority list and, thanks to KG's friends, I had a really great program to follow to prepare for the cert. I ended up signing a year-long contract with their gym specifically because of the community they'd cultivated. Often there were group outings and social events, all things I emphatically desired. After taking only two classes, I'd met some nice people and felt like there was potential to make a good group of friends. The only problem was, they all lived in Somerville, just outside of Boston, and I lived in the heart of the city in Back Bay. I still needed another outlet to break up the monotony of my "eat, sleep and wait for emails from Mr. Bates" routine.

After a few texts from the coffee shop guy I'd coined "Jaylen Fitness," I decided I would meet with him to talk about the blog I wanted to start and couldn't stop thinking about. Since meeting in Boston, we'd connected on social media and he seemed to know a lot about the online space, and "start a blog" was also on my to-do list. Plus, he'd mentioned wanting to help me, over text.

Unsure of how exactly he'd be of help, I agreed to meet him for coffee confident that at the very least we'd have fitness to discuss.

The first time I tried to meet him (warning, women, do not try this at home), he wanted me to meet him at his apartment and then we'd walk to a coffee shop together. It sounded kind of sketchy—and seemed even more so when I got to a quiet suburban neighborhood with zero coffee shops or places to walk to nearby. I called him when I saw the blue house next to a green house, which is where he said he lived. He said he was outside, but on the quiet, unfamiliar street, there was no Jaylen in sight. I thought someone was going to jump me in my car at any moment.

It turns out I followed my GPS to the incorrect 404 Elmhurst Avenue, in Quincy, and not the Elmhurst Avenue in Somerville. The fact that there was a green house next to a blue one was an odd coincidence. Instead of rerouting to see him, I decided to just go home and meet him another time—something about the whole thing just felt weird.

* * *

Jaylen: Let's make a deal.

Me: ?

Jaylen: You teach me gymnastics. I'll teach you powerlifting.

The text message offer was witty and silly and sounded fun. Plus, I was bored. One week later, we met to lift together. This time, we actually met at his apartment.

After an awkward hello, he told me to get into his car so we could drive together. (Again, ladies, don't try this at home.) From Somerville, he drove us about 15 minutes to another neighborhood in Medford.

Where was the gym?

He parked at the end of a residential driveway and started to get out.

Were we making a stop somewhere I wasn't informed of?

He grabbed a weightlifting belt out of his car and began walking down the long driveway. At the end, there was a small garage gym with a lot of insanely strong people inside lifting oversized dumbbells, large tires and even cars! It was a private, invite-only strength training gym and I felt more out of place than I did in Boston altogether.

Once we walked into the open-garage gym and a few ladies smiled at me, my anxiety let up a bit. From the moment we started stretching, he made me giggle.

"Ouchhhhh," I complained as I tried to stretch my calves in a downward-facing dog position.

"Oh, lit me come help ya with that," he said in a Scottish accent as he approached me, reaching for my calves.

The entire time he massaged my tight calf muscles, he spoke in the silly tone, distracting me from the pain. I scream-laughed at his kind-of funny jokes in lieu of screaming through tight muscle pain. At some points, he was funny like my brother Hunter (which is a *huge* compliment), and other times, it was like a bad movie where the short guy tries too hard but really comes off as either a jerk, not funny or annoying.

He taught me a few things that day—memorably, the deadlift. It seemed quite simple, yet he seemed obsessed with it. I didn't get it.

"It's just picking something up, right?" I asked quite bluntly.

He later told me that was an offensive question to ask a globally ranked powerlifter.

After lifting, we went on a walk down a nearby Medford public trail. The flow of lifting to walking seemed natural. I dare not say it was a date. However the vibe was more like friends hanging out than a business meeting because as we strolled, his questions took a very personal tone and included inquiries about my dating life. Since I was neither attracted to him physically nor trying to impress him, I wasn't shy about divulging several personal things. Clearly I needed to chat—I'd only had my mom and

Michelle to chat with the past couple weeks, and I was going mad with all the alone time.

Jaylen would ask one question and follow up with seven more before I could ask him a question of my own. He wanted to know so much about me and pried into my past relationships, reasons why I moved and everything in between.

On the subject of my kettlebell training, KG came up, as he was the "why" I got started. Feelings welled up inside me and the inflection of my voice changed slightly as I told him about this "older guy I kind of dated" and how we had kind of reconnected before I left Chicago. I also told him how I had recently gone through a breakup with a guy from Nashville. That led to my complicated feelings about the breakup and the move. As he pulled and pried more and more out of feeble me, he'd quickly become privy to much more than I'd have liked.

Regardless, his ear—anyone's ears—stifled my loneliness like one strong martini.

CHAPTER 38.

A DINNER, A DATE AND A BREAKUP IN ONE WEEK

August 2014

I'd lived in Boston for almost two months and only been out to dinner twice—once with my cousins and once with KG. Approaching my third month, I was en route to my third dinner, heavy work bag in tow, to meet Jaylen at a sushi place near the Boston Common.

Walking from Back Bay, I felt effortlessly sexy that night, despite the unusual juxtaposition of a professional leather briefcase and beachy cut-off jean shorts with a sheer lace blouse that loosely hung over a black lace bandeau top. The casual outfit gave me some confidence—the kind workout clothes, sticky sweat and chalky hands don't lend themselves to. As I approached the restaurant, I remember thinking it was a shame to have a work thing and not a date lined up!

Punctual Patty me became annoyed when Jaylen showed up late, on his phone and seemingly disinterested in our planned meeting, but I reminded myself I had nowhere else to be. He ordered a beer, so I decided to order a cocktail.

After some fitness small talk, conversation segued into my new blog idea, and he tried to convince me that I needed a website like his and offered to connect me with his web developer. I appreciated the help, but starting a blog seemed like a big enough endeavor at the moment, and I had a plan in place.

Sips, smiles and jovial banter, I enjoyed the way Jaylen spoke so madly about fitness and online coaching, as if he'd been in the industry 20 years, knew it all, loved it like a beginner and wanted everyone to join his sphere. I still couldn't quite wrap my brain around what exactly it was that he did, but I wrote down the name of his website and planned to read some of his stuff.

I admired his passion, but as the night trailed on, his tone took an overzealous tone—and not in an intimidating, know-it-all, Ren Man kind of way. I mean, Ren Man actually did know it all and he spoke with confidence and knowledge. Jaylen spoke with this kind of preachy, arrogant air that was too passionate, too happy, too knowledgeable. After we'd finished our sushi, I felt myself being coaxed into his inner circle of powerlifting and fitness by way of this "everyone has a place in fitness," "everyone can do this—you can, too" sales-pitchy vibe. Nice became pushy and I was ready to say goodbye.

After dinner (he paid like it was a date, but I didn't dare think it, especially because he joked it was a business expense), he asked me to go for a walk. Extending a friendly hangout on the Sunday night before Labor Day with no work the next day didn't bother me; all I had was time.

"Sure, since it's Labor Day weekend," I said, accepting his request. Immediately, my brain toggled back one year: me seducing KG in Boystown.

What a year it had been ...

Walking next to basically a stranger created an opposite feeling of comfort; in fact, it made me feel even more alone in my new city. Aside from my cousins, who were always busy, the human contact I was experiencing was with a stranger, a stranger with whom I'm not sure I would've wanted or needed to get to know if I were still in Chicago.

This must be what making adult friends is like at first. You feel a common connection and decide to spend time together, right? Whereas before, all my friends had been made quite simply: You go to class together, party together and pick from the pool of hundreds of young adults around you at college, whose main goal is to make friends.

It was misting outside, and my face was damp. I think he could tell I felt alone.

"You know, you're never alone here. You got that? I am here for you, always," he said very firmly.

My heart dropped as I realized that he almost tried to hold my hand.

Shit, was this a date?

As we entered the Boston Common, the scene for the most romantic date was set. Jaylen put the old faded hat he was wearing backward on my head as if to protect me from the rain, a gentlemanly gesture. The drizzle wasn't terrible, but the thought was so kind, I couldn't say no. Had I been romantically interested in the man who put it there, the hat would've comforted me rather than make me feel like I was balancing a bowling ball on my head. With each step, he began walking closer to me. Looking around at the stunningly lit-up Boston Common park, I wished I was there with someone else, although I'm not sure who. But definitely not Jaylen.

Was I judging him for his short stature?

I could not be that girl. He seemed nice enough. Maybe it was just that my heart had been through the ringer and seeing a new guy had no place on my agenda. Before I knew it, he stopped and turned right in front of me. His body was squared up against mine. The same height, we stood inches apart, literally eye to eye.

"Can I kiss you?"

I paused. More like, I froze. I didn't know what to say; I had nowhere to run. I noticed that without his hat, he was baldish. I liked his scruff, but not his height. What agitated me the most was that I never saw the night going this way—*it was intended to be a business thing!* But within seconds of my bewilderment (which may have looked lustful? I'm not sure what my own face does when it senses this "oh shit, he might kiss me" situation), he kissed me. Then we started making out for like 10 seconds.

I gave in, apparently seeking the connection? The attention? His approval?

He was a great kisser, but it still felt odd. Like I craved the emotional connection of a man, but he was not what I was looking for. If I still lived in Chicago, this definitely wouldn't have happened.

But I wasn't in Chicago. I was alone in Boston now. This was my reality. This was a successful, funny, smart guy.

It was just a kiss. It couldn't hurt anything, right?

I told him I needed to go home about five minutes after the kiss and he told me to wear the hat home as I hailed a cab. Pulling it off my head, I felt the embroidery on the front of it and looked to see it had an Israeli army emblem on it. By the looks of how beat-up it was, I knew the hat carried some significance, so I made him take it back.

"Maybe I'll see you after my kettlebell certification's over," I said out of the cab window, letting him down easy.

* * *

The next weekend, I had my kettlebell certification, which required flying to Philadelphia. While there, KG texted me good luck, wished me luck on Facebook and even said "I love you" in a late-night text. I was baffled by all of this (Are we friends now? Is this an apology?) and was determined not to let him interfere with crushing the cert for which I'd trained for months.

Even more baffling was that on the way home Sunday afternoon, I saw on Facebook that Jaylen and KG had become friends. Curious and bored me decided to call Jaylen to figure it out.

"Hi, Jaylen, it's me! This is totally random, but I saw that you and KG are now Facebook friends. Small world! You guys are similar in your coaching styles. He and I kind of had a thing a while back, and he was recently in Boston to visit me. We are great friends! Give me a call back when you get a chance. I still want to meet up for coffee this week to talk about my website."

And that voicemail is how Jaylen was reminded that KG and I have a past and learned that he'd been to Boston to see me.

* * *

After a Monday full of Instagram scrolling, Stride and Strength workout writing and nutritional reading, I had a weak, lonely moment and paused to feel my emotions. Emptiness, hurt and loneliness crept through my veins.

After God knows how many minutes of this, I pulled myself together from crying. My curly hair was a mess, and I was sitting up on the edge of my bed staring at my phone. I could barely see through the makeup smeared over my eyes.

"I need to talk to you," I texted KG.

He called me.

"What's up?" he said with doubt and depression in his voice.

"I don't know. I'm just really sad. I am confused as to why you came here, and why you won't talk to me or open up to me. I look up to you and I just know ..."

A year ago, the Hail Mary Heartbreak Letter had broken the seal of me unveiling my feelings to him; now I was ready to tell him how I felt on the phone, directly. But as many times as I had practiced what to say and how I'd say it, I made little sense. The only apparent thing was my creaky, sad voice.

"Nicole, you need to grow up!" KG yelled, interrupting me.

I assumed he was referring to my crying.

Stabbed.

Pierced.

My heart was broken. But not a "falling out of love" broken; it was an "I did this to myself, I am an idiot and a failure" kind of broken heart. Not only did the guy I want not like me, but he didn't seem to respect me, and maybe it was because I didn't respect myself? What did I really do wrong?

"You don't get it; maybe you're the one who should grow up." I said, before hanging up and throwing my phone to the ground.

I couldn't take being in my apartment alone anymore, especially because I could picture KG in it, so I walked to the rooftop to watch the sunset. With the dimming light out in the distance, I felt like a lonely princess in my tower up high, wondering when I'd come down to friends, community and freedom to live in the present.

CHAPTER 39.

GIVING ME THE FINAL PUSH

Tewksbury, MA, September 2014

I looked down at my scuffed-up, three-inch heels that were too high for a town hall meeting in Tewksbury, Massachusetts. No matter what you wear, you stand out when you're the youngest professional in the room by at least 15 years.

The town hall meeting was about to begin, and as a front-row attendee, I needed to pay attention. Swam and Associates needed permits for a 3,207-square-foot gas station for Oil City. As the developer, I was there to manage and oversee the civil engineer, Phil, land attorney, John, and traffic engineer, Jeff, who'd all come to plead our case for special permits and variances. We were last on the agenda; it was going to be a late night.

Phil had a genuine smile; I liked hearing about his wife and daughters when we made small talk; to him, they were royalty. Sometimes he made parenthood sound hard; dance recitals and diaper changes challenged his manhood. But talk with him for five minutes and you'd know he was the most loving father. He was also a damn good engineer. When he got stressed or flustered, his cheeks became a rosy pink under his dark, tan skin. Anytime we needed permits or variances, I hoped Phil was the one assigned to the project.

Working with Phil and John was refreshing because they were outsiders, third parties. They technically worked for Swam and Associates, not with us; since they weren't on the inside of the company, they didn't know that my job felt like a sham. My counterparts at Swam, Kathy and Cody, both knew I was reaching around in the dark when it came to projects most of the time, but not these guys. To them, I was in charge. I had a plan. I was the team leader. Although in the meetings, John ran the show, thank God.

On the drive to these town hall meetings, I'd give myself pep talks. I'd pretend I was acting and the camera was rolling. I had to have the "fake it 'til you make it" mentality because I literally didn't have a clue what was going on most of the time. Not because I didn't care or I was lazy, but because Mr. Bates kept me out of the loop. But not this particular night. I got this.

John began his introduction to the planning board.

"Hi, Mr. Chairman of the Board. My name is John Smoller, and I am the counsel on the Oil City proposal this evening. Here with me is Phil Check, the civil engineer, and Nicole Winston, vice president of real estate."

It always sounded so good.

Technically, the title on my card said "Assistant Vice President of Real Estate," but I wasn't going to correct him. It made me chuckle, which lifted my spirits, especially after the tearful conversation I'd had with my dad earlier that day.

This time, the tears weren't his doing. Ever since he helped move me into Back Bay, we'd been talking on the phone at least once a week. This was monumental for us. No arguments yet, and he seemed to be more engaged than usual. I knew he was making an effort, and I would too. But I also needed him as my dad. Before I set off into the jumbled world of Boston traffic for the meeting, I'd given him a call.

"Dad, please don't think I'm crazy, but my job feels fake. I swear it's not a real job," I complained.

"Nicole, what do you mean? They moved you there because they see you of value, they need you, or else they wouldn't have done such a thing," he said with care.

"Dad, think about it … You know what I mean." I paused.

He was silent.

"I'm beginning to think that Swam hired me just to get to you. I know about the $13 million deal. And you know I know because we were all on the same email. You can't ignore this."

"Nicole, as far as I am concerned, they don't have a penny from me at this point."

"But you know that they want to get you to sign off on this project. I mean, is it a good deal for you?"

"I'm working with Chris on it—he's planning to help us market and sell off the parts of it we don't need once the deal is done—but again, no papers have been signed as of now," he replied.

My dad never likes to assume that people want his money. He tries so hard to forget about his net worth, I think sometimes he actually convinces himself he's got nothing. He also hates it when I talk about money with him because his biggest fear is that I am "spoiled" or "entitled." I'm sure that this conversation alone agitated him.

Switching gears, my dad actually began asking me about my fitness goals. He seemed to genuinely care about what was going on with my blog, too; I decided to drop my concerns about Swam for the time being.

I missed my dad and, more than anything, I wished I could tell him about the other hurt I was going through with KG, but I knew he wouldn't understand and that I couldn't tell him some of the details that would help him understand. Instead, I told him that I was about to launch the blog in two days. He said he was proud of me. And those words alone were enough to get me through the long night ahead, listening to complex discussions on gas station architectural plans—or subjects that would be filed under "topics I don't care about."

* * *

I was getting ready for yet another meeting. Even though I was ready for fall clothes, I decided to wear my favorite yellow dress that revealed a little too much shoulder one more time. I threw a $600 gray blazer from J. Crew over the dress, grinning as I remembered that I bought it on sale for only $200.

I had to "run" over to Gardner, Massachusetts, for an informal 9 a.m. meeting—which is hyperbole since Gardner is over an hour's drive. Good news? Phil would be there and an equally awesome attorney named Tom. Bad news? Jack, the real estate director of Oil City, would be there as well. He wanted to make good with the town planner behind the scenes of formal meetings.

I had met Jack him during a New England tour a couple months back. He had a soft, raspy voice and was probably a little older than my dad, who'd just turned 50.

He had kids my age and, for the first months of my time on the job, he didn't speak to me directly. He only spoke to Mr. Bates. I'd be like a ghost in the back seat listening and taking notes verbatim for Mr. Bates while he bullshitted bits of information about the trade area.

Although his body language was more cordial than The Directors', Jack intimidated me with his more quiet, serious side.

No matter how much of your shit you have together, Mondays will always feel like Mondays when Jack's there, especially when applying for underground storage tank licenses, a crucial component to getting the project up to the construction point.

The long drive ahead reminded me that so far as a New England resident, my main contribution to Swam and Associates was driving to rural towns for meetings Mr. Bates didn't want to attend himself.

The Gardner deal was the only deal Mr. Bates had really given me free rein on. Ironically, it was becoming quite complex—a four-piece assemblage with three of the parcels of land having severe environmental contamination to remedy. I walked into the meeting, all senses heightened. (You never know when Mr. Bates will make a surprise appearance.)

I'd never suspect yellow to be a commanding color, but from the moment I walked into the room, I led the meeting like John Smoller typically would, introducing Jack, the attorney Tom, and myself, the (assistant) vice president of real estate, to the chairman of the board. I ran the meeting, got the board's approvals and felt like my business of being in Boston just might be legit.

During the entire 70-minute drive home, I voice-recorded myself "talk-writing" articles for my soon-to-be-published blog. I was on a roll!

CHAPTER 40.

CROSSROADS OF FITNESS

Boston, September 2014

As soon as I hit "publish," I felt the same anxiety one might feel before jumping off a cliff. OK, that was grave. Maybe how you feel before dropping in on a steep double black diamond ski run. Either analogy works. I felt ill with "I might die" nerves.

I put the link to my blog, "Crossroads of Fitness," on Facebook and hit "enter."

It was done. It was up. It was out there. I made myself vulnerable, and I was sharing my thoughts on health, wellness, strength training and nutrition. It was the scariest thing I had ever done—scarier than leaving Chicago.

I ran barefoot upstairs to the rooftop deck in my bathing suit and snagged a sun chair. The vacant, calm roof space was a godsend; my anxiety was screaming. All I could hear was my hyperventilating breath and traffic on Massachusetts Avenue.

Sobbing, I called KG, knowing he was on Facebook and had more than likely seen my post and shared the link to my blog.

It took about four solid sob sounds after he said hello for me to gather words.

"I don't know what to do. I'm so scared; I'm so embarrassed. I am ... I ... I ... I..."

Trying to catch my breath, I freaked out further, realizing the last time we spoke he had hurt me. Why was I leaning on him? No idea.

"Shhhhh, Nic. It's OK. Where are you? Are you OK? Take a deep breath. One more. One more. Shhhhhh," he said.

"I ... I ... I ... I am so sorry," I murmured.

"It's fine; you did it!" he said. "You're going to be OK."

"I know, I know. I'm just embarrassed. I'm freaking out, and I'm so sorry to bother you; I didn't know who to call. Putting yourself out there is so scary," I said, thankful he was somehow being a friend.

Hearing his voice soothed me and I felt lucky that he answered. For me it was like he saw it as burying the hatchet when my hatchet was still in my apartment. Parts of me wondered if I should've called someone else.

"It is scary, but you did it. You're going to help people," he said. Then he added, "I'm about to teach; can I call you later?"

"Yes, thank you for answering my call. I appreciate it," I said. "Remind me to tell you about my upcoming trip to Chicago later."

I stayed on my rooftop under the hot sun for the next 40 minutes until Matt Donahue called; his call was my only Swam responsibility that day. I pulled myself together, took the call and headed down to my desk. During the real estate call, KG, my friend Katie, my mom and three of my best friends all shared links to my blog. The ball was now in motion.

* * *

Jaylen called me a few days later and left a voicemail.

"Hey, we need to get together. Congrats on your blog. I didn't know you were calling it Crossroads. I don't get it, but, hey, it's live! But you need to start a website. It will be much easier for people to read and helpful for you. Let's meet at my place next week and go over the next steps."

It was weird. First of all, the compliment felt backhanded. Second, although I was thankful for his help, his tone made me nervous and intimidated. Yet, he was not my boss but made me think I had done something wrong. Third, it was called "Crossroads of Fitness" because I'm from Indiana, the "Crossroads of America," and I wanted the blog to have a name *and* a mantra—the mantra being "dare to move."

A few days later, we met for coffee. He seemed to be in a ticked-off mood. After giving me a quick "congrats" again, he told me that he was appalled that one of the videos I posted on my blog featured me in a bikini. (For the record, it was an inspirational video series called "Dare to Move" about people moving in creative and challenging new ways to imbue a sense of confidence and to feel good).

After just putting myself out there online and literally exposing my body to motivate others with the idea that nobody's body is perfect, his unwarranted criticism crushed me. He continued to lecture me about my video choices, making an uneasiness fall over me. My knee-jerk reaction was to defend myself to Jaylen, still a quasi-stranger.

Looking back, I wished I'd had the guts to tell him to mind his own business and that I could post whatever I wanted. He had no place to tell me how to act, look, dress or speak.

Instead of telling him to F off, I explained to him that my aim was to demonstrate confidence, proving that any woman could do what they wanted in a bikini. The back-and-forth continued with more reprimands from him.

In that moment, young Nicole thought: Oh well. I would work on it. I would do better, or at least he made me feel like I had to do better. Why he had any power over me? I'm unsure. Perhaps it was because he seemed to have more experience in the online field.

Someday, older Nicole would say: F him for telling you that you did anything wrong. Good for you for getting started; it's the hardest part. Avoid that guy, who seems to have a power trip—you owe him no explanation.

CHAPTER 41.

JAYLEN'S SPELL IS CAST

Boston, October 2014

Teaching my first Stride and Strength class, achieving my StrongFirst certification and launching my blog were all highs within my first few months in Boston. However, as far as the fitness hustle went, there were actually more lows than I'd expected.

Adding fitness to my 8-to-5 job was supposed to make life more fun, but instead, it was knocking me down. I'd landed the job at the spin studio in Back Bay, but they'd given me the worst schedule of all time. They wanted me to teach 8 a.m. on Sunday mornings and Wednesday nights at 8 p.m. I took them but knew I'd be lucky to get more than five people in class.

When Nike got back to me about being a run club leader, I learned they only needed a run leader on Thursday nights at 7, just before I had to teach at S&S, which wouldn't work. Nike Training Club was, in fact, coming to Boston in a few months, but they were looking at more well-known Boston instructors for the Nike trainer position—aka my colleagues from Stride and Strength.

Keeping my head up, I hoped that having an SFG kettlebell certification might make me an attractive candidate to Somerville Sweat, which was looking for part-time and substitute coaches. By October, I'd hoped wrong, and they chose my training partner to be their new assistant coach instead of me.

Those three letdowns told me I didn't have any authority to be writing about fitness. If Nike, Somerville Sweat and Back Bay Spin didn't believe in me, why should anyone else?

Adding to all of this internal conflict was the watchful, judgmental eye of Jaylen, who was reading everything I published. He'd like my post online, following up with criticism that never quite felt constructive.

Enter writer's block.

The thing about writer's block is that it feels like recovering from an injury—you just gotta wait it out. So, I spent my time sitting on my oversized couch reading my nutrition certification book when I got bored or lonely. I figured I could knock out that certification now that I'd finished the kettlebell one. Having these qualifications would add power to my name and allow me to write with more authority.

Re-enter Jaylen.

He noticed through the second half of September and the beginning of October that I hadn't been writing. I agreed to meet him for coffee again and tell him about my struggles and insecurities in writing. He told me to write more, worry less, to be vulnerable and not give a shit about what other people thought. (Wasn't that what I'd tried to do with the bikini video blog back in September?)

In some weird way, his opinion began to matter to me. Could it have been that he was being tough on me to make me care about his judgments and want to appease him? Either way, I was too nervous to write about the nutrition stuff until after my nutrition certification exam. So for most of my first New England autumn, I'd read until I'd get bored or fall asleep. Then I'd try to write a little, decide it sucked, check my email and doze off again. Sometimes I wouldn't remember if it was Friday or Monday night—it didn't matter either way.

CHAPTER 42.

I'VE BEEN DROWNING

October 2014

An official Swam and Associates employee for over a year, it was time to have a performance review phone call with Mr. Swam himself. Nervous? I was not! Ready to tell him how I really felt? Yes. Ballsy Nicole was still alive and well.

I'll admit, I had no clue what to expect. The last time we'd spoken on the phone was when I had been in Nashville, six months into my employment, with Ren Man listening in and the whole conversation revolving around my dad. And six months later? Not many of my opinions had changed about my lack of work, communication with Mr. Bates and autonomy on projects. I'd complained my way through the frustration, and I was ready for either big changes or clear guidance in my job and a better understanding of what the hell to do in Boston.

Despite my clear-cut aims for the call, I sincerely hoped he wouldn't ask me the same question everyone in the office asked me: *What deals have you closed?* He should be the first to know deals take around two years, and I'd been there only for one. It's not like any of the deals were really "mine" anyway; my negotiating power was at the mercy of Mr. Bates' email responses.

"Nicole, how are you? How's life in Boston? Are you enjoying it there?"

Insert fake happy response.

On this call, Mr. Swam spoke less about my dad and more about me. Frustrated and helpless, I took a chance and conveyed my issues with Mr. Bates. Was it risky to speak about the star employee this way? Sure. Did I care? At this point, no. I had changed my life for this job and, no matter what I did, I was always waiting for feedback, approval or direction from Mr. Bates.

"Nicole, you need to just go out there and dive right in. I'm not going to let you drown; nobody will let you drown. But I'd rather have to come get you out of the ocean than have you standing on the shore wondering if the water is cold or not," he said.

As far as I was concerned, that is exactly what I had been doing, driving to all these towns—Woburn and Needham and Malden and Reading and Concord—and sending LOIs. But eventually, Mr. Bates needed to be in the picture since he had the relationship with Jack, the real estate director for Oil City.

"Mr. Swam, I've been driving almost every day, and even compiling the letters of intent I want to send to various sellers and then submitting them to Mr. Bates. However, since it isn't my territory, I can only do so much without his approval."

"Yeah, he is not the best leader/people person, and I get that. Just do as much as you can."

The conversation was going nowhere. The only way things would ever change is if I had my own territory. Stew was beeping in on my other line as Mr. Swam and I wrapped things up.

Do more, ask less.

Got it. Click.

"Hey, Stew, how's it going? Any word on Goffstown, New Hampshire?"

"Apparently, the seller doesn't want to meet with us onsite. He doesn't want to scare one of the current tenants. We have a call with them Friday."

"Friday works for me."

"Did Mr. Bates tell you what prices we should start in with the offer?"

Mr. Bates hadn't responded to any of my emails about this subject.

"I think we should go in at $45K on both the larger parcels. The smaller ones are tiny but crucial, so I think it's fine to start around $33K."

He paused to see if I was going to finish with "let's wait to see what Mr. Bates says."

Not this time.

"I'll send the LOI drafts at those prices to Jack, and once he looks them over, we can send them out this afternoon," I said.

The truth was that if Mr. Bates really cared or worried, he would've responded to my emails asking about the deal. Plus, Mr. Swam had given me a little more guts to go get shit done.

I hung up with Stew and drafted an email to Jack. I knew Kathy often reached out directly to him. In her words, "as long as you appear that you very much have a handle on the deal, speak as the expert and are only seeking approval on economics for the deal, it is OK to send emails to Jack."

The email said:

> "Jack,
>
> Attached are the LOIs for all four parcels in this potential Goffstown, New Hampshire, assemblage. All sellers are open to discussing. We have reason to believe our offers are attractive as Swam tried to do another business deal with the corner piece here years ago. I've attached records of former LOIs to reference. Please let me know if you want to change any of the language of the environmental. Otherwise, I'll send these out today.
>
> Thanks."

Moments later, my email dinged.

> "Thank you, Nicole. I look forward to the update.—Jack"

At least one person knew how to use technology and respond to my email.

CHAPTER 43.

DATING TO QUELL THE LONELY GRIND

"Hello?" I said as I awoke on Sunday night at 9 to answer Jaylen's call. My voice was so weak, I repeated myself. "Hello, Jaylen?"

I had gone to bed early because even Netflix was beginning to bore me in Boston.

"Say something else," he ordered.

"Um, what do you mean?" I asked, realizing that this was him flirting.

"That voice. Your voice. It's so sexy," he said like he'd just taken a bite out of a cookie.

"I am so sorry. I was sleeping," I added, speaking slowly.

"I want a recording of it. It is so sexy," he chuckled, adding, "I can tell you were sleeping."

OK, he's definitely into me.

One logical side of my brain thought, "Oh shit," because initially I was not attracted to him nor was I looking for anything. But the emotional side yearned the high of someone flirting with me.

"I'm sorry to wake you, but I wanted to see if you want to grab dinner or drinks this week? Maybe Tuesday?"

It was a date, *like an actual one.*

Emotional side wins.

* * *

Tuesday night, I walked into Saloon, a speakeasy-type bar, feeling like myself but not entirely. I was out of my element. This was the first "date" I had been on in this new city, and I felt like my style of dressing up was not going to match Jaylen's, which made me uncomfortable. Let's not forget how impeccably dressed my last boyfriend was—I had a habit of dressing up for even little things like coffee dates. Girly me loved any reason to wear something fun.

As I walked across the bar to sit with Jaylen, I realized I'd been there before—with KG. We'd come in for one drink after tacos with John and Mary on the last night of his stay. This was the bar that gave us the extra drinks we didn't need on the infamous night when he'd bruised me. I tried to shut off those thoughts.

Fresh slate.

But my fresh slate wasn't nearly as good-looking. Jaylen arrived to our date wearing some raggedy pants. Oh, and did I mention that he's not very tall? But he did have some great qualities. He listened to me, spewing out more questions if I paused even simply to breathe. So many, in fact, I barely got to ask him any. Either he wasn't ready to be vulnerable, or he had something to hide. And I'm guilty of always finding the good in people, so I told myself the former. He made me feel special and, as the conversation continued, I enjoyed his camaraderie in the warm, low-lit room.

After dinner, we walked back from Saloon to his apartment and he invited me inside. I knew I was putting myself in a situation where he might think I was into him when I agreed to come "hang out" inside. I'm certain that the term "hang out" is the worst term of my generation. I simply agreed because it sounded better than any more time spent alone in my apartment.

Sitting next to each other on his couch with about a foot between us, we spoke for 30 seconds before he did a leaping lean over and kissed me. Bam. It happened so quickly, his lips on mine. His aim was quite good. Reminding me of high school at first, the vibe switched as the kiss continued. I could feel his whole heart in that kiss—or so I thought at that moment. Looking back, I think I was feeling my own wounded heart being bandaged by a kind soul.

Like many wounded soldiers fall for their nurses in old-time movies, I fell under his spell far enough for a passionate makeout session that night. On the drive home, I was a little pissed off, because I think he would've tried to go all the way with me and that bothered me—his expectation of sex, that was. In reality, if I'd liked him, it wouldn't have mattered when or how it happened. Two seconds later, my mental gears shifted to my upcoming weekend trip to Chicago, where I planned to stay with KG.

CHAPTER 44.

GETAWAY TO HELL, FROM PURGATORY

Chicago and Boston, November 2014

You know that feeling when you eat a cookie when you're on a diet? Like you somehow messed up, so you go ahead and order a pizza or eat three more cookies? Well, wasting energy on KG somehow seemed like that.

Dwelling on KG was still my favorite self-sabotaging activity. It was safe because the heartbreak was predictable. It felt less risky. And self-deprecating, I know. It was better to call him and avoid thinking about Ren Man. There were so many things I wasn't sure about with Ren Man, and subconsciously, I was still trying to convince myself that I didn't regret the breakup.

For the record, there'd only been one text between us since our breakup. I'd sent Ren Man a text about Dan and Shay's new album, and he followed it up with stories about more new stuff coming from artists we'd both liked. I randomly checked his Instagram in between texts to see what he was up to (naturally, we'd unfollowed one another after the breakup) and saw a new girl in his photos. And not just any girl, but a taller, blonder, skinnier version of me wearing the same dress I'd picked out to wear to the CMAs with Ren Man. The conversation was short from there, and I immediately called Michelle to gossip while mentally duct-taping the Ren Man filing box in my head so I could not go there again.

With more answers now than I'd wanted to have about Ren

Man, KG would stay in my thoughts, regardless of how terrible this was. Holding on to him was like holding on to a box of your most prized possessions. Letting go of him would feel like watching that box slip out of my hands into Lake Michigan, my Chicago past drifting away, like my first months in the Real World were all a dream.

Enough time had passed since KG's visit in July, and via texts and calls, we'd been communicating briefly. I'd planned to be in town for a fitness workshop in November, and although the workshop was canceled one week before the event, I didn't cancel my trip. It was the perfect excuse to leave Boston to see my BFF Shannon, who'd moved to Chicago, and KG, who said I could crash with him.

I'll spare you the details but will let you know that the short trip was hell. I taught three morning Tred11 classes, got wasted Saturday, day-drank on Sunday, lost my phone and ran out of KG's apartment sobbing harder than ever. The worst part? The weekend had started on such a high when KG cooked me dinner in his place, once again leading my hopeless heart to want more.

The lesson I relearned that weekend? He will never love me *that way.*

* * *

Back in Boston and driving to Maine on a Monday night for a town hall meeting, I thought about KG the entire way. Self-sabotage can be a hard cycle to break. I knew I needed to just let go of him. Ha-ha, like it was a simple decision.

It had been over a month since I'd run out of his apartment crying, and nothing about the way he'd treated me was OK. Ren Man had shown me how I deserved to be treated and, logically, I had absolutely no idea why I would even consider dating KG. I also hadn't a clue why I was hyperfocused on him.

Maybe it was the challenge? Maybe it was a messed-up thing I did to myself because I had low self-esteem about my body image and didn't feel I deserved more? Wait, doesn't every girl have body image issues? Maybe I yearned for something I connected to in Chicago.

When I got to Maine, I had dead time before my meeting, and I called Michelle. She gave me an unforgettable pep talk. It was like for the first time I actually listened to her. After she gave me a couple of empathetic "I knows" and a few "he sucks" and "you rocks," I got in the car and let myself sob one more time before taking her advice and letting go of everything KG.

I cried for loneliness.

I cried for missing my friends.

I cried for the unknown.

I cried knowing that I was hooking up with a guy who I didn't think I'd ever date seriously and because I felt bad about it.

Perhaps my sadness wasn't solely fueled by KG.

Jaylen must have been magically reading my thoughts because at that moment, he called.

I answered it and couldn't hide the creakiness in my voice. He knew I had been crying. I told him it was my nervousness about writing and publishing articles. It was kind of true—that was a thought on my mind. Putting yourself out there is scary as hell. But he didn't know the half of my tears.

However, something about his interest in my life made me feel like I was going to be OK, and I agreed to stay up later than my 9 p.m. bedtime and meet him and his friend Alex for dinner later that night.

CHAPTER 45.

A BUSINESS AND A BOYFRIEND

Boston

When I shower, I think about the big and little things. I savor closing my eyes, tilting my head back as I wash my hair and letting my mind drift off.

Especially in my new apartment, I loved doing it with the door open, allowing just enough light to come in from my large windows. Plus, in the fall, I'd open my windows and let rushes of fresh, cool air inside. When they mixed with the shower steam, it made me feel alive, the perfect space for deep thinking.

More and more, I had been ruminating over how fake my job felt. I'd run out of things to do—even ideas of things I thought I could do for Mr. Bates, who continued to evade me.

What's worse is that the civil engineers and attorneys were beginning to call me for answers when Mr. Bates evaded them as well. I felt like an idiot when I couldn't help them.

What did I want to do with my life? Where was I going?

Finally, I was ready to answer my first question: I wanted to help people. I wanted to help them lose weight.

I jumped out of the shower and posted an Instagram photo of myself doing a backbend with a kettlebell in the frame from the photo shoot I'd done in August with Lucie—the one where I asked her to make me look like I have abs. The photos were all pretty awesome—better than I'd expect to see of the depressed version of myself. I posted the athletic image with the caption:

"Now taking two more clients for my nutrition program in the month of December."

An hour later, I had two people signed up.

* * *

"Amy, please see my comments in red below," I typed rather feverishly.

I sounded like Mr. Bates. Every fifth or eighth time I sent him questions, he would respond, "Nicole, see my comments below in red."

It was the easiest way to make an email sound conversational and to stay on task.

Now I was doing the same thing, but with rough drafts of nutrition plans I'd sent to new clients.

Amy was my first client for my online business; the Instagram posts and fitness/nutrition articles I'd begun publishing were gaining speed and I had seven clients within a two-week period. I was helping clients like Amy crush their fat loss goals. The best part? I was creating the program on my time!

I'd set up their calorie and protein guidelines and then they were to create a rough draft of how to hit their target numbers. Then I would give them tweaks to make or minor corrections in order for them to hit the numbers more easily. After all that, we'd have weekly phone calls to discuss actionable steps to implement and own the new behaviors.

Just after I finished my email to Amy and hit "send," my apartment door opened. It was Jaylen.

"Hey, babe, how's it going? What job are you working on?"

That's another thing—somehow one coffee date, one dinner date and afternoon hangout in the park and Jaylen decided to ask me to be his girlfriend on Halloween. I wasn't sure how I felt about it. It was like I blinked and I had a boyfriend. What I did know was that he supported me, made me laugh and seemed much more focused and hardworking than Ren Man.

CHAPTER 46.

BUSY BEE

Early November

Moving to Boston didn't slow down my travels. It's just that plane time became car time. Trying to get to Tewksbury from my apartment in under an hour with traffic was impossible, and trips to Gardner were never less than 90 minutes. At least I could go home to my own bed and avoid lost luggage and long lines, but I was still in constant motion.

On this particular day, after an early morning meeting in Gardner, I had to rush to Tewksbury for an important neighborhood association event. The neighbors in this blue-collar community were outraged by the potential Oil City gas station project. Mr. Bates suggested we make the residents feel like they had a say in the project, so we—really I—led a series of meetings so they could voice their concerns.

Early to the meeting, I sat in my car waiting for a client call from a girl named Abby, whom I'd met in college. When I told her about my fat loss program and that the cost of my coaching was $200, she said OK without hesitation.

Crossroads of Fitness client count: eight.

Abby was so excited to gain confidence through fat loss, I swear I could hear her tearing up on the phone. Calls like these—which often happened inside my old, beat-up Touareg in the random parking lots of rural Massachusetts—helped me survive the move to Boston.

I hung up with Abby just as Phil pulled up to the Tewksbury Country Club. While waiting for John Smoller to arrive, we spoke about the impending meeting. We'd been dealt a rowdy, opinionated bunch who looked at us with hateful glares and disappointed eyes each time we walked into the room.

Despite the 159 complaints that I had to type up notes on and send in by the 10 a.m. conference call the next day, the meeting went well. Lesson? People enjoy being heard.

After such a long day, the last thing I wanted to do was go anywhere but "home." However, "the boys" never invited me anywhere, and when Mac Genter, the seller of our Tewksbury land and owner of the country club (and a lot of other Massachusetts real estate), asked John, Phil and me to grab a drink at the only neighborhood restaurant nearby, O'Malley's, I had to say yes.

Moments later, we were all seated around a tiny, tall table in the corner of the bar snacking on popcorn. They all ordered beers. I had a Diet Coke.

"Nicole, Nick told me he had to help you with your tire last time you guys were here in Tewksbury? Did you get it fixed?" Phil asked, referring to his business partner.

"Yes, thank goodness. I was so glad he noticed it! It's almost time for a new car. Our director, Jack, made fun of me last week in Littleton, New Hampshire. He joked that he was surprised my car even made it there."

"Oh, wow, Nicole, you must be all over New England. You cover New Hampshire, too?" asked Mac.

"Yes, and Maine. Technically, it's my colleague Mr. Bates' territory, but I help him manage it," I said.

"Did you always want to do real estate?" asked John.

"No, the job kind of found me," I said, unsure of how to exactly fake job enthusiasm.

"And you live in Back Bay, right?" asked Phil.

I didn't blame them for the questions. After all, after working with them for over a year, this was the first time I was sitting with them outside of a town hall meeting.

"Must be nice," said John, referring to my Boston zip code.

Being in the real estate business, they knew the price tag of Back Bay living. I felt like they assumed I was taken care of by my parents or something. Not a kept woman per se, but perhaps I was kept by my job.

"I really love where I live. It makes up for me missing Chicago," I said.

You could tell they all had a lot more questions for me, but I hated that I was the center of the conversation. Like since there was a woman at the table, they couldn't have their own normal conversation. So I shifted gears.

"Phil, how long ago did you start your business?"

Phil went on about his business, but that flowed into more about his passion for where he lived. He loved Lawrence, Massachusetts. He spoke with a smile from ear to ear. Besides Ren Man, I'd never met someone so passionate about their hometown.

That night, I went home and made a Facebook post about how I actually dislike Lawrence, Massachusetts, but the way Phil spoke about it made me want to move there immediately. Lesson No. 2 of the day? Passion is contagious.

CHAPTER 47.

STRIKE ONE

Late November 2014

"Nicole!"

Jaylen's voice was deep and angry. I could feel the fumes emanating from his body as he stood next to the bed leaning over me in a hoodie. In the five-second pause that followed—it felt like an hour—my mind was racing.

What could he be mad about? What did I do?

At that moment, I knew: He had looked through my phone and seen the text from KG.

"Did you text KG?" he demanded.

"Um," I said with that sleepy, "it's 3 in the morning" kind of voice. "Um, I think he texted me the other day, why?"

"Show me," he insisted as he handed me my phone to unlock.

Really? The only way he could have known about the text is if he had looked through it already. I was 99 percent sure he knew my code.

"Why do you think I texted him?"

"Just a feeling," he said sternly.

"You can look. He texted me about some dream he had," I said.

"What was the dream? And what did you say?!" he barked.

"I don't know, Jaylen; it's 3 in the morning. Something about him having a dream with me dating some Blackhawks hockey player ..." I trailed off, trying to hold on to my sleepy feeling.

"And what did you say?" he repeated.

"I don't remember. Something like 'LOL' or 'Mmmm … I wouldn't mind!' Come on, Jaylen. It was a dream about me dating a celebrity. He could have said Leonardo DiCaprio or Brad Pitt. It doesn't matter; it was not like I was flirting with *him*."

For the next two hours, until the sun came up, Jaylen berated me for flirtatiously texting another man and scolded me on how inappropriate my behavior was—like I was a misbehaving child.

"Do you realize how wrong that is? Are you trying to go behind my back? You're being shady," he barked.

Name-calling was one thing, but attacking my moral character was wrong. Worse? Instead of walking away or standing up for myself, young Nicole became remorseful and apologetic, believing him and his self-perceived almighty ways.

"I was not flirting. I'm sorry I texted him back. I know I said I wouldn't. But I was just responding to a harmless text."

"You swore to me that you would never ever contact him again when you told me how he hurt you in the past. You lied to me and you broke a promise. Do you know how wrong that is of you?" he scolded.

On that chilly, late November night, I didn't realize that I was being controlled, how he was creating this power struggle where he was the good guy and I was the bad guy who had done something criminally wrong. I had to earn his desire to stay with me, the terrible wrongdoer, and I'm embarrassed to admit I begged for him to stay when he threatened to break up with me. Was it because he was all I had?

We'd been dating just barely a month, and he literally never left my side. Despite that red flag, I couldn't see how insecure he was because I barely knew a moment without him. All I could see was that someone was questioning my commitment level, sincerity and trustworthiness, and I didn't like it. My knee-jerk reaction was to try to prove that I was being honest and had nothing to hide.

"I chose to be your girlfriend. I chose to date you. He's not here and, if anything, he might be a friend. But if you want, I'll block him, delete him on social media—whatever you think."

"You need to delete him immediately, if that helps you. You're the one struggling to keep your word. I don't want to force you, but you should if that will keep you from doing it."

It was so messed up; I didn't know what to do besides prove my genuine self. Proving myself was a weird reaction to some serious manipulation. However, the thing about manipulation is that you don't realize you're being manipulated when it first happens.

Anger still spewed out of his skin and the darkness surrounding him lingered, even when the sun came up. I was scared to be near him but fearful of what might happen without him. The evil he projected would suggest he didn't like me or want me, but his words and controlling ways signified I was a prize he wanted to win. I felt like a prisoner.

KG's Facebook was deleted right before Jaylen's eyes. We hugged, said we were sorry and my laptop was slammed shut. No need for it to be open while he "worked from home" via my apartment.

The moment I stepped out my apartment door to go lift, the hallway became like a temporary haven. I was the character in a movie that escaped the bad guy. Even though he wasn't really gone, that's how I felt, combined with the sense of relief you get after an argument. Truce. Moving on. But we weren't really.

Looking back, I should have been more observant. His rage was not normal.

* * *

At the gym that morning, I felt sick, a combination of self-disgust and physical exhaustion from lack of sleep. The mental hangover was so bad, I felt dizzy.

How would I tell my new friends at the gym that the guy I just told them I was dating was no longer going to be my boyfriend? People would think I was the crazy one.

I couldn't picture any other men in my life—Hunter, Wyatt, Ren Man, my dad—acting the way he did. I was even more embarrassed that I wasted my own hours of sleep begging for him not to leave. This was a whole new level of crazy.

What the hell?

Distraught, I had to leave the gym and call my mom back. I had begun telling her the story on my way to the gym. My car was the only safe place I could talk—Jaylen was always at my apartment.

"Mom, it's fine. He was being super-irrational, but I'm sure it will be fine."

"Nicole, that is ridiculous. I told Barry about it and, seriously, you need to get him out of there. No guy has the right to frighten you in *your* apartment in the middle of the night. Regardless of what the text message said, it was *your* phone in *your* apartment. He is crazy."

If my mom was telling Barry, she was clearly concerned. Barry is her easygoing boyfriend of several years, and she doesn't open up to him about everything. But this, apparently this was big to her, and now bigger to me.

I knew she was right, and I hated it. The worst part was that not only had we recently told people we were a couple, but we also booked a last-minute trip to New Orleans for my birthday.

"Nicole, first of all, you shouldn't even be talking to KG. But regardless, what if KG texts you while you're in the shower in the hotel room and Jaylen sees it and freaks out? You will be out of town. That scares me. You need to change your password on your phone right now."

"But what if he tries to go into my phone and sees that I changed it and gets even madder?"

"Shoot. I don't know. I think you should still do it, but I really don't want you going on that trip with him."

Red Flag No. 1.

* * *

For whatever dumb and naive reason, I still went to New Orleans with Jaylen for an early birthday celebration. After an easy flight and cab ride to our hotel, we walked to the famous Acme Oyster House.

We'd both fully planned to indulge in all the unhealthy foods we could find, and we started with a fried appetizer sampler at Acme. I bit into something and saw part of a fish head. It totally grossed me out. Then I reached for something else on the platter, a hot fried doughball.

"I can't believe ..." I started to describe how buttery it tasted, but my phone buzzed in my lap, catching me off guard. I'd been very cautious about not leaving my phone face up anywhere. I kept it in my purse or face down in my lap. Secretly, KG had been directed not to text me, and I'd even called him to tell him about the mini freak-out and asked him to please not contact me because it bothered Jaylen.

Red Flag No. 2.

The text was KG. He'd not only sent a message—he'd sent a photo.

Shit, a photo? That is the last thing I want him to be sending.

"Look what I just found," it read.

It was a photo of my old street in Chicago, North Wilton Avenue. If you looked closely, you could see the frontage of my old place.

What a sweet, nostalgic text! But I couldn't enjoy it with Jaylen there. It had to stop.

I wondered why he sent it. I wondered if he missed me. I knew he probably didn't, but I missed that street, that's for sure.

Not wanting Jaylen to think I was hiding anything, I told him about the photo and said, "I'm choosing to be here with you. He is choosing to send this. It's out of my control, and I'm telling you about it. OK?"

"OK," he said with a sigh. He knew it was irrational to be mad,

I thought. But perhaps being in public had some sort of leash on him.

CHAPTER 48.

WORST BIRTHDAY OF ALL TIME

Boston, December 9, 2014

My terrible, horrible, no-good, very bad 24th birthday had only one shining moment: 12 beautifully decorated, vegan, gluten-free cupcakes sent by Mom and delivered by my doorman. (They never brought packages upstairs!)

By 10 a.m., I had the cupcakes sitting out on my countertop, each with a single bite taken out of them. *Ha,* I chuckled to myself. *The perks of living alone.*

Well, I wasn't really living alone. Jaylen was still my "boyfriend" (no matter how weird it was to call him that) and still pretty much living with me. Aside from going to his apartment to pick up mail on Fridays, he worked from home with me and only left my place on Mondays, Wednesday and Fridays when he coached from 6 a.m. until 2 p.m. in downtown Boston.

Besides the cupcakes, the day was turning out to be a downer—and not just because of the crappy, rainy weather. My not-so-great birthday began when I failed at single-arm-pressing a 24-kilogram kettlebell that morning at Somerville Sweat, a cute goal I had for my 24th birthday. Next were the calls I made that went straight to voicemail—for both Matts, Stew and Mr. Bates (no surprise there).

Sweeping my dusty place out of boredom, I thought about my romantic 23rd birthday with Ren Man in Nashville, which naturally progressed to remembering the Michael Jordan text from KG. It made me want to reach out to him even more than I did when he'd texted me the photo when I was in New Orleans. Clearly unfriending him on Facebook hadn't stopped him from sending a photo to me via text; maybe he would answer if I texted him?

I couldn't text! What if Jaylen found it?

Red Flag No. 3.

But what if I were to call him?

I grabbed my phone and started dialing but stopped. I didn't want to have to explain myself to Jaylen, who would ask me, like he always did, if I'd spoken to KG. If I didn't tell him, I'm sure he'd see the record in my phone. I had a feeling he'd been looking through it at night when I was asleep.

Red Flag No. 4.

KG texted me before more boredom could tempt me to call him first. Without hesitation, I opened my phone and called him.

"Hey," he answered.

"Hey," I replied quietly, as if I had to whisper.

After the social media disconnects, both of our "heys" carried a lot of weight. To me, they meant, "I miss you, and I'm sorry, and I know we aren't social media friends, but it's your birthday and we actually are friends; your birthday still means something to me."

Ever since KG sent the photo of my old apartment in New Orleans, I'd been carefully planning out a speech to explain why I had to unfriend him, how much I missed him and that I wanted him to still be my friend. I respected him as a coach and wanted his respect in return.

He heard me inhale to unload the speech I'm sure he knew I'd practiced.

"I'm gonna stop you right there," he said. "I have something you need to know."

Because I'm that strong-willed, though, I interrupted him. Half-scared of not being able to say my piece, I wanted to be first.

"I miss you and I want to be friends. I know that everything ended weird, but it's important that you know I unfriended you on Facebook to appease Jaylen. He is very insecure about my past with you. He doesn't like that we had a thing, but I still want you to know that I want you as a friend," I said in one enormous breath.

Before I could ramble further, KG spoke. "Hey. Stop. Hey. Look, happy birthday. I miss you and want to be friends, too, and only friends."

I began having heart palpitations. It was hard to breathe.

"I've been seeing someone," he declared.

I swallowed and then inhaled like I was preparing for a breath-holding contest.

A few months back, I would've felt a stab in the chest, but this was like the best birthday present he could've given me, even if parts of me were jealous and curious. Jaylen had warped my sense of reality so much that he'd pretty much convinced me I was trying to cheat on him (looking back, I know it's insane—Red Flag No. 5). At that moment, I was overjoyed to be able to tell Jaylen that KG had moved on!

But crap, that would mean I'd have to tell him that we spoke!

My mind was going a mile a minute, and then KG shocked me further.

"But here's the thing," he added. "She lives in Back Bay. I've been to Boston three times since last July, and I will be there this weekend. I figured I should tell you before I end up running into you somewhere."

What? How could he have met someone in Boston?

He added, "I'd like to see you for lunch maybe on Friday while my girlfriend is at work, if that's OK with him," he said, referring to Jaylen.

Girlfriend? Why is he doing long distance with her?

I knew I wanted to see him, but if I did, there was no way I could tell Jaylen about it. I just couldn't. He didn't understand this relationship. I didn't even get it.

I decided I'd sit on the offer and contemplate whether it was OK to keep something from Jaylen.

* * *

Later that day, as I was on my way to Stride and Strength to take a class, I brainstormed how I could tell Jaylen about KG's girlfriend. Telling him I knew when they weren't Facebook official would mean I'd spoken with him privately. But telling Jaylen would help me prove that KG doesn't want to date me and that when he likes my Instagram posts, it's because he's a friend and a friend only. That would make everything better, right?

Maybe the mere fact that KG has a girlfriend would be good enough news to overshadow the fact that I broke his rule and my word that I wouldn't talk to him anymore. Time and vodka at dinner soon would tell.

For now, I had another problem to worry about—saving my job.

A week earlier, Stride and Strength owners Max and Kevin had sat me down and basically ripped me apart for not "showing up"—meaning that I wasn't active enough in the S&S community, both online and in real life. If I were more present, they argued, I would have higher attendance rates in my Thursday night class.

"We aren't paying you a lot, and you aren't making us a lot of money, so what are we even doing here? Do you want to be here?" Kevin asked rather bluntly as he and Max sat across a small cafe table decked out in perfect athleisure wear.

I choked back tears because I felt so misunderstood, ganged up on and judged.

If given the opportunity, I would rock their world! I would sell out! But they'd given me one class—Thursday at 7:40 p.m.—which began in July when everyone either travels or gets drunk on outdoor patios. Plus, it was hard to be "present" often, especially with an 8-to-5 job. Not to mention, it was intimidating! I was the non-shredded instructor. I was the new girl. And, hello? New Englanders are not friendly. The few mid-class/mid-locker room ice-breaking conversations I'd tried to have went over as smoothly as driving on gravel. I'd felt more comfortable spending my mornings doing powerlifting and kettlebell training at Somerville Sweat, where I had more friends and felt just a tiny bit at home.

"I want to be here. I simply thought you guys didn't want to have me. My efforts to market classes are present on my Instagram; I posted a photo about the new merchandise this morning. It's tough for me to teach or take classes midday, but like I said in the beginning, I'm still interested in teaching 5 a.m. and 6 a.m. classes."

I wanted them to know the Nicole who handed out 30-some resumes in the July heat in Chicago. I wanted them to want me to teach more and know that I would deliver!

"Really? I didn't see that. To us, it seems like you don't care about S&S. I haven't seen your posts and you're definitely not selling out classes. And make sure you respond to sub requests! That's the best way to get exposure," added Kevin.

"I always respond immediately to the ones I can sub. Since July, I've asked to take several weekend and morning sub opportunities, but didn't get them," I said.

"Say, 'I fucking want all of these classes' when you respond to sub requests," said Kevin. "Be bold."

It's not my nature to demand things nor is it to cuss. I thought by raising my hand to take the three or four I could was good enough. But I never got the classes I offered to teach. They went to the veteran instructors.

"It's tough because we think you could be great, but nobody knows you, and we want to put you in as a substitute in weekend classes, but we risk people not coming because they don't know you. So start by taking more classes."

"Understood," I replied, mimicking the way Mr. Bates would talk to First Aid Farm directors when they used a commanding tone with him.

I left that meeting trying not to cry, thankful not to be fired, and booked the earliest class I could take with my schedule, even if it meant going on my birthday.

* * *

Eight minutes into class, I sneezed. And then again and again. I couldn't breathe.

Someone near me or in the previous class must have owned a cat or pet rabbit. I could tell by the allergens in the air. My throat was closing up. Kevin had just announced that a newish instructor was in class, on Treadmill 2, and I sneezed while waving at strangers looking my way.

Two minutes into the run, I had to walk because I was wheezing so badly. It's not cool to be the new instructor and walking—we're supposed to be the #fitspo.

I didn't have my rescue inhaler for my asthma and ran out of class to grab a tissue and see if by chance there was an inhaler behind the desk. I couldn't stop sneezing and wheezing.

No luck. Benedryl would save me if I could get some. Crushing class would have to happen another time.

Immediately, I grabbed my phone and called for an Uber. No cars were available. It was pouring rain, and the city was gridlocked at 6:45 p.m. and getting Benedryl to calm the sneezing, could also (hopefully) prevent a serious asthma attack. In flight-or-fight mode, I ran out into the rain in shoes without socks trying not to cry out of embarrassment, fear, loneliness and frustration.

Sobbing through my puffy, swollen eyes, I somehow landed in the deepest puddles every time I tried to dodge one while running from Chauncy Street to Tremont in the dark. Crying felt good, though.

Having spent my 24th birthday being shocked at the news of KG's new girlfriend and that he'd been in Boston multiple times without seeing me, and hating this city for its traffic and inability to understand me, I cried hard. I needed an ugly cry—and Benadryl.

When I made it to Walgreens, I pounded four children's Benadryl and then rushed to the sushi place two blocks away, where I was meeting Jaylen for dinner. I was thankful to be greeted with a warm smile by my favorite waiter, Ben. Although a hug from Mom would've been better, at this point anything would do.

Unfortunately, Jaylen was fighting the gridlocked traffic without luck and wouldn't be there for another 45 minutes. I wasn't sure why he'd been at his apartment in Somerville. My best guess? Getting the mail early so he could get more work done on Friday.

By the time he got there, my allergies and asthma had dissipated.

A combination of vodka and Benadryl coaxed me into spilling the details of my day.

It must have been a birthday miracle: After telling him my big news, Jaylen's eyes glazed over like mine did after taking the Benadryl. Apparently, it *was* a positive in his mind. Thankful for Benadryl and company, my night ended better than predicted. Unfortunately, I'd come to know that my 24th year would not bestow brilliant birthday miracles like Jaylen's calm demeanor when I broke the news about talking to KG.

CHAPTER 49.

HOW MANY RED FLAGS EQUAL STRIKE TWO?

New Year's Eve, 2014

"It's been so weird without you!" I said in a cheery I-get-to-see-you-soon tone.

"I know, tell me about it. At least you've been surrounded by family and having a blast skiing. I'm just working here alone, without you."

I was in Snowmass, Colorado, for a ski vacation with my family during Christmas break, the first time Jaylen and I had been apart for more than two days since we started dating.

In my family, bringing boyfriends and girlfriends on family trips is frowned upon unless they've been around a few years. Since we had been dating just shy of two months, I didn't dare ask if he could come with me to Snowmass.

Plus, it may have been slightly awkward if he came. I'm a huge fan of Christmas, but Jaylen didn't have a reason to cherish this time of year the same way as I did. He was born and raised in the Jewish community. Through birthright trips and small social groups, he was very involved with the Jewish faith and even flew a mini Israeli flag from inside his backpack (it poked out of the top zipper). He spoke Hebrew and his nickname for me? "Habibi," which means something to the effect of "my adored love."

"Well, I am coming back now, so no need to worry. We will have a chill New Year's Eve," I said.

"Good. I have a surprise for you and I'm so glad you don't want to go out-out. I like lying low and want you all to myself."

His comment seemed dramatic at first, but on second thought, it was very much in line with his intense romantic professions. In fact, he'd told me he was madly in love with me. But I knew it was puppy love, that first-love infatuation type. I actually thought that about Ren Man, too, when he first told me he loved me. They both said it really, really early in the relationship. I always kind of thought you need a good six months to know if you mean it.

In college, my serious boyfriend Paul waited six months. When we finally confessed our love to one another, it felt as real as I'd ever felt anything.

Though Ren Man told me just two months in, I felt our love was mutual by month four; but not yet with Jaylen.

Still, I was very happy that I would be seeing him that night—until I actually saw him.

* * *

My blue Touareg pulled up to the terminal with Jaylen behind the wheel. He looked at me through the window with a cool, blank stare, the bone-chilling kind. As soon as he saw me, his eyes jetted away from mine, and he left me with an unreciprocated smile, like your hand hanging out in the air when someone doesn't realize you are waiting for a high-five. He got out of the car to help me with my luggage, and I skipped over to him, thinking maybe he was just too excited to wait another second to see me and smile back.

He grabbed my bags and said hi without any eye contact. I could feel the same anger emanating from him that I'd felt when he stood over me in bed at 3 a.m. back in November.

"Are you OK?" I asked.

"Yeah, I'm good," he said as he walked to get into the car, still with no eye contact.

All the way down Storrow Drive, I tried to break the ice that shouldn't have been there.

He was stiff. He was cold. He was mad.

"Are you sure you're OK?" I asked again.

"No. No, actually I'm not," he boomed without looking at me.

"You know why," he added, kind of like a statement but kind of like he was asking me, too.

If it was a question, I was actually clueless to the answer.

It'd been five hours since our very pleasant, hour-long call and I had no idea what I could've possibly done to warrant this anger during my flight. Not to mention, we'd been apart for those hours, so even if I had been texting KG (which for the record, I hadn't been), he couldn't have sneakily peeked at my phone to see it.

"Nicole. You liked Flash Fitness's Instagram. I saw it, you know. I can see those things," he stammered.

Flash Fitness was KG's gym. I'd liked a photo that showed my old workout buddies doing a New Year's Eve workout. I missed them. I liked the photo. KG wasn't even in the photo. Still angry over KG? O-M-G.

What??

Red Flag No. 6.

New Year's Eve or not, I was not going to stand for this behavior. Being around my family instilled more confidence in me. They reminded me of who I am: a strong girl who is loved, supported and not alone. Being far away often made me forget things like that, which may have been why I'd let Jaylen control me or put me down.

I put my foot down and said, "So what."

His fists gripped the steering wheel hard as he shook his head, veering the car toward the Fenway exit. We were almost home, but the fight was just beginning. Saying "so what" felt way better than it should have.

"I should be able to text whomever I want, whenever I want,

and if it's KG, who cares! I am dating *you*. And for the record, he isn't even in the photo!" I was firm. Back down? I would not.

We drove in silence, and I wondered how or why he'd seen that I liked the photo and it made me uneasy. Thinking back to our conversation earlier, he'd told me that he had surprises for me in the apartment, and the last thing I wanted were gifts from an angry man. I didn't even want to be around him. But the sad part was that being alone in this city I still didn't love—on a holiday—sounded worse.

We needed to come to an agreement. He was not going to control my life; I'd been disillusioned by his jealousy and paranoia for long enough. The jealousy was unattractive. The controlling part, even more. Nausea bubbled inside me as I realized this unreasonably furious guy was about to come back to my apartment and sleep next to me that night. I knew then he wasn't for me, but breaking up with him at that moment felt as far off as trying on a bikini did when I was chubby and not quite done with puberty.

Riding the elevator up to the apartment was like crawling into a dark, scary tunnel. Instead of letting the fear of Jaylen's anger and what might go down on what should've been a fun night shut me up, I fought it, taking command.

"I will not sleep next to you or even think about going to bed until we talk about this and how crazy it is that you're mad at me. I will not accept it," I said, halting outside the elevator, refusing to walk toward the apartment door.

Jaylen was silent.

"Hell, I don't want to see any nice things you did that can trick me into not being upset with you. I want to believe you're not actually mad at me. Can you let this go?" I asked bluntly.

He looked at me and waved his hand, head bowed down a bit. "Come on," he said, walking toward the door.

When I walked into the warm apartment, which smelled like chocolate and butter, I felt horrible for everything: fighting with him, being angry with him, having him express unwarranted anger at me. Seeing the gifts he showered me with was like the most gorgeous, enormous Band-Aid—the kind that doesn't stay on well. There was a new side table for the couch; a new, full-length mirror in my bedroom; an extravagant dinner he had made paired with chocolate-covered strawberries he had dipped himself. He showed me how he cleaned the place spic and span.

I said thank you and then sat on the couch and pulled on my hair; I wanted to rip it out, I was so frustrated.

This was nuts. I realized if I gave into his anger, I was weak and he won. If I stood up for myself, we quarreled and became a couple who fights a lot.

Red Flag No. 7.

I needed to get my anger off my chest and tell him his jealous and controlling tone toward me was not OK. Despite the gifts surrounding us, we fought for an hour and then made up with apologies and hugs, which led to makeup sex.

Hours after Jaylen fell asleep, I lay captive in what was my fresh-slate apartment with this person I couldn't understand. Did he really think I was a bad person? Why was I always doing something wrong (in his eyes)? Sadly, seeing him upset made me actually begin to think more about KG and Ren Man, who looked like saints compared to him.

At this point, Jaylen now had two strikes in my book (the first being when he yelled at me in the middle of the night). Promising myself I'd give him only one more strike made me feel like I'd retained some sense of power, which finally helped me fall asleep.

CHAPTER 50.

VALENTINE'S DAY DEVIL

February 2015

Sleeping in on Saturdays awakes my inner princess and puts me in a jovial mood. However, on Valentine's Day 2015, the late morning hour brought no whimsical headspace. Worse, I sensed the intense enmity only Jaylen could imbue when he got into one of his angry moods. Yawning audibly, I rolled over to an empty bed, and a pit grew in my stomach like the one I felt on New Year's Eve, and the same one I felt when he woke me up at 3 a.m. on that dark night in November.

Then Jaylen walked into my bedroom, smiling, with two cups of coffee in hand.

Surely, my senses were off—he wouldn't be mad on Valentine's Day.

"Good morning, babe! Happy Valentine's Day!" I said with the same zest one has for the first Valentine's Day they share with a new partner.

"Hi, habibi," he said softly, kissing my cheek and handing me the coffee mug.

I smiled at him. "I can't wait to give you the card I made."

"Look in front of you," he directed.

I gazed past my cup and saw photos of us strewn about my dresser. As I reached to put the coffee cup on my nightstand and get out of bed, I saw two more sweet photos of us smiling in

New Orleans. I hugged him and said thank you with a kiss on his cheek.

"There's more," he said excitedly. I no longer sensed the angry cloud around him and mentally sighed with relief.

"Can I go to the bathroom first, please?"

"Sure," he said, smiling even more broadly.

In the bathroom, the toilet paper was gone, and as I reached for a new roll under the sink, photos of us fell onto the tile floor.

"Babeeee!" I yelled through the door. "You are the best!" I chirped, acknowledging the sweet surprise.

Walking into the kitchen, I was about to head back to the bedroom to grab my coffee but stopped when I saw more photos taped to the cabinets. Coffee could wait!

"Aw! These are adorable!"

"I thought you'd like them. I was up late last night printing them and placing them," he said proudly.

"Thank you so much, sweet guy! I really appreciate this. The memories are so great, and you know how much I love photos!" I said as I opened the door to the fridge. More photos fell out.

"Can I make you breakfast? And then give you the card I made you?"

"There's more; keep looking! And then something else!" he said.

I looked toward the family room for more photos and noticed the powerlifting shoes he had given me as an early Valentine's Day present sitting on the couch. Walking over toward them, I noticed there was a deck of cards, wait, two decks of cards sitting inside the shoes.

"Open them," he said, beaming.

Pieces of paper were taped to each card. Each piece of paper taped to the card either displayed a reason why he loved me, a sweet compliment, an inside joke or an affirmation of unconditional love.

You can't count.

You laugh at my jokes.

You buy me bacon.
Go Eagles!
Make the announcement!

It took a while to get through all the reasons—all 104 of them. It was very romantic. You'd think we'd been dating for years, we had so many inside jokes and photos together.

There was a card for me on the table, too.

"Babe, you shouldn't have. This is so sweet!"

"There's more," he said, nodding toward the kitchen.

"Well, I'm going to start making you breakfast because you need to eat!"

We kissed and ate breakfast together, after I gave him a card. Moments after eating, we both got started on some work—that's all he ever wanted to do on Saturdays. I started to sense that angry vibe again. I felt guilty that I sensed it, but I knew something was up, even on a romantic day like Valentine's Day.

* * *

"Nicole!" he roared literally out of nowhere at about 4 p.m.

Startled, I jumped in my own desk chair. My stomach dropped at the all-too-familiar tone.

I had suspected this anger upon waking; my recent inklings that he'd been going through my phone (again) were on point.

A few days prior, I'd texted Ren Man to tell him I was planning to see one of his musician friends, Sam Hunt, in concert. During the exchange, Ren Man told me that the after-party would probably be way later than my bedtime, but that it should be a good show.

Why would those texts bother him? We'd never fought about Ren Man before. Talking to myself, I confirmed I was going mad and looked up at him with confusion on my face.

"Do you still talk to Ren Man?" he asked.

Not mad, apparently.

I answered with my hand to the Bible. "Yeah, I text him now

and then," I said, adding, "I touched base with him the other day, actually."

"Why did you text him?"

"I asked him if he could get me Sam Hunt's number or something for the concert next week."

"It was a short conversation," I added, as if he hadn't read the messages.

The fact that I had to divulge these meaningless details in a defensive manner on Valentine's Day was so disheartening. *Who had I become?*

More and more, it was clear I was the victim. Since New Year's Eve, I'd begun reading a lot about domestic abuse, per my mom's suggestion. Besides manipulation, there were two behaviors abusers exhibited: one, putting down and blaming the victim, and two, unwarranted anger. Jaylen again was making me feel like the wrongdoer, even though I was genuinely innocent. No part of me wanted Ren Man, and I'd moved on from KG.

Red Flag No. 8.

We fought about it for about three hours. It was like when a bully tells a little girl dressed up as a princess that fairy tales aren't real. I took off my crown and put on my running shoes. Sweating it out on the treadmill downstairs sounded like the only thing that could make my day better.

* * *

Quarreling in the afternoon threatened but did not disrupt our Valentine's dinner plans. Neither did Snowpocalypse—what they were calling the series of snowstorms in Boston. After not leaving the apartment for two days, we needed fresh air.

While I curled my hair and did some quick makeup, I tried to repress some facts I knew to be true but wasn't ready to admit. There were three reasons why I knew I hadn't broken up with him yet:

1. There was a blizzard putting everything on hold.

Since January, Mother Nature had been dropping boulder-sized snowballs on Boston. Until March, shovels were required just to leave your house, and few people walked in the most walkable U.S. city. The novelty of the whiteouts had long dissipated by this point, but we weren't sick of each other. We were all each other had in the city, which created a codependent relationship by nature, not nurture.

2. I felt trapped. If Jaylen and I hadn't been spending every second together in *my* apartment, some personal time to reflect would've told me to show him the door.
3. I had no friends or family nearby to run to and perhaps discuss some of the bouts of rage.

For a strong girl, I was getting really good at weak. For now, strong eyeliner became my short-term fix.

After I was done putting on makeup, I asked him if he liked my dress and then we drove to Pier 6 for a seven-course prix-fixe meal. While we were indulging in high-calorie, savory foods, the subject of nutrition and fat loss came up.

"Sometimes I feel like there is just no way I could get defined abs. Like my body won't do it," I said in the same frustrated tone every former dieter knows all too well.

"You can; it's definitely possible. But a lot of the people whom I know you look up to in the industry take things to make it easier," said Jaylen.

"What do you mean? Like the girls I follow on Instagram?" I asked, disheartened.

"Oh, yeah, absolutely. They take 'weightlifting' supplements," he said, with a wink.

At this point, dear reader, I'll let you draw your own conclusion.

"I always wondered if Ren Man took weightlifting supplements because he was super lean and seemed to have a relatively balanced life—you know, he drank now and then and ate candy. I mean, I highly doubt it, but ..."

"He definitely did not," Jaylen interjected.

I titled my head and gave him a look like, *How would you know?*

"I mean, based on what you told me about him and all of his nutrition-store supplements, he wasn't doing them."

"What do those have to do with anything?" I asked.

"These weightlifting supplements trump all that stuff. If you're on more intense things, you don't waste your time or money with any of that."

I looked him in the eye and knew he had something to say.

"Do you know people who do them?" I asked, then nervously added, "Do your clients take them?"

I could tell by his relaxed demeanor that he was tipsy at this point. We both were.

"Some do, yes, but we don't really talk about it unless they directly want advice from me," he said.

"Oh, yeah, you were around some guys using that stuff at that powerlifting camp you went to after high school, right?" I asked, remembering the stories he'd told me about certain mentors who had suggested he try taking them.

"Yes. Remember the story I told you about my mentor, Alex, and how he put them in the bathroom and told me to go in there and explore? And I told you I saw the weightlifting supplements and just walked out?"

This couldn't be happening.

"Well, I lied. I did them. I still do them. I'm on a cycle now."

So many thoughts rushed to my head. First and foremost, I felt the weight of the biggest burden on my chest. He'd just dropped a huge secret on me to bear. Being judgmental would not help me learn more about him or have a mature conversation, so I took a deep breath in through my nose and swallowed the wine in my mouth. It was hard to even know how to respond, especially given the fact that I was feeling a little drunk. As soon as I gulped, I asked, "Who else knows?"

He told me three names of people who knew—people who were also users.

I wanted to know *how* they worked. I wanted to know *why* he did them. I wanted to know *how* he did them. I wanted to know *when* he did them.

"You know when I go home on Fridays to get the mail?" he asked.

In that moment, it hit me that I'd been sleeping next to a guy who had been lying to me and it scared me. Knowing that while lying to me he'd also been accusing me of being emotionally unfaithful made me irate.

What else is he lying about?

But that night, I did not flip out on him. I didn't yell. I didn't cry. I didn't get upset. Whether it was from the booze or shock, instead of me getting angry, our night ended with me inquiring all about weightlifting supplements.

What were the side effects? Why did he do them? How long had he been on them while dating me? Do girls take them? Should I take them? Could I take them? Would they hurt me? Do any of our mutual friends take them?

It was 21 questions, and Jaylen was a proud respondent.

As he spilled all the details, the pieces began fitting together. The rage. The baldness. His short height. The nodules I once felt in his glutes while giving him a massage. The jealousy.

It all made sense now.

Holy shit!

CHAPTER 51.

CUTTING HIM OFF

After the big secret's reveal on Saturday night, Jaylen and I spent all of Sunday together. His presence helped me hold up the secret's weight on my chest. I didn't want to fight about anything, and I hadn't yet processed much; I only knew deep down that something felt wrong.

When Monday rolled around, though, and I had to bear it by myself, the weight became too big to carry. Crying as I drove to Somerville Sweat to go lift, I called Michelle and told her in a voicemail that I had to tell her something important.

Since I couldn't text her to call me because I was scared Jaylen would eventually see the exchange, Gchat seemed like a good idea. After all, when Michelle and I worked at Alessor, we used it every day.

"Hey! Just like old times? Call me when you get a chance," I wrote before entering the gym.

As I looked around during my workout and saw other trainees working so hard to get better, get stronger and improve themselves the natural way, everything seemed unfair. It made me nauseous to realize a very prominent coach would do something to have an unfair advantage.

How could I be dating the motivational guy who preached all of this "authenticity" bullshit, this "work hard and keep going" hustle mentality, telling others that they too can make sacrifices and get ahead when he wasn't walking the walk? His business was booming and, yes, he was a great coach, but it was hard to ignore the big fat lie he was telling every day.

"You can be strong, too."

"Powerlifters can be lean."

And yet, he had just finished telling me that most bikini competitors are on weightlifting supplements and can eat more freely thanks to better nutrient partitioning with the product.

I was dumbfounded. I wanted to talk to someone; I *needed* to talk about it with someone.

If I told my mom, she'd threaten to fly to Boston if I didn't break up with him, I was sure. Ever since that night in November, she was not on Team Jaylen.

Red Flag No. 9.

But I was scared. I was scared to end it, scared to tell him I didn't agree, scared to even talk about it because the thought of how he might react was terrifying.

I had a few more exercises to do, but when Michelle called me, I stepped out. My ability to lift heavy was compromised by the boulder-sized load of this secret.

* * *

"Hey, Nicky, what's going on?" asked Michelle.

"Michelle, I need to tell you something you can share with nobody. I have to talk to someone about it, and I really don't know who to tell. You live far away in the Midwest; you have nothing to do with fitness, and you are one of my closest friends, so ..."

"Oh, God. Tell me! Tell me!" she said excitedly.

"It's not exciting; it's not juicy-fun drama. It's kind of confusing and scary and I don't know what to do," I said and then spilled.

She acted as I suspected and expressed sincere concern for my well-being. Similar to what I had been thinking, she felt the issue of supplements themselves was a huge red flag, but unlike how I felt, it was a no-brainer for her. He had to stop using them and I had to make him, if I wanted to be with him.

She said it for me. She said what I was scared to admit: I couldn't be with someone who did weightlifting supplements.

Jaylen had been continuing to tell me he wanted to marry me, and Michelle knew this.

"Nic, you can't raise kids with someone doing this," she said.

"I know, there's no way I'm going to have to hide paraphernalia in our home someday. Absolutely not. You're right. I am so not OK with this. I can't even believe I am talking about this," I lamented, adding, "Even worse, he has sworn me to secrecy."

She told me she had to go, but that we should Gchat about it so that he wouldn't see texts about it on my phone.

Red Flag No. 10.

Later that day, we spoke about it at length and she even created a Google Doc for me to read. "How to confront J," it said at the top. Considering this was going to be one of those conversations you don't want to have, Michelle made the sheet for me to make it as easy as possible. It was a rather good plan, too. It was not, however, quite as fun as the strategic plan from our last Google Doc: "How to seduce KG."

I bit my lip imagining how this might go down. Scared that he would go into a bout of rage, flip out on me and automatically know that I'd told someone, I wondered if I should actually confront him. Luckily, I was raised to know that doing the right thing is not always easy. Still, my mind ran wild. I knew myself: There was no way I could be around him and not bring it up. He needed to know the moment he came home we were going to talk.

Michelle called me one more time right before he came home to review the steps. She also told me that if I didn't text her within an hour, she would call to make sure I was OK.

"I'm nervous he's going to come home early and hear us on the phone, so I gotta go. I'll Gchat you," I said.

Red Flag No. 11.

* * *

Jaylen came home and I immediately said, "Come sit with me. There's something I need to chat with you about."

By the grim look on his face, I knew my "we need to talk" text message I sent earlier had been more than enough to indicate a serious conversation was about to go down.

In the past, I'd never sensed a nervous, "always guilty" side of him, but now it was more apparent. No wonder he was always on edge and seemingly insecure; it was because he was probably either thinking everyone was wondering if he was a fraud or assuming others were frauds themselves. Think about it: If he could keep a huge secret like this, couldn't everyone else?

I went through the steps Michelle and I had planned very precisely. I said what we rehearsed. Made sure not to waiver. This was not a "maybe you might want to stop" kind of thing; this was an "I need you to stop immediately."

At first, he was skeptical and demeaning.

"You were even interested in them the other night! You asked about what they would do for you! You were curious about them, too! You were OK with it the other night!!!"

With Michelle's voice in my head, I held my ground. "Yes, I was intoxicated and needed time to process everything. I also didn't want to fight in a restaurant. It felt surreal because I hadn't a clue about this side of you."

Then he told me about several other famous coaches and powerlifters who have kids and are healthy and made up some lie about how he gets "checked" at the doctor every few months to make sure he is fertile and everything is working OK.

Sadly, I believed him.

He went on to say that he can't stop doing them right away, but that he wouldn't ever put our future kids in danger.

So he plans to keep a separate apartment in which to do weightlifting supplements forever?

In defense of the next part of my argument on how terrible it would be for him to be caught with these substances on him, he replied, "They don't go after users; they go after dealers. I am not going to get caught."

I started to cry.

He didn't get it.

"You're being so defensive; can't you see that the girl you supposedly love is telling you she's upset about your actions and the thought of changing them isn't your knee-jerk reaction?"

Insert more defensive words from Jaylen.

Then I dropped the bomb I was most scared to drop.

"Look, I've read up on this supplement. The two most common side effects? Jealousy and rage. We've been fighting since we met. How long have you been on them?" I asked, then added, "I've never fought this much in any of my relationships."

"You're being offensive. I'm only reacting to your words," he said. "You wanting to talk to your exes behind my back has nothing to do with this," he added.

"No ..." I began.

He interrupted me. "Your actions—being secretive and dishonest—they are not appropriate behaviors," he scolded.

I finally played my last card, the "scared, crying girlfriend" card—which I realized might remind him of his mother's reactions toward his abusive father.

Burying my face in my hands, through sobs, I yelped, "Can't you see? Your behavior—whatever the cause—is scaring me. Hell, I was scared to even have this conversation. I should not be made to feel scared in my own apartment by the person I'm dating."

This got through to him.

He began to cry and, for a slight moment, he let his walls down and said he felt like his dad. He cried to me for about a minute and put his head on my lap, promising to stop.

"But I can't right now, not right away; you have to cycle off of it to do this the healthy way."

"As long as you promise to get off of them," I said.

I wanted the secrecy and this stuff gone. I didn't want to have to lie to my family moving forward. Nobody in my family would do anything like this. Why was I dating someone who did?

CHAPTER 52.

WERE THINGS GETTING BETTER? OR IS SOMETHING THAT'S DOOMED DOOMED?

March 2015

There was still snow on the ground in New England, but most of Boston was just wet with the melt-off from the Snowpocalypse as Jaylen and I hopped over puddles on the way out of gymnastics, laughing at the fact that we wearing shorts in March and stomping through snow and slush. You could say my anger had melted.

The thing about Midwesterners? We forgive and forget, then we pray about it. I forgave Jaylen for keeping the secret from me and trusted that he would get off the weightlifting supplements as soon as he could—he just had to wean himself off of them.

Jaylen and I had done a great job of co-existing while trapped indoors during the Snowpocalypse, making it work by taking work breaks in the apartment building's gym, seeing movies on occasion and eating sushi on Friday nights.

We also were spending a few Saturday afternoons at open adult gymnastics classes to get out of the house and do something active. After months of grueling preparation for a powerlifting meet we both participated in, we were trying to broaden our horizons and have fun with exercise. Enter gymnastics class.

It reminded me of what I did as a little girl. I enjoyed going because it was the only active thing Jaylen and I did together when he didn't turn on his coaching demeanor with me. I was the expert in this realm. He was a good coach, though, I thought to myself as he grabbed my hand in the car. I might only have one close friend in the city (Candace was her name and we were starting to hang out here and there), but I had convinced myself that Jaylen was better than having a lot of friends because he was always with me, always available in this dreary season and not-so-lovely city.

Oh, and if you're wondering, Jaylen did have friends—three of them, to be exact. Two were from high school and one from lifting. But he didn't see them often.

As we headed back to the apartment, I realized the highlight of the day was now over. For much of the remainder of Saturday, he would be on his laptop, typing away while I did my own blog-writing at my usual spot at the table. I knew Candace would be going out that night, but she was single and I dare not think to go out, especially without Jaylen.

All I knew were the white walls of my apartment and his company.

The other thing about Midwesterners? We are as punctual and rhythmic with our lives as the cows and crops are on Indiana lands. X amount of time together and living together (God forbid) insinuates marriage is to come, and I'd be lying by omission if I didn't tell you that Jaylen brought the subject up in May.

Why did I consider him—someone whom I wasn't fully attracted to and fought with often—as a candidate? He supported my dream career of only doing fitness and building my online blog/fitness business.

Jaylen knew I wanted only to do one job—one that made me feel purposeful—so we had made a deal. We figured since he was always at my place, we could officially move in together and split the rent come September, when his lease was up. Then, as soon as I could make $3,000 a month (with my fitness coaching and online business combined) for three months in a row, I would quit my real estate job. We'd stay in Boston potentially one more year and then we'd travel for a year. He wanted to travel, and I liked the idea of it.

"You're gonna make more money than me soon," he'd say every time I got a new client.

I laughed. "Yeah, yeah."

"You think I'm kidding," he said with a cocky but confident tone.

He had a great smile.

Subconsciously, I worried because he was the most codependent and antisocial person I'd ever met. However, I liked his companionship most days. Maybe this was to be my new life?

"What are you working on?" I asked. "Can we go to the store soon to get stuff for dinner?"

"Emails, work, work. I have a lot to do; gymnastics took a lot of time," he said.

"I know, but it's good to get out. Maybe we could see a movie tonight if we make dinner here?"

"Let me see how much I can get done. But, yes, we can go to the grocery store soon for dinner stuff."

For the record, the store was in the building behind my apartment. So not far.

Anytime I asked him to do something that wasn't work-related, he made me feel guilty. I liked his silly side, but I saw him more as cute than sexy. I looked at him that night and knew I'd I fallen in love with him as a person—a hardworking, driven guy—but not in love with him as a partner. I yearned to love him in a more romantic way, but I think I knew in my gut I couldn't.

That night, we went to bed cuddling, and for probably the 80th time, I awoke to Jaylen yelling, blocking his head and tucking his small body into the fetal position in his sleep. He was constantly tormented by nightmares about his childhood.

"Shhhhhhh, it's OK, babe; I'm here, go to sleep. I'm right here. It's OK. Shhhhhhhhh," I whispered as I hugged him tightly.

CHAPTER 53.

KG IS BACK

Things that were normal for me in Chicago were becoming rare, special occasions with Jaylen in Boston. Example? Going out for a night on the town with friends.

In his defense, nobody really wanted to go out often during Snowpocalypse, but I was going stir crazy by mid-March. So when Jaylen had a nice gift card to a fancy restaurant in the South End, I decided to really go all out and wear this special dress I bought for my trip to NYC with Ren Man that in the end was never worn. It was a black, long-sleeved, backless dress with a plunging neckline and such thick material that you could only wear it in the wintertime. Everything from my makeup to handholding in the car felt right leading into the soiree.

To make the evening more of an event, I texted my cousins mid-dinner to see if they wanted to meet us out. I also sent a message to my coaches from Somerville Sweat and had Jaylen text his friend, EJ, from high school.

Why not make it a big night?

After a really splendid dinner in a dark French restaurant called Aquitaine (which was pleasantly quiet for how crowded and cluttered the small space was), we were slightly buzzed and eager to drink more.

The social hour began by meeting my cousin Elizabeth and her fiancé Carlo at a nearby hole-in-the-wall bar. The weather outside was cold enough to make the short jaunt feel like a near-death experience. But we were determined! At the bar, we texted my cousin Andrew, Elizabeth's brother, to come meet us as well.

The bar was one of the only ones left in Boston where smoking was still allowed and it was cash-only. While Jaylen faded into the smoke on his way to the ATM with Carlo, I stood across the bar at a round table, dodging the fog with Elizabeth; my phone buzzed. It was John, my coach from Somerville Sweat. He, Mary and some other coaches from the gym were at a bar called Lir right by my apartment.

This was perfect! I was going to have a real night out with multiple friends and bars like I used to have in Chicago!

"Hey, Jaylen," I yelled as he turned to come back toward us with drinks. "Guess who just reached out? John! He wants us to come by Lir in Back Bay!" I said with tipsy enthusiasm. "It sounds fun!"

"OK, sure, is Andrew coming? Can he meet us there?" Jaylen replied.

"Andrew is almost here; let's wait for him to get here and then go."

This was cool: Both of my cousins, my boyfriend, his one high school friend and my gym friends were all going to hang out! In Boston! I have friends!

Just then, my phone died. As we chugged our drinks and left the smoky time warp, Jaylen sent an "on our way" text to my coaches.

Apparently, we were all giggly, minus our sober driver, EJ. Jaylen and Carlo were practicing their thickest Boston accents. Carlo, who is half-Dutch and half-Portuguese, sounded so funny attempting the Boston persona; we were all tickled inside.

Pulling up to the bar, I stopped giggling. Suddenly, I remembered that earlier in the day I'd seen a photo of John, Mary, KG and his Boston girlfriend training at Somerville Sweat.

Shit. What if he's with them? They wouldn't have asked me to come, I don't think, if they knew ...

There was a weird feeling in the air as I walked into the bar ahead of my cousins while Jaylen went to park with EJ. I stared at the bouncer who checked my ID, too scared to look into the bar and see KG.

Young Nicole would've hoped the plunging neckline would at least make KG's heart skip a beat, but Jaylen had killed that sexy, flirtatious and curious side of me. Instead, I feared my cortisol was going to kill me. Physically unprepared to break up a fight between KG and Jaylen (I was wearing stilettos after all), mentally incapable of fighting with Jaylen nor emotionally available to meet KG's new girlfriend, the night was doomed.

When I saw him, it was too late to turn around or duck for cover in the crowded bar because I literally bumped into his shoulder the moment I noticed him. Just brushing his body sent the coldest chill through mine in the toasty-warm bar. Dodging my eye contact, he looked right past me with a blank stare in his eyes and kept walking toward the back of the bar, without saying hi.

Still alive.

Next move: Locate Jaylen immediately.

Almost seconds later, Mary appeared in the sea of people (thank goodness the bar was packed), and I could tell from her eyes and the pitch of her voice that she was a little drunk.

"Nicole, I am so sorry. I didn't know John texted you; he didn't realize how awkward this would be."

"It's OK, I appreciate your concern. It's fine. We can be adults. I just have to make sure Jaylen is OK." I turned around to try to catch Jaylen at the doorway.

"Babe," I said to him. "KG is here. He is not letting this ruin his night, so please don't let it ruin yours. He is with his new girlfriend, and they are hanging out with John and the gym people."

"I'm not going to talk to him. But sure, OK. It's fine," he replied curtly.

I was actually impressed with how well Jaylen composed himself. No heart attacks yet. There were several times that the two of them stood just feet apart from one another in the back area of the bar.

I did not say hello to KG's girlfriend.

My cousin Andrew walked in 10 minutes past awkward and I had to tell him what was going on because he'd met KG while having drinks the summer before, and Andrew is one of those people who would remember a face and say hi without knowing what was going on and why it was socially uncomfortable.

For the 90 minutes we spent at Lir, I sat on the edge of conversation between Andrew and Jaylen, who was getting deep about religion, and the group of people KG had come with. Standing in between two groups of people, I felt alone, even though this was my first night out ever with Boston friends, a boyfriend and family.

Digesting it all in my own little bubble outside of Andrew and Jaylen's conversation, holding my purse a little too tight, I knew this: This is not how it was supposed to go. The person to blame? I wanted to blame Jaylen. I wanted to blame my coaches, but really I had to blame myself for the entire mess. And I had to convince myself that I wanted to go home with Jaylen and commend him for not causing a scene.

For about an hour, I chimed in on conversations with my coaches on my left and with Jaylen and Andrew on my right, but never did I speak directly to KG. Hearing my voice must have upset him because I was in earshot, and soon after we'd arrived, he left with his girlfriend. As he brushed past me, I said goodnight, wondering if I'd transformed into a ghost because he looked right through me again, said nothing and left me wondering if he was a ghost, given the white, pale look on his face. It was the most stoic I had ever seen him. I wasn't sure if he was mad at me, mad at her or upset because she was mad at him; surely, she knew about me.

That night we went home and I lay in bed motionless as if the vodka I'd had was actually espresso. Rattled and trying to place my finger on my feelings, I searched KG on Instagram. Seeing his face made me miss him, or maybe miss the me that used to like him. Who was I now? A girl who was scared her boyfriend would see her search history on Instagram.

CHAPTER 54.

FIRED AT 24

May 2015

Ever since that 6 a.m. call with Mrs. Fleming—the one I took in my pink bath towel and negotiated a salary on the fly—I knew to expect the unexpected when she called. Like the Colorado weather above the tree line, she was unpredictable. Obviously, I hadn't anticipated her suggesting I move to Boston or telling me to pick up more fitness classes when work slowed, but what would be next?

"Hi, Mrs. Fleming," I said.

Jaylen gave me the curious eyebrow raise from across the room.

"Hi, Nicole! How are you?" she asked.

"I'm good, just working from home."

"And how is the fitness stuff going?" she asked.

It was always rather odd that she asked me about my side business more than my actual role with Swam. As my business grew and I began truly spending more of my dead workday on Crossroads of Fitness, I would get anxious when anyone in the office asked about it.

Without any more small talk, Mrs. Fleming came right out and told me that the company was downsizing, partly due to Oil City slowing down.

"This might be a great time for you to explore other options."

Wait, what? Am I being fired? It hasn't even been a year in Boston! Didn't she just tell me to re-sign my $3,000-per-month lease?

"We are not 100 percent sure if we will need you, so out of respect for you, we'd like to give you 60 days to see what else is out there."

It was like: "I am going to let you go, but not really. Well, we think we will, but in case we don't, we aren't officially firing you yet."

A lot of things swarmed around my brain, but the one thing right in front of my face, my initial reaction, was: *Hell yes; now I can do fitness full time.*

And you're probably wondering how the heck I'd pay that crazy rent with a fitness income and without the real estate salary.

Before I could worry or wonder, Mrs. Fleming interjected.

"Don't worry about your lease. If you decide to stay, which I'm not sure what you'll want to do, you can rest assured knowing that we will still pay the agreed-upon portion of your rent."

WOW! What a relief: I could do fitness, run my business and stay here with Jaylen. It was such an exciting thing to hear on first thought, I hadn't a second to feel what one must feel when they get "fired."

Even better were her next words.

"And don't worry. We can tell people whatever you want; we can say you're moving on. We can say you were let go—totally your call."

Now those last words, on second thought, actually sounded peculiar, weirded me out. Hurt and anger began to brew inside me.

It all made sense now.

You see, the first time I saw Chris' letter of intent to my dad for $13 million, I tried to repress thoughts that maybe they were using me.

Then in May 2014 when they offered me a $12,000 increase in

my salary, a sick apartment pretty much paid for and never gave me work to do, Ren Man told me it was all in my head.

"Babe, they wouldn't go to the length of relocating you if they were using you to get to your dad," he said when we were discussing the move to Boston.

"Can't they see that I'm not even on good terms with my dad?"

"Exactly, they don't even know the total story, so it can't be that," said Ren Man.

But now in late May 2015 with the deal done, it so was *that*. Swam had what he needed from my dad, and therefore no use for me (I texted my dad to confirm while still on the phone with Mrs. Fleming).

I hung up and before I could tell Jaylen what I was thinking, he grabbed my shoulders, squeezed them with strength, then lifted my chin up and kissed me.

"You needed this push. Now you are free! Now you can do what you want and work your online business and teach classes and write in your free time."

"They tried to tell me the account is slowing down. I don't know what to think," I said, holding back tears of confusion.

I could not believe they were going to fire me (or "let me go") and still give me $2,000 a month toward rent for a year.

"It doesn't matter. This is happening for a reason and this is what you've always wanted anyway. It's the best possible outcome," cheered Jaylen as he rested his hands firmly on my shoulders.

As scary as losing the whole reason I uprooted my life was, he was right. I was now going to be able to write my own ticket and do what I love without the intense rent stressor! Paying a third of my rent was doable, especially since Max and Kevin were starting to give me more classes—finally!

In the next 60-day window when I should have been "job hunting," as Mrs. Fleming said, I was ramping up my online coaching business instead and actively looking to take on more coaching jobs in person.

CHAPTER 55.

A CHANGE IN THE AIR

July 2015

In late June I'd been granted four more S&S classes. Spending more hours at the S&S studio meant less time in my boring apartment. Even better? Max and Kevin hooked me up with a new spinning concept opening in Boston. Taking on the new fitness role came with perks: 10 new colleagues who became instant friends.

As my social network began expanding, Jaylen seemed to be put off. For instance, when I went out for my friend Candace's birthday, I mentioned that I didn't want to be out too late, and so he offered to pick me up. I said I'd be fine, that I could grab a cab, but he insisted on picking me up. Midst texting while out, I mentioned I'd probably come home soonish and he quickly said, "OK, I'll come get you."

I really wasn't ready to leave but felt I had no option. What's worse? When he arrived, it was pouring down rain and he scolded me for making him come out in the middle of a busy work week in bad weather.

The next time we were invited out was in July, with my own family. They were in town for Elizabeth's wedding, and it was coincidently my brother Wyatt's birthday. Thursday night before the wedding weekend, we went out in Back Bay for Wyatt's birthday dinner—the first time I'd see my mom and brothers in my new city in the year I'd lived there. I was eager to go. Even better, Hunter's new Australian girlfriend would be there, too!

After pushing through a day of teaching 5 and 7 a.m. spin classes and then 6:30 and 7:40 p.m. classes at Stride and Strength, I taxied straight to Sonsie for the special dinner.

"Nicole, I heard there's a pool on a rooftop right by our hotel! Might you guys want to join us tomorrow?" Britt asked in her Australian accent.

"Oh, I forgot about that! I've never been and would love to!" I replied quickly. Fridays were never too busy for me with work, especially now that I no longer was working for Swam.

Jaylen reached his hand over my shoulder and pulled me in closer to him as he spoke. "We actually have work to do, don't we, sweetie?" he said coyly, giving me side-eye to catch my attention.

I think my mom actually moved two inches when she cringed.

After dinner, we all walked to the bar next door to meet up with Elizabeth and her immediate family for a mini birthday celebration for Wyatt. One drink in and Jaylen suggested we leave, ASAP. I hadn't seen my family in a month and they'd never been to Boston to see me, but at the time, I thought, "He's right, I have an early morning."

It was like I'd drunk the "Jaylen is almighty" Kool-Aid, fueling me to believe that we were meant to spend every single second together, save for when I taught classes.

* * *

The wedding weekend didn't make things better.

As a bridesmaid, I had duties all day Saturday, leaving Jaylen to ride out to the ceremony on his own with my family on the chartered bus.

By the time we saw each other after the ceremony, I thought he'd greet me by telling me how pretty I looked and how he missed me, but it was quite the opposite.

After my cousin's beautiful wedding ceremony, I'd quickly run to put my flowers away and grab my purse in the bride's room. I wanted to have my ID for the bar. Next up on the agenda was a pre-reception cocktail hour at a very scenic outdoor terrace.

On my way from the bride's room, I turned quickly to run right into Jaylen, who was already waiting in this magnificent patio space encircled with flowers overlooking the green space below. When he approached me, I smiled, and he gave me a fake "there you are, get over here" smile that didn't sit well with me.

"Hey, what's wrong? Are you OK? Wasn't that a beautiful ceremony?" I said a little annoyed.

"Um, yeah, but I've been waiting for you, like, all day. Good to see you. Did you have fun?"

"Yes, it was nice! How was your day? What did you do?"

"I had to work; it's a busy day. But then getting here took forever. I had to come by myself, so it's been a long day," he said with an annoyed tone.

"But you knew that this was the plan, and you know my brothers and my mom, so you weren't alone" is what I wanted to say.

I could feel an all-too-familiar fight brewing, and yet I was more interested in socializing with family, so instead I brashly rolled my eyes and walked away to go talk to my cousins from Florida. Pissed off, he followed me, so I stepped aside to continue the disgruntled conversation.

Old Nicole would have said, "I'm sorry, that was rude," and stood by him. But New Nicole was emerging. She was partially stooping to his low level of anger, but also partially empowered to stand up for herself. She'd had it.

"I do not like your attitude," I said, shocked at myself for being so blunt with him.

At the time, I wasn't aware of what was happening, but hindsight is 20/20. The comfort of my family had given me the confidence to say how I really felt to him and hold him to the standard I normally would in another time and place—not in Boston where I had such a small support group.

"Are you eff-ing kidding me?" I yelled at him.

"Yeah, I'm fucking serious," he hollered, heading from the outdoor tent to the indoor facility.

My tone didn't sit well with him and he sauntered off, sulking and whining. Until the sit-down dinner, we walked around the celebration separately. My mom could tell something was up.

At the stunning dinner tables with shimmering silverware and golden lights strung all around in the outdoor tent, our fighting continued over his frustrations about coming to the wedding.

"Fuck this shit, I'm out of here," he said, throwing his sport coat over his shoulder as he headed for the parking lot.

"I will not stand for that kind of behavior. You cannot act like this. I want you to dance with me and support this. Fuck you." I stooped down low enough to say the words I never wanted to say again.

"No way in hell I'm dancing with you. Is that a joke?" he said as he walked off.

Running awkwardly in stilettos to chase him, I yelled, unabashed by my surroundings.

"If you really wanted me you'd do whatever it takes—dancing, chartered buses, going out...." I trailed off.

His head was down in his phone; I could tell he was trying to summon Uber from rural Massachusetts.

"This is you! You leaving, your anger, your decision. Fine." I yelled as I walked back toward the party.

He didn't like that he couldn't control me, our situation, our setting, our schedule. Worse was the aggravated grimace he wore as he walked back outside to the wedding tent, reluctant to tell me no cabs were available. He rode back with me to Boston after the wedding, keeping face until we were back in the apartment, where he crumpled up in a ball on my bed, fetal position and all, crying until 1 a.m. about how I didn't love him.

And he was right when he said it: "I know I'm not the one for you; I know it, you know it and it sucks."

CHAPTER 56.

BREAKS NEVER WORK

The day after my cousin's wedding, Jaylen and I took a "break." Luckily, I had my brother Wyatt to hang out with. Together, we sat alongside the Boston Public Library, eating Sweetgreen salads, reflecting on all my failed relationships.

My spirit was 70 percent in pure flight-or-fight, "I need a friend" mode and 30 percent "FREEDOM!!" mode.

The 30 percent of me that was stretching my arms out with eagerness and ready to fly wanted to reach out to Ren Man simply because now I could—nobody would be going through my phone at night, peering over my shoulder or fixating on my personal text conversations, assuming the irrational.

I told Wyatt of this desire, but he told me to wait a few days. What I could not be patient with was calling KG—he and I had a lot to talk about. Because I had to excommunicate him completely (unfriend him and block his number to appease Jaylen), I wanted to make peace ASAP and work toward being friends.

After lunch, Wyatt had to catch a flight and I called KG on a walk in a park near my apartment.

Selfishly, I didn't think about how KG would feel about me calling him. But he answered. He heard my story. He was there in the moments I needed him. Considering all sides of my issues with Jaylen, he encouraged me to be safe and remain hopeful.

After hearing my woes, he even opened up to me about his most recent relationship. It had ended the week before.

Deja vu?

All in all, it was 20 minutes of impactful conversation—just like the time when I didn't know what to do about Ren Man.

I would be OK.

I would get through this.

I opened up to KG about everything except the supplements—the rage, the controlling behavior, the fact that we were on a break and how I wanted to stay friends with Jaylen.

"Just know that if you tell him that, be prepared to have him be against being friends. You will probably break his heart if he wants to try and work it out and you break it off. Most likely, he will not be your friend," said KG.

"I understand. We will see how this goes. Thank you," I replied.

"Please call me or text me later and let me know how it goes and then go change your locks," he said.

I was silent.

"I'm serious—change your locks," he added in a brotherly tone.

* * *

When I got back to my apartment, Jaylen had beat me inside. We had planned for him to come back to my place that evening to grab most of his things and make the break more official.

"I was out for a walk," I said, like I had to explain myself.

I knew my plan: Break it off completely.

But what would he say? How would he take it?

Jaylen handed me a Fresca and gave me a hug.

It was over. We both felt it in that one hug.

It needed to end.

And we both cried.

Halfway through the "I'm sorrys" and the "No, I'm sorrys" and the "I'll miss yous," I made a half-assed attempt to convince him to make it work, oddly enough. I think it was because I wanted him to feel like he was doing it and not me. Deep down, I'd known for a while it needed to be over and hadn't owned up to my feelings. For this, I felt very guilty.

Out of nowhere, we had breakup sex and, from it, I tried to pull out any joy. I was excited and ready to move on amicably. We decided to be friends and even to attend a couples dinner in two days' time, even though we were technically broken up.

As soon as he left, I texted KG, "best breakup ever."

CHAPTER 57.

A HATE SEANCE

The next morning, I woke up to a photo message from KG—a selfie of me. It was from a day I probably would've never remembered—a busy fall Sunday during The Grind— if not for this pic. I quickly took a quick photo of my neck to prove that I was still wearing the same necklace from that day. "I don't know why you even still have that photo!" I texted back.

Nostalgia fell over me, and hopefulness filled me up. No matter what might come in the next few weeks, I could feel myself coming back to me. I could reach out to friends, sleep in, text whomever, and it felt alright! All I had to do was attend one more outing with Jaylen before I'd truly be free.

* * *

The dinner had been booked weeks in advance, so we didn't want to cancel. I think Jaylen and I also wanted an excuse to see each other because anytime you go through a breakup, the initial stages involve odd feelings of withdrawal.

It was a warm Friday evening in August, slightly reminiscent of our first date, and there we were, a month shy of our one-year anniversary, at the same sushi place we'd met for a business dinner.

We sat at dinner with our hands on each other's knees or

around each other's shoulders. We acted like a couple. We drank a lot. And we sure as hell told nobody of our private situation.

After a few martinis convinced us to take the night a step further, the four of us decided to go back to my rooftop and have more to drink.

As I became gracefully wasted on my own rooftop, I felt comfort in the fact that Jaylen was there and that nothing could go wrong. I was too drunk to realize this was actually the most he'd ever had to drink, at least with me, and I'd actually never seen him belligerent or wasted.

When midnight approached and security gently reminded us of the building curfew, I offered to show the couple my apartment quickly on their way out. For some bizarre reason, which I can only attribute to the fact that I was drunk, I decided to share this really sweet card with them that Jaylen had written for me that was displayed on the fridge. It was a very personal, funny card. Together we laughed, hugged them goodbye and ended what could have been a terribly awkward evening.

As soon as the door closed behind them, Jaylen's voice boomed. "You are such a fraud!"

"What? What are you talking about? I thought my friends would find it funny and I loved that card!" I said, still trying to read him.

"You fucking lied to me. You texted KG, and what? You're on dating apps? Yeah, fuck right, you missed me. You're happy to break up. You're a fraud. You never loved me."

Unbeknownst to me, he'd been snooping through my phone again.

Panic is a really hard feeling to describe, but something waved over my body. Some percentage of it was fear but also anger and sadness.

Like a scared rabbit, I knew I needed to run away, go somewhere, so I burrowed into my closet in my bedroom.

Crying really hard, I drunk-dialed KG from my closet. He calmed me down as we FaceTimed through my sobs.

After I was able to take deep breaths, I went to check on Jaylen in the bathroom. As I opened the door, he kind of kicked his leg at me to get away as he sat on the floor by the toilet. I defensively kicked back, missing.

I went to my bed and passed out.

* * *

"WAKE UP!!!!" he boomed.

It was bone-chilling.

"You need to see something, you lying, scum-of-the-earth, worse-than-my-abusive-father human! Come into the living room right now! I hope you know what a terrible, absolutely disgusting person you are," he screamed.

As I rounded the corner of my bedroom door into the living room, I saw something quite terrifying. He had taken all the playing cards with reasons why he loved me on them and put them in the formation of a swastika on the floor. In between the carefully positioned cards, he'd placed photos of us.

It was like a hate memorial séance.

"I saw the selfie to KG. I saw the 'best breakup ever' text. You've loved him all along, you bitch," he yelled.

He explained again how he'd seen texts to my friends about me matching up with some guy on the dating app Hinge. (In my defense, I only downloaded it after we broke up—my friend Taylor claims that putting dating apps on your phone is the best way to get through a breakup.)

Worst of all, somehow or another he drunkenly stumbled through my Gchat (or had known all along) to find the conversations I had with Michelle about his secret.

Jaylen was livid to know that I had told another soul, not realizing how heavy the weight of that secret had been for me to bear. He cut me with words and thank God I was drunk because the alcohol made me less fearful than I would've been sober. I remember trying to actually slap him—something I'm not proud of. But when I missed, it was a huge wake-up call—I was still drunk and needed to go to bed, as did he.

"You're not driving," I yelled as I stumbled back to bed and slammed the door.

* * *

At 5 a.m., I heard something and rolled over, still in my floral dress from the double date. Jaylen was in my room, sitting on a bench against the wall, facing me. As soon as he saw my eyes open, he stood up and walked over to the bedside.

Standing over me, with anger emanating like a familiar earthquake, he said the scariest, meanest, most piercing words another human has ever spoken to me. Rushing out of him, the words forcefully blew me out of bed and up against a wall; there I was, planted there like a target. Each insult soared at me rapidly like an arrow, but he couldn't hit me. They scared the crap out of me, but I was beyond being hurt. At that moment, I had an invisible shield in front of me. Witnessing his ferocious anger made it easy to see he was not the guy for me, thus he could no longer hurt me.

After the slew of evil words, I was awake enough to process the fact that he was about to leave with my keys in hand.

"Please leave your keys!" I tried to yell like you do in a dream but your voice barely comes out.

I should've changed the locks, I thought as I went back to bed.

CHAPTER 58.

SILENCE SINKING IN SLOWLY

Later that morning, I awoke again with a slight taste of an alcohol hangover in my mouth and the feeling of an emotional hangover all over my body. My muscles ached, my heart felt heavy and my skin felt tingly, like it does when you're scared in the dark.

Please say it was all a dream.

But what part?

The dating? The whole relationship? The fight?

The cards! OMG, was that real? Did that happen?

Mustering the energy to get up, I went into the living room. There I found two photos of Jaylen and me on the table. Then another one on the chair and yet another on the couch.

I looked away and went into the kitchen to make breakfast and pretend like my life was together. As I opened up my big bag of gluten-free oats, three playing cards with reasons why he loved me on them were sitting inside. I dropped the bag; it was so creepy!

Picking them up from the floor and putting them in the trash, I stood up and reached to grab a spoon; there were cards in the silverware drawer! Then I found cards stuffed inside my powerlifting shoes.

But nowhere to be found? His keys to my apartment.

* * *

The next day, I was in my apartment all alone, surrounded by white walls. Everything around me was silent, but my thoughts were loud and my body still numb.

This quiet was eerily familiar. It was exactly like the previous summer when I had just moved into my Boston apartment. My mom had left me. Her job was done. I was all moved in ... *now what?*

Now what? I echoed.

The summer before, I'd been emotionless and numb from the depression I didn't know I was feeling. What was this feeling now? Loneliness? I welcomed his exit. Sadness? I was glad to be free. Helplessness? I could handle this. Fearful? I was safe now.

New, positive Nicole stepped up and realized that I was not back to square one. Instead of staring at the Verizon Jetpack from Swam or waiting on emails from Mr. Bates, my email was buzzing from fitness clients and I was staring at the cover of my first-ever e-book that was featured on my own business's website for free. In a year's time, in spite of the depression and confusion, I'd found the power to create.

Things would be weird for an uncertain amount of time, but what was for certain: New Nicole was alive and well and unbreakable.

PART IV.

NO JOB, NO JAYLEN

CHAPTER 59.

GIRL BOSS

August 20, 2015

After Jaylen left, I felt restless for a few days. Getting over the silence was a challenge, but getting over him? A cinch. The weekend passed, as did the bizarreness of being alone in my apartment again. Monday morning, I got up with the sun, ready to set the world on fire.

I could feel it in my bones—that same sense of urgency to live life as I did at 22, peering out the car window, craning my neck to scope out my new Lincoln Park neighborhood. In that moment of 2013, I was a girl with a passion for fitness. Now in 2015, I had an online fitness business, I worked for Stride and Strength (the Holy Grail of fitness) and my 9-to-5 job was long gone. Further than I've ever imagined, I wondered, *What would be next?*

The question answered itself in real time! I started going to the beach. I enrolled in every online dating app possible. I got new eyelash extensions and, oh yes, I enrolled in a bodybuilding competition.

Nicole 2.0 coming right up!

Thrilled at the idea of meeting someone whom I'd actually find attractive sounded fun and sexy. Of course, finding Prince Charming was on my agenda, but I was in no rush. More than anything, I aimed to make new friends. It helped that I was very much available, working for the new spinning studio and making up my schedule these days.

And that's how it began, this enthusiastic vibe of August, when if I wasn't teaching or writing or filming exercises for my website—without input from Jaylen!—I was planning my bodybuilding routine or setting up a social calendar. I finally felt in control of my own destiny again.

* * *

I liked to call it "going fishing," an activity I'd do during my self-made workday to hook new clients. Sitting in my working chair at my kitchen table, wearing my grandpa's old flannel hunting shirt, it felt right to be going fishing. My grandfather was the most astute businessman with a wild passion for the outdoors. Not a day goes by that I don't think about him.

Going fishing worked like this: I would think about a story or incident that had happened to me and share it with my newsletter followers in a story format so that: 1) They were entertained. 2) They could learn something. 3) They could relate to me and then hopefully I would "catch" a new client.

Interacting with my newsletter recipients was like going fishing in a stocked pond. It was a game of time. As long as you are consistently there, interacting with a captive audience (the fish), you will eventually catch something. With each email blasted, I received at least one personal note.

As I sat there going fishing in shorts and my grandpa's old shirt with my apartment window open and an oddly cool breeze for an August day blowing in, I wondered how or if he would have started his business differently had he had access to social media and more do-it-yourself business tools. All he had were the wherewithal and guts to put money down on land and erect a building to open a car dealership.

My grandfather was raised by a single mom. As the stories go, he hunted turtles and rabbits for her to cook and shared a one-bedroom apartment with his sister and mom.

My own dad didn't grow up without resources, but to a point, he grew up without his dad around since Grandpa was working diligently on the business he started. Like my dad, both my brothers and I had all we needed, but not everything we wanted, as kids.

Seeing my mom's single-mom hustle inspired me to always count on myself. Having a dad who didn't just hand me money (although he could have) made me feel the drive to work hard.

And there I was, a business owner at 24 without any idea of where I was taking it—just the same wherewithal and guts my grandpa had when he first started his business.

Without a steady salary (gasp!) to pay my bills, I worked nonstop, building my Crossroads of Fitness business, teaching spinning, training clients and teaching 5 a.m. classes at Stride and Strength Monday through Thursday (my bosses added more classes due to the success I had at 0-dark-thirty). On top of that, I also had taken on a few clients from a trainer in my apartment building. The Hustle was real.

Was it exhausting? Some days. But the cool part? I got to wake up every day and do things I truly enjoyed.

It felt like being in college again—where the goal is to learn, explore, make friends and focus on topics you want to know more about.

But unlike college, I felt I needed to be versed in everything—from how to market myself online with new social media tools to the latest nutrition research—to make my business thrive. Studying and putting things into motion at once is no easy feat.

Welcome to my mid-twenties.

Fortunately, the regimen of bodybuilding actually helped me to stay focused. The lifestyle of counting calories, fueling with protein, lifting and resting and planning my every move so I could look good half-naked on stage gave me the structure I needed as a new entrepreneur without a boss and work rules.

Now for the record, most bodybuilders hire a coach to prepare for the "show," as they call it. But seeing as though my main profession was now "fat loss coach," I wanted to show that I could do it myself and practice what I preached. Thank God for my mom, who truly became my mental coach.

And my hard work was paying off. For the first time in my life, people were giving me dramatic compliments, like: "Oh my gosh, I've never seen you this skinny!" Or, "Wow, what a dramatic transformation; you look incredible." And, "OMG, your glutes have grown!"

Sure, it was weird to feel more socially accepted due to my outward appearance. ("Hello? I have the same mind and I still offer the same skillset!") But I was selling out more classes, getting more clients and insanely dialed into my work, that it was all icing on the cake and, hopefully, an asset for dating.

The kicker? I also got hair extensions, a necessary evil for competition day. Closely resembling Barbie (and hence checking off my childhood dream of having "Barbie hair"), I was the most confident in my own skin as I'd ever been.

CHAPTER 60.

SINGLEDOM

October-November 2015

Despite all the hustling I was doing as a newly single person, I felt like I had all the time in the world. My social calendar was contingent on nobody but me! You see, when you're single, all you really have is time. Time to be selfish. Time to flirt. Time to make dinner for one. Time to spend three hours at the hair salon.

You can even sit at a coffee shop for three hours on a Tuesday night and nobody will wonder where you are. In fact, you could stay there until midnight without receiving 90 text messages that demand a response ("U there?" "Where are you?").

Some might be fantasizing about all the time I had on my hands, but when you're single, it kind of sucks. Especially when you're dating, time can drag on for eternity. To prove my point, here's a quick, scientific explanation of how time feels for single people waiting to hear back from someone they're interested in:

One minute: When you are waiting for a text, every minute is like an hour.

One day: If a full day goes by, you go through the motions of everything that would happen in a month—new projects, end-of-month reports, paying bills, cleaning the house, etc.—just to keep your mind preoccupied.

One week: Now this is tricky because if you've recently dated someone like Jaylen (a Stage 5 clinger), it feels like a year. But actually, one week is known as the "accidental ghosting period."

One month: In the dating world, this is equivalent to a lifetime. Either the person you're waiting to hear from really did die or the amazing date you shared actually never happened and you're 100 percent being ghosted. Being ghosted sucks. It's when they cease all communication completely, as if they've died.

Now that we're clear on how time works in the dating world, I'll let you in on my courageous attempts at capturing a mate. Remember how bold I was during the KG era when I made a plan to seduce him? Well, I used the same tactic in Boston—and had disappointing results.

For example, the first weekend I was truly single, I went to the beach with my friend Candace. We didn't drink; we simply observed day drinkers and caught up with each other until the heat was too much to bear. By late afternoon, we ventured off to a local taco joint in Southie. For whatever reason, the waiter kept putting his hands on my shoulders, holding eye contact extra long and even went as far as to ask us about our dating lives. I took that as a hint that he might be flirting with me (call me crazy), so I left my number on the receipt.

He never called. Maybe I didn't tip enough!

During this single phase, I also did a lot of power walking through Back Bay in my free time to blow off steam and get out of my bland apartment. I'd often wear headphones, even though I believe it can make you look unapproachable. However, every time I saw a cute guy, I would smile and turn down my headphones in case he wanted to stop and say hello. That never happened.

Confident in my online image, sometimes I'd even direct-message some of my flirty Instagram friends, Instagram crushes and even Instagram celebs. (If you're not DM-ing, you're not trying! #nevergiveup) For the record, it didn't work.

If I'm being honest, I also became very generous with "likes" on Facebook to cute guys' posts.

At the end of August, my friends dared me to ask a hot Man

Bun (popular douchey hairstyle I was into) for his number at a bar in Southie. So I did, awkwardly, of course.

"Hi, I'm Nicole. I wanted to come say hi. What's your name?" I asked, juxtaposing the bold move with sheepish eyes.

"Uh, hi. I'm Ben." Awkward pause. "Maybe, uh, I could take down your number?"

That counts, right?

I never heard from Man Bun Ben.

There were times I'd stay out later than I should've, waiting for Prince Charming. There were also times I knowingly went home with the opposite of Prince Charming, hopeless and frustrated, but down to settle with a hot-not-always-steamy makeout sesh. Little did I know, Prince Charming wasn't going to magically appear at a bar.

Nor would he appear at a gym, but it took me a minute to realize this. As a fitness instructor, I often see some handsome, fit-looking guys come into my classes, but when this one incredibly sexy guy arrived early to my Stride and Strength class one morning, my jaw almost hit the floor. During class, his energy was infectious. I'm pretty sure that along with his hooting and hollering during class (clearly LOVING my playlist) that he even clapped a few times. Naturally, his shirt came off once he broke a sweat (many people go shirtless at S&S) and I had to deflect my eyes to the other side of the classroom.

At the end of class, he was hanging inside the studio to stretch—a good sign. I know this because in the two prior instances of an attractive male lingering afterward "to stretch," the situation ended with an invitation for drinks or dinner. (ICYW: One guy ended up canceling our date without ever rescheduling and the other ghosted me after a not-so-steamy makeout).

Sexy shirtless man (also wearing a half man bun—two points!) walked slowly toward me and I gulped. His ab veins were sweating.

I smiled at him and said, "Thank you so much for coming; you killed it! I loved your energy."

He winked at me, reached for the door to push it open and, as he did, popped his back leg up and said, "Thanks! I'm totally a woo girl!"

Gay. Damn it.

* * *

Having more time alone and no luck in the romance department made me start looking back (always fondly) on the relationships that didn't end with swastikas on the floor. I specifically found my mind wandering back to Nashville. I missed the scent of Ren Man's apartment and yearned for his loving ways—the youthful, idealistic side of him that used to piss me off now became enchanting, especially after living with Jaylen's negativity.

I finally was once again breaking down the walls I'd put up around my relationship with Ren Man when something else happened to make me shut the box quickly. (If you remember, last time I'd checked his Instagram, I'd been hash-tag-blessed with images of his much hotter, taller, skinnier, blonder new girlfriend).

And thus, because of my wandering, lustful and yearning mind, I opened Instagram and saw …

A ring.

…

A brilliant, sparkly, giant gorgeous diamond on the ring finger of said blonde.

It was really over. She was The One.

I sat there, scared to click over to her page, as if hers would tell me that this was all legit. I frantically wondered which girlfriend I'd call first to vent to. Michelle came to mind, but I couldn't do it. Not yet. Something felt weird. Not the "I need to cry" weird, because I'd been mentally checked out. But knowing Ren Man was no longer in the realm of possibility in this lifetime was hard to grasp. Out of respect for his future wife, I felt I couldn't contact him, like, ever again.

Fortunately, I'd been busy enough to only spend late nights reminiscing about Ren Man. And thank God I was busy because Busy kept me from Lonely. Lonely made me sad, and I'd choose the stressful side effects of Busy over struggling to deal with Lonely any day.

Enter KG, who also helped push Lonely away.

We were FaceTiming—strictly as friends—every single day to discuss life, love and business.

"Nickyyyyy MONEYYYYY!" he'd always say upon answering the phone.

"Hi to you, too," I'd say with a grin.

He was pleasant and clear-eyed on FaceTime, and dialed into a very evident self-improvement phase of his life. When he'd read something, he'd tell me about it. When he ate something, he'd tell me about it. I knew everything, and I told him everything, especially when it came to my dating life.

Frustrated, I'd divulge that I found dating much different in Boston than in Chicago. In Chicago when I was 23, I'd get asked out by nines and tens and go out with stellar guys because I was bored. I wouldn't even like half the nice Midwestern guys who would take me on very sweet, thoughtful dates (probably because I was preoccupied chasing KG).

In Boston, I'd try to attract the attention of fours and fives, sometimes talk a six into getting drinks and either wait 30 minutes for his late ass to show up or get a "let's raincheck" text an hour before the date.

After a number of dates ended with me coming home to FaceTime KG, I realized things were developing into an odd dynamic between us.

How was I supposed to meet someone if I was leaving the date to go talk to another guy?

Were there feelings for KG? Sure, but they'd transformed into friendship and adoration, obviously with the caveat that our friendship had "we've hooked up in the past" stamped on it. Regardless, the feelings of lust were gone, the sex was not even an actual possibility. Without ever saying it, we could both feel (I'm speculating here) that we wanted to be in each other's lives, share online coaching ideas and support each other in the current time and space.

And right now that space was singledom, which looked very different for him than it did for me. KG wasn't looking, yet women still sought him out. To get any information about his dates or drama, I'd have to pry them out of him, because they weren't on his Top 10 topic list. Unfortunately for him, dating was always something I wanted to discuss. To my luck, he'd always listen, constantly offer "be patient" advice and readily make jokes about all the weirdos I'd encounter. By the fall, KG had met someone and I had not; it made me want to take his "care less" approach, but I wasn't ready to give up.

* * *

Nothing made me feel more single than being home in Indiana. Not only was everyone over the age of 23 in a committed relationship, but even if people were single, there isn't much of a social scene.

OK, so there *is* something that can make you feel more single: being home in Indiana and going to my grandma's 80th birthday bash on a riverboat with a bunch of 70- and 80-somethings swapping stories of 40-year marriages, their grandkids' engagements and baby announcements.

Worse were the conversations they'd have with me that reminded me how single I was:

"Do you have a boyfriend?"

No.

"Are you married?"

Do I look like I'm married?

"Oh, sweetie, you'll find someone eventually; it's best you don't settle."

Yeah, yeah.

Their sweet, "it's going to be OK" comments that were supposed to make me feel better did nothing but dig into sore wounds.

I thought I'd heard it all—then along came Mrs. Beauregard.

"Hi, Nicole! How are ya? How's the dating world?" she asked with such enormous enthusiasm, I contemplated jumping into the muddy river.

I couldn't hide my disdain for dating any longer. She'd known me long enough to know that I was clearly upset—actually physically ill—about dating. In case she wasn't, I gave her a 30-second synopsis of how many times I'd been stood up, about the guy who unasked me out and about the four guys who'd all dated me while they had girlfriends. And let's not forget the dejected divorced men.

After an empathetic eye roll, she smiled as she prepared for what I was certain would be a great pep talk. Boy, was I wrong.

"You know, I have a niece down in Texas. Not sure if she's well, you know, but anyhow, she never married, always focused on her career, that kind of thing. Like you, she truly wanted her own kids. Having a family was important to her. So you know what she did?"

She leaned in closer, like her secret was gold.

"And let me caution you, I would never really advise this if you don't have to, but you seem like the kind of girl who could do it ... she went to a sperm bank."

I stared at her, trying not to glare. Surely, she wasn't suggesting ...

"So you could totally do that, too! Don't stress; there is always that option! Let me know if you ever have questions. Her kids are healthy," she said, nudging me with her elbow.

I wanted to turn to a girlfriend and be like, "Can you believe that?" But there was nobody, just another older woman who'd been eavesdropping; when I glanced at her, she raised her eyebrows as if to say, "Such a great idea for you!"

And in this moment, being single felt like some type of handicap.

Could it get any worse?

I won't bore you with any more stories but I'll let you in on this: By the end of 2016, I'd had 55 dates under my belt with 35 unique individuals, including a drug lord, a dentist who modeled, an ex-air force bull rider, a gay cat lover, a guy named Nathan who was the "king of first dates," a guy named Drake who took me out once and canceled three other planned rendezvous before I realized he had a full-blown girlfriend, a crazy neighbor who became a friend with benefits and a few Bumble and Hinge dates that were nothing short of horrendous. The things a girl's gotta do to meet her Prince Charming.

CHAPTER 61.

TURNING A QUARTER OF A CENTURY

December 2015

I opened my eyes to see bright white everywhere. I quickly shut them.

As I lay there mentally preparing to reopen them, I could hear my head throbbing. I squinted my eyes open again and saw white shades over the floor-to-ceiling windows, white marble floors and white sheets.

The blue T-shirt I wore was on backward and it was definitely not mine. One of my kind friends must have dressed me.

My best friends' voices drifted from the kitchen into the fancy guest bedroom where I sprawled. Painfully, I pulled myself into a sitting position and gazed down at the white marble floors. My clothes were everywhere. Trying to figure out a strategy to dismount the bed and not trip on a stiletto or random item out of my exploding suitcase blocking my path to the bathroom, I was not ready for this.

Procrastinating, I slowly looked to my right; my college friend Karly was sleeping next to me. I looked down at myself again.

My red thong was twisted around my hips and bunched up inside my lululemon leggings.

Yup, somebody definitely dressed me.

It was the morning before my 25th birthday, a morning much different than I'd envisioned when I was in highschool.

Sure, I had a lot to be proud of. After winning second place in the bodybuilding competition, rocking a few fitness photo shoots and seeing a large increase in business income, life post-Jaylen wasn't too shabby. And I wasn't anywhere near stopping. The day after the bikini competition in November, I'd signed up for a powerlifting meet in January.

But my whole life I'd always thought I'd probably be with the man of my dreams (and possibly with child) by 25. My mom had me at that age, so perhaps it set some weird benchmark for me. Plus, I hadn't been single on my birthday since I was 15. This year, there was no man in sight. But I had something better than that—very dear friends.

I stumbled into the kitchen to find Shannon and Jordin sipping coffee and laughing about the night before. Motherly Jordin was in a long white robe, the kind you get in a hotel suite, and Shannon was half-naked, per usual.

They gave me Ibuprofen as soon as I walked in and handed me coffee in a white mug from the Nespresso machine. We walked from the kitchen to find refuge on the plush couches decked with impeccably designed pillows.

"How did you meet Ross again?" asked Shannon, ignoring the mug of coffee in her hands.

"He was Ren Man's friend, right?" asked Jordin, as she sipped the perfectly steamed cappuccino. Like me, she appreciated good caffeine.

"Yeah," I butted in. "I met him two years ago with Ren Man when we came to New York for Ren Man's birthday."

"He was seriously so sweet," Shannon cooed.

"Yeah, he didn't have to get us a black car! We would've never gotten into those cool spots without him last night," Jordin said with a twinkle in her eyes.

She was right. We went to some really neat spots. The Gramercy Park Hotel was the last place … wait. The last place I remembered was some really loud club with flashing lights and trees.

"Wait, guys. Did we go into some dark jungle-looking club after the Gramercy Park Hotel?"

"Yeah, I hated that place; it was cool to hop the line, but way too loud," said Jordin.

"We all wanted to go and you needed to go home," said Shannon.

I grabbed my forehead like someone just beat me with a baseball bat.

"This is like a happy-sad movie," I said, pulling a pillow over my head to doze off.

I fell back to sleep trying to figure out how I had gotten there—a moment wherein I felt safe and loved by the greatest, sweetest friends taking care of my hung-over self for my 25th birthday as we lounged inside a multimillion-dollar apartment in the Baccarat Hotel in New York City—perks of Jordin dating a 40-something-year-old billionaire whom we'd met on college spring break three years ago. But that's a story for another time.

This was 25: hung-over, dressed by my friends and giggling about our night out in NYC at 10 a.m. on a sunny Saturday morning in December.

Two hours later, I woke up to a text from KG.

"Make it back OK?" he asked.

"Headed back on a late bus tonight; amazing trip, but ready to get back to work."

The truth was, I wanted to go back and bury myself in work so that I could avoid thinking about my next move. Literally. The last six months were cool in Boston but the current decision at hand? Would I stay six more months and then go back to Chicago? Or would I re-sign my lease and stay in Boston?

Everyone knew how I felt about dating in Boston and the 5-foot-9 five-second rule/joke I'd coined (if you see a guy over 5-foot-9, wait five seconds and you'll see either his wedding band, wife or child), but I felt so far away from life in Chicago. Finally having built some social momentum in Boston, I feared it wasn't enough to keep me there, but I wasn't sure if my business would continue to flourish in Chicago. The most worrisome was the potential price tag of the impending decisions.

CHAPTER 62.

A CREATURE OF HABIT

January 2016

If you really want to own a city, get up at 4 a.m. and go somewhere before 5 a.m.

Without the boisterous daytime mess, the city feels quaint, cozy and calm as you hold the power to travel from one end to the other without pause. You can run any red light. You can choose any lane without signaling. You own the city.

As you zip through the silent space, you feel alone. Nobody else is awake. And the times I truly appreciate the silence are the times I feel the most alone. After Jaylen left, I had more time to enjoy the delicate mornings because I didn't worry about waking him up when I left or what mood he might be in when I got home. When he left, my internal noise quieted to a degree where I could hear the external environment more clearly.

Driving in Boston at 4:45 a.m. to teach morning classes reminded me of how I got closer to Chicago: It's like the cityscapes are naked and you can see them in their purest form, lit by the just-rising sun. You can see them fully, not blocked by traffic or people. Their glory is characterized by the overlooked blemishes; their giant facades mask the secrets they keep inside.

There's no clutter.

There's no noise.

The city is yours.

Having shared those intimate moments with Chicago, my old

friend of a city, and Boston, the new, unwanted temporary fix of a city, I found it odd that regardless of my disdain for one town and pure adoration of the other, I could not discern one from the other during the docile morning moments.

Maybe it was just my love of the morning time?

These were the thoughts I contemplated when I realized the only thing holding me to this city was my 5 a.m. teaching job. These moments, this ridiculously early hour and these giant buildings I could see so clearly. Were they enough to make me stay?

One of the things I really loved about coaching the 5 a.m. classes in Chicago, besides the class itself, was driving there. The only country station in Chicago would play new country hits before 5 a.m. Like clockwork in early 2014, Dan and Shay's hit, "19 You and Me" would always be playing at 4:32 a.m. when I got in the car to drive to Tred11. Something about seeing the music duo's dreams come to life lit a fire inside me.

And then it happened.

I was running late in 2016 to go teach at Stride and Strength.

I hopped in my car at 4:40—five minutes later than usual.

I heard a very Shay Mooney-like voice …

Could it be? The new Dan and Shay album dropped?

As I drove in the dark to teach such brave and committed souls, I pictured myself in the same black leggings, black tank top (but with "Tred" written on it) in the same blue Touareg, pulling out of North Wilton Avenue in Chicago, driving under the L, making a left onto Sheffield for just a second before going left onto Lincoln and heading to Old Town to teach at Tred11, listening to Dan and Shay.

Now I was in Boston driving down Boylston (the street I despised at all other times of the day), and in the moment, Boston was mine.

Being consistent had paid off.

Teaching the morning classes had paid off. Forty people were waiting for me.

I now had the lifestyle—teaching fitness only—that I'd dreamed of during those early morning drives in Chicago. But here in Boston? It couldn't be! When I drove by the Boston Common, all of a sudden the geography seemed more familiar than the shops and bars and restaurants on Halsted that I used to pass on my way to Old Town. I'd now been living in Boston almost one entire year longer than Chicago, there were more friendly faces in the larger studio and I had a bigger fitness following.

But wasn't home Chicago?

I still felt lonely in Boston—no boyfriend, few family members and no BFFs to grab Mista's pizza with at night. Yet, I had the work life I'd always dreamed of ... Is having both too much to ask for?

CHAPTER 63.

DECISION TIME

January 2016

The first week of January was one of the hardest weeks of my life due to barely eating for powerlifting weigh-ins, training like a 25-year-old athlete, teaching spin classes and running my business. In sum, these were wildly invigorating, inspirational months in my life, but they were also quite lonely. Individual sports are obviously isolating (you're in the zone by yourself), so for a girl without many friends in a city that still felt new, who was following a strict diet and going to bed at 8:30 in order to get up at 3:30 to teach 5 a.m. classes, spreading my social butterfly wings was a tough task.

Initially, I made Jaylen the scapegoat for my lack of a social circle, projecting that he'd very much thwarted any chances at my having a social life for a full year. But by January, I'd soul-searched enough to know he wasn't responsible; I was. I gave him the power. I'd (for whatever reason) prioritized him—manipulated or not—and needed to stand in my own power and do what my soul wanted. If I had the power to change my body, I could work on my mindset toward myself and accept the mistakes I'd made in the past.

Training for bikini competitions and powerlifting helped me better relate to my clients; it amplified my role as a leader and coach in the fitness space and further exemplified my goal of "inspiring others to believe in themselves." But, even more, it continued to provide a huge distraction from the larger issue at hand.

After Swam let me go (it did so less than a month after I'd re-signed my lease), I committed to staying one more year since it'd still be paying two-thirds of the rent. Thrilled that I'd finally figured out how to do exactly what I'd wished for my career when I lived in Chicago, a huge piece of my heart thought, *This is it.* And so, since August 1, I'd been blissfully living in a world "on pause," putting off making my next move until 2016, enjoying the non-9-to-5 lifestyle.

But I blinked and it was 2016.

Without a clue on how I'd make the economics work if I stayed (particularly in the same building, which cost $3,500 a month including utilities) or what I'd do to make money if I moved back to Chicago, I turmoil brewed inside me.

* * *

In spite of the anxiety of said overhanging decision, my apartment was growing on me. After the powerlifting meet, which was in Chicago (yes, KG was present; no we didn't decide to date—he still had a girlfriend), I walked into my apartment and was overcome with joy. Kind of like the feeling you have when your family dog runs up to you when you walk in the door after a while of being away.

I loved my apartment, probably because it was all mine. It was the one reliable, private and comforting thing I had in Boston. It was a space I'd created, where I felt safe. The first year of Boston was characterized by feelings of "Is this really my home?" when I walked in, but for the first time something had shifted and I welcomed my own place, where I was growing and adapting.

But after the initial 30 seconds of euphoria, the silence sank in.

It was empty. It was dark. It was a Saturday night and I had nothing to do but work. The happiness started to dissipate as I sat uncomfortably alone in the space.

With nobody to text, "I'm back! What are you doing?!" I wasn't accustomed to the quiet yet. I'd been with my loud family at Christmas, and then a week later, visiting old friends and coaches in Chicago; my former loneliness-induced depression was now making crystal-clear sense: This wasn't life.

For the first time in six months, I turned on my TV for background noise. I couldn't focus in the silence. I did some work, watched a movie on Netflix and went to bed. Nothing was "right," but nothing was inherently "wrong." My gut instinct was to make changes the best I could, before giving up and moving "home" to somewhere in the Midwest.

* * *

By mid-February, I'd been having the happy feeling on numerous occasions. I'm not talking about ordinary, overarching happiness; I'm talking about that almost pre-orgasm buildup of quivering euphoria. The feeling you get inside your mind, in your heart and then also physiologically. It's a bodily response paired with an emotional tie.

The first inklings of this sensation occurred in the aforementioned occasion when I re-entered my own empty, bland, but now homey apartment in Boston after Christmas vacation.

Take that back; it first happened in the cab ride home after winter vacation. The view from my car window: the sunset, dazzling against the calm water of the Charles River, runners on the Esplanade mimicking the hustle and speed that is Boston life in the foreground, turning me on as we weaved down Storrow Drive. But as quick as you come, you fade and I suddenly pictured myself strolling down the Esplanade aimlessly, killing time, trying to make sense of life, love and jobs lost while wandering through a quite beautiful scene. At least it was a comfortable place to contemplate.

Then it happened when I had two of my regular 5 a.m. Stride

and Strength clients show up to take my class on a Saturday and they couldn't take it because it was full—sold out.

And then again, a Saturday night in February. I was sitting in what was once Jaylen's work chair at my kitchen table. My friend Jonathon was sitting Indian-style directly across from me on a sectional. My friend Stevie was in the chair I sit on when I do work. Her boyfriend, Sam, was on a beanbag on the floor, and Jill was cuddled up in an oatmeal-colored blanket on my couch.

People.

People who were friends.

Friends who were hanging out in my apartment, my home, my place in my city.

I chose them; they chose me.

It was organic; it was real. And the camaraderie was so nice.

I sat leaning up against the wall, thankful to be wearing a sweater so nobody would notice the goosebumps on my arms because, for the first time in almost two years, I had friends sitting in my apartment, having drinks and chatting.

I created this. I found this. For the first time in Boston, I felt whole and not alone.

CHAPTER 64.

CATEGORIZING MY LIFE

March 2016

I sat in a middle-aged woman's dingy minivan. As an Uber driver, she seemed a little clueless and I was content in my own hurricane of thoughts until she began to ask questions to quell the traffic boredom. It's funny, though, because depending on your mood, questions can seem dumb or endearing. Fed up with red taillights, superfluous traffic directors and way too much exhaust fuming for the small city, I decided to indulge her in conversation by asking her how long she'd been driving for Uber.

I fully intended to give the whole "my ex used to drive for Uber in Nashville" story not only to start a conversation but to make myself seem relatable—not like some fancy Bostonian who is above talking to their Uber driver.

But this hippie driver was an undercover college professor. My guess would've been another job in yoga, but when she told me she taught journalism and business, the traffic suddenly became a godsend, halting time further so I could talk to her about the studies I missed so much.

"You know, the journalism professors I had almost scared me out of the major," I said.

It was true. Many collegiate hours were spent being lectured on the sad shell of an industry that the newspaper biz was becoming by professors who painted a somber picture of the dying beast. We all vacillated between days of feeling like pioneers of the digital media age and washed-up idiots chasing a dream far extinct.

"But I started a business over a year ago on my writing alone! I write health and wellness articles, post them on Facebook and send them to my e-newsletter and boom! Just like that, I get nutrition clients. So basically, I get to tell stories for a living!"

"You know, that doesn't surprise me. I taught my students a lot about the portfolio lifestyle," she said.

In her rearview mirror, I must have looked as puzzled as I actually was.

"Portfolio lifestyle?" I asked with an eyebrow raise.

She added, "You know, it's exactly what you do—and your friends do; all you millennials have side hustles."

"I think if there was a definition of 'portfolio lifestyle,' my photo would be next to it in the dictionary. It's neat that you taught your students about that. I was groomed to think I needed to pick a company with good benefits, strong leadership and positive retention rates," I said, adding, "So much for that."

She was so right; all of my friends were wading through what to do when you don't find a 9-to-5 that you want to get married to and have a 401(k) baby with that you labor over for the next 10 to 20 years.

No chance. Most of my friends had changed jobs at least once by their first year out of college.

That conversation stuck with me for the next three months. Every time I wasn't sure what I was doing, I tried to remind myself that my friends, my fellow Gen-whatevers and I were all trailblazers of getting paid to be ourselves—or paid to be the most relatable person at the new start-up that just hired us via Facebook.

I got this, I'd say.

I made over $8,000 on my business alone in January, but what next? What if I moved to Chicago and there was no word of mouth about my business there? Should I make my business more diversified? Should I offer more? Do I have to write an e-book to sell on my website?

Those questions would fill my brain for an hour or so and then I'd drift off to imagining my future life.

I was rarely in the present from January to May of 2016. I spent half my days thinking back to how whimsical Chicago seemed, how warm and comforted I felt in Nashville, and you wouldn't imagine how angry I'd get when I pictured my innocent, clueless self agreeing to get in my Touareg and drive across the country to Boston.

But then I'd pause and think about the future. I'd meditate on hope.

When I pictured myself in Chicago, it was fuzzy. I couldn't remember enough to visualize it clearly. What would it be like now? Was it really a good idea to move there hoping to find Prince Charming? I wanted so badly to have a home but also yearned for a life with more party in it. Simply having someone to share my good or bad news with sounded like a dream.

Was the lack of a partner a side effect of my portfolio lifestyle? I knew I wouldn't know for at least 30 years—not until my fellow Gen-whatevers started studying stats about what happened to us. Too soon to say.

The security I felt when I worked at Alessor was a fixture of rules and guidelines with an authority to hold me to them. I had to be at my desk by 8 a.m. I was allowed to leave by 5 p.m. I was confined to certain roles and spaces for a huge part of my day, just like high school. Was it fun or sexy? No. Was it predictable? Yes. I relied on someone else. When you have a portfolio lifestyle, you can only rely on yourself. After meeting that Uber driver, I gained a sense of relief to know that other people are doing this stuff too.

It'd be nice to meet some of them, I thought.

A seed was planted in my head that this entrepreneurial space existed. I was in it, wading through it like thick mud in Boston. This could work! And "this" happened in Boston.

CHAPTER 65.

FINDING A CONSTANT

I slept with fewer pillows now; two to be exact. It was a stark contrast from the seven that had surrounded me for as long as I could remember. It made me feel like there was absolutely room for one more person. I sighed and rolled away from the window. Loneliness. On second thought, fewer pillows in my queen-size bed reminded me more of the emptiness I felt. It was 8:01 a.m. and officially the latest I had stayed in bed thus far in Boston.

The weather seemed mild and the sun brighter than I wanted it to be as light crawled in through the large gap in the blinds I needed to get fixed. Out of nowhere, I thought about going for a run.

Maybe it was the warmer weather …

I remembered the early morning laps I used to do around Wrigley Field in Chicago. Fenway was probably the same distance from my apartment in Back Bay. If I did laps around Fenway tomorrow morning would that mean I could leave Boston? Would everything come full circle with a sign that I should go? Or would that make me feel more at home here?

I kind of feared it would make Boston feel more permanent … *but how could it?*

This was supposed to be temporary.

It still felt temporary.

I closed my eyes and tried to picture running the laps. I didn't even know what I would see. I'd only been around Fenway for a couple of late dinners when it was dark outside. Surely, running laps around Fenway would make the city seem more foreign to me.

Would it all feel new again?

I wasn't sure. I got in the shower (where I do all my really deep thinking) and contemplated the idea of permanence. Many people fear permanence, like it's brutal monotony. But I kind of like it. I kind of seek it, I think. It would be nice, I'd thought, if Boston could be more of a constant for me, but for that to happen, I needed more social interaction and, perhaps, a love interest. With those things, I thought I'd like to explore Boston. At this point, what I knew was all I cared to know.

I then pictured a typical home in the '80s, like my grandparents' house. I pictured the dad who comes home from work in the afternoon and checks the mail, even though the wife's probably already picked it up. Perhaps there's a little kid's bike misplaced in the front yard. The front door to the house is open, but the glass door is shut. And the house sits like that for years and years until it's a permanent thing. Timeless. A vision ingrained in not only the family members' minds but also in those of the neighbors and regular passersby. Even if and when the family moves, that home will still be there chiseled in memory.

My mom's house in Indiana was that constant for me to hold. Even if she moves, the house I grew up in from the time I was 7½ years old will forever be a constant in my life.

When will I have built my own constant?

I pictured a linear graph of a line going up very steeply and wondered: When does mine level out? Sure, in my mind steepness indicated rapid growth and development, but I wanted to experience that with someone else, or slow down and feel at ease in one place. How do you find a partner and a home and a place where you want to stay?

Is that even a thing for millennials?

And if so, did I really want to plant lasting roots in Boston and make it my constant? Not really.

The longer I lived there, the more I came to realize how much wealth the locals actually had. Compared to my yuppie, less fancy Lincoln Park neighborhood in Chicago, it served as a constant reminder that no matter how long I ended up staying in Boston, I wasn't in Kansas anymore, and it was never going to feel like home. I should never get used to this Back Bay reality where Ferrari sightings are common and parking in a garage is $48 per hour. I never want this to be normal.

Living in this bubble of luxury and opulence and being put up in my fancy Back Bay apartment on the 11th floor had me feeling like a kept woman; yet, instead of a rich husband or father paying for my lifestyle, it was my "surrogate father"—aka Swam and Associates. They'd be paying for my rent another six months. After that? The only thing that'd quasi-felt like home for two years would likely be unaffordable. Knowing this reminded me that I was an outsider as I walked past the stunning Newbury Street brownstones worth millions of dollars.

Even if I wanted to belong, at points it seemed Bostonians wouldn't have had me! I didn't come from New England money, attend an Ivy League school, work at Mass General or work for a tech startup. I was an outsider looking in. In it, yet not in it. Does that make sense?

My theory was proven once when two men flirted with me enough to ask me out but opted for women of a higher social status when it came time for a famous charity ball in Boston. My family had money, but they weren't in Boston, so technically I didn't count?

It wasn't just the men who projected that "I'm too good for you" attitude. I took issue with how cold some (not all) of the retailers were, and I dare not smile at passersby. Almost two years in and I'd learned that smiles were unwarranted, that smiling at a stranger meant you were weird or suspicious.

The upside of kind-of affording the 02115 zip code was that

Newbury Street, the Charles River Esplanade and iconic Back Bay landmarks were just a hop, skip and a jump away from my apartment, and I liked walking around the area to clear my mind. I'd start on Massachusetts Avenue, wind down Boylston Street and then up Newbury. When I'd turn the corner from ultra-luxurious Newbury to Commonwealth Avenue, I'd think, *What a difference a street makes.* There was a calming effect with people walking in the sparse grassy patches between the busy one-way streets. Then I'd chuckle as I made my way to Beacon Street, where young parents would be taking kids out of car seats, old women were strolling along with walkers and cleaning ladies would be leaving buildings as the sun set.

Just two streets over on busy Boylston, between Ladder 59 and Mass Avenue, I'd often pass musicians from Berklee College of Music who were playing on mini-drums and cellos or singing a cappella style. Other times, I'd see youngsters heading over to Fenway to catch a game. It was always a mess of people, but as long as you weren't driving, it was enjoyable.

Several Back Bay streets, each with their own character, providing space for all types of unique characters. There was space for anyone, even me. But did I really want there to be space for me?

Sunken in my lows of March 2016, I felt like a prisoner in my own uncertainty.

Until one day I thought, *Enough!* I called my mom to tell her I was ready to make a decision.

"Mom when I come home to visit this weekend, I want to return to Boston with a firm plan. I need to make up my mind and if I'm going to leave, I have to tell Max and Kevin ASAP."

And as soon as the words came out, I knew my decision. I would have to leave this place. Leave this loneliness and get on with my life. But first, I needed Indiana to affirm my decision. Going home to my constant would remind me of who I am, and what I've always wanted. Mom's not a bad career counselor either.

CHAPTER 66.

BREAKING THE NEWS

April 1, 2016

My parents' voices echoed through my head on the plane ride back to Boston.

"Nicole, I don't like that you call me all the time because you're sad or bored. You've given Boston a great shot. But maybe Chicago will make your life more fun," said Mom.

"Yeah, Nicole, I think it sounds like it's going to be too expensive there. If Chicago is cheaper and your friends are there, then that makes sense! You'll be close to home! We'd love that!" said April.

"If you don't like it, you should come back to the Midwest; it's better here and we can see you more," Dad encouraged.

Following direct plans from my parents was not my MO, but in this case, I heeded their advice. Midwest was the resounding answer!

Before takeoff back to Boston, a lighthearted feeling came over me; with the Indiana soil under me for fleeting moments, everything made sense. However, by the time I landed on the East Coast, I shook in my own steps. For a gutsy girl, I didn't know if I had it in me to break the news to Max and Kevin.

It'd be gut-wrenching to tell them my news, but I had to be a big girl and do it. The last thing I'd wanted was to put them out or leave them hanging after they'd given me a chance in an unfamiliar city. Maybe their former Wall Street selves would appreciate my aim to save money by leaving Boston. They would get it, I hoped.

Aside from the financial aspect, they'd fully grasp my emotional drive to leave, too. After all, Max and Kevin were both married with kids. Teaching was their "work" and then they had family time after work. For me, teaching in rooms full of fitness enthusiasts, I was the motivator, the support, the leader. But after all the classes were over, I was alone. I went home to my computer to do work (emotionally supporting my fat loss clients) or watch Netflix. Sure, I'd begun to meet more people. But aside from Meg, my student from S&S who was becoming a good friend; Lauren, a girl who owned my favorite local spray tan business; and Dee from the spinning place, nothing was making me feel attached.

* * *

During my 30-minute walk to the S&S studio to break the news, I thought back to the time I nervously met with the owners of Tred11 in Chicago to tell them I was leaving for Boston. Secretly hoping they'd offer me a place in their company so I could avoid moving to Boston, I had taken deep breath before I walked into Sally and Tawny's office.

I could help them develop new Tred11 locations ...

I could help them hire and train new trainers ...

I could manage a store ...

I took back the last one, though, after my career counselor (mom) pointed out that I'd have to be at the fitness studio all the time if I were managing it.

Nothing would ever compare, I thought when leaving Tred11.

Nothing would be as fun.

Nothing would help me meet as many people.

Similar doubts and questions swirled inside my head as I got closer to S&S.

Had I failed?

Was I giving up?

Was I a quitter?

Was the reason I wasn't making friends because I was mean and closed off and a loner?

Would my sprouting friendships dissipate?

Was I a self-fulfilling prophecy that just didn't make it work because I said it wouldn't?

Upon entering the studio, I fought back tears and felt angry feelings flaming in my stomach. I was sad to be giving up but continued to convince myself I was moving on to better things.

Waiting in the lobby, I went through one of several iPhone notes titled "Pros and Cons."

"Nic! Hey baby, come on in; Kevin forgot so it's just going to be me and you," Max said with a sincere smile.

"Ah, no worries, it won't take too long. I appreciate you meeting with me," I responded.

I put my bag down in the secret spot under the desk where I'd always stashed it and took one last deep breath, before following Max into the studio. Inside I found a seat on a workout bench.

"What's going on, Nic?" he asked calmly, sitting on the floor and leaning up against the classroom wall mirror, still a little sweaty from his workout.

The speech I'd so perfectly crafted spewed out like an overflowing pot of boiling soup. Tears started to stream the second I opened my mouth. This was going to be harder than I thought.

Choking out my words, I began. "Max, you know Boston wasn't where I'd always planned to live. It was supposed to be a year and I was so thankful to meet you guys. This, Stride and Strength, is the one place that feels like home. But while this is thankfully my home, it's all I have. And I feel like at 25, I should have more. Living here in such an expensive city, far away from my real home without much selling me on it, doesn't feel right. You see, in Chicago, I loved Tred11; it was great. But at the end of every class, I sighed with relief that the awesome workout was over and I could go on with my day. If I missed my Mom, I could drive home in two hours. Here, when I take a class and it's over, I feel sad because all I have to look forward to is sleeping or Netflix. S&S is my 'event' each day. I've tried so hard to have a social life, but with my 5 a.m. schedule and night classes on Thursdays and Fridays, it's hard to be social. I love you guys but . . ."

"Nic, it's OK," he interjected, his fatherly side surfacing to try to stop my tears.

"I want you guys to know that I don't really want to leave." My voice squeaked like a 10-year-old's. "I want more out of Boston, but it just isn't happening—and I'm trying!" I said, crying harder.

"It's the hardest decision I've had to make. But, economically speaking, without my former company paying two-thirds of my rent, I don't want to pay so much to live in a city that I only half-love."

"Nic, it makes total sense. Kevin and I want you to love it more. We want you to be happy; we want you to have more fun. When I was 25, I was going crazy in New York. You need to do that. If you want more money or a schedule change, we could work on that, but a better social life? We can't fix that for you."

He hugged me hard and made me feel better. I wiped my tears enough to sneak out without too many people noticing my sadness and began to walk through the sprinkling rain to go work out at the gym down the street. Naturally, I called my mom and told her about Max's empathy and that I was glad I got it off my chest.

By the time I'd started lifting, Kevin had texted me.

"Nicky, Max told me the news and I really don't want to lose you, but I want you to know that I think it will be good for you. And hopefully S&S will be in Chicago soon and you can teach there."

I sent him a quick thank-you text back, reiterating how hard it was for me to make the decision, and he replied, "So pumped for you! xoxo."

By the time I got home from lifting, Kevin and Max had sent me an email to tell me that they would wait until I was ready to make any sort of an announcement. *Phew.* I knew I loved them. One of my biggest fears was spending my last weeks in Boston feeling like a lame duck, and I was thankful they would keep my secret. This way, I didn't have to fully deal with it yet.

It wasn't real until it was on Instagram anyway. And the fact that I, the girl who shares everything on Instagram, wasn't itching to post a word about this impending move was a sign I wasn't totally sold on it.

CHAPTER 67.

THE ESCAPE PLAN

That night, Shannon called me and I told her the news, and out poured tears of joy on the other end of the line.

"Finally, Nicky-baby, you need to get back here! I'm so thankful you made this decision. Time to come home."

"It just sucks; I know it's the right decision, but I'm scared I'll flounder in Chicago. Not to mention, it's also gonna suck to drive back."

"Nic, here's what we're gonna do. Call me crazy, but I want to fly there and stay the night with you, then drive with you all the way back. But here's why: I want us to go stop at Niagara Falls. My boyfriend, Parks, has a cousin who lives nearby Niagara and we could stay one night there. It will make the drive home exciting instead of depressing like your drive to Boston."

At that moment, the Escape Plan had commenced. I held on to it like the golden ticket.

But the weird part is that, despite a picture-perfect, movie-like plot to exit Boston, instead of a countdown to the Big Escape, I kept a countdown to May 1st. That was how long I had to re-sign my lease. Shannon, Max and Kevin and my parents were all clued in to my plans, but to everyone else, I was becoming a New Englander day by day, learning how to complain about the weather and traffic as a form of endearment toward Boston. To be safe I started looking at other apartment options in case I lost my white-walled haven and wanted to stay in Boston somewhere cheaper.

Coincidentally, Shannon was coming to stay with me in Boston for a wedding she and Parks were attending in Cape Cod three weeks before I would have to renew my lease to keep my space. Either she'd be there to help throw one last mini-party in the tiny, white-walled lair, or I'd be convincing her that staying was actually the better decision.

* * *

Shannon and Parks didn't actually get to my place until almost midnight. Shannon ransacked my closet and her suitcase, contemplating about seven different outfits before she chose one suitable enough to go meet Parks' high school friends at a bar down the street from my place. She's always been a glorious little torpedo and I love her for it. Ten minutes in Boston and my apartment was "Shannified," as I liked to call her unique ability to make a mess in a minute. Mess or no mess, I loved the company.

We were only at the bar for about an hour before it closed down, but long enough to get drunk and stumble to another bar that stayed open until 2 a.m.

Parks, Shannon and Parks' three high school friends all came back to my place afterward and we danced and sang to Justin Bieber until about 3 a.m., then just Shannon, Parks and I remained.

Shannon was drunk when she said it, but as she put her head full of pretty blonde curls in my lap, she saw right through me—I was second-guessing my decision to leave.

"Nic, I know you. I can tell you're thinking about staying. But I also know you want kids. I know you want a husband. I know you want those things," she said a bit slurred.

"Look around you," she continued. "You aren't going to meet anyone in this apartment writing every day. You are productive and you have your business and that's amazing. But you are so lucky, you can take that anywhere. And if you're scared about leaving S&S because of the income, we can live together. I got the rent. We can get a cheap place and I can cover it. You want to start a business? I have money saved. I will invest in you, Nicky-baby. We can do this. You gotta get out of here."

I felt like I was listening to a girl who wasn't me as I replied.

"But Shannon, I have so many great things going on here with S&S and I'm scared. I'm scared of not knowing what I will do for work in Chicago besides my business. S&S directly feeds my business. I mean, I have always dared to do the things that scare me, and both options are frightening; but I think I need to see this through."

I cried as I spoke. She started to cry a little, too. I didn't have a clue where these words were coming from; agreeing with her would've been so easy.

My gaze shifted outward, landing near my lamp across the room and then shifting directly over Parks' head. He was pretending to look through my photo album. He sat far enough across the room to give us space for this conversation, but he was obviously hearing it all, seeing the tears, and somehow I started to think he knew this talk was coming all night. Maybe they'd even talked about it together—about how she was going to pitch me. And I had talked about this talk with myself all week. After all, Shannon was the best salesperson I knew. (I always say, "My best friend could sell you a pair of old, dirty shoes and you'd go home and tell your family you got the best deal in the world.") It was going to be tough to convince her that I should stay.

I think she knew something was up too, because in one month's time since I told her I was moving, I hadn't made any plans with her yet regarding the physical move to Chicago. She could see I was still looking for a reason to stay. We'd agreed to be roommates, but I'd failed to start the apartment hunt with her. If I had told her I was reconsidering my decision, I knew she'd fight me on it.

"What about your rent? It's so expensive," she argued.

"I have money saved!" I could've said. Instead, I just shook my head, telling her she was right, but unable to hide my hesitation.

And I was scared that it was all sales talk. *What if she's wrong?*

But the tears didn't lie.

My pounding heart didn't lie.

Chicago was the right answer.

"So dare to move back, Nicole," she said.

At that moment, the decision was crystal-clear.

I nodded that I would and hugged her tight, but something inside me wasn't going to give in just yet. I was going to make her sell me harder because to me, clearly more clarity was required.

CHAPTER 68.

A WRENCH IN THE PLAN

May 2016

You could call it laziness; you could call it depression. I called it survival. With all of my 3:30 a.m. wakeups to teach 5 a.m. classes, I had to begin programming naps into my day. I started doing it in February, but it took me until May to feel OK about it. I felt guilty since the 8-to-5 lifestyle had been so ingrained in me.

With the stress of not knowing where I was going to wind up living come July, the naps sometimes turned into hours of staring at the ceiling with heavy clouds hanging over my head as I'd lie there procrastinating on other projects I knew I should be doing. When you're your own boss, there's always something to be doing.

Right after dozing off into what felt like an hour-long nap, I jolted awake as my phone rang right by my face.

It was a Massachusetts number. In the past with real estate work, I always answered my phone because I was "on the clock." Now with my own business, the only people who'd call were my clients, friends or family and I didn't have to answer unless it was convenient for me.

But something struck me about the Massachusetts number, so I answered it.

"Hi, this is Nicole Winston," I said as I tried to mask my sleepy voice.

"Nicole. Matt Rogue," he said in his thick Boston accent. Matt

Rogue, as in my old-real-estate-broker-in-Massachusetts Matt Rogue.

When he said, "How are you?" The "r" was silent. Oh, how I missed his tonality.

"Hi, Matt!" I said, a bit confused as to why he was calling.

"Nicole, I'm gonna cut to the chase because I haven't got a lot of time. I'm working with a new client these days and your name came up. I need someone young and hip and someone who knows Boston well. The client, Cafe Fern, wants to get a lot of deals done fast and I think you'd be the perfect person for the job. Do you know Cafe Fern?"

"Wow, I appreciate you thinking of me, Matt," I said feeling very frustrated that I couldn't break out of my sleepy voice. "I do know Cafe Fern; I love the brand and so do all of my fitness friends. There's a store right near Stride and Strength."

"What have you been up to? Do you have time for such a project?"

"Well, I've been writing a book, running my online business and teaching fitness classes," I replied very matter-of-factly.

Matt chuckled.

"Nicole, out of all the things I expected you to say, I would have never guessed any of those things." He said in an even thicker accent than I remembered.

"It's been fun and it definitely keeps me busy. I am considering moving because I feel as though I haven't quite found the right social group here in Boston. It's been a tough city to crack and I really miss Chicago. The beauty of an online business is that I can go anywhere."

Considering, ha! I'd already told Shannon, Max and Kevin I was moving, plus, my lease had expired.

"Nicole, I totally understand. I don't picture you antisocial, but I can imagine it's hard since you're not from here. In my twenties, I worked all the time, so I didn't really notice feeling lonely, but at the same time, I'm from here, so I guess I knew if I wanted the friends or community, I had them at my disposal. I will send you an email with more info in case the stars align and you do not move to Chicago."

"Thank you, Matt," I said.

As soon as I hung up, I realized I was mentally checking out of Boston. The Escape Plan was overtaking me. I knew I needed to focus more on the group nutrition programs and getting a response from the Chicago apartment broker than following up with Matt. Getting the apartment you want is like trying to find a golden ticket in that market.

After a few moments of processing the call and the offer, a part of me was flattered, so I sent Matt a thank-you email and asked if he knew any brokers in Chicago. Within 20 minutes, he replied that he didn't know anyone off the top of his head but would think about it. He reminded me that the door was open to become his associate should I want the opportunity, and he'd pay me a stipend to work for him before I started closing deals and could make commission. Oddly, it was the same amount I used to get from Swam and Associates for living expenses—and that got me contemplating, again.

CHAPTER 69.

NOW OR NEVER

May 2016

Here's the thing: I didn't plan on moving to Boston and launching my own fitness business. What I truly wanted to do after college was to stay in Chicago to be close to Indy so I could step into the family business and work my way up. But after so many attempts to appeal to my family (I'd even had a secret meeting with my dad's VP John Winston when he was in Chicago for work), my skillset, drive and tools didn't make the cut. After I fought with my dad in Berlin, I left the trip convinced that working in the business would never happen. Worse, almost a year later, we got into another fight on my 25th birthday, while at dinner in Boston. The birthday quarrel ensued after I told him how proud I was that my business was one year and one month old and he asked me the name of it …

I could give up on my dreams of working in the family business, but not on my dreams of a steady relationship with my father. Whether it was April coaching him to try harder, me forgiving and forgetting or God's work at hand, by May of 2016, my dad and I'd grown into a more cordial relationship, one that'll probably always be "a work in progress." The conversations we'd been having on the phone were so dramatically different that I'd even mentioned it to my mom.

In a low moment at the tail end of May, while I was feeling

overcome by the darkness of uncertainty, my dad called. I answered to have company amongst my scary thoughts.

Unable to hide my tears, I divulged my worries, and spoke to him about my options:

1) Moving to Chicago and working on writing and Crossroads of Fitness until S&S would open in Chicago

2) Staying in Boston with expensive rent

Same options, same pros and cons, same dance, same song. But for whatever reason, the conversation shifted to my frustrations with dating. There I was in the best shape of my life and felt the most confident, but it seemed nobody was even attracted to me.

"Nicky, you don't have to move to Chicago, you know," he said. "You could move to Indiana."

I rolled my eyes and let out a loud sigh.

"Dad, if I'm having trouble dating in a city this big, I doubt I'll find someone in Indiana where half of the people are married by age 23. There's no single life; plus, there's no Stride and Strength. I'd have to hustle to find work in fitness."

"Well, the right guy will come at the right time. You never know," he said, shocking me with actual advice.

"Maybe ..." I trailed off with an unenthusiastic tone.

"I don't want to waste money here, but I don't want to make the wrong move to Chicago and wait too long before S&S opens there. They don't have an opening date until at least January 2017."

"You could always work for us," my dad said.

My jaw hit the floor. *WHAT?*

Hearing those words was like I'd struck gold, like I'd won the lottery. They echoed in my mind, and felt like more than 100 times the number of Band-Aids I needed from all the wounds he'd caused over the years.

"Are you serious?" is what I wanted to say.

However, I was so scared that I'd dreamt the words and that they weren't real, so I paused. Grandpa was looking down on me; he heard my prayers, I'm sure.

"Wow. I'd love to help out, Dad. I really, truly want to be a part of it and help in whatever way I can."

I didn't care that my business would have to take a back seat if I chose this path. I'd highly consider his offer, but he'd have to give me a real offer first for me to budge.

* * *

Through all the contemplation about whether I should stay or go, KG had said something that kept ringing true.

"Stop trying all the time," he said once midst contemplation-filled phone call. It soon became a line he'd say each time we spoke, always pissing me off as much as it did the first time.

Why wouldn't I want to put in the effort? Why would I want to give up?

Since July 2015, I'd constantly tell him all about me trying to fit in, trying to have fun plans, trying to find a social group.

It hit me: I had been TRYING for two years.

But for my potential "last weekend" in Boston, I'd planned to keep trying: I had a volleyball match with the random summer league I'd joined, a Strong Woman training camp, a Red Sox game (my first!) and a night out at a club with the spinning crew.

Going into the weekend, I knew it wasn't going to be my actual last weekend, but for months I'd planned for it to be the last social weekend. I then still had two weeks until The Escape Plan commenced.

But even after all the highs of my fake last week in Boston, I'd had a poor week. Several new friends canceled plans, and I felt bored with work and lonely. I still worried that I'd lost a sense of "normal" for a twenty-something—or at least what I thought normal should be. Remember, it's too early to tell if I'm an average millennial or not … not enough studies on us yet!

And even if S&S and my business made me happy, work's not everything. What's more? I knew I was more productive when

I'm my happiest self. The time to try to fix things was running out, yet I still was running in circles.

KG's words had originally made me think that cutting out "trying," and that meant returning to Chicago. But what if I just stopped trying as much here in Boston?

Thursday night, I called Shannon and shared my doubts about moving back, that perhaps I was giving up too early.

"It's not about giving up," Shannon responded. "You don't need to keep trying. You are just choosing happiness. You are choosing to be in a place where you have friends to laugh with at dinner on a Tuesday night. Work will always be there. You have always worked hard and found money. And people will still follow you. People always ask me how you are doing. So many people will want you back."

"I know, I know. I can't stay in this same apartment doing the same things and hoping for a different outcome. I just need to go now and DARE to move back. It scares the shit out of me, but it feels right."

Hindsight is 20/20 but at the time what felt right was logic. Comfortable was home nearby. Safe was cheaper rent. Familiar was a city with friends.

We decided to apply for one more apartment together; I promised to scan the documents first thing in the morning.

Immediately, I hung up the phone to call KG and tell him the news that he didn't even know was news (last time we spoke I was moving to Chicago).

"Dude, you're gonna get back here for one week and be like, 'Thank God, I came back.' You won't think twice about Boston. This is home. You're gonna have an epic summer and redevelop a drinking problem. I cannot wait for you to meet my girlfriend."

Warm, gushy feelings in my heart and goosebumps on my arms—my white walls were old news and I could not wait for more color, imagining what my new Chicago apartment might look like.

"You're gonna be fine," he added. "You're making the right decision."

What I didn't know was that as soon as we'd hung up, he got a text from Shannon: "Our girl is coming home."

CHAPTER 70.

GETTING ALL THE ANSWERS

June 2016

It was a day Shannon had been anticipating all week long, the day we would find out if the apartment we'd put an offer on would be ours. I'd put it out of my head during the week, head down in coaching mode, until Thursday night when Shannon FaceTimed me from the two-bedroom apartment in Lincoln Park. She'd scurried across the city during rush hour to meet the broker, and in less than 24 hours, we'd know if we were to be the lucky winners of the urban space.

I saw it first. The Chicago broker lamented in a brief email that we were not the lucky winners, and I felt nothing. But then, relief.

Instead of shooting Shannon a text to say, "Let's keep checking Craigslist, we got this," I did something far opposite.

"Matt," I quickly typed into an email. "Is there any way that your offer to work with Cafe Fern is still on the table?"

Sent.

Next, I sent an email to my building manager. The window to re-sign my lease had expired May 1st. During that first week of May, I felt the effects of a breakup. But now I wanted to see if we still could make the relationship work.

"Hi, is there any way my apartment is still on the market? If so, could it be taken down so that I can re-sign for another year?"

Sent.

Immediately, I received a response.

Hyperventilating, I clicked "Open."

"Yes, your apartment is still available, but we will need an answer by the end of next week."

Next, I called my dad to ask about an offer. The week prior, I had sent him an email about how I could create a tax-deductible wellness plan and work in HR, a department in his business that greatly needed help.

"Dad, what would you be able to pay me?" I said. "I can help in whatever area you need help with, but I want to make sure it's step up for me career-wise. I don't want to make less than I did with Swam."

"Ah, I don't know, like $40,000 or something?"

I wanted to cuss him out. He knew I had made $64,000 in salary and $24,000 on top of that for my living expenses with Swam—plus I had the income coming in from my online business and teaching.

It hurt like hell that my own father didn't value me (at least not yet) and that he had said something without thinking it through: "You can come work for me" was like a fake offer because he really didn't have a job for me.

At least now I knew there was no real opportunity in Indiana. I made a conscious effort not to let the salary number slap me in the face and to focus instead on the positive invitation itself. We were on the mend. And I had decisions to finalize, not time to waste.

After we hung up, I received an email from Matt: Yes, the offer was still on the table and the stipend would cover my costs of living.

But wait, there's more. When I contacted Kevin and Max to let them know I was going to stick around, they were thrilled! Not only did they allow me to write my dream work schedule (no more Thursday and Friday night classes killing my social life), but they also gave me a raise!

Now things were looking up. Less financial stress if I stayed.

Leaning over the kitchen table, I put my head in my hands, sighing.

How am I ever going to break the news to Shannon?

* * *

It was now June 3rd and Shannon still had a one-way flight to Boston for June 28th. The Escape Plan to Chicago had always made the move back more appealing. There'd be no better way to leave than driving with my best friend to Niagara Falls, off to begin a new chapter. What would come after Niagara Falls didn't matter in my daydreams—I only pictured it like a movie where the photo op in front of the Falls was the happily-ever-after, end scene.

But I knew this to be true: The true test of a friendship is when you can break plans with your BFF, an act that could break their heart, but you need not worry because you know it won't change a thing. Their love is unconditional—they're a rare breed, but they're real.

Shannon is that kind of friend. I might break her heart (and mine), fully knowing this whole plan could backfire, but she'd still be there for me. The other reason she's amazing? She had to support whatever decision I made, angry or not, selflessly knowing that if it goes awry, she'll be on the rescue team. But friends do this because they know you'd do it for them. They are the family you choose.

The night I planned to call her was a nightmare. First, I got home and decided to clean before calling—she'd probably be at work anyway, right? Then I decided to bake protein muffins. Before I could actually dial, I got lost scrolling Instagram while nearly eating all the muffins I'd baked.

Finally, I called. I wasted no time with small talk and when I broke the news, the call was short. She had "to go." I understood the sadness and I felt like I'd committed a crime. Knowing she'd still be my friend made me mad that I'd done this to her. Worse,

I had a dinner date directly after with my new friend Meg, who I adored, but something about it made me feel guilty, like I was cheating or moving on from Shannon.

When I got to dinner, I felt like I could tell Meg that my decision to stay was final. She was as lukewarm about it all as I was, understanding my millennial strife. I told her about Matt and the opportunity and she seemed really impressed, but then we both laughed about the timing of it all. As girlfriends do, conversations shifted to guys and we joked about all my horrible woes of singledom, her offering hope as she spoke of her long-term boyfriend.

After dinner, we walked down the glowing streets in almost-summer evening light with hands over each other's shoulders. I threw my head back laughing when Meg made a witty comment about an asshole I'd been seeing and realized this is what I had been missing: close friends in the city. Someone to eat with, walk with, laugh with. I finally found it, kind of. Just in time.

As we continued walking, laughing our heads off about silly stuff, I paused and looked down the glowing Newbury Street at dusk. The sun sets later in June and the evening rainstorm had dissipated, leaving this afterglow that made magic before my eyes.

"I gotta capture this," I said, grabbing my phone out of my jean shorts pocket and jogging right out into the four-way stop, adding, "Doing it for the Insta!" as I ran out into the middle of the street.

"Oh, Nicky, be careful!" she hollered behind me, letting me do my thing.

I bowed down into an awkward kneel to get the right angle of the brilliant sun setting and the tourists walking by.

As soon as I snapped the photo, I got up quickly like a football player does after an awesome tackle and jogged back to the safety of the sidewalk. Right as I crossed the threshold that was out of traffic's way, Meg to my right shoulder, I heard my name called.

"Nicky!" someone yelled from afar. And while I contemplated

if I'd really just heard my name, the person must have begun to jog over toward me. A few seconds later, I heard it again, from a much closer range.

"Nic!" he yelled.

Meg saw it first and whispered, "Holy shit, Nic!"

I turned and saw Ren Man.

CHAPTER 71.

COFFEE AND PEACE

He was standing right there in front of me. In a perfect jean jacket, tight jeans, a fashion necklace and his favorite Rolex with leather boots, he was a cartoon character left unchanged. He looked the same, maybe a little better.

"Hey, Nicky, how are you?" he said, going in for the hug.

He smelled good like I remembered.

Shell shocked, Meg introduced herself. "Hi, I'm Meg. Nicky's friend from S&S," she said.

I felt no need to pretend to tell Meg who he was; she knew. As girlfriends do, we had divulged our relationship pasts, career dreams and family woes, fully explaining our pasts via Instagram photos and Facebook profile pics. She'd actually never met anyone from my past, not even Jaylen, but if interviewed, she could give complete, impeccable physical descriptions.

"Hi. Oh my, gosh. Hi, how are you? Wait, what are you doing here?" I said bluntly, while struggling to get my cellphone back into my back pocket. It was as if my arms stopped working, my neurons weren't firing correctly. Plus, my heart was beating physically out of my chest like I was the cartoon character in this situation.

"Ah, man, so good to see you, Nic. I'm here for a few cigar meetings. I've been doing some independent cigar brokering on my own and there are some bigwigs in town. Plus, Jimmie is playing in northern Mass tonight, so I'm gonna head there in an hour or so and fly out tomorrow afternoon."

"Wow. I wouldn't have expected that, but it sounds right up your alley! You always loved cigars," I said, trying to act like my respiration rate was normal.

He swooped his left hand up into his hair to brush it back and the wedding ring glared at me. So bizarre.

"Do you live around here?" he asked.

"I do, actually, about less than a quarter mile over there on Mass Avenue by Berklee. It's a convenient spot, for sure," I said, adding, "Is your wife here with you?"

"That's awesome. I love this street. The shopping is nice," he said, accentuating the word "nice."

"She's actually traveling for work in Spain, so no, but we were here last summer and she loved it, so I wish she were here now."

"That's so cool!" I said with way too much fake enthusiasm; I could literally hear Meg's eyes roll.

"Hey, you want to hang out tomorrow or something? I have a ton of time to kill before my flight. Maybe we could catch up?"

"Yeah, that would be great! I don't think I've seen you in the flesh since before I even moved here. What? Like a little over two years ago?"

"Crazy," he said.

"Let's meet here tomorrow? I could do 11 a.m."

"Sure," he said, leaning in for a hug. "I'll see you then."

* * *

Never an ugly duckling but never a beauty queen (at least not until my bodybuilding-Barbie days), I always had my insecurities. And, to Ren Man's misfortune, they were most heightened in our months together. Whether it was his good looks (for the record he was an ugly duckling as a child) making me feel out of my league, the gorgeous women around Nashville or the vanity of most Nashvillians (teeth whitening, veneers, hair extensions,

Botox, etc.) from 2013 to 2014 in my own mind, I was less than or not enough. But all of that changed post-Jaylen. Nicole 2.0 had the abs, the 24-inch waist, the hair extensions, the incredible headshots and fitness photos for Instagram, and somewhere along the lines of all the physical changes, my surface matched my internal drive and confidence. Therefore, when it came time to primp for coffee with Ren Man, I wasn't nervous at all, just more ready to reveal my newer self to him.

He arrived at the corner of Newbury and Gloucester wearing the same version of his outfit from the day before, except this time his tight-fitting tee was striped. I smiled when I saw him, but wondered what we'd talk about. My business? My dating life? My decision to stay? God, I hoped we wouldn't discuss the latter. I didn't want him to convince me to leave.

"Hey, Nicky," he said, hugging me again.

"Hi! Wanna duck into the little coffee shop on the garden level of this building?"

"Definitely! I just gotta meet some people at 1 at that new restaurant Saltie Girl a few blocks down," he said.

As he scanned the menu inside the local coffee spot, my mind begged for answers to so many questions.

How did he know she was the one?

How did he meet her?

What did she do?

Did he marry her so quickly because she was pregnant?

Knowing I had to keep it formal and only about the present to be respectful of his wife, I focused then on what else I would tell him about myself. Walking over to a corner booth, I wondered, *How did he remember me?*

"How's it been going?" he said so casually.

"Good, good. I actually just decided to stay in Boston one more year after like six months of contemplating. So that's my big news. But other than that, just navigating the portfolio lifestyle: running my business, beginning to work on a real estate client called Cafe Fern and teaching. What about you? Are you still thinking about working for your dad?"

"Wow, Nic, that's a lot! But super cool. You nailed the whole portfolio lifestyle thing. I get that, for sure. I've been doing this side business selling and distributing fine cigars, but I'm also still helping Mitchell produce songs, laying drum tracks when I can and helping my dad with the new build-out of a luxury car store. He's no longer with Lexus."

"Amazing. All things you love, except no more Uber, I suppose?" I said jokingly.

"Ha! Thank GOD," he said, literally face-palming himself. "What a nightmare. It was great cash at first but they changed a bunch of shit and it turned out to be a waste of time."

"And how's married life?" I asked in a fake "I'm so excited for you" tone.

"Good. Always work, but overall good. She travels a lot—we both do—but she's supportive and creating a home together has been fun," he explained so genuinely.

"How did you meet?" I asked

"I DM'ed her on Instagram, ha! And she responded. She was gonna be in Nash for a weekend so we decided to meet up. From Texas originally, she's a true southern belle," he said with pride.

"Just what you wanted!"

For the next 20 minutes, I opened up about my dating woes. The apps, the setups, the jerks and more. I made the sad comical, but he could see through it.

"Nic, I know it's tough, but you gotta keep your head up and be positive. You were dating a short guy for some time though, right? I thought I saw some bald guy on your Instagram?"

"Yeah, yeah, that was nuts. He was very driven, from Boston, but a few months in, I found out he was doing weightlifting supplements and accusing me of liking you and KG. Super weird situation. I stayed longer than I should have."

"Nic, I don't wanna sound mean or intense, but you were in a rough place when we broke up. I was really, truly worried about you. Hell, I texted your mom about it. I tried really hard to move on and prayed that you'd heal, hoping that you'd go back to the happy-go-lucky giggling Nicole I witnessed on our snowboarding trip to Aspen. That's the girl I loved. But you'd become so dark, stressed and angry."

"I was ..." I tried to say something but didn't know what to say.

"Look," he added, "I know you were going through a lot, I do. But you really hurt me with your words. It was hard to forgive and harder to forget, but once I did, I really prayed that you'd find yourself and be that shiny, driven, focused and strong girl whom I'd gotten to know."

His words came out gracefully, poignant but true, hard to hear but medicinal. Is this what therapy feels like?

"Ren, I'm sorry that I hurt you and even more sorry that I got to that place. It was dark—you're right. And to be honest, it stayed dark for a while. The highs of bodybuilding and self-improvement have been awesome, but I think part of why dating has sucked is because I still haven't known what I really want, at least as far as my living situation goes. Picking a city has been harder than picking a man!"

Ren Man then dropped some C.S. Lewis lines to inspire me, told me to stay hopeful and revealed that he thought my decision not to move would be great, adding, "I've been doing some residential real estate myself; it's a fun game! I get why you like it, and I know you'll excel with Cafe Fern."

"Thank you," I said with a smile. Looking into his eyes felt good, like they knew my whole soul, the good, the bad and the very ugly, but improving side. He knew me like family and cared for me as a friend. Hearing all of this was like opening the Ren Man box in my head and going through it together. He took some of his things back and I kept the good memories. We could be friends.

Minutes passed as we caught up on family, more about my business and his and then it was time to part. I hugged him goodbye, wondering if I'd ever see him again. No part of me wanted to be with him and his lifestyle, a realization for which I'm thankful (one portfolio lifestyle is enough for a relationship), but he did have all the characteristics I did want in a partner. Even better? He reminded me of the good parts of my soul, the parts I wanted and needed to find, and then showcase in order to be ready for Prince Charming, should he arrive in Boston.

CHAPTER 72.

MAKING SENSE OF THE SEARCH

January 2017

As a little girl, I had to travel near and far to spend time with my dad. After my parents' divorce, from age 7 until 13, I'd guide my brothers through airports and keep them busy on bus rides to go see Dad in Idaho, Vegas, Colorado and Florida at his respective air force bases. It was never easy navigating the foreign terminals. Hanging out with other young kids flying solo in dark, scary holding cells during layovers made me uneasy; but it was all worth it when we got to see Dad. He'd take us on adventures—waterskiing, camping, hiking, fishing. If it was outdoors, adventurous or away from regular society, we did it.

When we were little, it seemed that Dad planned these outdoor excursions, but now that I'm almost the age he was during his single-dad phase, it's clear to me that he was just doing what he loved doing on the fly and bringing us along for the ride.

At night, after long days on the lake or in the woods, we'd all pile onto the small couch in his air force base home in Mountain Home, Idaho. Sometimes we'd avoid falling asleep on the couch and crawl into the purple-framed double bed he had on base in Las Vegas, or plop down on the futon in Dad's favorite teepee (regular tents were too normal) when we'd go camping in Colorado. Thus, Dad's life assured me that it's OK to dare to be different if it made me happy. In any of the tiny, unfamiliar places we'd go to with Dad, snuggling up together and watching scary adventure movies about bears or sharks made everything feel all right! We'd listen to Dad's stories of ice climbing, hunting or something that would definitely keep our attention in spite of the late hour.

But what I loved most were the times when we'd fall asleep watching wildlife shows on the Discovery Channel. Dad would always fall asleep first, somehow still rubbing Wyatt's back or with his arm around Hunter, his other hand holding the remote. Parents seem to develop an additional type of sleep—where they aren't totally knocked out, but their slumber is deep enough to slightly snore yet light enough to be aware of their surroundings.

Once everyone appeared to be asleep, I'd look around the dark room or tent with the zipper-door ajar, noticing that the TV was too loud, food was left out or the campfire was still blazing—scenes that you'd never see at Mom's. It's that image of my dad passed out, completely relaxed, that imbued a greater sense of relaxation in me. Like it's OK that proper bedtime didn't occur; it's OK that there are open cans and paper plates on the coffee table; it's OK that we are all snuggling together; reality is safe and disparate from the startling scenes on television or from the scenes imagined from Dad's stories.

These were the highlights of life with my dad, and we lived for these moments, since regular life was with Mom in boring Fishers, Indiana. If there was one thing I was ultimately searching for in my early twenties, it was this type of OK-ness; it was the sense of security I'd felt in small doses that I sought.

I was after it the moment I set foot in Chicago. From Day One in the Real World, I'd positioned myself in a city with familiar faces, multiple jobs and income streams, a steady roommate and family nearby.

Realizing that this sense of home, this search for place were driving me, I began to understand why Ren Man and I worked, when we worked. It helped me comprehend my own decision-making when I would get on oddly timed flights just to spend a day in his apartment. My yearning for a safe space made Ren

Man's lair so attractive—cozy bed, family nearby, friends abounding. So secure. Predictable.

The safe asylum I'd created in Chicago was pulled out from under me when I got to Boston, and I hadn't a clue how to recreate it without my college friends built in, a roommate to go get dinner with or an office full of young people like me. It's like I needed a Ren Man to show me Boston and include me in a community, a support system, something. But instead, I got Jaylen, who kept me holed up in my apartment.

It was only after my decision to re-sign my lease and stay in Boston when my search for OK-ness and community reignited in earnest. But it was daunting—Boston was the Actual Real World. I would now go back to having a "real job" part-time via Cafe Fern. Still struggling to make close adult friends, I often wondered: *How was I to find other people to go out with?*

Fuck, without having to teach weekends, how was I supposed to spend Saturdays?

Initially, I was happy. Social outings were made easier by summer weather; days at the beach led to weeknights out on the town with friends in the fall.

But then I began having second thoughts as I went back to Chicago and Indiana for bachelorette parties, weddings and my dad's birthday in the second half of 2016, feeling the pull of the Midwest yet again.

By Thanksgiving, I noticed my savings account had dwindled after almost six months of luxury living, and I began to feel nervous. What would I have to show for after a full second year in Boston that was coming with a price tag of nearly $40,000 in rent?

After time with my family at Thanksgiving and friends in a November 2016 wedding, I was looking at January 1 as a nice move-out date. Chicago was still alive and well, and not only did I plan to visit there for my 26th birthday, I'd also get to take an S&S class in the brand-new studio, completed earlier than anticipated! Knowing that I'd be in Chicago soon, I realized I could potentially see some apartments. Therefore, on December 1st I had a meeting with my building manager to discuss how to break my lease. My discovery? I'd face some financial recourse, but the punitive charge would be a tenth of what living there for seven more months would cost.

After a lot of consideration before Christmas, I decided that moving in the middle of winter midst the holidays was unrealistic, and if things got worse, I could move in the spring or just stick it out six more months. Nevertheless, business was going well, and the only thing that truly was the worst was dating.

There was no fire in the romance department. By December of 2016, I'd gone on several dates with a nice guy whose middle name was "Friend Zone." I'd been ghosted two more times, and unfortunately also was roofied on the night of an early birthday celebration at a very popular Boston restaurant. Things took a turn for the worse (if that's even possible) when I received unsolicited selfies from a cab driver who'd asked for my business card because he said he wanted help with fat loss. But the ultimate kicker was a picture of a man's you-know-what from Bumble after I refused an unsolicited FaceTime call.

Weirder than worse was a call I received from Jaylen.

Butt dial?

Nope. He wanted to catch up, see how I was doing, shoot the shit.

What?

In his mind, time and space had healed "us" and this was appropriate. More bizarrely, he called me at 4:30 in the morning since he had insomnia, knowing that I'd be awake. On that phone call, January 15, 2017, he reminded me of our first date with 21 questions and no information about himself. Asking why I blasted my social media with so much about S&S, why I was still staying in Boston and inquired all about my family members, I felt overwhelmed and wished I hadn't answered. After the brief call, he texted me, "Come meet me in Vegas this weekend?"

Was he high?

I hated men and was ready to swear them off for good when, on January 24, one of the sweetest women I'd ever had the pleasure of coaching emailed me.

"Garrett! Hi! This is unrelated to fitness, but I read a lot of your newsletters and follow up on your social media and I think you're still single? This may be too personal, but I would like to set you up with a guy I work with. He's super nice and outdoorsy and I'm not saying that you'll be perfect for each other, but you're both perfect in your own way. Can I give him your email?"

Nope.

I couldn't be bothered.

"Hell no," I began to type.

Backspace, backspace.

"Hi, Denise! Thank you so much for thinking of me! You are so sweet to reach out. Yes, I am single and it's safe to say I've had a really rough go with dating, but you know me, never giving up!" I typed with forced enthusiasm.

Immediately after sending the email, I went to her company's LinkedIn page to see if any of her male coworkers were even slightly attractive. Of the 12 who even had profiles, there was only one guy who looked under the age of 50. His name was Jeff. Jeff was hot.

Just before bed, my email dinged. It was Denise!

"Great, Garrett! If anything, you'll make a new friend! Stay tuned for an email from Jeff."

My interest was piqued. This could be something.

I said a little prayer and wondered if maybe I'd wake up to an email from a Jeff the next morning.

* * *

Two days later, I woke up, still no email from any men from Denise's company. It was a Thursday and I had already taught three 5 a.m. classes that week. I was dragging. On my birthday,

I'd mystically decided that the 26th day of each month of my 26th year would be magical because it was going to be my Lucky Year (26 is my lucky number), but that morning I felt the furthest from lucky. I felt annoyed and silly for hoping for something so elusive.

As I walked into the S&S studio to teach, the front desker looked at me like she needed to tell me something. After a smile, she said, "Garrett! Oh my gosh, my boyfriend's roommate matched with you on Bumble! He really wants you to message him." (Bumble is the app where the woman has to reach out first).

After rudely rolling my eyes, I walked past her like Eeyore, yelling as I went to the locker room,"Tell him not to hold his breath. I gave up on dating. Dating is the worst. I deleted Bumble."

The negativity I embodied was grossing me out. In the private bathroom stall, I gave myself a pep talk. "Pull yourself up, Nicole. There's more to life than dating. Just enjoy what you have and if you're gonna give up, give up without a care. But whatever you decide, own it and don't be negative around clients! It's ugly!"

CHAPTER 73.

DONE DATING

January 28, 2017

Sitting at my desk chair, I fired away three last-minute emails before closing out and finishing up my coffee. T minus one hour until my first date with Jeff. It was 6:15 a.m. and I still needed to curl my hair. As my email window disappeared, a PDF popped up: "How to Break a Lease at Mass Ave. Living."

Instead of closing out of it, I simply put my computer to sleep and carried my coffee with me into the bathroom.

With each curl I made, I wondered why:

Why spend time on another jerk after two men sent unsolicited, inappropriate photos two days ago?

Why waste my work time when the last date I went on (five days ago) walked out of the restaurant mid-drink without reason?

Why meet a stranger and drive an hour north to go snowboard?

Then came the "at leasts":

At least I'll get out of my apartment and see some nature.

At least I'll breathe fresh air.

At least I'll have an excuse to step away from my email for a day.

Thirty-four hours had passed since we e-met the afternoon of January (lucky!) 26 when Jeff had sent me a very upbeat email asking me out. Thankfully, my Instagram had a snowboarding #TBT video up, a professional headshot and a fitness post within the most recent posts for Jeff to discover.

During the 34-hour window from e-meeting to our first date,

we'd discussed each other's family dynamics and shared a little bit about our work life. He'd suggested we go snowboarding for our first date—we both had a mutual passion for shredding the New England hills. He'd be the driver, and I was going to bring coffee and my favorite protein pumpkin muffins.

I sighed deeply remembering the tone of his texts, trusting my intuition that he would be a good (hopefully tall!) guy.

Before I went to bed the night before, he'd sent me a closing text: "It feels like Christmas Eve!"

I sprayed a few curls and went over to check the state of my board bag.

Packing my snowboard meant I'd have to pull it out of the corner of the living room area of my apartment, where it had been leaning up against the wall ever since I moved to Boston. Just walking over to that part of the room was odd. Since Jaylen left, I'd sat on my own couch only twice, keeping mostly to the kitchen table that served as my desk from 3:30 a.m. until 9 at night.

But I'd had some fun in 2016, too, including friends visiting me, sunny beach days when I brought sand home with me, late nights out that turned into hot makeout sessions and some late-night dates that ended in tears. I was proud of all the things this snowboard bag had witnessed, and a fire burned inside me steadily now. If the date wasn't "the one," I'd be OK; I got this.

So many times before I had done my makeup and picked out a new dress, all to have a date let me down. But this one? While it would appear to be a larger risk, given that we were traveling an hour north for our first date, I felt comfort in the fact that I was wearing my favorite leggings, my sturdy Sorel hiking boots and a cozy sweater, and bringing my favorite muffins. My kind of date. I only hoped he wouldn't think I was overdone, given that I put on makeup for a 7 a.m. date. I wasn't going to not put my best foot forward. #stilltrying

"Good morning! It feels like Christmas! How are you? I'm headed to you in 15!"

My heart fluttered. I hoped he was as genuine as he seemed and not cheesy.

I touched up a few more curls, finished my mascara and tied my boots.

As I threw my snowboard bag over my shoulder, I promised myself not to talk about my Chicago contemplation on this date. I would talk about my move to Boston, sure, but not about actually my contemplating leaving in a few months. Not today. I'd give this a fair shot. Fresh slate fun day.

* * *

I sighed at the relief of locking eyes with a very attractive, at least 5-foot-10 man waiting for me outside of a giant silver lifted truck. His light brown hair flowed out of his beanie hat. When he walked toward me to take my bag, I began to feel like a princess. Further, he helped me into the truck before he'd come around to join me inside. The door closed behind him and he paused as if he were sitting down at a dinner table.

"How are you? I'm Jeff. Thanks for coming!"

I loved how he expressed a relaxed energy; he lacked a sense of urgency. I was the event, and we were going on an adventure. All we needed was us—and maybe some (more) coffee.

I handed him the to-go cups I stole from my building's concierge. His hands were trembling as he poured the coffee; my heart skipped another beat. Throughout the entire ride, I listened eagerly as he told me about his elk-hunting adventures in the Wyoming forest. There was a twinkle in his eye as he spoke and I was lost in his story. After telling me more about his family, his incredibly balanced work-life lifestyle and friends, he listened about my journey to Boston. He didn't judge, he didn't comment. He listened and offered compassion. His voice seemed proud of me.

"Well, I'm glad you're still here," he said with a smile. "I mean you have to see Sunapee to really understand and appreciate New England," he added, changing to a silly tone.

A few hours and cocktails into our date, we sat, facing downhill on our last run of the day. The booze coaxed me to share a little more about my trials and tribulations of dating, how frustrated I'd been and how thankful I was to be having so much fun.

He looked at me, smiled, put his hand on my knee and said, "You know what the problem was with your other boyfriends?"

I looked straight ahead at the run-in front of us, worried that whatever he was about to say would either be super-sweet, extremely cocky and condescending or very awkward.

"They didn't have a mustache!" he said before hopping up onto his feet to snowboard away.

I giggled hard, ticked at how he could turn my frown upside down and raced to catch up with him.

* * *

The date ended after 17 hours of drinking, eating and playing. I was home safely and he asked to see again—the next day. I agreed to meet him less than 17 hours later and fell asleep wondering if it had all been a dream. When I opened my computer to check my emails before bed, I closed the "Break Lease" PDF.

When I awoke, I called my mom, then my friend Meg, and texted my friend Dee on the way to meet my friend Lauren for yoga. I was home, and a potential Prince Charming lived nearby.

CHAPTER 74.

WHEN IT ALL MAKES SENSE

New Hampshire, 2017

Sitting on the front porch of the house Prince Charming bought for us in New Hampshire, I felt neutral, at ease, OK. Three months into dating, he'd asked for my support on his purchase and, without a shadow of a doubt, I leaned into the move. I wanted to help decorate the house and together we'd begun building a life.

From this OK-ness, I could think without pain, sorrow or confusion. It was all for a reason.

Chicago was like Ren Man, a dreamy place that didn't seem real at times. Fleeting, fun, but unfortunately a short chapter. Friends and family nearby, opportunities abounding and a chance to rise to the top as a youngster, Chicago was easy, and an easy way out of Boston for me, like my thoughts on how Ren Man often had it easy in life. And our relationship was seamless in its early stages. But we had to leave each other like I had to leave the Chi-Town. Letting go had been the only way for both of us to develop and grow our portfolio lifestyles.

Boston, on the other hand, fit the mold of the guy who comes into your life at the wrong time when you're dealing with something else. Take Jaylen. Barging right in at that moment when you're so not looking for it, you really don't even want to know what this person has to say or offer. But some way, somehow, they butt into your life and stake out a semipermanent spot. Out of nowhere, you feel something deeper. Like your first time drinking—a couple of strong drinks and your brain is drastically changed.

They touch you in places where you didn't know you could feel. You reveal a side of yourself you didn't know you had. It was like dating Jaylen inspired me to grow a layer to my character or my person, daring me to uncover something that'd been buried beneath insecurities and fear.

Whether it's because they need you, you need them or it's forced, it's a thing. You decide to see it through and, in the end, both parties part ways better for it.

Like Jaylen, my time in the Back Bay of Boston was short-term, and midst the experience, I always wondered, *How long will I stay?*

After Jaylen, I viewed Boston like I viewed dating. Maybe they're in your life for a little or they stay for a while. Frustratingly enough, you feel powerless, like they control when they exit your life and you have no say. Yet the fighter in you won't walk away, even when you want to give up. A concise and thrilling chapter is born, a chapter you wouldn't want to reread. Or, at least, one you don't think you want to read. All of the Back Bay Boston chapters will forever be those hard-to-read chapters but are something so unique that life wouldn't make sense without them.

And even if years from now you don't like what the chapter says, it will forever exist, because it changed you forever. And maybe, just maybe, the way you wrote it (lived it!) changed the readers a bit, too.

Regardless of the chapter, there'll always be struggle in your story, and there will always be unresolved issues from one chapter that carry into another. And no, they don't fit into perfect boxes to be placed on organized shelves where forever they'll rest in peace. Struggles (which may be from people, anxieties, contemplations, uncertainties) will live in you, sometimes dormant like viruses and other times like friendly spirits of the past, if that's how you want them to be.

Me? I made peace by friendship. Some people are not worth giving up on. KG and I stayed in contact and our evolution to friendship occurred quite gracefully. Our friendship grew into something valuable as we both grew up. He is real, still a character in my life, forever a story I enjoy reading.

For a girly girl fortunate to have spent most of my early twenties during the rebirth of feminism, I was shaped by men. The Directors made me feel like a toy, thus I experienced firsthand what it's like to feel devalued by men in business. Suddenly the plight of feminists on Instagram resonated with me. If I'd only worked with men like The Directors, I'd probably be a loud and proud feminist with a lot of anger for my professional inequality.

But my story is different: Mr. Bates made me wanna prove myself; Stew convinced me I was a rock star, and the way in which both Boston Matts respected me instilled in me the idea that I was a professional and that's how I'd approach my career. Kevin and Max didn't go easy on me, but I learned they didn't go easy on anyone; they set a high bar and working for them taught me for the first time in my life what it's like to miss the mark. Gathering at town hall meetings with attorneys like John Smoller and engineers like Phil Check, and having male coaches like Jeremy, John, Greg and KG's business partner Mike at Flash Fitness, I'd learned they saw value in me without their eyes.

And thanks to a combination of Ren Man's wisdom and all of the tumultuous dating, the woman who stayed in Boston, the woman who knew never to say the "F" word to her boyfriend, the woman who wanted to lay a foundation built on trust and openness was ready for Prince Charming when she met him and knew to make sure he was a man who loved his family as I loved mine.

And one more thing about Boston as it ties to men: Never give up. My roller-coaster relationship with my father is in some ways just the tip of the iceberg; however, now the iceberg has melted and the relationship is vastly simple. Everything we went through rests in the past and our communication continues to improve. I'd continued to press on with Boston, and so I did with my father.

Daring to stay while daring to think I should leave scared me into paralysis. However, somewhere in the contemplation phase it dawned on me: daring to make Boston my home meant settling in with myself. Prince Charming would have to be a second priority. Me first. If could get myself to a place of self-love, work balance, fulfilling community and healthy routine in a city I didn't despise, I'd be a better Princess Charming.

I'd created, I'd cried and I'd grown in my white-walled haven. Boring and bland, I could handle it a few more months. If I'd learned anything I came to know that nothing is permanent. I would stay, and more time in the city meant more friendly faces each and every day. I got this.

73947962R00220

Made in the USA
Middletown, DE
18 May 2018